*Praise for #1* **New York Times** *bestselling author*
**Debbie Macomber**

"Macomber is...an icon of the genre."
—*Publishers Weekly*

"Macomber's endearing characters offer courage and
support to one another and find hope and love in the
most unexpected places."
—*Booklist* on *204 Rosewood Lane*

"Debbie Macomber writes characters who are as warm
and funny as your best friends."
—#1 *New York Times* bestselling author Susan Wiggs

**Praise for** *USA TODAY* **bestselling author Jillian Hart**

"*A Handful of Heaven* is a refreshing look at love between
two people who weren't sure they'd find someone again.
Jillian Hart's pacing is excellent and the plot believable."
—*RT Book Reviews*

"Jillian Hart conveys heart-tugging emotional struggles
and the joy of remaining open to the Lord's leading."
—*RT Book Reviews* on *Sweet Blessings*

## DEBBIE MACOMBER

is a number one *New York Times* and *USA TODAY* bestselling author. Her recent books include *1225 Christmas Tree Lane*, *1105 Yakima Street*, *A Turn in the Road*, *Hannah's List* and *Debbie Macomber's Christmas Cookbook*, as well as *Twenty Wishes*, *Summer on Blossom Street* and *Call Me Mrs. Miracle*. She has become a leading voice in women's fiction worldwide and her work has appeared on every major bestseller list, including those of the *New York Times*, *USA TODAY*, *Publishers Weekly* and *Entertainment Weekly*. She is a multiple award winner, and won the 2005 Quill Award for Best Romance. Two of her Harlequin MIRA Christmas titles have been made into Hallmark Channel Original Movies. There are more than 100 million copies of her books in print. For more information on Debbie and her books, visit her website, www.debbiemacomber.com.

## JILLIAN HART

grew up on her family's homestead, where she helped raise cattle, rode horses and scribbled stories in her spare time. After earning her English degree from Whitman College, she worked in travel and advertising before selling her first novel. When Jillian isn't working on her next story, she can be found puttering in her rose garden, curled up with a good book or spending quiet evenings at home with her family.

# BESTSELLING AUTHOR COLLECTION

#1 *New York Times* Bestselling Author

# DEBBIE MACOMBER

*Thanksgiving Prayer*

**HARLEQUIN**®
entertain, enrich, inspire™

ISBN-13: 978-0-373-18060-8

Recycling programs
for this product may
not exist in your area.

THANKSGIVING PRAYER
Copyright © 2012 by Harlequin Books S.A.

The publisher acknowledges the copyright holders of the individual works as follows:

THANKSGIVING PRAYER
Copyright © 1984 by Debbie Macomber

A HANDFUL OF HEAVEN
Copyright © 2006 by Jill Strickler

www.Harlequin.com

**Printed in U.S.A.**

# CONTENTS

THANKSGIVING PRAYER        9
Debbie Macomber

A HANDFUL OF HEAVEN        213
Jillian Hart

Dear Friends,

I'm so pleased to see *Thanksgiving Prayer* published again after years of being out of print. I've received letters from readers looking for this book, which was first published back in the early 1980s and then reissued in 2000. You're going to enjoy reading Jillian Hart's book, *A Handful of Heaven*, too.

When I originally wrote *Thanksgiving Prayer*, my husband, Wayne, had just returned from working on the Alaska pipeline. He loved his time in Alaska and couldn't wait to share his adventures. In the years since, we've gone twice and I came to understand his fascination. My first visit was to do research for the "Midnight Sons" stories, which proved to be one of my most popular series.

I hope that in *Thanksgiving Prayer* I've captured even a small part of Alaska's appeal—and that you, too, will have an opportunity to visit the forty-ninth state. I also hope you enjoy Claudia and Seth's story, which has been refreshed so that outdated references won't distract you or jar you from it.

I always love hearing from my readers. You can contact me through my website at DebbieMacomber.com or my Facebook page, DebbieMacomberWorld, or through the mail at P.O. Box 1458, Port Orchard, WA 98366.

God's richest blessings to you and yours.

*Debbie Macomber*

# THANKSGIVING PRAYER

## Debbie Macomber

In memory of
Marie Macomber,
mother-in-law extraordinaire

# Chapter 1

The radiant blue heavens drew Claudia Masters's eyes as she boarded the jet for Nome, Alaska. Her heart rate accelerated with excitement. In less than two hours she would be with Seth—manly, self-assured, masterful Seth. She made herself comfortable and secured the seat belt, anticipating the rumble of the engines that would thrust the plane into the air.

She had felt some uncertainty when she boarded the plane that morning in Seattle. But she'd hastily placed a phone call during her layover in Anchorage and been assured by Seth's assistant that yes, he had received her message, and yes, he would meet her at the airport. Confident now, Claudia relaxed and idly flipped through a magazine.

A warmth, a feeling of contentment, filled her.

Cooper's doubts and last-ditch effort to change her mind were behind her now, and she was free to make her life with Seth.

Cooper had been furious with her decision to leave medical school. But he was only her uncle. He hadn't understood her love for her Alaskan oilman, just as he couldn't understand her faith in the Lord.

A smile briefly curved her soft mouth upward. Cooper had shown more emotion in that brief twenty-minute visit to his office than she'd seen in all her twenty-five years.

"Quitting med school is the dumbest idea I've ever heard," he'd growled, his keen brown eyes challenging the serene blue of hers.

"Sometimes loving someone calls for unusual behavior," she had countered, knowing anything impractical was foreign to her uncle.

For a moment all Cooper could do was stare at her. She could sense the anger drain from him as he lowered himself into the desk chair.

"Contrary to what you may believe, I have your best interests at heart. I see you throwing away years of study for some ignorant lumberjack. Can you blame me for doubting your sanity?"

"Seth's an oilman, not a lumberjack. There aren't any native trees in Nome." It was easier to correct Cooper than to answer the questions that had plagued her, filling her with doubts. The choice hadn't been easy; indecision had tormented her for months. Now that she'd decided to marry Seth and share his life in the Alaskan wilderness, a sense of joy and release had come over her.

"It's taken me two miserable months to realize that my future isn't in any hospital," she continued. "I'd be a rotten doctor if I couldn't be a woman first. I love Seth. Someday I'll finish medical school, but if a decision has to be made, I'll choose Seth Lessinger every time."

But Cooper had never been easily won over. The tense atmosphere became suddenly quiet as he digested the thought. He expelled his breath, but it was several seconds before he spoke. "I'm not thinking of myself, Claudia. I want you to be absolutely sure you know what you're doing."

"I am," she replied with complete confidence.

Now, flying high above the lonely, barren Alaska tundra, Claudia continued to be confident she was doing the right thing. God had confirmed the decision. Seth had known from the beginning, but it had taken her much longer to realize the truth.

Gazing out the plane window, she viewed miles upon miles of the frozen, snow-covered ground. It was just as Seth had described: a treeless plain of crystalline purity. There would be a summer, he'd promised, days that ran into each other when the sun never set. Flowers would blossom, and for a short time the tundra would explode into a grassy pasture. Seth had explained many things about life in the North. At first she'd resented his letters, full of enticements to lure her to Nome. If he really loved her, she felt, he should be willing to relocate in Seattle until she'd completed her studies. It wasn't so much to ask. But as she came to know and love Seth, it became evident that Nome was more than the location of his business. It was a way of life, Seth's life. Crowded cities, traffic jams and shopping malls would suffocate him.

She should have known that the minute she pushed the cleaning cart into the motel room. Her being a housekeeper at the Wilderness Motel had been something of a miracle in itself.

Leaning back, Claudia slowly lowered her lashes as the memories washed over her.

Ashley Robbins, her lifetime friend and roommate, had been ill—far too sick to spend the day cleaning rooms. By the time Ashley admitted as much, it was too late to call the motel and tell them she wouldn't be coming to work, so Claudia had volunteered to go in her place.

Claudia had known from the moment she slid the pass key into the lock that there was something different, something special, about this room.

Her hands rested on her slender hips as she looked around. A single man slept here. She smiled as she realized how accurate she was becoming at describing the occupants of each room, and after just one day. She was having fun speculating. Whoever was staying in here had slept uneasily. The sheet and blankets were pulled free of the mattress and rumpled haphazardly at the foot of the king-size bed.

As she put on the clean sheets, she couldn't help wondering what Cooper would think if he could see her now. He would be aghast to know she was doing what he would call "menial work."

As she lifted the corner of the mattress to tuck in the blanket, she noticed an open Bible on the nightstand, followed by the sudden feeling that she wasn't alone. As she turned around, a smile lit up her sky-blue eyes. But her welcome died: no one was there.

After finishing the bed, she plugged in the vacuum. With the flip of the switch the motor roared to life. A minute later she had that same sensation of being watched, and she turned off the machine. But when she turned, she once again discovered she was alone.

Pausing, she studied the room. There was something about this place: not the room itself, but the occupant. She could sense it, feel it: a sadness that seemed to reach out and touch her, wrapping itself around her. She wondered why she was receiving these strange sensations. Nothing like this had ever happened to her before.

A prayer came to her lips as she silently petitioned God on behalf of whoever occupied this room. When she finished she released a soft sigh. Once, a long time ago, she remembered reading that no one could come to the Lord unless someone prayed for them first. She wasn't sure how scriptural that was, but the thought had stuck with her. Often she found herself offering silent prayers for virtual strangers.

After cleaning the bathroom and placing fresh towels on the rack, she began to wheel the cleaning cart into the hallway. Again she paused, brushing wisps of copper-colored hair from her forehead as she examined the room. She hadn't forgotten anything, had she? Everything looked right. But again that terrible sadness seemed to reach out to her.

Leaving the cart, she moved to the desk and took out a postcard and a pen from the drawer. In large, bold letters she printed one of her favorite verses from Psalms. It read: "May the Lord give you the desire of your heart and make all your plans succeed." Psalm 20:4. She didn't question why that particular verse had come to mind. It didn't offer solace, even though she had felt unhappiness here. Perplexed and a little unsure, she tucked the card into the corner of the dresser mirror.

Back in the hall, she checked to be sure the door had locked automatically. Her back ached. Ashley hadn't been kidding when she said this was hard work. It was that and more. She was so glad that had been her final room for the day. A thin sheen of perspiration covered Claudia's brow, and she pushed her thick, naturally curly hair from her face. Her attention was still focused on the door when she began wheeling the cart toward the elevator. She hadn't gone more than a few feet when she struck something. A quick glance upward told her that she'd run into a man.

"I'm so sorry," she apologized immediately. "I wasn't watching where I was going." Her first impression was that this was the largest, most imposing man she'd ever seen. He loomed above her, easily a foot taller than her five-foot-five frame. His shoulders were wide, his waist and hips lean, and he was so muscular that the material of his shirt was pulled taut across his broad chest. He was handsome in a reckless-looking way, his hair magnificently dark. His well-trimmed beard was a shade lighter.

"No problem." The stranger smiled, his mouth sensuous and appealing, his eyes warm.

Claudia liked that. He might be big, but one look told her he was a gentle giant.

Not until she was in her car did she realize she hadn't watched to see if the giant had entered the room where she'd gotten such a strange feeling.

By the time Claudia got back to the apartment, Ashley looked better. She was propped against the arm of the sofa, her back cushioned by several pillows. A hand-knit afghan covered her, and a box of tissues sat on the coffee table, the crumpled ones littering the polished surface.

"How'd it go?" she asked, her voice scratchy and unnatural. "Were you able to figure out one end of the vacuum from the other?"

"Of course." Claudia laughed. "I had fun playing house, but next time warn me—I broke my longest nail."

"That's the price you pay for being so stubborn," Ashley scolded as she grabbed a tissue, anticipating a sneeze. "I told you it was a crazy idea. Did old Burns say anything?"

"No, she was too grateful. Finding a replacement this late in the day would have been difficult."

Fall classes at the University of Washington had resumed that Monday, and Ashley had been working at the motel for only a couple of weeks, one of the two part-time jobs she had taken to earn enough to stay in school.

Claudia knew Ashley had been worried about losing the job, so she'd been happy to step in and help. Her own tuition and expenses were paid by a trust fund her father had established before his death. She had offered to lend Ashley money on numerous occasions, but her friend had stubbornly refused. Ashley believed that if God wanted her to have a degree in education, then He would provide the necessary money. Apparently He did want that for her, because the funds were always there when she needed them.

Ashley's unshakable faith had taught Claudia valuable lessons. She had been blessed with material wealth, while Ashley struggled from one month to the next. But of the two of them, Claudia considered Ashley the richer.

Claudia often marveled at her friend's faith. Everything had been taken care of in her own life. Decisions had been made for her. As for her career, she'd known from the time she was in grade school that she would be a doctor, a dream shared by her father. The last Christmas before his death he'd given her a stethoscope. Later she realized that he must have known he wouldn't be alive to see their dream fulfilled. Now there was only Cooper, her pompous, dignified uncle.

"How are you feeling?"

Ashley sneezed into a tissue, which did little to muffle the sound. "Better," she murmured, her eyes red and watery. "I should be fine by tomorrow. I don't want you to have to fill in for me again."

"We'll see," Claudia said, hands on her hips. Ashley was so stubborn, she mused—she seemed to be surrounded by strong-willed people.

Later that night she lay in bed, unable to sleep. She hadn't told Ashley about what had happened in the last room she'd cleaned. She didn't know how she could explain it to anyone. Now she wished she'd waited to see if the stranger outside had been the one occupying that room. The day had been unusual in more ways than one. With a yawn, she rolled over and forced herself to relax and go to sleep.

The clouds were gray and thick the next morning. Claudia was up and reading over some material from one of her classes when Ashley strolled into the living room, looking just as miserable as she had the day before.

"Don't you ever let up?" she complained with a long yawn. "I swear, all you do is study. Take a break. You've got all quarter to hit the books."

With deliberate slowness Claudia closed the text-book. "Do you always wake up so cheerful?"

"Yes," Ashley snapped. "Especially when I feel I could be dying. You're going to be a doctor—do something!"

Claudia brandished the thick book, which happened to be on psychology. "All right," she said. "Take two aspirin, drink lots of liquids and stay in bed. I'll check on you later."

"Wonderful," Ashley murmured sarcastically as she stumbled back into her bedroom. "And for this she goes to medical school."

A half hour later Claudia tapped lightly before letting herself into Ashley's bedroom. "Feel any better?"

"A little." Ashley spoke in a tight voice. She was curled into a ball as if every bone ached.

"You probably have a touch of the flu to go along with that rotten cold."

"This isn't a touch," Ashley insisted vehemently. "This is a full-scale beating. Why did this have to happen to me now?"

"Don't ask me," Claudia said, as she set a tray of tea and toast on the nightstand. "But have you ever stopped to think that maybe your body has decided it needs a rest? You're going to kill yourself working at the motel and the bookstore, plus doing all your coursework. Something's got to give, and in this instance it's your health. I think you should take warning."

"Uh-oh, here it comes." Ashley groaned and rolled over, placing the back of her hand to her forehead. "I wondered how long it would take to pull your corny doctor routine on me."

"It's not corny." Claudia's blue eyes flashed. "Don't you recognize good advice when you hear it?"

Ashley gestured weakly with her hand. "That's the problem, I guess. I don't."

"Well, trust me. This advice is good," Claudia said and fluffed up a pillow so Ashley could sit up comfortably.

"I'm better, honest," Ashley said and coughed. "Good enough to work. I hate the thought of you breaking another fingernail."

"Sure you do, Ash, sure you do."

Claudia wheeled the cleaning cart from one room to the next without incident. The small of her back ached, and she paused to rub it. She hadn't exactly done much housecleaning in her life.

Her fingers trembled when she inserted the pass key into the final room—the same one she had finished with yesterday. Would she feel the same sensations as before? Or had it all been her imagination? The room looked almost identical to the way it had yesterday. The sheets and blankets were rumpled at the foot of the bed, as if the man had once again slept restlessly.

Her attention flew to the mirror, and she was pleased to note that the card was gone. Slowly she walked around the room, waiting to feel the sensations she'd had yesterday, but whatever she had felt then was gone. Maybe she had conjured up the whole thing in her mind. The brain could do things like that. She should know. She'd studied enough about the human mind these past couple of years.

She was placing the fresh white towels in the bathroom when a clicking noise was followed by the sound of the door opening.

She stiffened, her fingers nervously toying with the towel as she pretended to straighten it.

"Hello." The male voice came from behind her, rich and deep.

"Hello," she mumbled and managed a smile as she turned. The man she had bumped into yesterday was framed in the doorway. Somehow she had known this was his room. "I'll be out of your way in a minute."

"No," he insisted. "Don't go. I want to talk to you."

Turning away from him, she moistened her suddenly parched lips.

"Do I frighten you?" he asked.

Claudia realized that his size probably intimidated a lot of people. "No," she answered honestly. This man could probably lift a refrigerator by himself, yet he wouldn't hurt an ant. She wasn't sure how she knew that, but she did.

"Are you the one who left this?" He pulled the card she'd placed in the mirror from his shirt pocket.

Numbly she nodded. She didn't know anything about motel policy. What if she'd gotten Ashley into trouble?

His thick brows lifted, as if he'd expected more than a simple movement of her head. "Why?" The single word seemed to be hurled at her.

"I...I don't really know," she began weakly, surprised at how feeble her voice sounded. "If it offended you, then please accept my apology."

"I wasn't displeased," he assured her. "But I was a little curious about your reasons." He released her gaze as he put the card back into his shirt pocket. "Do you do this often?"

Claudia looked away uneasily. "No. Never before."

His dark eyes narrowed on her. "Do you think we could have a cup of coffee somewhere when you're through? I really would like to talk to you."

"I..." She looked down at the uniform skirt the motel had provided and noticed a couple of smudges.

"You look fine."

No doubt he assumed she did this full-time, which made his invitation into an interesting opportunity. So many times she had wished she could meet someone without the fear of intimidating him with her brains and financial situation. Although she wasn't an heir to millions, she would receive a large sum of cash at age thirty or the day she married—whichever came first.

"I'd like that." Obviously this stranger needed to speak to someone. The open Bible on his nightstand had convinced her that he was a Christian. Was it because he was lonely that she had felt that terrible sadness in the room? No, she was sure it was more than loneliness—a lot more.

"Can we meet someplace?" he suggested. "There's a coffee shop around the corner."

"Fine," she said, and nodded, knowing Cooper would have a fit if he knew what she was doing. "I can be ready in about twenty minutes."

"I'll see you there." He stepped aside, and she could feel him studying her as she moved back toward her cart. What was the matter with her? She had never done anything as impulsive as agreeing to meet a stranger for coffee.

Finished for the day, Claudia returned the cart to Mrs. Burns, who thanked her for helping out again. Next she made a stop in the ladies' room. One glance in the mirror made her groan at her reflection. Her hair was an unruly auburn mass. She took the brush from her purse and ran it through her long curls until they practically sparked with electricity. Her thick, naturally curly hair had always been a problem. For several years now she had kept it long and tied away from her face with a ribbon at the base of her neck. When she first applied and was accepted into medical school, she'd been determined to play down her femininity. Women weren't the rarity they once were, but she didn't want her gender, combined with her money, to prejudice any of her classmates against her. There had been some tension her first year, but she had long since proved herself.

The coffee shop was crowded, but her searching gaze instantly located the stranger, who towered head and shoulders above everyone else. Even when he was sitting down, his large, imposing build couldn't be disguised. Weaving her way between chairs, she sauntered toward him.

The welcome in his smile warmed her. He stood and pulled out a chair for her. She noticed that he chose the one beside him, as if he wanted her as close as possible. The thought didn't disturb her, but her reaction to him did. She wanted to be close to him.

"I suddenly realized I don't know your name," she said after sitting down.

"Seth Lessinger." He lifted a thick eyebrow in silent inquiry. "And yours?"

"Claudia Masters."

"I'm surprised they don't call you Red with that hair."

In any other family she might well have been tagged with the nickname, but not in hers. "No, no one ever has." Her voice sounded strangely husky. To hide her discomfort, she lifted the menu and began studying it, although she didn't want anything more than coffee.

The waitress arrived, and Claudia placed her order, adding an English muffin at Seth's urging. He asked for a club sandwich.

"What brings you to Seattle?" Claudia asked once the waitress was gone. She found herself absently smoothing a wrinkle from the skirt.

"A conference."

"Are you enjoying the Emerald City?" She was making small talk to cover up her nervousness. Maybe meeting a strange man like this wasn't such a good idea after all.

"Very much. It's my first visit to the Northwest, and I'll admit, it's nicer than I expected. Big cities tend to intimidate me. I never have understood how anyone can live like this, surrounded so many people."

Claudia didn't mean to smile, but amusement played at the edges of her mouth. "Where are you from? Alaska?" She'd meant it as a joke and was surprised when he nodded in confirmation.

"Nome," he supplied. "Where the air is pure and the skies are blue."

"You make it sound lovely."

"It's not," he told her with a half-smile. "It can be dingy and gray and miserable, but it's home."

Her coffee arrived, and she cupped the mug, grateful to have something to do with her hands.

He seemed to be studying her, and when their gazes clashed, a lazy smile flickered from the dark depths of his eyes.

"What do you do in Nome?" she asked to distract herself from the fact that his look was disturbingly like a gentle caress. Not that it made her uncomfortable; the effect was quite the opposite. He touched a softness in her, a longing to be the woman she had denied for so long.

"I'm a commissioning agent for a major oil company."

"That sounds interesting." She knew the words came out stiff and stilted.

"It's definitely the right job for me. What about you?"

"Student at the University of Washington." She didn't elaborate.

A frown creased the wide brow. "You look older than a college student."

She ignored that and focused her gaze on the black coffee. "How long will you be in Seattle?"

If he noticed she was disinclined to talk about herself, he didn't say anything. "I'll be flying back in a few days. I'd like to be home by the end of the week."

A few days, her mind echoed. She would remember to pray for him. She believed that God brought everyone into her life for a specific reason. The purpose of her meeting Seth might be for her to remember to pray for him. He certainly had made an impression on her.

"How long have you been a Christian?" He inquired.

"Five years." That was another thing Cooper had

never understood. He found this "religious interest" of hers amusing. "And you?" Again she directed the conversation away from herself.

"Six months. I'm still an infant in the Lord, although my size disputes that!" He smiled, and Claudia felt mesmerized by the warmth in his eyes.

She returned his smile, suddenly aware that he was as defensive about his size as she was about her money and her brains.

"So why *did* you leave that Bible verse on the mirror?"

This was the crux of his wanting to talk to her. How could she explain? "Listen, I've already apologized for that. I realize it's probably against the motel policy."

A hand twice the size of her own reached over the table and trapped hers. "Claudia." The sound of her name was low-pitched and reassuring. "Don't apologize. Your message meant more to me than you can possibly realize. My intention is to thank you for it."

His dark, mysterious eyes studied hers. Again Claudia sensed more than saw a sadness, a loneliness, in him. She made a show of glancing at her watch. "I...I really should be going."

"Can I see you again? Tomorrow?"

She'd been afraid he was going to ask her that. And also afraid that he wouldn't.

"I was planning on doing some grocery shopping at the Pike Place Market tomorrow," she said without accepting or refusing.

"We could meet somewhere." His tone held a faint challenge. At the same time, he sounded almost unsure.

Claudia had the impression there wasn't much that unsettled this man. She wondered what it was about her that made him uncertain.

"All right," she found herself agreeing. "But I feel I'd better warn you, if you find large cities stifling, downtown Seattle at that time of the day may be an experience you'd rather avoid."

"Not this time," he said with a chuckle.

They set a time and place as Seth walked her back to the motel lot, where she'd left her car. She drove a silver compact, even though Cooper had generously given her a fancy sports car when she was accepted into medical school. She'd never driven it around campus and kept it in one of Cooper's garages. Not that she didn't appreciate the gift. The car was beautiful, and a dream to drive, but she already had her compact and couldn't see the need for two cars. Not when one of them would make her stand out and draw unnecessary and unwanted attention. Never had she been more grateful for the decision she'd made than she was now, though. At least she wouldn't have to explain to Seth why a hotel housekeeper was driving a car that cost as much as she made in a year.

"Hi," Claudia said later as she floated into the apartment, a Cheshire Cat grin on her face.

"Wow!" Ashley exclaimed from the sofa. "You look like you've just met Prince Charming."

"I have." Claudia dropped her purse on the end table and sat on the sofa arm opposite the end where Ashley was resting. "He's about this tall." She held her hand high above her head. "With shoulders this wide." She held her hands out ridiculously wide to demonstrate. "And he has the most incredible dark eyes."

"Oh, honestly, Claudia, that's not Prince Charming. That's the Incredible Hulk," Ashley admonished.

Claudia tilted her head to one side, a slow smile spreading over her mouth. "'Incredible' is the word, all right."

Not until the following morning, when Claudia dressed in her best designer jeans and cashmere sweater, with knee-high leather boots, did Ashley take her seriously.

"You really did meet someone yesterday, didn't you?"

Claudia nodded, pouring steaming cocoa into a mug. "Want some?"

"Sure," Ashley said, then hesitated. "When did you have the chance? The only place you've been is school and—" she paused, her blue eyes widening "—the Wilderness and back. Claudia," she gasped, "it isn't someone from the motel, is it?"

Two pieces of toast blasted from the toaster with

the force of a skyrocket. Deftly Claudia caught them in the air. "Yup."

For the first time in recent history, Ashley was speechless. "But, Claudia, you can't…I mean…all kinds of people stay there. He could be *anyone.…*"

"Seth isn't just anyone. He *is* a big guy, but he's gentle and kind. And I like him."

"I can tell," Ashley murmured with a worried look pinching her face.

"Don't look so shocked. Women have met men in stranger ways. I'm seeing him this afternoon. I told him I have some grocery shopping to do." When she saw the glare Ashley was giving her, Claudia felt obliged to add, "Well, I do. I wanted to pick up some fresh vegetables. I was just reading an article on the importance of fiber in the diet."

"We bought a whole month's worth of food last Saturday," Ashley mumbled under her breath.

"True." Claudia shrugged, then picked up a light jacket. "But I think we could use some fresh produce. I'll be sure and pick up some prunes for you."

Seth was standing on the library steps waiting when Claudia arrived. Again she noted his compelling male virility. She waited at the bottom of the stairs for him to join her. The balmy September breeze coming off Puget Sound teased her hair, blowing auburn curls across her cheek. He paused, standing in front of her, his eyes smiling deeply into hers.

The mesmerizing quality of his gaze held her motionless. Her hand was halfway to her face to remove the lock of maverick hair, but it, too, was frozen by the warmth in his look, which seemed to reach out and caress her. She had neither the will nor the desire to glance away.

The rough feel of his callused hand removing the hair brought her out of the trance. "Hello, Claudia."

"Seth."

"You're beautiful." The words appeared to come involuntarily.

"So are you," she joked. The musky scent of his aftershave drifted pleasantly toward her, and an unwilling sigh broke from between her slightly parted lips.

Someone on the busy sidewalk bumped into Claudia, throwing her off balance. Immediately Seth reached out protectively and pulled her close. The iron band of his arm continued to hold her against him far longer than necessary. His touch warmed her through the thin jacket. No man had ever been able to awaken this kind of feeling in her. This was uncanny, unreal.

# Chapter 2

"Are you ready to call it quits?" Claudia asked. Seth had placed a guiding hand on her shoulder, and she wondered how long his touch would continue to produce the warm, glowing sensation spreading down her spine.

"More than ready," he confirmed.

The Pike Place Market in the heart of downtown Seattle had always been a hub of activity as tourists and everyday shoppers vied for the attention of the vendors displaying their wares. The two of them had strolled through the market, their hands entwined. Vegetables that had been hand-picked that morning were displayed on long tables, while the farmers shouted their virtues, enticing customers to their booths. The odd but pleasant smell of tangy spices and fresh fish had drifted agreeably around them.

"I did warn you," she said with a small laugh. "What's the life expectancy of someone from Nome, Alaska, in a crowd like this?"

Seth glanced at his watch. "About two hours," he said. "And we've been at it nearly that. Let's take a break."

"I agree."

"Lunch?"

Claudia nodded. She hadn't eaten after her last class, hurrying instead to meet Seth. Now she realized she was hungry. "Sounds good."

"Chinese okay?"

For once it was a pleasure to have someone take her out and not try to impress her with the best restaurant in town, or how much money he could spend. "Yes, that's fine."

He paused. "You sure?"

She squeezed his hand. "Very sure. And I know just the place."

They rode the city bus to Seattle's International District and stepped off into another world. Seth looked around in surprise. "I didn't know Seattle had a Chinatown."

"Chinatown, Little Italy, Mexico, all within a few blocks. Interesting, isn't it?"

"Very."

They lingered over their tea, delaying as long as possible their return to the hectic pace of the world outside.

"Why do you have a beard?" Claudia asked curiously. She didn't mean to be abrupt, but his beard fascinated her—it looked so soft—and the question slipped out before she could stop herself.

Seth looked surprised by the question, rubbing the dark in question with one hand as he spoke. "Does it bother you? I can always shave it off."

"Oh, no," she protested instantly. "I like it. Very much. But I've always been curious why some men choose to grow their beards."

"I can't speak for anyone else, but my beard offers some protection to my face during the long winter months," he explained.

His quick offer to shave it off had shocked Claudia with the implication that he would do it for her. She couldn't understand his eagerness.

"I've about finished my shopping. What about you?" She hated to torture him further.

The tiny teacup was dwarfed by his massive hands. "I was finished a long time ago."

"Want to take a walk along the waterfront and ride the trolley?" she suggested, looking for reasons to prolong their time together.

"I'd like that."

While Seth paid for their meal she excused herself to reapply her lipstick and comb her hair. Then, hand in hand, they walked the short distance back to the heart of downtown Seattle. They paused in front of a department store to study a window display in autumn colors.

Her eyes were laughing into his when he placed a possessive hand around her waist, drawing her close to his side. Then they stepped away from the window and started down the street toward the waterfront.

It was then that Claudia spotted Cooper walking on the opposite side of the street. Even from this distance she could see his disapproving scowl, and she felt the blood drain from her face. The differences between these two men were so striking that to make a comparison struck her as ludicrous.

"I'll get us a taxi," Seth suggested, his eyes showing concern. "I've been walking your legs off." Apparently he thought her pale face was the result of the brisk pace he'd set.

"No, I'd rather walk," she insisted, and reached for his hand. "If we hurry, we can make this light."

Their hands were still linked when she began to run toward the corner. There had never been any chance of their reaching the crosswalk before the light changed, but even so, she hurried between the busy shoppers.

"Claudia." Seth stopped, placing his arm over her shoulders, his wide brow creased with concern. "What's the matter?"

"Nothing," she said hesitantly, looking around. She was certain Cooper had seen them, and she didn't want him to ruin things. "Really, let's go." Her voice was raised and anxious.

"Claudia."

Cooper's voice coming from behind her stopped her heart.

"Introduce me to your friend," he said in a crisp, businesslike tone.

Frustration washed over her. Cooper would take one look at Seth and condemn him as one of the fortune hunters he was always warning her about.

"Cooper Masters, this is Seth Lessinger." She made the introduction grudgingly.

The two men eyed each other shrewdly while exchanging handshakes.

"Masters," Seth repeated. "Are you related to Claudia?"

Cooper ignored the question, instead turning toward Claudia. "I'll pick you up for dinner Sunday at about two. If that's convenient?"

"It was fine last week and the week before, so why should it be any different this week?"

Her uncle flashed her an impatient glance.

"Who is this man?" Seth asked, the look in his eyes almost frightening. Anger darkened his face. He dropped his hand to his side, and she noted how his fist was clenched until his knuckles turned white.

Claudia watched, stunned. *He thinks I'm Cooper's wife.* Placing a hand on his forearm, she implored, "Seth, let me explain."

He shook his arm free. "You don't need to say anything more. I understand. Do you do this kind of thing often? Is this how you get your thrills?"

For a moment she was speechless, the muscles of

her throat paralyzed with anger. "You don't understand. Cooper's my uncle."

"And I believe in Santa Claus," Seth returned sarcastically.

"I've warned you about men like this," Cooper said at the same time.

"Will you please be quiet!" she shouted at him.

"There's no excuse for you to talk to me in such a tone," Cooper countered in a huff.

People were beginning to stare, but she didn't care. "He really is my uncle." Desperately her eyes pleaded with Seth, asking for understanding and the chance to explain. *His* eyes were dark, clouded and unreasonable.

"You don't want to hear, do you?" she asked him.

"We definitely need to have a discussion, Claudia," Cooper interrupted again.

"You're right, I don't." Seth took a step away from her.

Claudia breathed in sharply, the rush of oxygen making her lungs hurt. She bit her lip as Seth turned and walked away. His stride was filled with purpose, as if he couldn't get away from her fast enough.

"You've really done it this time," she flared at her uncle.

"Really, Claudia," he said with a relieved look. "That type of man is most undesirable."

"That man—" she pointed at Seth's retreating figure "—is one of the most desirable men I've ever known." Without waiting for his response, she turned and stalked away.

An hour later, Claudia was banging pans around in the kitchen. Ashley came through the front door and paused, watching her for a moment. "What's wrong?"

"Nothing," Claudia responded tersely.

"Oh, come on. I always know when you're upset, because you bake something."

"That's so I can eat it."

Ashley scanned the ingredients that lined the counter. "Chocolate chip cookies," she murmured. "This must really be bad. I'm guessing you had another run-in with Cooper?"

"Right again," Claudia snapped.

"You don't want to talk about it?"

"That's a brilliant deduction." With unnecessary force, she cracked two eggs against the mixing bowl.

"You want me to quit interrogating you, huh?"

Claudia paused, closing her eyes as the waves of impatience rippled over her. "Yes, please."

"All right, all right. I'm leaving."

Soon the aroma of freshly baked cookies filled the apartment, though Claudia didn't notice. Almost automatically she lifted the cookies from the baking sheet and placed them on a wire rack to cool.

"I can't stand it anymore." Ashley stumbled into the kitchen dramatically. "If you don't want to talk, fine, but at least let me have a cookie."

Claudia sighed, placed four on a plate and set it on the kitchen table.

Ashley poured herself a tall glass of milk and sat down, her eyes following Claudia's movements. "Feel like talking now?" she asked several minutes later. There was a sympathetic tone in her voice that came from many years of friendship.

Ashley had been Claudia's only friend as a child. Ashley's mother had been Claude Masters's cook and housekeeper, and she had brought her daughter with her to keep the lonely Claudia company. The two of them had been best friends ever since.

"It's Seth," Claudia admitted and sighed, taking a chair opposite Ashley.

"Seth? Oh, the guy you met at the motel. What happened?"

"We ran into Cooper, and he had a fit of righteous indignation over seeing me with someone who wasn't wearing a business suit and a silk tie. To complicate matters, Seth apparently thought Cooper and I were married, or at least used to be. He didn't wait for an explanation."

Ashley's look was thoughtful. "You really like him, don't you?"

Claudia worried the soft flesh of her bottom lip. "Yes," she said simply. "I like him very much."

"If he's so arrogant that he wouldn't wait for you to explain, then I'd say it was his loss," Ashley said, attempting to comfort her.

"No." Claudia shook her head and lowered her

gaze to the tabletop. "In this case, I think I'm the one who lost."

"I don't think I've ever heard you talk this way about a man. What makes him so special?"

Claudia's brow furrowed in concentration. "I'm not really sure. He's more attractive than any man I can remember, but it's not his looks. Or not only his looks, anyway." She smiled. "He's a rare man." She paused to formulate her thoughts. "Strong and intelligent."

"You know all this and you've only seen him twice?" Ashley sounded shocked.

"No." Claudia hung her head, and her long auburn curls fell forward to hide her expression. "I sensed more than I saw, and even then, I'm only skimming the surface. This man is deep."

"If he's so willing to jump to conclusions, I'd say it's his own fault—"

"Ashley, please," Claudia interrupted. "Don't. I know you're trying to make me feel better, but I'd appreciate it if you didn't."

"All right." Ashley was quiet for a long time. After a while she took a chocolate chip cookie and handed it to Claudia.

With a weak smile, Claudia accepted the cookie. "Now, that's what I need."

They talked for a while, but it wasn't until they headed into the living room that Claudia noticed Ashley's suitcase in front of the door.

"You're going away?"

"Oh, I almost forgot. I talked to Mom this morning, and she wants me home for a few days. Jeff and John have the flu, and she needs someone there so she can go to work. I shouldn't be any more than a couple of days, and luckily I'm not on the schedule to work until the weekend. You don't mind, do you?"

"Not at all," Claudia said with a smile. Although Ashley's family lived in the nearby suburb of Kent, Ashley shared the apartment with Claudia because it was easier for her to commute to school. But she occasionally moved back home for a few days when her family needed her.

"You're sure you'll be all right?"

"Are you kidding?" Claudia joked. "The kitchen's full of cookies!"

Ashley laughed, but her large blue eyes contained a knowing look. "Don't be too hard on Cooper," she said, and gave Claudia a small hug before she left.

What good would it do to be angry with her uncle? Claudia thought. He had reacted the only way he knew how. Anger wouldn't help the situation.

The apartment felt large and lonely with Ashley gone. Claudia turned on the television and flipped through the channels, hoping to find something interesting, feeling guilty because she was ignoring her schoolwork. Nothing interesting on. Good, she decided, and forced herself to hit the books. This quarter wasn't going to be easy, and the sooner she sharpened her study habits, the better.

Two hours later she took a leisurely bath, dressed

in a long purple velour robe, curled up on the sofa and lost herself in a good book. Long ago she'd recognized that reading was her escape. When things were really bothering her, she would plow through one mystery after another, not really caring about the characters or the plot so long as the book was complicated enough to distract her from her troubles.

The alarm rang at six, and she stumbled out of bed, then stepped into the shower. As she stood under the hot spray, her thoughts drifted to Seth Lessinger. She felt definitely regretful at the way things had ended. She would have liked to get to know him better. On Sunday she would definitely have a talk with Cooper. She was old enough to choose who she wanted to date without his interference. It was bad enough being forced to endure a stilted dinner with him every Sunday afternoon.

She dressed in jeans, a long-sleeved blouse and a red sweater vest. As she poured herself a cup of coffee, she wondered how long she would have to force thoughts of Seth from her mind. The mystery novel had diverted her attention last night, but she couldn't live her life with her nose in a book. Today and tomorrow she would be busy with school, but this was Thursday, and she wasn't looking forward to spending the evenings and weekend alone. She decided to ask a friend in her psych class if she wanted to go to a movie tonight.

She sat sipping from her mug at the kitchen table,

her feet propped on the opposite chair, and read the morning paper. A quick look at her watch and she placed the cup in the sink and hurried out the door for school.

Claudia pulled into the apartment parking lot early that afternoon. It seemed everyone had already made plans for this evening, so she was on her own. Several of her friends were attending the Seahawks game. She loved football, and decided to microwave popcorn and watch the game on television. She had no sooner let herself into the apartment and hung up her jacket when the doorbell rang.

The peephole in the door showed an empty hall. Odd, but it could be her neighbor's son collecting for the jogathon. Claudia had sponsored the ten-year-old, who was trying to earn enough money for a soccer uniform. Todd had probably seen her pull into the parking lot. She opened the door and looked out into the hallway.

"Claudia?" There was surprise in his tone as he stepped away from the wall he'd been leaning on.

"Seth." Her heart tripped over itself.

"What are you doing here?" they both asked at the same time.

Claudia smiled. It was so good to see him, it didn't matter what had brought him here.

"I was looking for Ashley Robbins, the motel maid," he told her.

"Ashley?" Her curiosity was evident in her voice.

"Come in," she said, then closed the door after him. "Ashley's gone home for a few days to be help out her parents. Do you know her?"

"No." He stroked the side of his beard. "But I was hoping she could tell me how to find you."

"We're roommates," she explained, no doubt unnecessarily. "So...you were looking for me? Why?"

He looked slightly ill at ease. "I wanted to apologize for yesterday. I could at least have stayed and listened to your explanation."

"Cooper really is my uncle."

"I should have known you wouldn't lie. It wasn't until later that I realized I'd behaved like an idiot," he said, his face tight and drawn. "If I hadn't reacted like a jealous fool, I would have realized you would never lead anyone on like that."

"I know what you thought." She paused and glanced away. "And I know how it looked—how Cooper wanted it to look."

Seth ran a hand over his face. "Your uncle." He chuckled. Wrapping his arms around her, he lifted her off the ground and swung her around. Hands resting on the hard muscles of his shoulders, she threw back her head and laughed.

Soon the amusement died as their gazes met and held. Slowly he released her until her feet had securely settled on the carpet. With infinite gentleness, his hand brushed her face, caressing her smooth skin. It was so beautiful, so sweet, that she closed her eyes to the sensuous assault. Her fingers clung to his arms as he drew her into his embrace, and her lips trembled, anticipating his kiss.

Seth didn't disappoint either of them as his mouth settled firmly over hers. His hand slid down her back, molding her against him, arching her upward to meet the demand of his kiss.

Claudia felt her limbs grow weak as she surrendered to the sensations swirling inside her. Her hands spread over his chest, feeling she belonged there in his arms.

When he freed her mouth, his lips caressed the sensitive cord along the side of her neck.

"Does this mean you'll give me another chance?" he murmured, his voice faintly husky from the effects of the kiss.

"I'd say the prognosis is excellent," she replied, her breathing still affected. "But I'd like to explain a few things."

She led the way into the kitchen, poured mugs of coffee and added sugar to his the way she'd seen him do.

When she set his cup on the table, Seth reached for her hand and kissed her fingers. "Your family has money?" he asked.

"Yes, but I don't," she explained. "At least not yet. Cooper controls the purse strings for a little while longer. My father was Claude Masters. You may or may not have heard of him. He established a business supply corporation that has branch offices in five states. Dad died when I was in high school. Cooper is president of the company now, and my legal guardian." Her soft mouth quirked to one side. "He takes his responsibility seriously. I apologize if he offended you yesterday."

Humor glinted briefly in his expression. "The only thing that could possibly offend me is if you were married." He laughed, and she stared at him curiously. "I'll never wear five-hundred-dollar business suits. You understand that?"

Nodding, she smiled. "I can't imagine you in a suit at all."

"Oh, I've been known to wear one, but I hate it." Again she smiled.

"Do you hate having money?" He was regarding her steadily, his wide brow creased.

"No," she replied honestly. "I like having money when I need it. What I hate is being different from others, like Ashley and you. I have a hard time trusting people. I'm never really sure whether they like *me*. I find myself looking at any relationship with a jaundiced eye, wondering what the other person is expecting to receive from my friendship." She lowered her gaze, her fingers circling the top of the mug. "My father was the same way, and it made him close himself off from the world. I was brought up in a protected environment. I fought tooth and nail to convince Cooper I should attend the University of Washington. He wanted to send me to study at a private university in Switzerland."

"I'm glad you're here."

Claudia watched as Seth clenched and unclenched his hands.

"Do you think the reason I came back is because I figured out you have money?" he finally asked.

Something in his voice conveyed the seriousness of the question. "No, I don't think you're the type of person to be impressed by wealth. Just knowing you this little while, I believe if you wanted money, you'd have it. You're that type of man." Having stated her feelings, she fell silent.

"God gives the very best." The throaty whisper was barely discernible, and she glanced up, her blue eyes questioning.

"Pardon?"

Seth took her hand and carried it to his lips. The coarse hairs of his beard prickled her fingertips. "Nothing," he murmured. "I'll explain it to you later."

"I skipped lunch and I'm hungry, so I was going to fix myself a sandwich. Would you like one?" she offered.

"I would. In fact, you don't even need to ask. I'm always hungry. Let me help," he volunteered. "Believe it or not, I'm a darn good cook."

"You can slice the cheese if you like." She flashed him a happy smile.

"I hope you don't have any plans for the evening," he said, easing a knife through the slab of cheese. "I've got tickets for the game. The Seahawks are playing tonight, and I…" He paused, his look brooding, disconcerted.

"What's wrong?"

He sighed, walked to the other side of the small kitchen and stuck his huge hands inside his pants pockets. "Football isn't much of a woman's sport, is it?"

"What makes you say that?"

"I mean…" He looked around uneasily. "You don't have to go. It's not that important. I know that someone like you isn't—"

She didn't give him the chance to finish. "Someone like me," she repeated, "would love going to that game." Her eyes were smiling into his.

Amusement dominated his face as he slid his arms around her waist. One hand toyed with a strand of her hair. "We'll eat a sandwich now, then grab something for dinner after the game. All right, Red?" He said the name as if it were an endearment. "You don't mind if I call you that, do you?"

"Only you," she murmured just before his mouth claimed hers. "Only you."

The day was wonderful. They spent two hours talking almost nonstop. Claudia, who normally didn't drink more than a cup or two of coffee, shared two pots with Seth. She told him things she had never shared with anyone: her feelings during her father's short illness and after his death; the ache, the void in her life, afterward; and how the loss and the sadness had led her to Christ. She told him about her lifelong friendship with Ashley, the mother she had never known, medical school and her struggle for acceptance. There didn't seem to be anything she couldn't discuss with him.

In return he talked about his oil business, life in Nome and his own faith.

Before they knew it, it was time to get going. Claudia hurried to freshen up, but took the time to spray a light perfume at her pulse points. After running a comb through the unruly curls that framed her face, she tied them back at the base of her neck with a silk scarf. Seth was waiting for her in the living room. Checking her appearance one last time, she noted the happy sparkle in her eyes and paused to murmur a special thank-you that God had sent Seth back into her life.

Seth helped her into her jacket. Then he lovingly ran a rough hand and down her arm as he brought her even closer to his side.

"I don't know when I've enjoyed an afternoon more," he told her. "Thank you."

"I should be the one to thank you, Seth." She avoided eye contact, afraid how much her look would reveal.

"I knew the minute I saw you that you were someone very special. I didn't realize until today how right my hunch was." He looked down at her gently. "It wasn't so long ago that I believed Christians were a bunch of do-gooders. Not long ago that I thought religion was for the weak-minded. But I didn't know people like you. Now I wonder how I managed to live my life without Christ."

Claudia tugged at Seth's hand as she excitedly walked up the cement ramp of the Kingdome. "The game's about to start." They'd parked on the street, then walked the few blocks to the stadium, hurrying up First Avenue. The traffic was so heavy that they were a few minutes later than planned.

"I love football," she said, her voice high with enthusiasm.

"Look at all these people." Seth stopped and looked around in amazement.

"Seth," she groaned. "I don't want to miss the kickoff."

Because the game was being televised nationwide, the kickoff was slated for five o'clock Pacific time. More than sixty thousand fans filled the Kingdome to capacity. Seahawk fever ran high, and the entire stadium was on its feet for the kickoff. In the beginning she only applauded politely so she wouldn't embarrass Seth with her enthusiasm. But when it came to her favorite sport, no one could accuse her of being unemotional. Within minutes she was totally involved with the action on the field. She cheered wildly when the Seahawks made a good play, then shouted at the officials in protest of any call she thought was unfair.

Seth's behavior was much more subdued, and several times when she complained to him about a call, she found that he seemed to be watching her more closely than the game.

There was something about football that allowed her to be herself, something that broke down her natural reserve. With her class schedule, she couldn't often afford the time to attend a game. But if at all possible she watched on TV, jumping on the furniture in exaltation, pounding the couch cushions in despair. Most of her classmates wouldn't have believed it was her. At school she was serious, all about the work, since she still felt the need to prove herself to her classmates. Although she had won respect from most of the other students, a few still believed her name and money were the only reasons she had been accepted.

"Touchdown!" Her arms flew into the air, and she leaped to her feet.

For the first time since the game had started, Seth showed as much emotion as she did. Lifting her high, he held her tight against him. Her hands framed his face, and it seemed the most natural thing in the world, as she stared into his dark, hungry eyes, to press her lips to his. Immediately he deepened the kiss, wrapping his arms around her, lifting her higher off the ground.

The cheering died to an excited chatter before either of them was aware of the crowd.

"We have an audience," he murmured huskily in her ear.

"It's just as well, don't you think?" Her face was

flushed lightly. She had known almost from the beginning that the attraction between them was stronger than anything she had experienced with another man. Seth seemed to have recognized that, as well. The effect they had on each other was strong and disturbing. He had kissed her only three times, and already they were aware of how easy it would be to let their attraction rage out of control. It was exciting, but it was also frightening.

After the game—which the Seahawks won—they stopped for hamburgers. When Seth had finished his meal, he returned to the counter and bought them each an ice cream sundae.

"When you come to Alaska, I'll have my Inuit friends make you some of their ice cream," he said. His eyes flashed her a look of amusement.

Claudia's stomach tightened. *When* she came to Alaska? She hadn't stopped to think about visiting America's last frontier. From the beginning she had known that Seth would be in Seattle for only a few days. She had known and accepted that as best she could.

Deciding it was best to ignore the comment, she cocked her head to one side. "Okay, I'll play your little game. What's Inuit ice cream?"

"Berries, snow and rancid seal oil."

"Well, at least it's organic."

Seth chuckled. "It's that, all right."

Claudia twisted the red plastic spoon, making circles in the soft ice cream. She avoided Seth's gaze, just as she had been eluding facing the inevitable.

Gathering her resolve, hoping maybe his plans had changed, she raised her face, her eyes meeting his. "When will you be returning to Nome?"

He pushed his dessert aside, his hand reaching for hers. "My flight's booked for tomorrow afternoon."

# Chapter 3

The muscles of Claudia's throat constricted. "Tomorrow," she repeated, knowing she sounded like a parrot. Lowering her gaze, she continued, "That doesn't leave us much time, does it?" She'd thought she was prepared. After all, she reminded herself yet again, she'd known from the beginning that Seth would only be in Seattle for a few days.

Lifting her eyes to his watchful gaze, she offered Seth a weak smile. "I know this sounds selfish, but I don't want you to go."

"Then I won't," he announced casually.

Her head shot up. "What do you mean?"

The full force of his magnetic gaze was resting on her. "I mean I'll stay a few more days."

Her heart seemed to burst into song. "Over the

weekend?" Eyes as blue as the Caribbean implored him. "My only obligation is dinner Sunday with Cooper, but you could come. In fact, I'd like it if you did. My uncle will probably bore you to tears, but I'd like you to get to know each other. Will you stay that long?" She tilted her head questioningly, hopefully.

Seth chuckled. She loved his laugh. The loud, robust sound seemed to roll from deep within his chest. She'd watched him during the football game and couldn't help laughing with him.

"Will you?" she repeated.

"I have the feeling your uncle isn't going to welcome me with open arms."

"No." She smiled beguilingly. "But I will."

The restaurant seemed to go still. Seth's gaze was penetrating, his voice slightly husky. "Then I'll stay, but no longer than Monday."

"Okay." She was more than glad, she was jubilant. There hadn't been time to question this magnetic attraction that had captured them, and deep down she didn't want to investigate her feelings, even though she knew this was all happening too fast.

Seth's slipped his arm around her waist as they walked to the car. He held open the door for her and waited until she was seated. Unconsciously she smoothed the leather seat cushion, the texture smooth against the tips of her fingers. The vehicle had surprised her. Seth didn't fit the luxury-car image, but she hadn't mentioned it earlier, before the game.

"This thing *is* a bit much, isn't it?" His gaze

briefly scanned the interior. The high-end sedan was fitted with every convenience, from the automatic sunroof to a satellite sound system to built-in Bluetooth technology.

"So why did you rent it?" she felt obliged to ask.

"Why did I—heavens, no! This is all part of the sisters' efforts to get me to sign the contract."

"The sisters?"

"That's a slang expression for the major oil conglomerates. They seem to feel the need to impress me. They originally had me staying at one of those big downtown hotels, in a suite that was over seven hundred dollars a night. I didn't feel comfortable with that and found my own place. But I couldn't refuse the car without offending some important people."

"We all get caught in that trap sometimes."

Seth agreed with a short, preoccupied nod. Although the game had finished over an hour earlier, the downtown traffic was at a standstill. Cautiously he eased the car into the heavy flow of bumper-to-bumper traffic.

While they were caught in the snarl of impatient drivers, Claudia studies his strong profile. Several times his mouth tightened, and he shook his head in disgust.

"I'm sorry, Seth," she said solemnly, and smiled lamely when he glanced at her.

He arched his thick brows. "You're sorry? Why?"

"The traffic. I should have known to wait another hour, until things had thinned out a bit more."

"It's not your fault." His enormous hand squeezed hers reassuringly.

"Don't you have traffic jams in Nome?" she asked, partly to keep the conversation flowing, and partly to counteract the crazy reaction her heart seemed to have every time he touched her.

"Traffic jams in Nome?" He smiled. "Red, Nome's population is under four thousand. Some days my car is the only one on the road."

Her eyes narrowed suspiciously. "You're teasing? I thought Nome was a major city."

He laughed as he returned both hands to the wheel, and her heartbeat relaxed. "The population of the entire state is only 700,000, a fraction of Washington's nearly seven million." A smile softened his rugged features. "Anchorage is the largest city in Alaska, with under 300,000 residents."

An impatient motorist honked, and Seth pulled forward onto the freeway entrance ramp. The traffic remained heavy but finally it was at least moving at a steady pace.

"I couldn't live like this," he said and expelled his breath forcefully. "Too many people, too many buildings and," he added with a wry grin, "too many cars."

"Don't worry. You won't have to put up with it much longer," she countered with a smile that she hoped didn't look as forced as it felt.

Seth scowled thoughtfully and didn't reply.

He parked the car in the lot outside her apartment building and refused her invitation to come in for coffee. "I have a meeting in the morning, but it shouldn't go any longer than noon. Can I see you then?"

She nodded, pleased. "Of course." She would treasure every minute she had left with him. "Shall I phone Cooper and tell him you're coming for dinner Sunday?"

"He won't mind?"

"Oh, I'm sure he will, but if he objects too strongly, we'll have our own dinner."

He reached out to caress the delicate curve of her cheek and entwined his fingers with the auburn curls along the nape of her neck. "Would it be considered bad manners to hope he objects strenuously?" he asked.

"Cooper's not so bad." She felt as if she should at least make the effort to explain her uncle. "I don't think he means to come off so pompous, he just doesn't know how else to act. What he needs is a woman to love." She smiled inwardly. "I can just hear him cough and sputter if I were to tell him that."

"*I* need a woman to love," Seth whispered as his mouth found hers. The kiss was deep and intense, as if to convince her of the truth of his words.

Claudia wound her arms around his neck, surrendering to the mastery of his kiss. *He's serious,* her mind repeated. *Dead serious.* The whole world seemed right when he was holding her like this. He covered her neck and the hollow of her throat with light, tiny kisses. She tilted her head to give him better access, reveling in the warm feel of his lips against the creamy smoothness of her skin. A shudder of desire ran through her, and she bit into her bottom lip to conceal the effect he had on her senses.

Taking a deep breath, he straightened. "Let's get you inside before this gets out of hand." His voice sounded raw and slightly uneven.

He kissed her again outside her apartment door, but this kiss lacked the ardor of a few minutes earlier. "I'll see you about noon tomorrow."

With a trembling smile she nodded.

"Don't look at me like that," he groaned. His strong hands stroked the length of her arms as he edged her body closer. "It's difficult enough to say good night."

Standing on tiptoe, she lightly brushed her mouth over his.

"Claudia," he growled in warning.

She placed her fingertips over her moist lips, then over his, to share the mock kiss with him.

He closed his eyes as if waging some deep inner battle, then covered her fingers with his own.

"Good night," she whispered, glorying in the way he reacted to her.

"I'll see you tomorrow."

"Tomorrow," she repeated dreamily.

Dressed in her pajamas and bathrobe, Claudia sat on top of her bed an hour later, reading her Bible.

Her concentration drifted to the events of the past week and all the foreign emotions she had encountered. This thing with Seth was happening too fast, far too fast. No man had ever evoked such an intensity of emotion within her. No man had made her feel the things he did. Love, real love, didn't happen like this. The timing was all wrong. She couldn't fall in love—not now. Not with a man who was only going to be in Seattle for a few more days. But why had God sent Seth into her life when it would be so easy to fall in love with him? Was it a test? A lesson in faith? She was going to be a doctor. The Lord had led her to that decision, and there wasn't anything in her life she was more sure of. Falling in love with Seth Lessinger could ruin that. Still troubled, she turned off the light and attempted to sleep.

Claudia was ready at noon, but for what she wasn't sure. Dressed casually in jeans and a sweater, she thought she might suggest a drive to Snoqualmie Falls. And if Seth felt ambitious, maybe a hike around Mount Si. She didn't have the time to do much hiking herself, but she enjoyed the outdoors whenever possible. The mental picture of idly strolling with Seth, appreciating the beautiful world God had provided, was an appealing one. Of course, doing anything with Seth was appealing.

When he hadn't shown up or called by one, she started to get worried. Every minute seemed interminable, and she glanced at her watch repeatedly.

When the phone rang at one-thirty, she grabbed the receiver before it had a chance to ring again.

"Hello?" she said anxiously.

"Red?" Seth asked.

"Yes, it's me." He didn't sound right; he seemed tired, impatient.

"I've been held up here. There's not much chance of my getting out of this meeting until late afternoon."

"Oh." She tried to hide the disappointment in her voice.

"I know, honey, I feel the same way." The depth of his tone relayed his own frustration. "I'll make it up to you tonight. Can you be ready around seven for dinner? Wear something fancy."

"Sure." She forced a cheerful note into her voice. "I'll see you then. Take care."

"I've got to get back inside. If you happen to think of me, say a prayer. I want this business over so we can enjoy what's left of our time."

*If* she thought of him? She nearly laughed out loud. "I will," she promised, knowing it was a promise she would have no trouble keeping.

Cooper phoned about ten minutes later. "You left a message for me to call?" he began.

Claudia half suspected that he expected her to apologize for the little scene downtown with Seth. "Yes," she replied evenly. "I'm inviting a guest for dinner Sunday."

"Who?" he asked, and she could almost picture him bracing himself because he knew the answer.

"Seth Lessinger. You already met him once this week."

The line seemed to crackle with a lengthy silence. "As you wish," he said tightly.

A mental picture formed of Cooper writing down Seth's name. Undoubtedly, before Sunday, her uncle would know everything there was to know about Seth, from his birth weight to his high school grade point average.

"We'll see you then."

"Claudia," Cooper said, then hesitated. Her uncle didn't often hesitate. Usually he knew his mind and wasn't afraid to speak it. "You're not serious about this—" he searched for the right word "—man, are you?"

"Why?" It felt good to turn the tables, answering her cagey uncle with a question of her own. Why should he be so concerned? She was old enough to do anything she pleased.

He allowed an unprecedented second pause. "No reason. I'll see you Sunday."

Thoughtfully she replaced the receiver and released her breath in a slow sigh. Cooper had sounded different, on edge, not like his normal self at all. Her mouth quivered with a suppressed smile. He was worried; she'd heard it in his voice. For the first time since he'd been appointed her guardian, he had showed some actual feelings toward her. The smile grew. Maybe he wasn't such a bad guy after all.

Scanning the contents of her closet later that afternoon, Claudia chose a black lace dress she had bought on impulse the winter before. It wasn't the type of dress she would wear to church, although it wasn't low-cut or revealing. It was made of Cluny lace and had a three-tiered skirt. She had seen it displayed in an exclusive boutique and hadn't been able to resist, though she was angry with herself afterward for buying something so extravagant. She was unlikely to find a reason to wear such an elegant dress, but she loved it anyway. Even Ashley had been surprised when Claudia had showed it to her. No one could deny that it was a beautiful, romantic dress.

She arranged her auburn curls into a loose chignon at the top of her head, with tiny ringlets falling at the sides of her face. The diamond earrings she popped in had been her mother's, and Claudia had worn them only a couple of times. Seth had said fancy, though, so he was going to get fancy!

He arrived promptly at seven. One look at her and his eyes showed surprise, then something else she couldn't decipher.

Slowly his gaze traveled over her face and figure, openly admiring the curves of her hips and her slender legs.

"Wow."

"Wow yourself," she returned, equally impressed. She'd seen him as a virile and intriguing man even without the rich dark wool suit. But now he was compelling, so attractive she could hardly take her eyes off him.

"Turn around. I want to look at you," he requested, his attention centered on her. His voice sounded ragged, as if seeing her had stolen away his breath.

Claudia did as he asked, slowly twirling around. "Now you."

"Me?" He looked stunned.

"You." She laughed, her hands directing his movements. Self-consciously he turned, his movements abrupt and awkward. "Where are we going?" she asked while she admired.

"The Space Needle." He took her coat out of her hands and held it open for her. She turned and slid her arm into the satin-lined sleeves. He guided it over her shoulders, and his hands lingered there as he brought her back against him. She heard him inhale sharply before kissing the gentle slope of her neck.

"Let's go," he murmured, "while I'm still able to resist other temptations."

Seth parked outside the Seattle Center, and they walked hand in hand toward the city's most famous landmark.

"Next summer we'll go to the Food Circus," she mentioned casually. If he could say things about her visiting Alaska, she could talk the same way to him.

Seth didn't miss a step, but his hand tightened over hers. "Why next summer? Why not now?"

"Because you've promised me dinner on top of the city, and I'm not about to let you out of that. But no one visiting Seattle should miss the Food Circus. I don't even know how many booths there are, all serving exotic dishes from all over the world. The worst part is having to make a decision. When Ashley and I go there, we each buy something different and divide it. That way we each get to taste more new things." She stopped talking and smiled. "I'm chattering, aren't I?"

"A little." She could hear the amusement in his voice.

The outside elevators whisked them up the Space Needle to the observation deck six-hundred-and-seven feet above the ground. The night was glorious, and brilliant lights illuminated the world below. Seth stood behind her, his arms looped over her shoulders, pulling her close.

"I think my favorite time to see this view is at night," she said. "I love watching all the lights. I've never stopped to wonder why the night lights enthrall me the way they do. But I think it's probably because Jesus told us we were the light of the world, and from up here I can see how much even one tiny light can illuminate."

"I hadn't thought of it like that," he murmured close to her ear. "But you have to remember I'm a new Christian. There are a lot of things I haven't discovered yet."

"That's wonderful, too."

"How do you mean?"

She shrugged lightly. "God doesn't throw all this knowledge and insight at us at once. He lets us digest it little by little, as we're able."

"Just as any loving father would do," Seth said quietly.

They stood for several minutes until a chill ran over Claudia's arms.

"Cold?" he questioned.

"Only a little. It's so lovely out here, I don't want to leave."

"It's beautiful, all right, but it's more the woman I'm with than the scenery."

"Thank you," she murmured, pleased by his words.

"You're blushing," he said as he turned her around to face him. "I don't believe it—you're blushing."

Embarrassed, she looked away. "Men don't usually say such romantic things to me."

"Why not? You're a beautiful woman. By now you must have heard those words a thousand times over."

"Not really." The color was creeping up her neck. "That's the floating bridge over there." She pointed into the distance, attempting to change the subject. "It's the largest concrete pontoon bridge in the world. It connects Mercer Island and Seattle."

"Claudia," Seth murmured, his voice dipping slightly, "you are a delight. If we weren't out here with the whole city looking on, I'd take you in my arms and kiss you senseless."

"Promises, promises," she teased and hurried inside before he could make good on his words.

They ate a leisurely meal and talked over coffee for so long that she looked around guiltily. Friday night was one of the busiest nights for the restaurant business, and they were taking up a table another couple could be using.

"I'll make us another cup at my place," she volunteered.

Seth didn't argue.

The aroma of fresh-brewed coffee filled the apartment. Claudia poured two cups and carried them into the living room.

Seth was sitting on the long green couch, flipping through the pages of one of the medical journals she had stacked on the end table.

"Are you planning on specializing?"

She nodded. "Yes, pediatrics."

His dark brown eyes became intent. "Do you enjoy children that much, Red?"

"Oh, yes," she said fervently. "Maybe it's because I was an only child and never had enough other kids around. I can remember lining up my dolls and playing house."

"I thought every little girl did that?"

"At sixteen?" she teased, then laughed at the expression on his face. "The last two summers I've worked part-time in a day care center, and the experience convinced me to go into pediatrics. But that's a long way down the road. I'm only a second-year med student."

When they'd finished their coffee, she carried the cups to the kitchen sink. He followed her, slipping his hands around her waist. All her senses reacted to his touch.

"Can I see you in the morning?" he asked.

She nodded, afraid her voice would tremble if she spoke. His finger traced the line of her cheek, and she held her breath, bracing herself as his touch trailed over her soft lips. Instinctively she reached for him, her hands gliding up his chest and over the corded muscles of his shoulders, which flexed beneath her exploring fingers.

He rasped out her name before his mouth hungrily descended on hers. A heady excitement engulfed her. Never had there been a time in her life when she was more gloriously happy. The kiss was searing, turbulent, wrenching her heart and touching her soul.

"Red?" His hold relaxed, and with infinite care he studied her soft, yielding eyes, filled with the depth of her emotions. "Oh, Red." He inhaled several sharp breaths and pressed his forehead to hers. "Don't tempt me like this." The words were a plea that seemed to come deep from within him.

"You're doing the same thing to me," she whispered softly, having trouble with her own breathing.

"We should stop now."

"I know," she agreed, but neither of them pulled away. How could she think reasonable thoughts when he was so close? A violent eruption of Mount St. Helens couldn't compare with the ferocity of her emotions.

Slowly she pulled back, easing herself from his arms.

He dropped his hands to his sides. "We have to be careful, Red. My desire for you is strong, but I want us to be good. I don't think I could ever forgive myself if I were to lead us into temptation."

"Oh, Seth," she whispered, her blue eyes shimmering with tears. "It's not all you. I'm feeling these things just as strongly. Maybe it's not such a good idea for us to be alone anymore."

"No." His husky voice rumbled with turmoil. A tortured silence followed. He paced the floor, raking his fingers through his thick brown hair. "It's selfish, I know, but there's so little time left. We'll be careful and help one another. It won't be much longer that we'll be able..." He let the rest of the sentence fade.

Not much longer, her mind repeated.

He picked up the jacket he'd discarded over the back of a chair and held out a hand to her. "Walk me to the door."

Linking her fingers with his, she did as he asked. He paused at the door, his hand on the knob. "Good night."

"Good night," she responded with a weak smile.

He bent downward and gently brushed her lips. Although the contact was light, almost teasing, Claudia's response was immediate. She yearned for the feel of his arms again, and felt painfully empty when he turned away and closed the door behind him.

They spent almost every minute of Saturday together. In the morning Seth drove them to Snoqualmie Falls, where they ate a picnic lunch, then took a leisurely stroll along the trails leading to the water. Later in the day they visited the Seattle Aquarium on the waterfront, and ate a dinner of fresh fish and crusty, deep-fried potatoes.

When she got home that night, there was a message from Cooper. When she called back, he said he just wanted to tell her that he was looking forward to getting to know Seth over Sunday dinner, a gesture that surprised her.

"He's a good man," her uncle announced. "I've been hearing quite a few impressive things about your friend. I'll apologize to him for my behavior the other day," he continued.

"I'm sure Seth understands," she assured him.

She hadn't known Seth for even a week, and yet it felt like a lifetime. Her feelings for him were clear now. She had never experienced the deep womanly yearnings Seth aroused within her. The attraction was sometimes so strong that it shocked her—and she could tell that it shocked him, too. Aware of their vulnerability, they'd carefully avoided situations that would tempt them. Even though Seth touched her often and made excuses to caress her, he was cautious, and their kisses were never allowed to deepen into the passion they'd shared the night they dined at the Space Needle.

On Sunday morning Claudia woke early, with an eagerness that reminded her of her childhood. The past week had been her happiest since before her father's death.

She and Seth attended the early morning church service together, and she introduced him to her Christian family. Her heart filled with emotion as he sat beside her in the wooden pew. There was nothing more she would ask of a man than a deep, committed faith in the Lord.

Afterward they went back to her apartment. The table was set with her best dishes and linen. Now she set out fresh-squeezed orange juice and delicate butter croissants on china plates. A single candle and dried-flower centerpiece decorated the table.

She had chosen a pink dress and piled her hair high on her head again, with tiny curls falling free to frame her face. Although Seth would be leaving tomorrow, she didn't want to deal with that now, and she quickly dismissed the thought. Today was special, their last day together, and she refused to let the reality of a long separation trouble her.

"I hope you're up to my cooking," she said to him as she took her special egg casserole from the oven.

He stood framed in the doorway, handsome and vital. He still wore his dark wool suit, but he held his tie in one hand as if he didn't want that silken noose around his neck any longer than absolutely necessary.

Just having him this close made all her senses pulsate with happiness, and a warm glow stole over her.

"You don't need to worry. My stomach can handle just about anything," he teased gently. He studied her for a moment. "I can't call you Red in a dress like that." He came to her and kissed her lightly. Claudia sighed at the sweetness of his caress.

"I hope I don't have to wait much longer. I'm starved."

"You really *are* always hungry," she teased. "But how can you think about food when I'm here to tempt you?"

"It's more difficult than you know," he said with a smile. "Can I do anything?"

Claudia answered him with a short shake of her head.

"Then are you going to feed me or not?" His roguish smile only highlighted his irresistible masculinity.

The special baked egg recipe was one Ashley's mother had given her. Claudia was pleased when Seth asked for seconds.

When he finished eating, he took a small package from his coat pocket. "This thing has been burning a hole in my pocket all morning. Open it now."

Claudia took the package and shook it, holding it close to her ear. "For me?" she asked, her eyes sparkling with excitement.

"I brought it with me from Nome."

From Nome? That was certainly intriguing. Carefully she untied the bow and removed the red foil paper, revealing a black velvet jeweler's box.

"Before you open it, I want to explain something." He leaned forward, resting his elbows on the table. "For a long time I've been married to my job, building my company. It wasn't until..." He hesitated. "I won't go into the reason, but I decided I wanted a wife. Whenever I needed anything in the past, I simply went out and bought it, but I knew finding a good woman wouldn't work like that. She had to be someone special, someone I could love and respect, someone who shared my faith. The more I thought about the complexities of finding that special woman, the more I realized how difficult it would be to find her."

"Seth—"

"No, let me explain," he continued, reaching for her hand. He gripped it hard, his eyes studying her intently. "I was reading my Bible one night and came across the story of Abraham sending a servant to find a wife for Isaac. Do you remember the story?"

She nodded, color draining from her features. "Seth, please—"

"There's more. Bear with me." He raised her hand to his lips and very gently kissed her fingers. "If you remember, the servant did as Abraham bade and traveled to the land of his master's family. But he was uncertain. The weight of his responsibility bore heavily upon him. So the servant prayed, asking

God to give him a sign. God answered that prayer and showed the servant that Rebekah was the right woman for Isaac. Scripture says how much Isaac loved his wife, and how she comforted him after the death of his mother, Sarah."

"Seth, please, I know what you're going to say—"

"Be patient, my love," he interrupted her again. "After reading that account, I decided to trust the Lord to give me a wife. I was also traveling to the land of my family. Both my mother and father originally came from Washington State. I prayed about it. I also purchased the engagement ring before I left Nome. And like Abraham's servant, I, too, asked God for a sign. I was beginning to lose hope. I'd already been here several days before you placed that card with the verse in the mirror. You can't imagine how excited I was when I found it."

Claudia swallowed tightly, recalling his telling her that the message had meant more to him than she would ever know. She wanted to stop him, but the lump in her throat had grown so large that speaking was impossible.

"I want you to come back to Nome with me tomorrow, Red. We can be married in a few days."

# Chapter 4

Claudia's eyes widened with incredulous disbelief. "Married in a few days?" she repeated. "But, Seth, we've only been together less than a week! We can't—"

"Sure we can," he countered, his eyes serious. "I knew even before I found the Bible verse in the mirror that it was you. Do you remember how you bumped into me that first day in the outside corridor?" Although he asked the question, he didn't wait for the answer. "I was stunned. Didn't you notice how my eyes followed you? Something came over me right then. I had to force myself not to run and stop you. At the time I assumed I was simply physically reacting to a beautiful woman. But once I found the Bible verse on the mirror, I knew."

"What about school?" Somehow the words made it past the large knot constricting her throat.

A troubled look tightened his mouth. "I've done a lot of thinking about that. It's weighed heavily on me. I know how much becoming a doctor means to you." He caught her hand and gently kissed the palm. "Someday, Red, we'll be able to move to Anchorage and you can finish med school. I promise you that."

Taking her hand from his, Claudia closed the jeweler's box. The clicking sound seemed to be magnified a thousand times, a cacophony of sound echoing around the room.

"Seth, we've only known each other a short time. So much more goes into building the foundation for a relationship that will support a marriage. It takes more than a few days."

"Rebekah didn't even meet Isaac. She responded in faith, going with the servant to a faraway land to join a man she had never seen. Yet she went," he argued.

"You're being unfair," she said as she stood and walked to the other side of the room. Her heart was pounding so hard she could feel the blood pulsating through her veins. "We live in the twentieth century, not biblical times. How do we know what Rebekah was feeling? Her father was probably the one who said she would go. More than likely, Rebekah didn't have any choice in the matter."

"You don't know that," he said.

"You don't, either," she shot back. "We hardly know each other."

"You keep saying that! What more do you need to know?"

She gestured weakly with her hands. "Everything."

"Come on, Red. You're overreacting. You know more about me than any other woman ever has. We've done nothing but talk every day. I'm thirty-six, own and operate the Arctic Barge Company, wear size thirteen shoes, like ketchup on my fried eggs and peanut butter on my pancakes. My tastes are simple, my needs few. I tend to be impatient, but God and I are working on that. Usually I don't anger quickly, but when I do, stay clear. After we're married, there will undoubtedly be things we'll need to discuss, but nothing we shouldn't be able to settle."

"Seth, I—"

"Let me see," he continued undaunted. "Did I leave anything out?" He paused again. "Oh yes. The most important part is that I love you, Claudia Masters."

The sincerity with which he said the words trapped the oxygen in her lungs, leaving her speechless.

"This is the point where you're supposed to say, 'And I love you, Seth.'" He rose, coming to stand directly in front of her. His hands cupped her shoulders as his gaze fell lovingly upon her. "Now, repeat after me: *I...love...you.*"

Claudia couldn't. She tried to say something, but nothing would come. "I can't." She had to choke out the words. "It's unfair to ask me to give up everything I've worked so hard for. I'm sorry, Seth, really sorry."

"Claudia!" His mouth was strained and tight; there was no disguising the bitter disappointment in his voice. "Don't say no, not yet. Think about it. I'm not leaving until tomorrow morning."

"Tomorrow morning." She closed her eyes. "I'm supposed to know by then?"

"You should know now," he whispered.

"But I don't," she snapped. "You say that God gave you a sign that I was to be the wife He had chosen for you. Don't you find it the least bit suspicious that God would say something to you and *nothing* to me?"

"Rebekah didn't receive a sign," he explained rationally. "Abraham's servant did. She followed in faith."

"You're comparing two entirely different times and situations."

"What about the verse you stuck in the mirror? Haven't you ever wondered about that? You told me you'd never done anything like that before."

"But…"

"You have no argument, Red."

"I most certainly do."

"Can you honestly say you don't feel the electricity between us?"

How could she? "I can't deny it, but it doesn't change anything."

Seth smoothed a coppery curl from her forehead, his touch gentle, his eyes imploring. "Of course it does. I think that once you come to Nome you'll understand."

"I'm not going to Nome," she reiterated forcefully. "If you want to marry me, then you'll have to move to Seattle. I won't give up my dreams because of a six-day courtship and your feeling that you received a sign from God."

Seth looked shocked for a moment but recovered quickly. "I can't move to Seattle. My business, my home and my whole life are in Nome."

"But don't you understand? That's exactly what you're asking *me* to do. My education, my home and my friends are all here in Seattle."

Seth glanced uncomfortably around the room, then directed his gaze back to her. His dark eyes were filled with such deep emotion that it nearly took Claudia's breath away. Tears shimmered in her eyes, and his tall, masculine figure blurred as the moisture welled.

Gently Seth took her in his arms, holding her head to his shoulder. His jacket felt smooth and comforting against her cheek.

Tenderly he caressed her neck, and she could feel his breath against her hair. "Red, I'm sorry," he whispered with such love that fresh tears followed a crooked course down her wan cheeks. "I've known all this from the first day. It's unfair to spring it on you at the last minute. I know it must sound crazy to you now. But think about what I've said. And remember that I love you. Nothing's going to change that. Now dry your eyes and we'll visit your uncle. I promise not to mention this again today." He kissed the top of her head and gently pulled away.

"Here." She handed him the jeweler's box.

"No." He shook his head. "I want you to keep the ring. You may not feel like you want it now, but you will soon. I have to believe that, Red."

Her face twisted with pain. "I don't know that I should."

"Yes, you should." Brief anger flared in his eyes. "Please."

Because she couldn't refuse without hurting him even more, Claudia agreed with an abrupt nod.

Since she certainly couldn't wear the ring, she placed the velvet box in a drawer. Her hand trembled when she pushed the drawer back into place, but she put on a brave smile when she turned toward Seth.

To her dismay, his returning smile was just as sad as hers.

Cooper knew something was wrong almost immediately. That surprised Claudia, who had never found her uncle to be sensitive to her moods. But when he asked what was troubling her, she quickly denied that anything was. She couldn't expect him to understand what was happening.

The two men eyed each other like wary dogs that had crossed paths unexpectedly. Cooper, for his part, was welcoming, but Seth was brooding and distant.

When they sat down to dinner, Seth smiled ruefully.

"What's wrong?" Claudia asked.

"Nothing," he said, shaking his head. "It's just this is the first time I've needed three spoons to eat one meal."

Cooper arched his thick brows expressively, as if to say he didn't know how anyone could possibly do without three spoons for anything.

Claudia looked from one man to the other, noting the differences. They came from separate worlds. Although she found Cooper's attitudes and demeanor boring and confining, she was, after all, his own flesh and blood. If she were to marry Seth, give up everything that was important to her and move to Alaska, could she adjust to his way of life?

During the remainder of the afternoon she often found her gaze drawn to Seth. He and Cooper played a quiet game of chess in the den, while she sat nearby, studying them.

In the few days they had spent together, she had been witness to the underlying thread of tenderness that ran through Seth's heart. At the same time, he was self-assured, and although she had never seen the ruthless side of his nature, she didn't doubt that it existed. He was the kind of man to thrive on challenges; he wasn't afraid of hardships. But would she?

Resting her head against the back of the velvet swivel rocker, she slowly lowered her gaze. The problem was that she also knew Seth was the type of man who loved intensely. His love hadn't been offered lightly; he wanted her forever. But most of all, he wanted her now—today. At thirty-six he had waited a long time to find a wife. His commitment was complete. He had looked almost disbelieving when she hadn't felt the same way.

Or did she? She couldn't deny that the attraction between them was powerful, almost overwhelming. But that was physical, and there was so much more to love than the physical aspect. Spiritually they shared the same faith. To Claudia, that was vital; she wouldn't share her life with a man who didn't believe as she did. But mentally they were miles apart. Each of them had goals and dreams that the other would never share. Seth seemed almost to believe medical school was a pastime, a hobby, for her. He had no comprehension of the years of hard work and study that had gotten her this far. The dream had been ingrained in her too long for her to relinquish it on the basis of a six-day courtship. And it wasn't only her dream, but one her beloved father had shared.

Seth hadn't understood any of that. Otherwise he wouldn't have asked her to give it all up without a question or thought. He believed that God had shown him that she was to be his wife, and that was all that mattered. If only life were that simple! Seth was a new Christian, eager, enthusiastic, but also unseasoned—not that she was a tower of wisdom and discernment. But she would never have prayed for anything so crazy. She was too down to earth—like Cooper. She hated to compare herself to her uncle, but in this instance it was justified.

Cooper's smile turned faintly smug, and Claudia realized he was close to putting Seth in check, if not checkmate. She didn't need to be told that Seth's mind was preoccupied with their conversation this morning and not on the game. Several times in the last hour he had lifted his gaze to hers. One look could reveal so much, although until that day she had never been aware just how *much* his eyes could say. He wanted her so much, more than he would ever tell her. Guiltily her lashes fluttered downward; watching him was hurting them both too much.

Not long afterwards he kissed her good night outside her apartment, thanking her for the day. The lump that had become her constant companion blocked her throat, keeping her from thanking him for the beautiful solitaire diamond she would probably never wear.

"My flight's due to take off at seven-thirty," he said without looking at her.

"I'll be there," she whispered.

He held her then, so tightly that for a moment she found it impossible to breathe. She felt him shudder, and tears prickled her eyes as he whispered, "I love you, Red."

She couldn't say it, couldn't repeat the words he

desperately longed to hear. She bit her tongue to keep from sobbing. She longed to tell him how she felt, but the words wouldn't come. They stuck in her throat until it constricted painfully and felt raw. Why had God given her a man who could love her so completely when she was so wary?

Claudia set the alarm for five. If Seth's flight took off at seven-thirty, then she should meet him at the airport at six. That early, he would be able to clear security quickly. On the ride back from Cooper's she'd volunteered to drive him, but he'd declined the invitation and said he would take a taxi.

Sleep didn't come easily, and when it did, her dreams were filled with questions. Although she searched everywhere, she couldn't find the answers.

Claudia's blue eyes looked haunted and slightly red when she woke up, though she tried to camouflage the effects of her restless night with cosmetics.

The morning was dark and drizzly as she climbed inside her car and started the engine. The heater soon took the bite out of early morning, and she pulled onto the street. With every mile her heart grew heavier. A prayer came automatically to her lips. She desperately wanted to do the right thing: right for Seth, right for her. She prayed that if her heavenly Father wanted her to marry Seth, then He would make the signs as clear for her as He'd apparently done for Seth. Did she lack faith? Was that the problem.

"No," she answered her own question aloud. But her heart seemed to respond with a distant "yes" that echoed through her mind.

She parked in the garage, pulled her purse strap over her shoulder and hurried along the concourse. *I'm doing the right thing,* she mentally repeated with each step. Her heels clicked against the marble floor, seeming to pound out the message—right thing, right thing, right thing.

She paused when she saw Seth waiting for her, as promised, in the coffee shop. The only word for the way he looked was "dejected." She whispered a prayer, seeking strength and wisdom.

"Morning, Seth," she greeted him, forcing herself to smile.

His expression remained blank as he purposely looked away from her.

This was going to be more difficult than she'd imagined. The atmosphere was so tense and strained, she could hardly tolerate it. "You're angry, aren't you?"

"No," he responded dryly. "I've gone beyond the anger stage. Disillusioned, perhaps. You must think I'm a crazy man, showing up with an engagement ring and the belief that God had given me this wonderful message that we were to marry."

"Seth, no." She placed a hand on his arm.

He looked down at it and moved his arm, breaking her light hold. It was almost as if he couldn't tolerate her touch.

"The funny thing is," he continued, his expression stoic, "until this minute I didn't accept that I'd be returning to Alaska alone. Even when I woke up this morning, I believed that something would happen and you'd decide to come with me." He took a deep breath, his gaze avoiding hers. "I've behaved like a fool."

"Don't say that," she pleaded.

He glanced at her then, with regret, doubt and a deep sadness crossing his face. "We would have had beautiful children, Red." He lightly caressed her cheek.

"Will you stop talking like that?" she demanded, becoming angry. "You're being unfair."

He tilted his head and shrugged his massive shoulders. "I know. You love me, Red. You haven't admitted it to yourself yet. The time will come when you can, but I doubt that even then it will make much difference. Because, although you love me, you don't love me enough to leave the luxury of your life behind."

She wanted to argue with him, but she couldn't. Unbidden tears welled in the blue depths of her eyes, and she lowered her head, blinking frantically to still their fall.

She held her head high and glared at him with all her anguish in her eyes for him to see. "I'm going to forgive you for that, because I know you don't mean it. You're hurting, and because of that you want me to suffer, too." Tugging the leather purse strap over

her shoulder, she stood and took a step back. "I can't
see that my being here is doing either of us any good.
I wish you well, and I thank you for six of the most
wonderful days of my life. God bless you, Seth." She
turned and stalked away down the corridor. For several
moments she was lost in a painful void. Somehow she managed to make it to a ladies' room.

Avoiding the curious stares of others, she wiped
the tears from her face and blew her nose. Seth had
been cold and cruel, offering neither comfort nor
understanding. Earlier she had recognized that his
capacity for ruthlessness was as strong as his capability for tenderness, but she'd never been exposed to
the former. Now she had. How sad that they had to
part like this. There had been so much she'd longed
to say, but maybe it was better left unsaid.

When she felt composed enough to face the outside world, she moved with quick, purposeful steps
toward the parking garage.

She had gone only a few feet when a hand gripped
her shoulder and whirled her around. Her cry of
alarm was muffled as she was dragged against Seth's
muscular chest.

"I thought you'd gone," he whispered into her hair,
a desperate edge to his voice. "I'm sorry, Red. You're
right. I didn't mean that—not any of it."

He squeezed her so tightly that her ribs ached.
Then he raised his head and looked around at the attention they were receiving. He quickly pulled her
into a secluded nook behind a pillar. The minute

he was assured they were alone, his mouth sought hers, fusing them together with a fiery kiss filled with such emotion that she was left weak and light-headed.

"I need you," he whispered hoarsely against the delicate hollow of her throat. He lifted his face and smoothed a curl from her forehead, his eyes pleading with her.

Claudia was deluged with fresh pain. She needed him, too, but here in Seattle. She couldn't leave everything behind, not now, when she was so close to making her dream come true.

"No, don't say it." He placed a finger over her mouth to prevent the words of regret from spilling out. "I understand, Red. Or at least I'm trying to understand." He sighed heavily and gently kissed her again. "I have to go or I'll never make it through security in time."

He sounded so final, as if everything between them was over. She blinked away the tears that were burning her eyes. No sound came from her parched throat as he gently eased her out of his embrace. Her heart hammered furiously as she walked with him to the security line.

A feeling of panic overcame her when she heard the announcement that Seth's plane was already being boarded. The time was fast approaching when he would be gone.

Once again he gently caressed her face, his dark

eyes burning into hers. "Goodbye, Red." His lips covered hers very gently.

In the next instant, Seth Lessinger turned and strolled out of her world.

Part of her screamed silently in tortured protest as she watched him go and longed to race after him. The other part, the more level-headed, sensible part, recognized that there was nothing she could do to change his leaving. But every part of her was suffering. Her brain told her that she'd done the right thing, but her heart found very little solace in her decision.

The days passed slowly and painfully. Claudia knew Ashley had grown worried over her loss of appetite and the dark shadows beneath her eyes. She spent as much time as she could in her room alone, blocking out the world, but closing the door on reality didn't keep the memories of Seth at bay. He was in her thoughts continually, haunting her dreams, obsessing her during the days, preying on her mind.

She threw herself into her studies with a ferocity that surprised even Ashley, and that helped her handle the days, but nothing could help the nights. Often she lay awake for hours, wide-eyed and frustrated, afraid that once she did sleep her dreams would be haunted by Seth. She prayed every minute, it seemed—prayed harder than she had about anything in her life. But no answer came. No flash of lightning, no writing on the wall, not even a Bible verse stuck to a mirror. Nothing. Wasn't God listening? Didn't He know that this situation was tormenting her?

Two weeks after Seth's departure she still hadn't heard from him. She was hollow-eyed, and her cheeks were beginning to look gaunt. She saw Ashley glance at her with concern more than once, but she put on a weak smile and dismissed her friend's worries. *No,* she insisted, *she was fine. Really.*

The next Saturday Ashley was getting ready to go to work at the University Book Store near the U. of W. campus when one of the girls she worked with, Sandy Hoover, waltzed into the apartment.

"Look." She proudly beamed and held out her hand, displaying a small diamond.

"You're engaged!" Ashley squealed with delight.

"Jon asked me last night," Sandy burst out. "I was so excited I could hardly talk. First, like an idiot, I started to cry, and Jon didn't know what to think. But I was so happy, I couldn't help it, and then I wasn't even able to talk, and Jon finally asked me if I wanted to marry him or not and all I could do was nod."

"Oh, Sandy, I'm so happy for you." Ashley threw her arms around her friend and hugged her. "You've been in love with Jon for so long."

Sandy's happy smile lit her eyes. "I didn't ever think he'd ask me to marry him. I've known so much longer than Jon how I felt, and it was so hard to wait for him to feel the same way." She sighed, and a dreamy look stole over the pert face. "I love him so much it almost frightens me. He's with me even when he isn't with me." She giggled. "I know that sounds crazy."

It didn't sound so crazy to Claudia. Seth was thousands of miles away, but in some ways he had never left. If anything was crazy, it was the way she could close her eyes and feel the taste of his mouth over hers. It was the memory of that last gentle caress and the sweet kiss that was supposed to say goodbye.

She was so caught up in her thoughts she didn't even notice that Sandy had left until Ashley's voice broke into her reverie.

"I wish you could see yourself," Ashley said impatiently, her expression thoughtful. "You look so miserable that I'm beginning to think you should see a doctor."

"A doctor isn't going to be able to help me," Claudia mumbled.

"You've got to do something. You can't just sit around here moping like this. It isn't like you. Either you settle whatever's wrong between you and Seth or I'll contact him myself."

"You wouldn't," Claudia insisted.

"Don't count on it. Cooper's as worried about you as I am. If I don't do something, *he* might."

"It isn't going to do any good." Claudia tucked her chin into her neck. "I simply can't do what Seth wants. Not now."

"And what *does* he want? Don't you think it's time you told me? I'm your best friend, after all."

"He wants me to marry him and move to Nome," Claudia whispered weakly. "But I can't give up my dream of a medical degree and move to some no-man's-land. And he just as adamantly refuses to move to Seattle. As far as I can see, there's no solution."

"You idiot!" Ashley flared incredulously. "The pair of you! You're both behaving like spoiled children, each wanting your own way. For heaven's sake, does it have to be so intense? You've only known each other a few days. It would be absurd to make such a drastic change in your life on such a short acquaintance. And the same thing goes for Seth. The first thing to do is be sure of your feelings—both of you. Get to know each other better and establish a friendship, then you'll know what you want."

"Good idea. But Seth's three thousand miles away, in case you'd forgotten, and forming a relationship when we're thousands of miles apart isn't going to be easy."

"How did you ever make the dean's list, girl?" Ashley asked in a scathing tone. "Ever hear of letters? And I'm not talking e-mail, either. I mean the real thing, pen on paper, to prove you put a little time and thought into what you're saying. Some people have been known to faithfully deliver those white envelopes as they fill their appointed rounds—through snow, through rain—"

"I get the picture," Claudia interrupted.

She had thought about writing to Seth, but she

didn't have his address and, more importantly, didn't know what she could say. One thing was certain, the next move would have to come from her. Seth was a proud man. He had made his position clear. It was up to her now.

Ashley left for work a few minutes later, and Claudia once again mentally toyed with the idea of writing to Seth. She didn't need to say anything about his proposal. As usual, her level-headed friend had put things into perspective. Ashley was right. She couldn't make such a major decision without more of a basis for their relationship than six days. They could write, phone and even visit each other until she was sure of her feelings. Because, she realized, she couldn't go on living like this.

The letter wasn't easy. Crumpled pieces of paper littered the living room floor. When it got to the point that the carpet had all but disappeared under her discarded efforts, she paused and decided it would go better if she ate something. She stood, stretched and was making herself a sandwich when she realized that, for the first time since Seth had left, she was actually hungry. A pleased smile spread slowly across her face.

Once she'd eaten, the letter flowed smoothly. She wrote about the weather and her classes, a couple of idiosyncrasies of her professors. She asked him questions about Nome and his business. Finally she had two sheets of neat, orderly handwriting, and she signed the letter simply "Claudia." Reading it over, she realized she'd left so much unsaid. Chewing on the end of her pen, she scribbled a postscript that said she missed him. Would he understand?

She had the letter almost memorized by the time she dropped it into a mailbox an hour later. She'd walked it there as soon as she'd finished writing it, afraid she would change her mind if she let it lie around all weekend. She hadn't even tried to find his address, even though she was sure she could track him down on the internet. She simply wrote his name and Nome, Alaska. If it arrived, then it would be God's doing. This whole relationship was God's doing.

Calculating that the letter would arrive on Wednesday or Thursday, she guessed that, if he wrote back right away, she could have something from him by the following week. Until then, she was determined to let it go and try to think of anything else. That night she crawled into bed and, for the first time in two and a half desolate weeks, slept peacefully.

All day Thursday, Claudia was fidgety. Seth would get her letter today if he hadn't already. How would he react to it? Would he be glad, or had he given up on her completely? How much longer would it be before she knew? How long before she could expect an answer? She smiled as she let herself into the apartment; it was as if she expected something monumental to happen. By ten she'd finished her studies, and, after a leisurely bath she read her Bible and went to bed, unreasonably disappointed.

Nothing happened Friday, either. Steve Kali, another medical student, asked her out for coffee after anatomy lab, and she accepted, pleased by the invitation. Steve was nice. He wasn't Seth, but he was nice.

The phone rang Saturday afternoon. She was bringing in the groceries and dropped a bag of oranges as she rushed across the carpet to answer it.

"Hello." She sounded out of breath.

"Hello, Red," Seth's deep, rich voice returned.

Her hand tightened on the receiver, and her heartbeat accelerated wildly. "You got my letter?" Her voice was still breathless, but this time it had nothing to do with hurrying to answer the phone.

"About time. I didn't know if I'd ever hear from you."

Claudia suddenly felt so weak that she had to sit down. "How are you?"

"Miserable," he admitted. "Your letter sounded so bright and newsy. If you hadn't added that note at the bottom, I don't know what I would have thought."

"Oh, Seth," she breathed into the phone. "I've been wretched. I really do miss you."

"It's about time you admitted as much. I had no idea it would take you this long to realize I was right. Do you want me to fly down there so we can do the blood tests?"

"Blood tests?"

"Yes, silly woman. Alaska requires blood tests for a marriage license."

# Chapter 5

"Marriage license? I didn't write because I was ready to change my mind," Claudia said, shocked. Did Seth believe this separation was a battle of wills and she'd been the first to surrender? "I'm staying here in Seattle. I thought you understood that."

Her announcement was followed by a lengthy pause. She could practically hear his anger and the effort he made to control his breathing. "Then why did you write the letter?" he asked at last.

"You still don't understand, do you?" She threw the words at him. "Someday, Seth Lessinger, I'm going to be a fabulous doctor. That's been my dream from the time I was a little girl." She forced herself to stop and take a calming breath; she didn't want to argue with him. "Seth, I wrote you because I've been miserable. I've missed you more than I believed possible. I thought it might work if you and I got to know one another better. We can write and—"

"I'm not interested in a pen pal." His laugh was harsh and bitter.

"Neither am I," she returned sharply. "You're being unfair again. Can't we compromise? Do we have to do everything your way? Give me time, that's all I'm asking."

Her words were met with another long silence, and for an apprehensive second she thought he might have hung up on her. "Seth," she whispered, "all I'm asking is for you to give me more time. Is that so unreasonable?"

"All right, Red, we'll do this your way," he conceded. "But I'm not much for letter writing, and this is a busy time of the year for me, so don't expect much."

She let out the breath she hadn't realized she'd been holding and smiled. "I won't." It was a beginning.

Seth's first letter arrived four days later. Home from her classes before Ashley, Claudia stopped to pick up the mail in the vestibule. There was only one letter, the address written in large, bold handwriting. She stared at it with the instant knowledge that it was from Seth. Clutching the envelope tightly, she rushed up the stairs, fumbled with the apartment lock and barged in the front door. She tossed her coat and books haphazardly on the couch before tearing open the letter. Like hers, his was newsy, full of tidbits of information about his job and what this new contract would do for his business, Arctic Barge Company. He talked a little about the city of Nome and what she should expect when she came.

Claudia couldn't prevent the smile that trembled across her lips. When she came, indeed! He also explained that when she packed her things she would have to ship everything she couldn't fit in her suitcases. Arrangements would need to be made to have her belongings transported on a barge headed north. The only way into Nome was either by air or by sea, and access by sea was limited to a few short weeks in the summer before the water froze again. The pressure for her to make her decision soon was subtle. He concluded by saying that he missed her and, just in case she'd forgotten, he loved her. She read the words and closed her eyes to the flood of emotions that swirled through her.

She answered the letter that night and sent off another two days later. A week passed, but finally she received another long response from Seth, with an added postscript that there was a possibility he would be in Seattle toward the end of October for a conference. He didn't know how much unscheduled time he would have, but he was hoping to come a day early. That, he said, would be the time for them to sit down and talk, because letters only made him miss her more. He gave her the dates and promised to contact her when he knew more. Again he told her that he loved her and needed her.

Claudia savored both letters, reading them so many times she knew each one by heart. In some ways, their correspondence was building a more solid relationship than having him in Seattle would have. If he'd been here, she would have been more easily swayed by her physical response to him. This way she could carefully weigh each aspect of her decision, and give Seth and the move to Nome prayerful consideration. And she *did* pray, fervently, every day. But after so many weeks she was beginning to believe God was never going to answer.

One afternoon Ashley saw her reading one of Seth's letters for the tenth time and laughingly tossed a throw pillow at her.

"Hey," Claudia snapped, "what did you do that for?"

"Because I couldn't stand to see you looking so miserable!"

"I'm not miserable," Claudia denied. "I'm happy. Seth wrote about how much he wants me to marry him and…and…" Her voice cracked, and she swallowed back tears that burned for release. "I…didn't know I would cry about it."

"You still don't know what you want, do you?"

Claudia shook her head. "I pray and pray and pray, but God doesn't seem to hear me. He gave Seth a sign, but there's nothing for me. It's unfair!"

"What kind of confirmation are you looking for?" Ashley sat beside Claudia and handed her a tissue.

Claudia sniffled and waved her hand dramatically. "I don't know. Just something—anything! When I made my commitment to Christ, I told Him my life was no longer my own but His. If He wants me digging ditches, then I'll dig ditches. If He wants me to give up medical school and marry Seth, then I'll do it in a minute. Seth seems so positive that it's the right thing, and I'm so unsure."

Ashley pinched her lips together for a moment, then went into her bedroom. She returned a minute later with her Bible. "Do you remember the story of Elijah?"

"Of course. I would never forget the Old Testament prophets."

Ashley nodded as she flipped through the worn pages of her Bible. "Here it is. Elijah was hiding from the wicked Jezebel. God sent the angel of the Lord, who led Elijah into a cave. He told him to stay there and wait, because God was coming to speak to him. Elijah waited and waited. When a strong wind came, he rushed from the cave and cried out, but the wind wasn't God. An earthquake followed, and again Elijah hurried outside, certain this time that the earthquake was God speaking to him. But it wasn't the earthquake. Next came a fire, and again Elijah was positive that the fire was God speaking to him. But it wasn't. Finally, when everything was quiet, Elijah heard a soft, gentle whisper. That was the Lord."

Ashley transferred the open Bible to Claudia's lap. "Here, read the story yourself."

Thoughtfully Claudia read over the chapter before looking up. "You're telling me I should stop looking for that bolt of lightning in the sky that spells out *Marry Seth*?"

"Or the handwriting on the wall," Ashley added with a laugh.

"So God is answering my prayers, and all I need to do is listen?"

"I think so."

"It sounds too simple," Claudia said with a sigh.

"I don't know that it is. But you've got to quit looking for the strong wind, the earthquake and the fire, and listen instead to your heart."

"I'm not even a hundred percent sure I love him. I don't think I know him well enough yet." The magnetic physical attraction between them was overwhelming, but there was so much more to love and a lifetime commitment.

"You'll know," Ashley assured her confidently. "I don't doubt that for a second. When the time is right, you'll know."

Claudia felt as if a weight had been lifted from her, and she sighed deeply before forcefully expelling her breath. "Hey, do you know what today is?" she asked, then answered before Ashley had the opportunity. "Columbus Day. A day worthy of celebrating with something special." Carefully she tucked Seth's letter back inside the envelope. "Let's bring home Chinese food and drown our doubts in pork fried rice."

"And egg rolls," Ashley added. "Lots of egg rolls."

By the time they returned to the apartment, Claudia and Ashley had collected more than dinner. They had bumped into Steve Kali and a friend of his at the restaurant, and after quick introductions, the four of them realized they could get two extra items for free if they combined their orders. From there it was a quick step to inviting the guys over to eat at their place.

They sat on the floor in a large circle, laughing and eating with chopsticks directly from the white carry-out boxes, passing them around so everyone could try everything.

Steve's friend, Dave Kimball, was a law student, and he immediately showed a keen interest in Ashley. Claudia watched with an amused smile as her friend responded with some flirtatious moves of her own.

The chopsticks were soon abandoned in favor of forks, but the laughter continued.

"You know what we're celebrating, don't you?" Ashley asked between bites of ginger-spiced beef and tomato.

"No." Both men shook their heads, glancing from one girl to the other.

"Columbus Day," Claudia supplied.

"As in 'Columbus sailed the ocean blue'?" Steve jumped up and danced around the room singing.

Everyone laughed.

The phone rang, and since Steve was right near it, he picked up the cordless. "I'll get that for you," he volunteered, then promptly dropped the receiver. "Oops, sorry," he apologized into the receiver.

Claudia couldn't help smiling as she realized she was having a good time. It felt good to laugh again. Ashley was right, this whole thing with Seth was too intense. She needed to relax. Her decision had to be based on the quiet knowledge that marriage to Seth was what God had ordained.

"I'm sorry, would you mind repeating that?" Steve said into the phone. "Claudia? Yeah, she's here." He covered the receiver with the palm of his hand. "Are you here, Claudia?" he asked with a silly grin.

"You nut. Give me that." She stood and took the phone. "Hello." With her luck, it would be Cooper, who would no doubt demand to know what a man was doing in her apartment and answering her phone, no less. "This is Claudia."

"What's going on?"

The color drained from her flushed cheeks. "Seth? Is that you?" she asked incredulously. Breathlessly, she repeated herself. "Seth, it is really you?"

"It's me," he confirmed, his tone brittle. "Who's the guy who answered the phone."

"Oh." She swallowed, and turned her back to the others. "He's a classmate of mine. We have a few friends over," she explained, stretching the truth. She didn't want Seth to get the wrong impression. "We're celebrating Columbus Day…you know, Columbus, the man who sailed across the Atlantic looking for India and discovered America instead. Do you celebrate Columbus Day in Alaska?" she asked, embarrassingly aware that she was babbling.

"I know what day it is. You sound like you've been drinking."

"Not unless the Chinese tea's got something in it I don't know about."

"Does the guy who answered the phone mean anything to you?"

The last thing Claudia wanted to do was make explanations to Seth with everyone listening. On the other hand, carrying the phone into her bedroom so they could talk privately would only invite all kinds of questions she didn't want to answer. "It would be better if we…if we talked later," she said, stammering slightly.

"Everyone's there listening, right?" Seth guessed.

"Right," she confirmed with a soft sigh. "Do you mind?"

"No, but before you hang up, answer me one thing. Have you been thinking about how much I love you and want you here with me?"

"Oh, Seth," she murmured miserably. "Yes, I've hardly thought of anything else."

"And you still don't know what you want to do?" he asked, his voice heavy with exasperation.

"Not yet."

"All right, Red. I'll call back in an hour."

\* \* \*

In the end it was almost two hours before the phone rang again. Steve and Dave had left an hour earlier, and Ashley had made a flimsy excuse about needing to do some research at the library. Claudia didn't question her and appreciated the privacy.

She answered the phone on the first ring. "Hello."

"Now tell me who that guy was who picked up the phone before," Seth demanded without even a greeting.

Claudia couldn't help it. She laughed. "Seth Lessinger, you sound almost jealous."

"Almost?" he shot back.

"His name's Steve Kali, and we have several classes together, that's all," she explained, pleased at his concern. "I didn't know you were the jealous sort," she said gently.

"I never have been before. And I don't like the way it feels, if that makes you any happier."

"I'd feel the same way," she admitted. "I wish you were here, Seth. Ashley and I walked by a skating rink tonight and stopped to watch some couples skating together. Do you realize that you and I have never skated? If I close my eyes, I can almost feel your arm around me."

Seth sucked in his breath. "Why do you say things like that when we're separated by thousands of miles? Your sense of timing is really off. Besides, we don't need skating as an excuse for me to be near you," he murmured, his voice low. "Listen, honey, I'll be in Seattle a week from Saturday."

"Saturday? Oh, Seth!" She was too happy to express her thoughts coherently. "It'll be so good to see you!"

"My plane arrives early that morning. I couldn't manage the extra day, but I'll phone you as soon as I can review the conference schedule and figure out when I'll be able to see you."

"I won't plan a thing. No," she said, laughing, "I'll plan everything. Can you stay over through Monday? I'll skip classes and we can have a whole extra day alone."

"I can't." He sounded as disappointed as she felt.

They talked for an hour, and Claudia felt guilty at the thought of his phone bill, but the conversation had been wonderful.

Did she love him? The question kept repeating itself for the next two weeks. If she could truthfully answer that one question, then everything else would take care of itself. Just talking to him over the phone had lifted her spirits dramatically. But could she leave school and everything, everyone, she had ever known and follow him to a place where she knew no one but him and would have no way to follow her dream?

Her last class on the day before he arrived was a disaster. Her attention span was no longer than a four-year-old's. Time and time again she was forced to bring herself back into reality. So many conflicting emotions and milestones seemed to be coming at her. The first big tests of the quarter, Seth's visit. She felt pounded from every side, tormented by her own indecision.

Steve walked out of the building with her.

"Why so glum?" he asked. "If anyone's got complaints, it should be me." They continued down the stairs, and Claudia cast him a sidelong glance.

"What have you got to complain about?"

"Plenty," he began in an irritated tone. "You remember Dave Kimball?"

She nodded, recalling Steve's tall, sandy-haired friend who had flirted so outrageously with Ashley. "Sure, I remember Dave."

"We got picked up by the police a couple of nights ago."

She glanced apprehensively at him. "What happened?"

"Nothing, really. We'd been out having a good time and decided to walk home after a few beers. About halfway to the dorm, Dave starts with the crazies. He was climbing up the streetlights, jumping on parked cars. I wasn't doing any of that, but we were both brought into the police station for disorderly conduct."

Claudia's blue eyes widened incredulously. Steve was one of the straightest, most clean-cut men she had met. This was so unlike anything she would have expected from him that she didn't know how to react.

"That's not the half of it," he continued. "Once we were at the police station, Dave kept insisting that he was a law student and knew his rights. He demanded his one phone call."

"Well, it's probably a good thing he did know what to do," she said.

"Dave made his one call, all right." Steve inhaled a shaky breath. "And twenty minutes later the desk sergeant came in to ask which one of us had ordered the pizza."

Claudia couldn't stop herself from bursting into giggles, and it wasn't long before Steve joined her. He placed a friendly arm around her shoulders as their laughter faded. Together they strolled toward the parking lot.

"I do feel bad about the police thing…" she said. Before she could complete her thought, she caught sight of a broad-shouldered man walking toward her with crisp strides. She knew immediately it was Seth.

His look of contempt was aimed directly at her, his rough features darkened by a fierce frown. Even across the narrowing distance she recognized the tight set of his mouth as he glared at her.

Steve's arm resting lightly across her shoulders felt as if it weighed a thousand pounds.

## Chapter 6

Claudia's mouth was dry as she quickened her pace and rushed forward to meet Seth. If his look hadn't been so angry and forbidding, she would have walked directly into his arms. "When—how did you get here? I thought you couldn't come until tomorrow?" Only now was she recovering from the shock of seeing him.

An unwilling smile broke his stern expression as he pulled her to him and crushed her in his embrace.

Half lifted from the sidewalk, Claudia linked her hands behind his neck and felt his warm breath in her hair. "Oh, Seth," she mumbled, close to tears. "You idiot, why didn't you say something?"

So many emotions were filling her at once. She felt crushed yet protected, jubilant yet tearful, excited but afraid. Ignoring the negatives, she began spreading eager kisses over his face.

Slowly he released her, and the two men eyed each other skeptically.

Seth extended his hand. "I'm Seth Lessinger, Claudia's fiancé."

She had to bite her lip to keep from correcting him, but she wouldn't say anything that could destroy the happiness of seeing him again.

Steve's eyes were surprised, but he managed to mumble a greeting and exchange handshakes. Then he made some excuse about catching a ride and was gone.

"Who was that?"

"Steve," she replied, too happy to see him to question the way he had introduced himself to her friend. "He answered the phone the other night when you called. He's just a friend, don't worry."

"Then why did he have his arm around you?" Seth demanded with growing impatience.

Claudia ignored the question, instead standing on the tips of her toes and lightly brushing her mouth over his. His whiskers tickled her face, and she lifted both hands to his dark beard, framing his lips so she could kiss him soundly.

His response was immediate as he pulled her into his arms. "I've missed you. I won't be able to wait much longer. Who would believe such a little slip of nothing could bring this giant to his knees? Literally," he added. "Because I'll propose again right here on the sidewalk if you think it will make a difference."

Claudia's eyes widened with feigned offense. "Little slip of nothing? Come on, you make me sound like some anorexic supermodel."

He laughed, the robust, deep laugh that she loved. "Compared to me, you're pint-size." Looping his arm around her waist, he walked beside her. She felt protected and loved beyond anything she had ever known. She smiled up at him, and his eyes drank deeply from hers as a slow grin spread over his face, crinkling tiny lines at his eyes. "You may be small, but you hold a power over me I don't think I'll ever understand."

Leaning her head against his arm, Claudia relaxed. "Why didn't you say anything about coming today?"

"I didn't know that I was going to make the flight until the last minute. As it was, I hired a pilot out of Nome to make the connection in Fairbanks."

"You could have called when you landed."

"I tried, but no one answered at the apartment and your cell went straight to voicemail."

She pulled the phone out of her purse and checked. "Oops. I turned it off during class, and I guess I forgot to turn it on again." She remedied that as she asked, "So how'd you know where to find me?"

"I went to your apartment to wait for you and ran into Ashley just getting home. She drew me a map of the campus and told me where you'd be. You don't mind?"

"Of course not," she assured him with a smile and a shake of her head. "I just wish I'd known. I could have ducked out of class and met you at the airport."

By then they had reached her car. Seth asked to drive, so she gave him her keys. It wasn't until they were stuck in heavy afternoon traffic that she noticed Seth was heading in the opposite direction from her apartment.

"Where are we going?" She looked down at her jeans and Irish cable-knit sweater. She wasn't dressed for anything but a casual outing.

"My hotel," he answered without looking at her, focusing his attention on the freeway. "I wanted to talk to you privately, and from the look of things at your place, Ashley is going to be around for a while."

Claudia knew just what he was talking about. Ashley was deep into a project that she'd been working on for two nights. Magazines, newspapers and pages of scribbled notes were scattered over the living room floor.

"I know what you mean about the apartment." She laughed softly in understanding.

He slowed the car as he pulled off the freeway and onto Mercer Avenue. "She's a nice girl. I like her. Those blue eyes of hers are almost as enchanting as yours."

Something twitched in Claudia's stomach. Jealousy? Over Ashley? She was her best friend! Quickly she tossed the thought aside.

Seth reached for her hand. Linking their fingers, he carried her hand to his mouth and gently kissed her knuckles. Shivers tingled up her arm, and she smiled contentedly.

The hotel lobby was bristling with activity. In contrast, Seth's room in the conference hotel was quiet and serene. Situated high above the city, it offered a sweeping view of Puget Sound and the landmarks Seattle was famous for: the Pacific Science Center, the Space Needle and the Kingdome.

The king-size bed was bordered on each side by oak nightstands with white ceramic lamps. Two easy chairs were set obliquely in front of a hi-def television and state-of-the-art gaming system. Claudia glanced over the room, feeling slightly uneasy.

The door had no sooner closed than Seth placed a hand on her shoulder and turned her around to face him. Their eyes met, hers uncertain and a little afraid, his warm and reassuring. When he slipped his arms around her, she went willingly, fitting herself against the hard contours of his solid body. Relaxing, she savored the fiery warmth of his kiss. She slipped her hands behind his neck and yielded with the knowledge that she wanted him to kiss her, needed his kisses. Nothing on earth came so close to heaven as being cradled in his arms.

Arms of corded steel locked around her, held her close. Yet he was gentle, as if she were the most precious thing in the world. With a muted groan, he dragged his mouth from hers and showered the side of her neck with urgent kisses.

"I shouldn't be doing this," he moaned hoarsely. "Not when I don't know if I have the will to stop." One hand continued down her back, arching her upward while the fingers of the other hand played havoc with her hair.

Claudia's mind was caught in a whirl of desire and need. This shouldn't be happening, but it felt so right. For a moment she wanted to stop him, tell him they should wait until they were married—*if* they married. But she couldn't speak.

Seth pulled away and paused, his eyes searching hers. His breath came in uneven gasps.

She knew this was the time to stop, to back away, but she couldn't. The long weeks of separation, the doubts, the uncertainties that had plagued her night and day, the restless dreams, all exploded in her mind as she lifted her arms to him. It had been like this between them almost from the beginning, this magnetic, overpowering attraction.

Slowly Seth lowered his mouth to hers until their breaths merged, and the kiss that followed sent her world into a crazy spin.

"I can't do it," he whispered hoarsely into her ear, the bitter words barely distinct. "I can't," he repeated, and broke the embrace.

His voice filtered through her consciousness, and she forced her eyes open. Seth was standing away from her. He wasn't smiling now, and his troubled, almost tormented, expression puzzled her.

"Seth," she asked softly, "what is it?"

"I'm sorry." He crossed his arms and turned his back, as if offering her the chance to escape.

Her arms felt as if they'd been weighed down with lead, and her heart felt numb, as if she'd been exposed to the Arctic cold without the proper protective gear.

"Forgive me, Red." Seth covered his eyes with a weary hand and walked across the room to stand by the window. "I brought you here with the worst of intentions," he began. "I thought if we were to make love, then all your doubts would be gone." He paused to take in a labored breath. "I knew you'd marry me then without question."

Understanding burned like a laser beam searing through her mind, and she half moaned, half cried. Her arms cradled her stomach as the pain washed over her. Color blazed in her cheeks at how close she had come to letting their passion rage out of control. It had been a trick, a trap, in order for him to exert his will over her.

Several long moments passed in silence. Claudia turned to Seth, whose profile was outlined by the dim light of dusk. He seemed to be struggling for control of his emotions.

"I wouldn't blame you if you hated me after this," he said at last.

"I...I don't hate you." Her voice was unsteady, soft and trembling.

"You don't love me, either, do you?" He hurled the words at her accusingly and turned to face her.

The muscles in her throat constricted painfully. "I don't know. I just don't know."

"Will you ever be completely sure?" he asked with obvious impatience.

Claudia buried her face in her hands, defeated and miserable.

"Red, please don't cry. I'm sorry." The anger was gone, and he spoke softly, reassuringly.

She shivered with reaction. "If...if we did get married, could I stay here until I finished med school?"

"No," he returned adamantly. "I want a wife and children. Look at me, Red. I'm thirty-six. I can't wait another five or six years for a family. And I work too hard to divide my life between Nome and Seattle."

Wasn't there any compromise? Did everything have to be his way? "You're asking for so much," she cried.

"But I'm offering even more," he countered.

"You don't understand," she told him. "If I quit med school now, I'll probably never be able to finish. Especially if I won't be able to come back for several years."

"There isn't any compromise," he said with a note of finality. "If God wants you to be a doctor, He'll provide the way later. We both have to trust Him for that."

"I can't give up my entire life. It's not that easy," she whispered.

"Then there's nothing left to say, is there?" Dark shadows clouded his face, and he turned sharply and resumed his position in front of the window.

There didn't seem to be anything left to do but to leave quietly. She forced herself to open the door, but she knew she couldn't let it end like this. She let the door click softly shut.

At the sound Seth slammed his fist against the window ledge. Claudia gave a small cry of alarm, and he spun to face her. His rugged features were contorted with anger as he stared at her. But one look told her that the anger was directed at himself and not her.

"I thought you'd gone." His gaze held hers.

"I couldn't," she whispered.

He stared deeply into her liquid blue eyes and paused as if he wanted to say something, but finally he just shook his head in defeat and turned his back to her again.

Her eyes were haunted as she covered the distance between them. She slid her hands around his waist, hugging him while she rested a tearstained cheek against his back.

"We have something very special, Red, but it's not going to work." The dejected tone of his voice stabbed at her heart.

"It *will* work. I know it will. But I want to be sure,

very sure, before I make such a drastic change in my life. Give me time, that's all I'm asking."

"You've had almost six weeks."

"It's not enough."

He tried to remove her hands, but she squeezed tighter. "We're both hurt and angry tonight, but that doesn't mean things between us won't work."

"I could almost believe you," he murmured and turned, wrapping her securely in his arms.

She met his penetrating gaze and answered in a soft, throbbing voice, "Believe me, Seth. Please believe me."

His gaze slid to her lips before his mouth claimed hers in a fierce and flaming kiss that was almost savage, as if to punish her for the torment she had caused him. But it didn't matter how he kissed her as long as she hadn't lost him.


They had dinner at the hotel but didn't return to Seth's room. They discussed his conference schedule, which would take up pretty much all of Saturday. His plane left Sunday afternoon. They made plans to attend the Sunday morning church service together, and for her to drive him to the airport afterward.

Her heart was heavy all the next day. Several times she wished she could talk to him and clear away the ghosts of yesterday. For those long, miserable weeks she had missed him so much that she could hardly function. Then, at the first chance to see each other again, they had ended up fighting.

Why didn't she know what to do? Was this torment her heart was suffering proof of love?

The question remained unanswered as they sat together in church Sunday morning. It felt so right to have him by her side. Claudia closed her eyes to pray, fervently asking God to guide her. She paused, recalling the verses she had found in the Gospel of Matthew just the other night, verses all about asking, seeking, knocking. God had promised that anyone who asked would receive, and anyone who sought would find. It had all sounded so simple and straightforward when she read it, but it wasn't—not for her.

When she finished her prayer and opened her eyes, she felt Seth's gaze burn over her, searching her face. She longed to reassure him but could find no words. Gently she reached for his hand and squeezed it.

They rode to the airport in an uneasy silence. Their time had been bittersweet for the most part. What she had hoped would be a time to settle doubts had only raised more.

"You don't need to come inside with me," he said as they neared the airport. His words sliced into her troubled thoughts.

"What?" she asked, confused and hurt. "But I'd like to be with you as long as possible."

He didn't look pleased with her decision. "Fine, if that's what you want."

The set of his mouth was angry and impatient, but

she didn't know why. "You don't want me there, do you?" She tried to hide the hurt in her voice.

His cool eyes met her look of defiance. "Oh, for goodness sake, settle down, Red. I take it all back. Come in if you want. I didn't mean to make a federal case out of this."

Claudia didn't want to argue again, not during this last chance to spend time together. Seth continued to look withdrawn as they parked in the cement garage and walked into the main terminal.

She reached out tentatively and rested her hand on his arm. "Friends?" she asked and offered him a smile.

He returned the gesture and tenderly squeezed her delicate hand. "Friends."

The tension between them eased, and she waited while Seth hit the check-in kiosk. He returned with a wry grin. "My flight's been delayed an hour. How about some lunch?"

She couldn't prevent the smile that softly curved her mouth. Her eyes reflected her pleasure at the unexpected time together.

Claudia noted that Seth barely touched his meal. Her appetite wasn't up to par, either. Another separation loomed before them.

"How long will it be before you'll be back?" she asked as they walked toward the security line.

There was a moment of grim hesitation before Seth answered. "I don't know. Months, probably. This conference wasn't necessary. If it hadn't been for you, I wouldn't have attended, but I can't afford to keep taking time away from my business like this."

Claudia swallowed past the lump forming in her throat. "Thanksgiving break is coming soon. Maybe I could fly up and visit you. I'd like to see the beauty of Alaska for myself. You've told me so much about it already." Just for a moment, for a fleeting second, she was tempted to drop everything and leave with him now. Quickly she buried the impulsive thought and clenched her fists inside the pockets of her wool coat.

Seth didn't respond either way to her suggestion.

"What do you think?" she prompted.

He inclined his head and nodded faintly. "If that's what you'd like."

Claudia had the feeling he didn't really understand any of what she'd been trying to explain about her dreams and what it would mean to her to move, or how big a step it was for her to offer to visit.

When he couldn't delay any longer and had to get in line to pass through the security screening process, her façade of composure began to slip. It was difficult not to cry, and she blinked several times, not wanting Seth to remember her with tears shimmering in her eyes. With a proud lift of her chin, she offered him a brave smile.

He studied her unhappy face. "Goodbye, Red." His eyes continued to hold hers.

Her hesitation before her answer only emphasized her inner turmoil. "Goodbye, Seth," she whispered softly, a slight catch in her voice.

He cupped her face with the palm of his hand, and his thumb gently wiped away the single tear that was weaving a slow course down her pale cheek. Claudia buried her chin in his hand and gently kissed his calloused palm.

Gathering her into his embrace, Seth wrapped his arms around her as he buried his face in her neck and breathed deeply. When his mouth found hers, the kiss was gentle and sweet, and so full of love that fresh tears misted her eyes.

His hold relaxed, and he began to pull away, but she wouldn't let him. "Seth." She murmured his name urgently. She had meant to let him go, relinquish him without a word, but somehow she couldn't.

He scooped her in his arms again, crushing her against him with a fierceness that stole her breath away. "I'm a man," he bit out in an impatient tone, "and I can't take much more of this." He released her far enough to study her face. His dark eyes clearly revealed his needs. "I'm asking you again, Claudia. Marry me and come to Nome. I promise you a good life. I need you."

Claudia felt raw. The soft, womanly core of her cried out a resounding yes, but she couldn't let herself base such a life-changing decision on the emotion of the moment. She didn't want to decide something so important to both of them on the basis of feelings. Indecision and uncertainty raced through her mind, and she could neither reject nor accept his offer. Unable to formulate words, she found a low, protesting groan slipping from her throat. Her brimming blue eyes pleaded with him for understanding.

Seth's gaze sliced into her as a hardness stole over his features, narrowing his mouth. Forcefully he turned and, with quick, impatient steps, joined the line of passengers waiting to pass security and head to their gates.

Unable to do anything more, she watched him until he was out of sight, and then she turned and headed dejectedly back to the garage. At least she'd canceled her regular Sunday dinner with Cooper, so she wouldn't have to put on a happy face for him, and could just go home and give in to her depression.

The following week was wretched. At times Claudia thought it would have been easier not to have seen Seth again than endure the misery of another parting. To complicate her life further, it was the week of midterm exams. Never had she felt less like studying. Each night she wrote Seth long, flowing letters. School had always come first, but suddenly writing to him was more important. When she did study, her concentration waned and her mind wandered to the hurt look on Seth's face when they'd said goodbye. That look haunted her.

She did poorly on the first test, so, determined to do better on the next, she forced herself to study. With her textbooks lying open on top of the kitchen table, she propped her chin on both hands as she stared into space. Despite her best intentions, her thoughts weren't on school but on Seth. The illogical meanderings of her mind continued to torment her with the burning question of her future. Was being a pediatrician so important if it meant losing Seth?

"You look miserable," Ashley commented as she strolled into the kitchen to pour herself a glass of milk.

"That's because I feel miserable," Claudia returned, trying—and failing—to smile.

"There's been something different about you since Seth went back to Alaska again."

"No there hasn't," Claudia denied. "It's just the stress of midterms." Why did she feel the need to make excuses? She'd always been able to talk to Ashley about anything.

Her roommate gave her a funny look but didn't say anything as she turned and went back to the living room.

Angry with herself and the world, Claudia studied half the night, finally staggering into her bedroom at about three. That was another thing. She hadn't been sleeping well since Seth had gone.

Ashley was cooking dinner when Claudia got home the next afternoon. After her exam, she'd gone to the library to study, hoping a change of scenery would help keep her mind off Seth and let her concentrate on her studies.

"You had company," Ashley announced casually, but she looked a bit flushed and slightly uneasy.

Claudia's heart stopped. Seth. He had come back for her. She needed so desperately to see him again, to talk to him.

"Seth?" she asked breathlessly.

"No, Cooper. I didn't know what time you were going to get home, so instead of waiting here, he decided to run an errand and come back later," Ashley explained.

"Oh." Claudia didn't even try to disguise the disappointment in her voice. "I can do without another unpleasant confrontation with my uncle. I wonder how he found out about how badly I did on that test already."

"Why do you always assume the worst with Cooper?" Ashley demanded with a sharp edge of impatience. "I, for one, happen to think he's nice. I don't think I've ever seen him treat anyone unfairly. It seems to me that you're the one who—" She stopped abruptly and turned back toward the stove, stirring the browning hamburger with unnecessary vigor. "I hope spaghetti sounds good."

"Sure," Claudia responded. "Anything."

Cooper didn't return until they had eaten and were clearing off the table. Claudia made a pot of coffee and brought him a cup in the living room. She could feel him studying her.

"You don't look very good," he commented, taking the cup and saucer out of her hand. Most men would have preferred a mug, but not Cooper.

"So Ashley keeps telling me." She sat opposite

him. "Don't do the dishes, Ash," she called into the kitchen. "Wait until later and I'll help."

"No need." Ashley stuck her head around the kitchen door. "You go ahead and visit. Shout if you need anything."

"No, Ashley," Cooper stood as he spoke. "I think that it might be beneficial if you were here, too."

Ashley looked from one of them to the other, dried her hands on a towel and came into the room.

"I don't mean to embarrass you, Ashley, but in all fairness I think Claudia should know that you were the one to contact me."

Claudia's gaze shot accusingly across the room to her friend. "What does he mean?"

Ashley shrugged. "I've been so worried about you lately. You're hardly yourself anymore. I thought if you talked to Cooper, it might help you make up your mind. You can't go on like this, Claudia." Her voice was gentle and stern all at the same time.

"What do you mean?" Claudia vaulted to her feet. "This is unfair, both of you against me."

"Against you?" Cooper echoed. "Come on now, Claudia, you seem to have misjudged everything."

"No I haven't." Tears welled in her eyes, burning for release.

"I think it would probably be best if I left the two of you alone." Ashley stood and excused herself, returning to the kitchen.

Claudia shot her an angry glare as she stepped past. Some friend!

"I hope you'll talk honestly with me, Claudia," Cooper began. "I'd like to know what's got you so upset that you're a stranger to your own best friend."

"Nothing," she denied adamantly, but her voice cracked and the first tears began spilling down her cheeks.

She was sure Cooper had never seen her cry. He looked at a loss as he stood and searched hurriedly through his suit jacket for a handkerchief. Just watching him made her want to laugh, and she hiccupped in an attempt to restrain both tears and laughter.

"Here." He handed her a white linen square, crisply pressed. Claudia didn't care; she wiped her eyes and blew her nose. "I'm fine, really," she declared in a wavering voice.

"It's about Seth, isn't it?" her uncle prompted.

She nodded, blowing her nose again. "He wants me to marry him and move to Alaska."

The room suddenly became still as he digested the information. "Are you going to do it?" he asked in a quiet voice she had long ago learned to recognize as a warning.

"If I knew that, I wouldn't be here blubbering like an idiot," she returned defensively.

"I can't help but believe it would be a mistake," he continued. "Lessinger's a good man, don't misunderstand me, but I don't think you'd be happy in Alaska. Where did you say he was from again?" he asked.

"Nome."

"I don't suppose there's a med school in Nome where you could continue your studies?"

"No." The word was clipped, impatient.

Cooper nodded. "You were meant to be a doctor," he said confidently as he rose to his feet. "You'll get over Seth. There's a fine young man out there somewhere who will make you very happy when you finally meet."

"Sure," she agreed without enthusiasm.

Cooper left a few minutes later, and at the sound of the door closing, Ashley stepped out of the kitchen. "You aren't mad, are you?"

At first Claudia had been, but not anymore. Ashley had only been thinking of her welfare, after all. And thanks to her friend's interference, now she knew where Cooper stood on the subject and what she would face if she did decide to marry Seth.

"Oh, Seth," she whispered that night, sitting up in bed. He hadn't contacted her since his return to Nome, not even answering her long letters, though she had eagerly checked the mail every day. Once again, she understood that the next move would have to be from her. Her Bible rested on her knees, and she opened it for her devotional reading in Hebrews. She read Chapter 11 twice, the famous chapter on faith. Had Rebekah acted in faith when the servant had come to her family, claiming God had given him a sign? Flipping through the pages of her Bible, she turned to Genesis to reread the story Seth had quoted when he had given her the engagement ring and they had argued. She had said that Rebekah probably didn't have any choice in the matter, but reading the story now, she realized that the Bible said she had. Rebekah's family had asked her if she was willing to go with Abraham's servant, and she'd replied that she would.

Rebekah had gone willingly!

Claudia reread the verses as a sense of release came over her. Her hands trembled with excitement as she closed the Bible and stopped to pray. The prayer was so familiar. She asked God's guidance and stated her willingness to do as He wished. But there was a difference this time. This time the peace she had so desperately sought was there, and she knew that at last she could answer Seth in faith, and that her answer would be yes.

Slipping out of the sheets, she opened the drawer that contained the jeweler's box holding the engagement ring. With a happy sigh she hugged it to her breast. The temptation to slip the ring on her finger now was strong, but she would wait until Seth could do it.

Claudia slept peacefully that night for the first time since Seth had left. And the next morning she stayed in her pajamas, with no intention of going to school.

Ashley, who was dressed and ready to go out the door, looked at her in surprise. "Did you oversleep?

I'm sorry I didn't wake you, but I thought I heard you moving around in your room."

"You did," Claudia answered cheerfully, but her eyes grew serious as her gaze met Ashley's. "I've decided what to do," she announced solemnly. "I love Seth. I'm going to him as soon as I can make the arrangements."

Ashley's blue eyes widened with joy as she laughed and hugged her friend. "It's about time! I knew all along that the two of you belonged together. I'm so happy for you."

Once the decision was made, there seemed to be a hundred things to be dealt with all at once. Claudia searched the internet for the number she needed, then phoned Seth's company, her fingers trembling, and reached his assistant, who told her that he had flown to Kotzebue on an emergency. She didn't know when he would be returning, but she would give him the message as soon as he walked in the door. Releasing a sigh of disappointment, Claudia replaced the headset in the charger.

Undaunted by the uncertainties of the situation, she drove to the university and officially withdrew from school. Next she purchased the clothes she would be needing to face an Arctic winter, along with a beautiful wedding dress. Finally, focusing on her luck in finding an available dress that was a perfect fit and not on the difficult conversation to come, she drove to Cooper's office.

He rose and smiled broadly when she entered.

"You look in better spirits today," he said. "I knew our little talk would help."

"You'd better sit down, Cooper," she said, smiling back at him. "I've made my decision. I love Seth. I've withdrawn from school, and I've made arrangements for my things to be shipped north as soon as possible. I'm marrying Seth Lessinger."

Cooper stiffened, his eyes raking over her. "That's what you think."

# Chapter 7

It was dark and stormy when the plane made a jerky landing on the Nome runway, jolting her back to the present, away from the memories of the difficult emotional journey that had brought her to this point. Claudia shifted to relieve her muscles, tired and stiff from the uncomfortable trip. The aircraft had hit turbulent weather shortly after takeoff from Anchorage, and the remainder of the flight had been far too much like a roller-coaster ride for her taste. More than once she had felt the pricklings of fear, but none of the other passengers had showed any concern, so she had accepted the jarring ride as a normal part of flying in Alaska.

Her blue eyes glinted with excitement as she stood and gathered the small bag stored in the compartment above the seat. There wasn't a jetway to usher her into a dry, warm airport. When she stepped from the cozy interior of the plane, she was greeted by a solid blast of Arctic wind. The bitter iciness stole her breath, and she groped for the handrail to maintain her balance. Halfway down the stairs, she was nearly knocked over by a fresh gust of wind. Her hair flew into her face, blinding her. Momentarily unable to move either up or down, she stood stationary until the force of the wind decreased.

Unexpectedly the small bag was wrenched from her numb fingers and she was pulled protectively against a solid male form.

Her rescuer shouted something at her, but the wind carried his voice into the night and there was no distinguishing the message.

She tried to speak but soon realized the uselessness of talking. She was half carried, half dragged the rest of the way down. Once on solid ground, they both struggled against the ferocity of the wind as it whipped and lashed against them. If he hadn't taken the brunt of its force, Claudia had a feeling she might not have made it inside.

As they neared the terminal, the door was opened by someone who'd been standing by, watching. The welcoming warmth immediately stirred life into her frozen body. Nothing could have prepared her for the intensity of the Arctic cold. Before she could turn and thank her rescuer, she was pulled into his arms and crushed in a smothering embrace.

"Seth?" Her arms slid around his waist as she returned the urgency of his hug.

He buried his face in her neck and breathed her name. His hold was almost desperate, and when he spoke, his voice was tight and worried.

"Are you all right?" Gently his hands framed her face, pushing back the strands of hair that had been whipped free by the wind. He searched her features as if looking for any sign of harm.

"I'm fine," she assured him and, wrapping her arms around him a second time, pressed her face into his parka. "I'm so glad to be here."

"I've been sick with worry," he ground out hoarsely. "The storm hit here several hours ago, and there wasn't any way your flight could avoid the worst of it."

"I'm fine, really." Her voice wobbled, not because she was shaky from the flight but from the effect of being in Seth's arms.

"If anything had happened to you, I don't know..." He let the rest fade and tightened his already secure hold.

"I'm glad we won't have to find out," she said and lightly touched her lips to the corner of his mouth.

He released her. The worried look in his eyes had diminished now that he knew she was safe. "Let's get out of here," he said abruptly, and left her standing alone as he secured her luggage. Everything she could possibly get into the three large suitcases— along with whatever she could buy locally—would have to see her through until the freight barge arrived in the spring.

They rode to the hotel she'd booked herself into in his four-wheel-drive SUV. They didn't speak, because Seth needed to give his full attention to maneuvering safely through the storm. Claudia looked out the windshield in awe. The barren land was covered with snow. The buildings were a dingy gray. In her dreams she had conjured up a romantic vision of Seth's life in Nome. Reality shattered the vision as the winds buffeted the large car.

The hotel room was neat and clean—not elegant, but she'd hoped for a certain homey, welcoming appeal. It was not to be. It contained a bed with a plain white bedspread, a small nightstand, a lamp, a phone, a TV and one chair. Seth followed her in, managing the suitcases.

"You packed enough," he said with a sarcastic undertone. She ignored the comment, and busied herself by removing her coat and hanging it in the bare closet. She gave him a puzzled look. Something was wrong. He had hardly spoken to her since they'd left the airport. At first she'd assumed the tight set of his mouth was a result of the storm, but not now, when she was safe and ready for his love. Her heart ached for him to hold her. Every part of her longed to have him slip the engagement ring onto the third finger of her left hand.

"How's everything in Seattle?" Again that strange inflection in his voice.

"Fine."

He remained on the far side of the room, his hands clenched at his sides.

"Let me take your coat," she offered. As she studied him, the gnawing sensation that something wasn't right increased.

He unzipped his thick parka, but he didn't remove it. He sat at the end of the bed, his face tight and drawn. Resting his elbows on his knees, he leaned forward and buried his face in his hands.

"Seth, what's wrong?" she asked calmly, although she was far from feeling self-possessed.

"I've only had eight hours' sleep in the last four days. A tanker caught fire in port at Kotzebue, and I've been there doing what I could for the past week. You certainly couldn't have chosen a worse time for a visit. Isn't it a little early for Thanksgiving break?"

She wanted to scream that this wasn't a visit, that she'd come to stay, to be his wife and share his world. But she remained quiet, guided by the same inner sense that she had to take this carefully.

Quietly Seth stood and stalked to the far side of the small room. She noticed that he seemed to be limping slightly. He paused and glanced over his shoulder, then turned away from her.

Uncertainty clouded her deep blue eyes, and her mind raced with a thousand questions that she didn't get a chance to ask, because he spoke again.

"I'm flying back to Kotzebue as soon as possible. I shouldn't have taken the time away as it is."

He turned around, and his eyes burned her with the intensity of his glare. His mouth was drawn, hard and inflexible. "I'll have one of my men drive you back to the airport for the first available flight to Anchorage." There was no apology, no explanation, no regrets.

Claudia stared back at him in shocked disbelief. Even if he had assumed she was here for a short visit, he was treating her as he would unwanted baggage.

Belying the hurt, she smiled lamely. "I can't see why I have to leave. Even if you aren't here, this would be a good opportunity for me to see Nome. I'd like to—"

"Can't you do as I ask just once?" he shouted.

She lowered her gaze to fight the anger building within her. Squaring her shoulders, she prepared for the worst. "There's something I don't know, isn't there?" she asked in quiet challenge. She wanted to hear the truth, even at the risk of being hurt.

Her question was followed by a moment of grim silence. "I don't want you here."

"I believe you've made that obvious." Her fingers trembled, and she willed them to hold still.

"I tried to reach you before you left."

She didn't comment, only continued to stare at him with questioning eyes.

"It's not going to work between us, Claudia," he announced solemnly. "I think I realized as much when you didn't return with me when I gave you the ring. You must think I was a fool to propose to you the way I did."

"You know I didn't. I—"

He interrupted her again. "I want a wife, Claudia, not some virtuous doctor out to heal the world. I need a woman, someone who knows what she wants in life."

White-lipped, she stiffened her back and fought her building rage with forced control. "Do you want me to hate you, Seth?" she asked softly as her fingers picked an imaginary piece of lint from the sleeve of her thick sweater.

He released a bitter sigh. "Yes. It would make things between us a lot easier if you hated me," he replied flatly. He walked as far away as the small room would allow, as if he couldn't bear to see the pain he was causing her. "Even if you were to change your mind and relinquish your lofty dreams to marry me, I doubt that we could make a marriage work. You've been tossing on a wave of indecision for so long, I don't think you'll ever decide what you really want."

She studied the pattern of the worn carpet, biting her tongue to keep from crying out that she knew what she wanted now. What would be the point? He had witnessed her struggle in the sea of uncertainty. He would assume that her decision was as fickle as the turning tide.

"If we married, what's to say you wouldn't regret it later?" he went on. "You've wanted to be a doctor for so many years that, frankly, I don't know if my love could satisfy you. Someday you might have been able to return to medical school—I would have wanted that for you—but my life, my business, everything I need, is here in Nome. It's where I belong. But not you, Red." The affectionate endearment rolled easily from his lips, seemingly without thought. "We live in two different worlds. And my world will never satisfy you."

"What about everything you told me about the sign from God? You were the one who was so sure. You were the one who claimed to feel a deep, undying love." She hurled the words at him bitterly, intent on hurting him as much as he was hurting her.

"I was wrong. I don't know how I could have been so stupid."

She had to restrain herself from crying out that it had never been absurd, it was wonderful. The Bible verse in the mirror had meant so much to them both. But she refused to plead, and the dull ache in her heart took on a throbbing intensity.

"That's not all," he added with a cruel twist. "There's someone else now."

Nothing could have shocked her more. "Don't lie to me, Seth. Anything but that!"

"Believe it, because it's true. My situation hasn't changed. I need a wife, someone to share my life. There's—" he hesitated "—someone I was seeing before I met you. I was going to ask her to marry me as soon as I got the engagement ring back from you."

"You're lucky I brought it with me, then!" she

shouted as she tore open her purse and dumped the contents out on the bedspread. Carelessly she sorted through her things. It took only a couple of seconds to locate the velvet box, turn around and viciously hurl it at him.

Instinctively he brought his hands up and caught it. Their eyes met for a moment; then, without another word, he tucked it in his pocket.

A searing pain burned through her heart.

Seth seemed to hesitate. He hovered for a moment by the door. "I didn't mean to hurt you." Slowly he lowered his gaze to meet hers.

She avoided his look. Nothing would be worse than to have him offer her sympathy. "I'm sure you didn't," she whispered on a bitter note, and her voice cracked. "Please leave," she requested urgently.

Without another word, he opened the door and walked away.

Numb with shock, Claudia couldn't cry, couldn't move. Holding up her head became an impossible task. A low, protesting cry came from deep within her throat, and she covered her mouth with the palm of one hand. Somehow she made it to the bed, collapsing on the mattress.

When Claudia woke the next morning the familiar lump of pain formed in her throat at the memory of her encounter with Seth. For a while she tried to force herself to return to the black cloud of mindless sleep, but to no avail.

She dressed and stared miserably out the window. The winds were blustery, but nothing compared to yesterday's gales. Seth would have returned to Kotzebue. Her world had died, but Nome lived. The city appeared calm; people were walking, laughing and talking. She wondered if she would ever laugh again. What had gone wrong? Hadn't she trusted God, trusted in Seth's love? How could her world dissolve like this? The tightness in her throat grew and grew.

The small room became her prison. She waited an impatient hour, wondering what she should do, until further lingering became intolerable. Since she was here, she might as well explore the city Seth loved.

The people were friendly, everyone offering an easy smile and a cheery good morning as she passed. There weren't any large stores, nothing to compare with Seattle. She strolled down the sidewalk, not caring where her feet took her. Suddenly she saw a sign proclaiming ARCTIC BARGE COMPANY— Seth's business. A wave of fresh pain swamped her, destroying her fragile composure, and she turned and briskly walked in the opposite direction. Ahead, she spotted a picturesque white church with a bell in its steeple. She was hopeful that she would find peace inside.

The interior was dark as she slipped quietly into the back pew. Thanksgiving would be here at the end of the month—a time for sharing God's goodness with family and friends. She was trapped in Nome with neither. When she'd left Seattle, her heart had nearly burst with praise for God. Now it was ready to burst with the pain of Seth's rejection.

She didn't mean to cry, but there was something so peaceful and restful about the quiet church. A tear slipped from the corner of her eye, and she wiped it aside. She'd left Seattle so sure of Seth's love, filled with the joy of her newfound discovery that she loved him, too, and was ready to be his wife. She'd come in faith. And this was where faith had led her. To an empty church, with a heart burdened by bitter memories.

She'd painted herself into a dark corner. She'd lost her apartment. In the few days between her decision and her flight, Ashley had already found herself a cheaper place and a new roommate. If she did return to school, she would be forced to repeat the courses she'd already taken—not that there was any guarantee she would even be admitted back into the program. Every possession she owned that wasn't in her suitcases had been carefully packed and loaded onto a barge that wouldn't arrive in Nome for months.

She poured out her feelings in silent prayer. She still couldn't believe that she had come here following what she thought was God's plan, and now it seemed she had made a terrible mistake. Lifting the Bible from the pew, she sat and read, desperately seeking guidance, until she caught a movement from the corner of her eye. A stocky middle-aged man was approaching.

"Can I help you?" he asked her softly.

She looked up blankly.

He must have read the confusion in her eyes. "I'm Paul Reeder, the pastor," he said, and sat beside her.

She held out her hand and smiled weakly. "Claudia Masters."

"Your first visit to Nome?" His voice was gentle and inquiring.

"Yes, how'd you know?" she couldn't help but wonder aloud.

He grinned, and his brown eyes sparkled. "Easy. I know everyone in town, so either you're a visitor or I've fallen down in my duties."

She nodded and hung her head at the thought of why she had come to Nome.

"Is there something I can do for you, child?" he asked kindly.

"I don't think there's much anyone can do for me anymore." Her voice shook slightly, and she lowered her lashes in an effort to conceal the desperation in her eyes.

"Things are rarely as difficult as they seem. Remember, God doesn't close a door without opening a window."

She attempted a smile. "I guess I need someone to point to the window."

"Would you feel better if you confided in someone?" he urged gently.

She didn't feel up to explanations but knew she should say something. "I quit school and moved to

Alaska expecting…a job." The pastor was sure to know Seth, and she didn't want to involve this caring man in the mess of her relationship. "I…I assumed wrong…and now…"

"You need a job and place to live," he concluded for her. A light gleamed in the clear depths of his eyes. "There's an apartment for rent near here. Since it belongs to the church, the rent is reasonable. As for your other problem…" He paused thoughtfully. "Do you have any specific skills?"

"No, not really." Her tone was despairing. "I'm in medical school, but other than that—"

"My dear girl!" Pastor Reeder beamed in excitement. "You are the answer to our prayers. Nome desperately needs medical assistants. We've advertised for months for another doctor—"

"Oh, no, please understand," Claudia said, "I'm not a doctor. All I have is the book knowledge so far."

Disregarding her objections, Pastor Reeder stood and anxiously moved into the wide aisle. "There's someone you must meet."

A worried frown marred Claudia's smooth brow. She licked her dry lips and followed the pastor as he pulled on his coat and strode briskly from the church and out to the street.

They stopped a block or two later. "While we're here, I'll show you the apartment." He unlocked the door to a small house, and Claudia stepped inside.

"Tiny" wasn't the word for the apartment. It was the most compact space Claudia had ever seen: living room with a sleeper sofa, miniature kitchen and a very small bathroom.

"It's perfect," she stated positively. Perfect if she didn't have to return to Seattle and face Cooper. Perfect if she could show Seth she wasn't like a wave tossed to and fro by the sea. She had made her decision and was here to stay, with or without him. She had responded in faith; God was her guide.

"The apartment isn't on the sewer," the pastor added. "I hope that won't inconvenience you."

"Of course not." She smiled. It didn't matter to her if she had a septic tank.

He nodded approvingly. "I'll arrange for water delivery, then."

She didn't understand but let the comment pass as he showed her out and locked the door behind them.

He led her down the street. "I'm taking you to meet a friend of mine, Dr. Jim Coleman. I'm sure Jim will share my enthusiasm when I tell him about your medical background."

"Shouldn't I sign something and make a deposit on the apartment first?"

Pastor Reeder's eyes twinkled. "We'll settle that later. Thanksgiving has arrived early in Nome. I can't see going through the rigmarole of deposits when God Himself has sent you to us." He handed her the key and smiled contentedly.

The doctor's waiting room was crowded with people when Claudia and Pastor Reeder entered. Every chair was taken, and small children played on the floor.

The receptionist greeted them warmly. "Good morning, Pastor. What can I do for you? Not another emergency, I hope."

"Quite the opposite. Tell Jim I'd like to see him, right away, if possible. I promise to take only a few minutes of his time."

They were ushered into a private office and sat down to wait. The large desk was covered with correspondence, magazines and medical journals. A pair of glasses had been carelessly tossed on top of the pile.

The young doctor who entered the room fifteen minutes later eyed Claudia skeptically, his dark eyes narrowing.

Eagerly Paul Reeder stood and beamed a smile toward Claudia. "Jim, I'd like to introduce you to God's Thanksgiving present to you. This is Claudia Masters."

She stood and extended her hand. The smile on her face died as she noted the frown that flitted across the doctor's face.

His handshake was barely civil. "Listen, Paul, I don't have the time for your matchmaking efforts today. There are fifteen people in my waiting room and the hospital just phoned. Mary Fulton's in labor."

Her eyes snapped with blue sparks at his assumption and his dismissive tone. "Let me assure you,

Dr. Coleman, that you are the last man I'd care to be matched with!"

A wild light flashed in Jim's eyes and it looked as if he would have snapped out a reply if Pastor Reeder hadn't scrambled to his feet to intervene.

"I'll not have you insulting the woman the good Lord sent to help you. And you, Claudia—" he turned to her, waving his finger "—don't be offended. Jim made an honest mistake. He's simply overworked and stressed."

Confusion and embarrassment played rapidly over the physician's face. "The Lord sent her?" he repeated. "You're a nurse?"

Sadly Claudia shook her head. "Medical student. Ex-medical student," she corrected. "I don't know if I'll be much help. I don't have much practical experience."

"If you work with me, you'll gain that fast enough." He looked at her as if she had suddenly descended from heaven. "I've been urgently looking for someone to work on an emergency medical team. With your background and a few months of on-the-job training, you can take the paramedic test and easily qualify. What do you say, Claudia? Can we start again?" His boyish grin offered reassurance.

She smiled reluctantly, not knowing what to say. Only minutes before she'd claimed to be following God, responding to faith. Did He always move so quickly? "Why not?" she said with a laugh.

"Can you start tomorrow?"

"Sure," she confirmed, grateful that she would be kept so busy she wouldn't have time to remember that the reason she had come to Nome had nothing to do with paramedic training.

A message was waiting for her when she returned to the hotel. It gave a phone number and name, with information for upcoming flights leaving Nome for Anchorage. Crumpling the paper, Claudia checked out of the hotel.

She spent the rest of the afternoon unpacking and settling into the tiny apartment. If only Cooper could see her now!

Hunger pangs interrupted her work, and she realized she hadn't eaten all day. Just as she was beginning to wonder about dinner, there was a knock on the door. Her immediate thought was that Seth had somehow learned she hadn't returned to Seattle. Though that was unlikely, she realized, since Seth was no doubt back in Kotzebue by now.

Opening the door, she found a petite blonde with warm blue eyes and a friendly smile. "Welcome to Nome! I'm Barbara Reeder," she said, and handed Claudia a warm plate covered with aluminum foil. "Dad's been talking about his miracle ever since I walked in the door this afternoon, and I decided to meet this Joan of Arc myself." Her laugh was free and easy.

Claudia liked her immediately. Barbara's personality was similar to Ashley's, and she soon fell into easy conversation with the pastor's daughter. She let

Barbara do most of the talking. She learned that the woman was close to her own age, worked as a legal assistant and was engaged to a man named Teddy. Claudia felt she needed a friend, someone bright and cheerful to lift her spirits from a tangled web of self-pity, and Barbara seemed like the answer to a prayer.

"Barbara, while you're here, would you mind explaining about the bathroom?" She had been shocked to discover the room was missing the most important fixture.

Barbara's eyes widened. "You mean Dad didn't explain that you aren't on the sewer?"

"Yes, but—"

"Only houses on the sewers have flush toilets, plumbing and the rest. You, my newfound friend, have your very own 'honey bucket.' It's like having an indoor outhouse. When you need to use it, just open the door in the wall, pull it inside and—*voilà*."

Claudia looked up shocked. "Yes, but—"

"You'll need to get yourself a fuzzy cover, because the seat is freezing. When you're through, open the door, push it back outside and it'll freeze almost immediately."

"Yes, but—"

"Oh, and the water is delivered on Monday, Wednesday and Friday. Garbage is picked up once a week, but be sure and keep it inside the house, because feral dogs will get into it if it's outside."

"Yes, but—"

"And I don't suppose Dad explained about ordering food, either. Don't worry, I'll get you the catalog, and you'll have plenty of time to decide what you need. Grocery prices are sometimes as much as four times higher than Seattle, so we order the nonperishables once a year. The barge from Seattle arrives before winter."

Claudia breathed in deeply. The concepts of honey buckets, no plumbing and feral dogs were almost too much to grasp in one lump. This lifestyle was primitive compared to the way things were in Seattle. But she would grow stronger from the challenges, grow—or falter and break.

Concern clouded Barbara's countenance. "Have I discouraged you?"

Pride and inner strength shimmered in Claudia's eyes. "No, Nome is where I belong," she stated firmly.

Jim Coleman proved to be an excellent teacher. Her admiration for him grew with every day and every patient. At the end of her first week, Claudia was exhausted. Together they had examined and treated a steady flow of the sick and injured, eating quick lunches when they got a few free minutes between patients. At the end of the ten-to-twelve-hour day, he was sometimes due to report to the hospital. She spent her evenings studying the huge pile of material he had given her to prepare for the paramedic exam that spring. She marveled at how hard he drove himself, but he explained that his work load wasn't by choice. Few medical professionals were willing to set up practice in the frozen North.

Barbara stopped by the apartment during Claudia's second week with an invitation for Thanksgiving dinner. Jim had also been invited, along with Barbara's fiancé and another couple. Claudia thanked her and accepted, but she must have appeared preoccupied, because Barbara left soon afterward.

Claudia closed the door after her, leaning against the wood frame and swallowing back the bitter hurt. When she'd left Seattle, she'd told Ashley that she was hoping the wedding would be around Thanksgiving. Now she would be spending the day with virtual strangers.

"Good morning, Jim," Claudia said cheerfully the next day as she entered the office. "And you, too, Mrs. Lucy."

The receptionist glanced up, grinning sheepishly to herself.

"Something funny?" Jim demanded brusquely.

"Did either of you get a chance to read Pastor Reeder's sign in front of the church this morning?" Mrs. Lucy asked.

Claudia shook her head and waited.

"What did he say this time?" Jim asked, his interest piqued.

"The sign reads 'God Wants Spiritual Fruit, Not Religious Nuts.'"

Jim tipped his head back and chuckled, but his

face soon grew serious. "I suggest we get moving," he said. "We've got a full schedule."

He was right. The pace at which he drove himself and his staff left little time for chatting. With so many people in need of medical attention and only two doctors dividing the load, they had to work as efficiently as possible. By six Claudia had barely had time to grab a sandwich. She was bandaging a badly cut hand after Jim had stitched it when he stuck his head around the corner.

"I want you to check the man in the first room. Let me know what you think. I've got a phone call waiting for me. I'll take it in my office and join you in a few minutes."

A stray curl of rich auburn hair fell haphazardly across her face as she stopped outside the exam room a few minutes later, and she paused long enough to tuck it around her ear and straighten her white smock.

Tapping lightly, her smile warm and automatic, she entered the room. "Good afternoon, my name's—"

Stopping short, she felt her stomach pitch wildly. Seth. His eyes were cold and hard, and his mouth tightened ominously as he asked, "What are *you* doing here?"

# Chapter 8

"I work here," Claudia returned, outwardly calm, although her heartbeat was racing frantically. She had realized it would be only a matter of time before she ran into Seth, and had in fact been mildly surprised it hadn't happened before now. But nothing could have prepared her for the impact of seeing him again.

His mouth tightened grimly. "Why aren't you in Seattle?" he demanded in a low growl.

"Because I'm here," she countered logically. "Why should you care if I'm in Seattle or Timbuktu? As I recall, you've washed your hands of me."

Her answer didn't please him, and he propelled himself from the examination table in one angry movement. But he couldn't conceal a wince of pain.

Clearly he was really hurting. "Jim asked me to look at you—now get back on the table."

"Jim?" Seth said derisively. "You seem to have arrived at a first-name basis pretty quickly."

Pinching her lips tightly together, she ignored the implication. "I'm going to examine you whether you like it or not," she said with an authority few patients would dare to question.

His dark eyes narrowed mutinously at her demand.

Winning any kind of verbal contest with him had been impossible to date. She wouldn't have been surprised if he'd limped out of the office rather than obey her demand. He might well have done exactly that if Jim Coleman hadn't entered at that precise minute.

"I've been talking to the hospital," he remarked, handing Claudia Seth's medical chart. Sheer reflex prevented the folder from falling as it slipped through her fingers. She caught it and glanced up guiltily.

Jim seemed oblivious to the tense atmosphere in the room. "Have you examined the wound?" he asked her, and motioned for Seth to return to the table.

Seth hesitated for a moment before giving in. With another flick of his hand, Jim directed Seth to lie down. Again he paused before lying back on the red vinyl cushion. He lay with his eyes closed, and Claudia thought her heart would burst. She loved this man, even though he had cast her out of his life, tossing out cruel words in an attempt to make her hate him. He had failed. And surely he had lied, as well. He couldn't possibly have decided to marry someone else so quickly.

Jim lifted the large bandage on Seth's leg, allowing Claudia her first look at the angry wound. Festering with yellow pus, the cut must have been the source of constant, throbbing pain. When Jim gently tested the skin around the infection Seth's face took on a deathly pallor, but he didn't make a sound as he battled to disguise the intense pain. A faint but nonetheless distinct red line extended from the wound, reaching halfway up his thigh.

"Blood poisoning," Claudia murmured gravely. She could almost feel his agony and paled slightly. Anxiously she glanced at Jim.

"Blood poisoning or not, just give me some medicine and let me out of here. I've got a business to run. I can't be held up here all day while you two ooh and ah over a minor cut." He spoke sharply and impatiently as he struggled to sit upright.

"You seem to think you can work with that wound," Jim shot back angrily. "Go ahead, if you don't mind walking on a prosthetic leg for the rest of your life. You need to be in the hospital."

"So *you* say," Seth retorted.

Stiff with concern, Claudia stepped forward when Seth let out a low moan and lay back down.

"Do whatever you have to," he said in a resigned tone.

"I'd like to talk to you in my office for a minute, Claudia," Jim said. "Go ahead and wait for me there."

The request surprised her, but she did as he asked, pacing the small room as she waited for him. He joined her a few minutes later, a frown of concern twisting his features.

"I've already spoken to the hospital," he announced as he slumped defeatedly into his chair. "There aren't any beds available." He ran a hand over his face and looked up at her with unseeing eyes. "It's times like these that make me wonder why I chose to work in Nome. Inadequate facilities, no private nurses, overworked staff...I don't know how much more of the stress my health will take."

She hadn't known Jim long, but she had never seen him more frustrated or angry.

"I've contacted the airport to have him flown out by charter plane, but there's a storm coming. Flying for the next twelve hours would be suicidal," he continued. "His leg can't wait that long. Something's got to be done before that infection spreads any farther." He straightened and released a bitter sigh. "I don't have any choice but to send you home with him, Claudia. He's going to need constant care or he could lose that leg. I can't do it myself, and there's no one else I can trust."

She leaned against the door, needing its support as the weight of what he was asking pressed heavily on her shoulders—and her heart. Despite the emotional cost to herself, she couldn't refuse.

Patiently Jim outlined what Seth's treatment would entail. He studied Claudia for any sign of confusion or misunderstanding, then gave her the supplies she would need and reminded her of the seriousness of the infection.

An hour later, with Seth strongly protesting, Claudia managed to get him into his house and into his bed. After propping his leg up with a pillow, she removed the bandage to view the open wound again. She cringed at the sight, thinking of how much pain he had to be in.

Her eyes clouded with worry as she worked gently and efficiently to make him as comfortable as possible. She intentionally avoided his gaze in an attempt to mask her concern.

He appeared somewhat more comfortable as he lay back and rested his head against a pillow. A tight clenching of his jaw was the only sign of pain he allowed to show on his ruggedly carved features. She didn't need to see his agony to know he was in intense pain, though.

"Why are you here?" he asked, his eyes closed as he echoed the question he'd asked when she walked into the exam room.

"I'm taking care of your leg," she replied gently. "Don't talk now, try to sleep if you can." Deftly she opened the bag of supplies and laid them out on the dresser. Then, standing above him, she rested her cool hand against his forehead. She could feel how feverish he was.

At the tender touch of her fingers, he raised his hand and gripped her wrist. "Don't play games with me, Red." He opened his eyes to hold her gaze. "Why are you in Nome?" The words were weak; there wasn't any fight left in him. Protesting Jim's arrangements had depleted him of strength. Now it took all his effort to disguise his pain. "Did you come back just to torment me?"

"I never left," she answered, and touched a finger to his lips to prevent his questions. "Not now," she whispered. "We'll talk later, and I'll explain then."

He nodded almost imperceptibly and rolled his head to the side.

Examining the cut brought a liquid sheen to her eyes. "How could you have let this go so long?" she protested. Jim had explained to her that Seth had fallen against a cargo crate while in Kotzebue. Claudia recalled that he'd had a slight limp the day he picked her up from the airport. Had he let the injury go untreated all that time? Was he crazy?

He didn't respond to her question, only exhaled a sharp breath as she gently began carefully swabbing the wound. She bit into her lip when he winced again, but it was important to clean the cut thoroughly. Jim had given Seth antibiotics and painkillers before leaving the office, but the antibiotics needed time to kick in, and as for the painkillers, their effect had been minor.

When she'd finished, she heated hot water in the kitchen, then steeped strips of cloth in the clean water. After allowing them to cool slightly, she placed them over his thigh, using heat to draw infection from the wound. His body jerked taut and his mouth tightened with the renewed effort to conceal his torment. She repeated the process until the wound was thoroughly cleansed, then returned to the kitchen.

"I'm going to lose this leg," Seth mumbled as she walked into the bedroom.

"Not if I can help it," she said with a determination that produced a weak smile from him.

"I'm glad you're here," he said, his voice fading.

She gently squeezed his hand. "I'm glad I'm here, too." Even if she did eventually return to Seattle, she would always cherish the satisfaction of having been able to help Seth.

He rested fitfully. Some time later, she again heated water, adding the medicine Jim had given her to it as it steamed. A pungent odor filled the room. As quietly as possible, so not to disturb him, she steeped new strips of fabric. Cautiously she draped them around the swollen leg, securing them with a large plastic bag to keep them moist and warm as long as possible. When the second stage of Jim's instructions had been completed, she slumped wearily into a chair at Seth's bedside.

Two hours later she repeated the process, and again after another two-hour interval. She didn't know what time it was when Jim arrived. But Seth was still asleep, and there didn't seem to be any noticeable improvement in his condition.

"How's the fever?" Jim asked as he checked Seth's pulse.

"High," she replied, unable to conceal her worry.

"Give him time," Jim cautioned. He gave Seth another injection and glanced at his watch. "I'm due at the hospital. I'll see what I can do to find someone to replace you."

"No!" she said abruptly. Too abruptly. "I'll stay."

Jim eyed her curiously, his gaze searching. "You've been at this for hours now. The next few could be crucial, and I don't want you working yourself sick."

"I'm going to see him through this," she said with determination. Avoiding the question in his eyes, she busied herself neatening up the room. She would explain later if she had to, but right now all that mattered was Seth and getting him well.

Jim left a few minutes later, and she paused to fix herself a meal. She would need her strength, but although she tried to force herself to eat, her fears mounted, dispelling her appetite.

The small of her back throbbed as she continued to labor through the night. Again and again she applied the hot cloths to draw out the infection.

Claudia fidgeted anxiously when she took his temperature and discovered that his fever continued to rage, despite her efforts. She gently tested the flesh surrounding the wound and frowned heavily.

Waves of panic mounted again a few minutes later

when he stirred restlessly. He rolled his head slowly from side to side as the pain disturbed his sleep.

"Jesus, please help us," Claudia prayed as she grew more dismayed. Nothing she did seemed to be able to control Seth's fever.

She'd repeatedly heard about the importance of remaining calm and clearheaded when treating a patient. But her heart was filled with dread as the hours passed, each one interminable, and still his fever raged. If she couldn't get his fever down, he might lose his leg.

His Bible lay on the nightstand, and she picked it up, holding it in both hands. She brought the leather-bound book to her breast and lifted her eyes to heaven, murmuring a fervent prayer.

Another hour passed, and he began to moan and mumble incoherently as he slipped into a feverish delirium. He tossed his head, and she was forced to hold him down as he struggled, flinging out his arms.

He quieted, and she tenderly stroked his face while whispering soothing words of comfort.

Unexpectedly, with an amazing strength, Seth jerked upright and cried out in anguish, "John... watch out...no...no...."

Gently but firmly she laid him back against the pillow, murmuring softly in an effort to calm him. Absently she wondered who John was. She couldn't remember Seth ever mentioning anyone by that name.

He kept mumbling about John. Once he even

laughed, the laugh she loved so much. But only seconds later he cried out in anguish again.

Tears that had been lingering so close to the surface quickly welled. Loving someone as she loved Seth meant that his torment became one's own. Never had she loved this completely, this strongly.

"Hush, my darling," she murmured softly.

She was afraid to leave him, even for a moment, so she pulled a chair as close as she could to his bedside and sank wearily into it. Exhaustion claimed her mind, wiping it clean of everything but prayer.

Toward daylight Seth seemed to be resting more comfortably, and Claudia slipped into a light sleep.

Someone spoke her name, and Claudia shifted from her uncomfortable position to find Seth, eyes open, regarding her steadily.

"Good morning," he whispered weakly. His forehead and face were beaded with sweat, his shirt damp with perspiration. The fever had broken at last.

A wave of happiness washed through her, and she offered an immediate prayer of thanksgiving.

"Good morning," she returned, her voice light as relief lightened her heart. She beamed with joy as she tested his forehead. It felt moist but cool, and she stood to wipe the sweat from his face with a fresh washcloth.

He reached out and stopped her, closing his hand over her fingers, as if touching her would prove she was real. "I'm not dreaming. It *is* you."

She laughed softly. "The one and only." Suddenly conscious of her disheveled appearance, she ran her fingers through her tangled hair and straightened her blouse.

His gaze was warm as he watched her, and she felt unexpectedly shy.

"You told me you never left Nome?" The inflection in his voice made the statement a question.

"I didn't come here to turn around and go back home," she said and smiled, allowing all the pent-up love to burn in her eyes.

His eyes questioned her as she examined his leg. The improvement was remarkable. She smiled, remembering her frantic prayers during the night. Only the Great Physician could have worked this quickly.

She helped Seth sit up and removed his damp shirt. They worked together silently as she wiped him down and slipped a fresh shirt over his head. Taking the bowl of dirty water and tucking his shirt under her arm, she smiled at him and walked toward the door.

"Red, don't go," he called urgently.

"I'll be right back," she assured him. "I'm just going to take these into the kitchen and fix you something to eat."

"Not now." He extended his hand to her, his look intense. "We need to talk."

She walked back to the dresser to deposit the bowl before moving to the bed. Their eyes locked as they studied each other. The radiant glow of love seemed to reach out to her from his gaze. She took his hand in her own and, raising it to her face, rested it against her cheek and closed her eyes. She didn't resist as the pressure of his arm pulled her downward. She knelt on the carpet beside the bed and let herself be wrapped in his embrace.

His breathing was heavy and labored as he buried his face in the gentle slope of her neck. This was what she'd needed, what she'd yearned for from the minute she stepped off the plane—Seth and the assurance of his love.

"I've been a fool," he muttered thickly.

"We both have. But I'm here now, and it's going to take a lot more than some angry words to pry me out of your arms." She pulled away slightly, so she would be able to look at him as she spoke. "I need to take some responsibility here," she murmured, and brushed the hair from the sides of his face. He captured her hand and pressed a kiss against her palm. "I'd never once told you I loved you."

His hand tightened around hers punishingly. "You love me?"

"Very much." She confirmed her words with a nod and a smile. "You told me so many times that you needed me, but I discovered I'm the one who needs you."

"Why didn't you tell me when you arrived that you intended to stay?" He met her eyes, and she watched as his filled with regret.

"I'm a little slow sometimes," she said, ignoring

his question in favor of explaining how she'd come to realize she loved him. She sat in the chair but continued to hold his hand in hers. "I couldn't seem to understand why God would give you a sign and not say anything to me. I was miserable—the indecision was disrupting my whole life. Then one day I decided to read the passage in Genesis that you'd talked about. I read about Abraham's servant and learned that Rebekah had been given a choice and had made the decision to accompany the servant. I felt as if God was offering me the same decision and asking that I respond in faith. It didn't take me long to recognize how much I loved you. I can't understand why I fought it so long. Once I admitted it to myself, quitting school and leaving Seattle were easy."

"You quit school?"

"Without hesitation." She laughed with sudden amusement. "I'd make a rotten doctor. Haven't you noticed that I become emotionally involved with my patients?"

"What about your uncle?"

"He's accepted my decision. He's not happy about it, but I think he understands more than he lets on."

"We'll make him godfather to our first son," Seth said, and slipped a large hand around her nape, pulling her close so her soft mouth could meet his. The kiss was so gentle that tears misted her eyes. His hands framed the sides of her face as his mouth slanted across hers, the contact deepening until he seemed capable of drawing out her soul.

\* \* \*

Jim Coleman stopped by later, but only long enough to quickly check Seth's leg and give him another injection of antibiotic. He was thrilled that the fever had broken, but he spoke frankly with Seth and warned him that it would take weeks to regain the full use of the leg.

He hesitated once, and Claudia was sure he'd noticed the silent communication and emotional connection that flashed between her and Seth. Jim's eyes narrowed, and the corner of his mouth twitched. For a fleeting moment she thought the look held contempt. She dismissed the idea as an illusion based on a long night and an overactive imagination. Jim left shortly afterward, promising to return that evening.

She heated a lunch for the two of them and waited until Seth had eaten. He fell asleep while she washed the dishes. When she checked on him later, her heart swelled with the wonder and joy of their love. How many other married couples had received such a profound confirmation of their commitment as they had? He had spoken of a son, and she realized how much she wanted this man's child.

Smiling, she rested her hands lightly on her flat stomach and started to daydream. They would have tall lean sons with thick dark hair, and perhaps a daughter. A glorious happiness stole through her.

Content that Seth would sleep, she opened the other bedroom door, crawled into the bed and drifted into a deep sleep. Her dreams were happy, confident of the many years she would share with Seth.

When she awoke later she rolled over and glanced at the clock. Seven. She had slept for almost five hours. Sitting up, she stretched, lifting her arms high above her head, then rotated her neck to ease the tired muscles.

The house was quiet as she threw back the covers and walked back to Seth's room. He was awake, his face turned toward the wall. Something prevented her from speaking and drawing attention to herself. His posture said that he was troubled, worried. What she could see of his face was tight. Was he in pain? Was something about his business causing him concern?

As if feeling her regard, he turned his head and their eyes met. His worried look was gone immediately, replaced by a loving glance that sent waves of happiness through her.

"Hello. Have you been awake long?" she asked softly.

"About an hour. What about you?"

"Just a few minutes." She moved deeper into the room. "Is something troubling you, Seth? You had a strange look just now. I don't exactly know how to describe it...sadness, maybe?"

His hand reached for hers. "It's nothing, my love."

She felt his forehead, checking for fever, but it was cool, and she smiled contentedly. "I don't know about you, but I'm starved. I think I'll see what I can dig up in the kitchen."

He nodded absently.

As she left the room, she couldn't help glancing over her shoulder. Her instincts told her that something wasn't right. But what?

A freshly baked pie was sitting in the middle of the kitchen table, and she glanced at it curiously. When had that appeared? She shrugged and opened the refrigerator. Maybe Seth had some eggs and she could make an omelette. There weren't any eggs, but a gelatin salad sat prominently on the top shelf. Something was definitely going on here. When she turned around, she noticed that the oven light was on, and a quick look through the glass door showed a casserole dish warming. Someone had been to the house when she'd been asleep and brought an entire meal. How thoughtful.

"You didn't tell me you had company," she said a little while later as she carried a tray into the bedroom for him.

He was sitting on the edge of the mattress, and she could see him clench his teeth as he attempted to stand.

"Seth, don't!" she cried and quickly set the tray down to hurry to his side. "You shouldn't be out of bed."

He sank back onto the mattress and closed his eyes to mask a resurgence of pain. "You know, I think you're right about that."

"Here, let me help you." With an arm around his shoulders, she gently lifted the injured leg and propped it on top of a thick pillow. When she'd finished, she turned to him and smiled. She couldn't hide the soft glow that warmed her eyes as she looked at this man she loved.

Sitting up, his back supported by pillows, he held his arms out to her and drew her into his embrace. His mouth sought hers, and the kisses spoke more of passion than gentleness. But she didn't care. She returned his kisses, linking her hands around his neck, her fingers exploring the black hair at the base of his head. His hands moved intimately over her back as if he couldn't get enough of her.

"I think your recovery will impress Dr. Coleman, especially if he could see us now," she teased and tried to laugh. But her husky tone betrayed the extent of her arousal. When Seth kissed her again, hard and long, she offered no resistance.

Crushed in his embrace, held immobile by the steel band of his arm encircling her waist, she submitted happily to the mastery of his kisses.

When they took a break to breathe, she smiled happily into his gleaming eyes. "There are only a few more days before Thanksgiving," she murmured, and kissed him. "I have so much to thank God for this year—more happiness than one woman was ever meant to have. I had hoped when I first came that we might be married Thanksgiving week. It seemed fitting somehow." She relaxed as she realized that she truly had no more doubts. She was utterly his.

Although Seth continued to hold her, she felt again the stirring sense of something amiss. When she leaned her head back to glance at him, she saw that his look was distant, preoccupied.

"Seth, is something wrong?" she asked, worried.

A smile of reassurance curved his lips, but she noticed that it didn't reach his eyes. "Everything's fine."

"Are you hungry?"

He nodded and straightened so that she could bring him the tray. "You know me. I'm always hungry."

But he hardly touched his meal.

She brought him a cup of coffee after taking away the dinner tray, then sat in the chair beside the bed, her hands cupping her own hot mug.

"If you don't object, I'd like Pastor Reeder to marry us," she said, and took a sip of coffee.

"You know Paul Reeder?" He looked over at her curiously.

She nodded. "I'm very grateful for his friendship. He's the one who introduced me to Jim Coleman. He also rented me an apartment the church owns—honey bucket and all," she said with a smile. "I'm going to like Nome. There are some wonderful people here, and that very definitely includes Pastor Reeder."

"Paul's the one who talked to me about Christ and salvation. I respect him greatly."

"I suspected as much." She recalled Seth telling her about the pastor who had led him to Christ. From the first day she had suspected it was Pastor Reeder. "Jim needed help with an emergency, so I didn't get to church last Sunday to hear him preach, but I bet he packs a powerful sermon."

"He does," Seth said, and looked away.

Claudia's gaze followed his, and she realized that Jim Coleman had let himself into the house. The two men eyed each other, and an icy stillness seemed to fill the room. She looked from one man to the other and lightly shook her head, sure she was imagining things.

"I think you'll be impressed with how well Seth is doing," she said, and moved aside so Jim could examine the wound himself.

Neither man spoke, and the tension in the room was so thick that she found herself stiffening. Something was wrong between these two, *very* wrong.

Claudia walked Jim to the front door when he was done with the exam. Again he praised her efforts. "He might have lost that leg if it hadn't been for you."

"I was glad to help," she said, studying him. "But I feel God had more to do with the improvement than I did."

"That could be." He shrugged and expelled a long, tired sigh. "He should be okay by himself tonight if you want to go home and get a good night's sleep."

"I might," she responded noncommittally.

He nodded and turned to leave. She stopped him

with a hand on his arm. "Jim, something's going on between you and Seth, isn't it?"

"Did he tell you that?"

"No."

"Then ask *him*," he said, casting a wary glance in the direction of Seth's bedroom.

"I will," she replied, determined to do just that.

Seth's eyes were closed when she returned to his room, but she wasn't fooled. "Don't you like Jim Coleman?" she asked right out.

"He's a fine Christian man. There aren't many doctors as dedicated as he is."

"But you don't like him, do you?"

Seth closed his eyes again and let out a sharp breath. "I don't think it's a question of how I feel. Jim doesn't like me, and at the moment I can't blame him," he responded cryptically.

She didn't know what to say. It was obvious Seth didn't want to talk about it, and she didn't feel she should pry. It hurt a little, though, that he wouldn't confide in her. There wasn't anything she would ever keep from him. But she couldn't and wouldn't force him to talk, not if he wasn't ready. She left him to rest and went into the kitchen to clean up.

An hour later she checked on him and saw that he appeared to be asleep. Leaning down, she kissed his brow. She was undecided about spending another night. A hot shower and a fresh change of clothes sounded tempting.

"Seth," she whispered, and he stirred. "I'm going

home for the night. I'll see you early tomorrow morning."

"No." He sat up and winced, apparently having forgotten about his leg in his eagerness to stop her. "Don't go, Red. Stay tonight. You can leave in the morning if you want." He reached for her, holding her so tight she ached.

"Okay, my love," she whispered tenderly. "Just call if you need me."

"I'll need you all my life. Don't ever forget that, Red."

He sounded so worried that she frowned, drawing her delicate brows together. "I won't forget."

Claudia woke before Seth the next morning. She was in the kitchen putting on a pot of coffee when she heard a car pull up outside the kitchen door.

Barbara Reeder slammed the car door closed and waved. Claudia returned the wave and opened the door for her friend.

"You're out bright and early this morning," she said cheerfully. "I just put on coffee."

"Morning." Barbara returned the smile. "How's the patient?"

"Great. It's amazing how much better he is after just two days."

"I was sorry to miss you yesterday." Barbara pulled out a chair and set her purse on the table while she unbuttoned her parka.

"Miss me?" Claudia quizzed.

"Yes, I brought dinner by, but you were in the bedroom sound asleep. From what I understand, you were up all night. You must have been exhausted. I didn't want to wake you, so I just waved at your patient, left the meal and headed out."

"Funny Seth didn't say anything," Claudia said, speaking her thoughts out loud.

Barbara's look showed mild surprise. "Honestly, that man! You'd think it was top secret or something." Happiness gleamed in her eyes, and she held out her left hand so Claudia could admire the sparkling diamond. "Teddy and I are going to be married next month."

# Chapter 9

"Teddy?" Claudia repeated. She felt as if someone had kicked her in the stomach. Seth hadn't been lying after all. There really was another woman. Somehow she managed to conceal her shock.

"It's confusing, I know," Barbara responded with a happy laugh. "But Seth has always reminded me of a teddy bear. He's so big and cuddly, it seemed natural to call him Teddy."

Claudia's hand shook as she poured coffee into two mugs. Barbara continued to chat excitedly about her wedding plans, explaining that they hoped to have the wedding before Christmas.

Strangely, after that first shock Claudia felt no emotion. She sipped her coffee, adding little to the conversation.

Barbara didn't seem to notice. "Teddy changed after John's death," she said, and blew on her coffee to. Cool it

"John," Claudia repeated. Seth had called out that name several times while his fever was raging.

"John was his younger brother, his partner in Arctic Barge. There was some kind of accident on a barge—I'm not sure I ever got the story straight. Seth was with him when it happened. Something fell on top of him and ruptured his heart. He died in Seth's arms."

Claudia stared into her coffee. From that first day when she'd walked into his room at the Wilderness Motel, she'd known there was a terrible sadness in Seth's life. She'd felt it even then. But he had never shared his grief with her. As much as he professed to love her and want her for his wife, he hadn't shared the deepest part of himself. Knowing this hurt as much as his engagement to Barbara.

"Could I ask a favor of you?" Claudia said and stood, placing her mug in the kitchen sink. "Would you mind dropping me off at my apartment? I don't want to take Seth's car, since I don't know when I'll be back. It should only take a minute."

"Of course. Then I'll come back and surprise Seth with breakfast."

He would be amazed all right, Claudia couldn't help musing.

She managed to maintain a fragile poise until Barbara dropped her off. Waving her thanks, she entered her tiny home. She looked around the room that had so quickly become her own and bit the inside of her cheek. With purposeful strides she opened the lone closet and pulled out her suitcases. She folded each garment with unhurried care and placed it neatly inside the luggage.

Someone knocked at the door, but she obstinately ignored the repeated rapping.

"Open up, Claudia, I know you're in there. I saw Barbara drop you off." It was Jim Coleman.

"Go away!" she called, and her voice cracked. A tear squeezed free, despite her determination not to cry, and she angrily wiped it away with the back of her hand.

Ignoring her lack of an invitation, Jim pushed open the door and stepped inside the room.

"I like the way people respect my privacy around here," she bit out sarcastically, wondering how she could have been foolish enough to leave her door unlocked. "I don't feel up to company at the moment, Jim. Another time, maybe." She turned away and continued packing.

"I want you to listen to me for a minute." Clearly he was angry.

"No, I won't listen. Not to anyone. Go away, just go away." She pulled a drawer from the dresser and flipped it over, emptying the contents into the last suitcase.

"Will you stop acting like a lunatic and listen? You can't leave now."

She whirled around and placed both hands challengingly on her hips. "Can't leave? You just watch me. I don't care where the next plane's going, I'll be on it," she shot back, then choked on a sob.

He took her in his arms. She struggled at first, but he deflected her hands and held her gently. "Let it out," he whispered soothingly.

Again she tried to jerk away, but, undeterred, he held her fast, murmuring comforting words.

"You knew all along, didn't you?" she asked accusingly, raising hurt, questioning eyes to search his face.

He arched one brow and shrugged his shoulders. "About Barbara and Seth? Of course. But about *you* and Seth? How could I? But then I saw the two of you, and no one could look at you without knowing you're in love. I was on my way to his house this morning when I saw Barbara with you. Something about your expression told me you must have found out the truth. Did you say anything to her?"

Claudia shook her head. "No. I couldn't. But why does it have to be Barbara?" she asked unreasonably. "Why couldn't it be some anonymous woman I could feel free to hate? But she's bright and cheerful, fun to be around. She's my friend. And she's so in love with him. You should have heard her talk about the wedding."

"I have," he stated, and rammed his hands into his pockets. He walked to the other side of the couch that served as her bed.

"I'm not going to burst that bubble of happiness. I don't think Seth knows what he wants. He's confused and unsure. The only thing I can do is leave."

Jim turned and regarded her steadily. "You can't go now. You don't seem to understand what having you in Nome means to me, to all of us. When Pastor Reeder said you were God's Thanksgiving gift to us, he wasn't kidding. I've been praying for someone like you for months." He heaved a sigh, his eyes pleading with her. "For the first time in weeks I've been able to do some of the paperwork that's cluttering my desk. And I was planning to take a day off next week, the first one in three months."

"But you don't know what you're asking."

"I do. Listen, if it will make things easier, I could marry you."

The proposal was issued sincerely, and his gaze didn't waver as he waited for her reaction.

She smiled "Now you're being ridiculous."

His taut features relaxed, and she laughed outright at how relieved he looked.

"Will you stay a bit longer, at least until someone answers our advertisement in the medical journals? Two or three months at the most."

Gesturing weakly with one hand, Claudia nodded. She was in an impossible position. She couldn't stay, and she couldn't leave. And there was still Seth to face.

Jim sighed gratefully. "Thank you. I promise you

won't regret it." He glanced at his watch. "I'm going to talk to Seth. Something's got to be done."

She walked him to the door, then asked the question his proposal had raised in her mind. "Why haven't you ever married?"

"Too busy in med school," he explained. "And since I've been here, there hasn't been time to date the woman I wanted." He pulled his car keys from his pocket.

There was something strange about the way he spoke, or maybe it was the look in his eyes. Suddenly it all came together for her. She stopped him by placing a hand on his arm. "You're in love with Barbara, aren't you?" If she hadn't been caught up in her own problems, she would have realized it long ago. Whenever Jim talked about Barbara there was a softness in his voice that spoke volumes.

He began to deny his feelings, then seemed to notice the knowing look in Claudia's blue eyes. "A lot of good it's done me." His shoulders slumped forward in defeat. "I'm nothing more than a family friend to her. Barbara's been in love with Seth for so long, she doesn't even know I'm around. And with the hours I'm forced to work, there hasn't been time to let her know how I feel."

"Does Seth love her?" Pride demanded that she hold her chin high.

"I don't know. But he must feel genuine affection for her or he wouldn't have proposed."

Both of them turned suddenly introspective, unable to find the words to comfort each other. He left a minute later, and she stood at the window watching him go.

She walked over to her suitcases and began to unpack. As she replaced each item in the closet or the drawers, she tried to pray. God had brought her to Nome. She had come believing she would marry Seth. Did He have other plans for her now that she was here? How could she bear to live in the same city as Seth when she loved him so completely? How could she bear seeing him married to another?

No sooner had the last suitcase been tucked away than there was another knock at the door.

Barbara's cheerful smile greeted her as she stuck her head in the front door. "Are you busy?"

Claudia was grateful that she had her back turned as she felt tears come into her eyes. Barbara was the last person she wanted to see. It would almost be preferable to face Seth. Inwardly she groaned as she turned, forcing a smile onto her frozen lips.

"Sure, come in."

Barbara let herself in and held out a large gift-wrapped box. "I know you're probably exhausted and this is a bad time, but I wanted to give this to you, and then I'll get back to Teddy's."

Numbly Claudia took the gift, unable to look higher than the bright pink bow that decorated the box. Words seemed to knot in her throat.

"I'll only stay a minute," Barbara added. "Jim Coleman came by. It looked like he wanted to see

Teddy alone for a few minutes, so I thought it was the perfect time to run this over."

"What is it?" The words sounded strange even to herself.

"Just a little something to show my appreciation for all you've done for Teddy. All along, Dad's said that God sent you to us. You've only been here a short time, but already you've affected all our lives. Teddy could have lost his leg if it hadn't been for you. And Dad said your being here will save Jim from exhausting himself with work. All that aside, I see you as a very special sister the Lord sent to me. I can't remember a time when I've felt closer to anyone more quickly." She ended with a shaky laugh. "Look at me," she mumbled, wiping a tear from the corner of her eye. "I'm going to start crying in a minute, and that's all we both need. Now go ahead and open it."

Claudia sat and rested the large box on her knees. Carefully she tore away the ribbon and paper. The ever-growing lump in her throat constricted painfully. Lifting the lid, she discovered a beautiful hand-crocheted afghan in bold autumn colors of gold, orange, yellow and brown. She couldn't restrain her gasp of pleasure. "Oh, Barbara!" She lifted it from the box and marveled at the weeks of work that had gone into its creation. "I can't accept this—it's too much." She blinked rapidly in an effort to forestall her tears.

"It's hardly enough," Barbara contradicted. "God

sent you to Nome as a helper to Jim, a friend to me and a nurse for my Teddy."

A low moan of protest and guilt escaped Claudia's parched throat. She couldn't refuse the gift, just as she couldn't explain why she'd come to Nome.

"How…how long have you been engaged?" she asked in a choked whisper.

"Not very long. In fact, Teddy didn't give me the ring until a few days ago."

Claudia's gaze dropped to rest on the sparkling diamond. She felt a sense of relief that at least it wasn't the same ring he'd offered *her*.

"His proposal had to be about the most unromantic thing you can imagine," she said with a girlish smile. "I didn't need a fortune-teller to realize he's in love with someone else."

Claudia's breathing grew shallow. "Why would you marry someone when he…?" She couldn't finish the sentence and, unable to meet Barbara's gaze, she fingered the afghan on her lap.

"It sounds strange, doesn't it?" Barbara answered with a question. "But I love him. I have for years. We've talked about this other girl. She's someone he met on a business trip. She wasn't willing to leave everything behind for Teddy and Nome. Whoever she is, she's a fool. The affection Teddy has for me will grow, and together we'll build a good marriage. He wants children right away."

With a determined effort Claudia was able to smile. "You'll make him a wonderful wife. And you're right, the other girl *was* a terrible fool." Her mouth ached with the effort of maintaining a smile.

Luckily Barbara seemed to misread the look of strain on Claudia's pale face as fatigue. Standing, she slipped her arms into her thick coat. "I imagine Jim's done by now. I'd better go, but we'll get together soon. And don't forget Thanksgiving dinner. You're our guest of honor."

Claudia felt sick to her stomach and stood unsteadily. The guest of honor? This was too much.

Together they walked to the door.

"Thank you again for the beautiful gift," Claudia murmured in a wavering voice.

"No, Claudia, *I* need to thank *you*. And for so much—you saved the leg and maybe the life of the man I love."

"You should thank God for that, not me."

"Believe me, I do."

Barbara was halfway out the door when Claudia blurted out, "What do you think of Jim Coleman?" She hadn't meant to be so abrupt and quickly averted her face.

To her surprise, Barbara stepped back inside and laughed softly. "I told Dad a romance would soon be brewing between the two of you. It's inevitable, I suppose, working together every day. The attraction between you must be a natural thing. I think Jim's a great guy, though he's a bit too arrogant for my taste. But you two are exactly right for one another. Jim needs someone like you to mellow him." A smile twinkled in her eyes. "We'll talk more about Jim later. I've got to get back. Teddy will be wondering what's going on. He was asleep when Jim arrived, so I haven't had a chance to tell him where I was going."

That afternoon Jim phoned and asked if Claudia could meet him at the office. An outbreak of flu had hit town, and several families had been affected. He needed her help immediately.

Several hours later, she was exhausted. She came home and cooked a meal, then didn't eat. She washed the already clean dishes and listened to a radio broadcast for ten minutes before she realized it wasn't in English.

The water in her bathtub was steaming when there was yet another knock at her door. The temptation to let it pass and pretend she hadn't heard was strong. She didn't feel up to another chat with either Barbara or Jim. Again the knock came, this time more insistent.

Impatiently she stalked across the floor and jerked open the door. Her irritation died the minute she saw that it was Seth. He was leaning heavily on a cane, his leg causing him obvious pain.

"What are you doing here?" she demanded. "You shouldn't be walking on that leg."

Lines of strain were etched beside his mouth. "Then invite me inside so I can sit down." He spoke tightly, and she moved aside, then put a hand on his elbow as she helped him to the couch.

Relief was evident when he lowered himself onto it. "We have to talk, Red," he whispered, his eyes seeking hers.

Fearing the powerful pull of his gaze, she turned away. The control he had over her senses was frightening. "No, I think I understand everything."

"You couldn't possibly understand," he countered.

"Talk all you like, but it isn't going to change things." She moved to the tiny kitchen and poured water into the kettle to heat. He stood and followed her, unable to hide a grimace of pain as he moved.

"Where are you going?" he demanded.

"Sit down," she snapped. The evidence of his pain upset her more than she cared to reveal. "I'm making us coffee. It looks like we can both use it." She moved across the room and gestured toward the bathroom door. "Now I'm going to get a pair of slippers. I was about to take a bath, and now my feet are cold." She'd taken off her shoes, and the floor was chilly against her bare feet. "Any objections?"

"Plenty, but I doubt they'll do any good."

She was glad for the respite as she found her slippers and slid her feet inside. She felt defenseless and naked, even though she was fully clothed. Seth knew her too well. The bathroom was quiet and still, and she paused to pray. Her mind was crowded with a thousand questions.

"Are you coming out of there, or do I have to knock that door down?" he demanded in a harsh tone.

"I'm coming." A few seconds later she left the bathroom and entered the kitchen to pour their coffee.

"I can't take this. Yell, scream, rant, rave, call me names, but for goodness sake, don't treat me like this. As if you didn't care, as if you weren't dying on the inside, when I know you must be."

She licked her dry lips and handed him the steaming cup. "I don't need to yell or scream. I admit I might have wanted to this morning, when I talked to Barbara, but not now. I have a fairly good understanding of the situation. I don't blame you. There was no way for you to know I was coming to Nome to stay." She made a point of sitting in the lone chair across the room from him, her composure stilted as she clutched the hot mug.

"Look at me, Red," he ordered softly.

She raised unsure eyes to meet his and time came to a halt. The unquestionable love that glowed in his dark eyes was her undoing. She vaulted to her feet and turned away from him before the anguish of her own eyes became obvious.

"No," she murmured brokenly.

He reached for her, but she easily sidestepped his arm.

"Don't touch me, Seth."

"I love you, Claudia Masters." His words were coaxing and low.

"Don't say that!" she burst out in a half-sob.

"Don't look! Don't touch! Don't love!" His voice was sharp "You're mine. I'm not going to let you go."

"I'm *not* yours," she cut in swiftly. "You don't own me. What about Barbara? I won't see you hurt her like this. She loves you, she'll make you a good wife. You were right about me. I don't belong here. I should be in Seattle with my family, back in medical school. I never should have come."

"That's not true and you know it," he said harshly, the blood draining from his face.

"Answer me something, Seth." She paused, and her lips trembled. For a moment she found it difficult to continue. "Why didn't you tell me about your brother?"

If possible, he paled even more. "How do you know about John? Did Barbara tell you?"

Claudia shook her head. "You called out to him that first night when your fever was so high. Then Barbara said something later, and I asked her to explain."

He covered his face with his hands. "I don't like to talk about it, Red. It's something I want to forget. That feeling of utter helplessness, watching the life flow out of John. I would have told you in time. To be frank, it hasn't been a year yet, and I still have trouble talking about it." He straightened and wiped a hand across his face. "John's death has been one of the most influential events of my life. I could find no reason why I should live and my brother should die. It didn't make sense. Other than the business, my life lacked purpose. I was completely focused on personal gain and satisfaction. That was when I talked to Pastor Reeder, seeking answers, and that led to my accepting Jesus Christ. And both John's death and my acceptance of the Lord led to my decision that it was time for me to get married and have a family."

Unable to speak, Claudia nodded. She had been with him the other night as he relived the torment of his brother's death. She had witnessed just a little of the effect it had had on his life.

"I'll be leaving Nome in a couple of months," she said. "Once Jim finds someone to help at the clinic. I want—"

"No," Seth objected strenuously.

"I'm going back to Seattle," she continued. "And someday, with God's help, I'll be one of Washington's finest pediatricians."

"Red, I admit I've made a terrible mess of this thing. When I told you God and I were working on the patience part of me, I wasn't kidding." His voice was low and tense. "But I can't let you go, not when I love you. Not when…"

"Not when Barbara's wearing your ring," she finished for him.

"Barbara…" he began heatedly, then stopped, defeated. "I have to talk to her. She's a wonderful woman, and I don't want to hurt her."

Claudia laughed softly. "We're both fools, aren't we? I think that at the end of three months we'd be at each other's throats." She marveled at how calm she sounded.

"You're going to marry me." Hard resolve flashed in his eyes.

"No, Seth, I'm not. There's nothing anyone can say that will prevent me from leaving."

He met her look, and for the first time she noticed the red stain on his pant leg. Her composure flew out the window. "Your wound has opened. It was crazy for you to have come here," she said, her voice rising. "I've got to get you home and back into bed."

"You enjoy giving orders, don't you?" he bit out savagely. "Marry Barbara. Go home. Stay in bed." He sounded suddenly weary, as if the effort of trying to talk to her had become too much. "I'll leave, but you can be sure that we're not through discussing the subject."

"As far as I'm concerned, we are." She ripped her coat off the hanger and got her purse.

"What are you doing now?"

"Taking you home and, if necessary, putting you back in bed."

Carefully Seth forced himself off the couch. The pain the movement caused him was clear in his eyes. Standing, he leaned heavily on the cane and dragged his leg as he walked.

"Let me help." She hastened to his side.

"I'm perfectly fine without you," he insisted.

Claudia paused and stepped back. "Isn't that the point I've been making?"

\* \* \*

The next days were exhausting. The flu reached epidemic proportions. Both Jim and Claudia were on their feet eighteen hours a day. She traveled from house to house with him, often out to the surrounding villages, because the sick were often too ill to come into the city.

When the alarm sounded early the morning of the fifth day, she rolled over and groaned. Every muscle ached, her head throbbed, and it hurt to breathe. As she stirred from the bed, her stomach twisted into tight cramps. She forced herself to sit up, but her head swam and waves of nausea gripped her. A low moan escaped her parted lips, and she laid her head back on the pillow. She groped for the telephone, which sat on the end table beside the bed, and sluggishly dialed Jim's number to tell him she was the latest flu victim.

He promised to check on her later, but she assured him that she would be fine, that she just needed more sleep.

After struggling into the bathroom and downing some aspirin, she went back to bed and floated naturally into a blissful sleep.

Suddenly she was chilled to the bone and shivering uncontrollably, unconsciously incorporating the iciness into her dreams. She was lost on the tundra in a heavy snowstorm, searching frantically for Seth. He was lost, and now she was, too. Then it was warm, the snowflakes ceased, and the warmest summer sun stole through her until she was comfortable once again.

"Red?" A voice sliced into her consciousness.

Gasping, Claudia opened her eyes, and her gaze flew to the one chair in the room. Seth was sitting there, his leg propped on the coffee table. A worried frown furrowed his brow. As she struggled to a sitting position, she pulled the covers against her breast and flashed him a chilling glare. "How did you get in here?" The words emerged in a hoarse whisper, the lingering tightness in her chest still painful.

"Jim Coleman got a key from Paul Reeder and let me in. He was concerned about you. I thought it was only right that I volunteer to watch over you. I owe you one."

"You don't owe me anything, Seth Lessinger, except the right to leave here when the time comes."

He responded with a gentle smile. "We'll talk about that later. I'm not going to argue with you now, not when you're sick. How are you feeling?"

"Like someone ran over me with a two-ton truck." She leaned against the pillow. The pain in her chest continued, but it hurt a bit less to breathe if she was propped up against something solid. Her stomach felt better, and the desperate fatigue had fled.

"I haven't had a chance to talk to Barbara," he said as his gaze searched her face. "She's been helping Jim and her father the last couple of days. But I'm going to explain things. We're having dinner tonight."

"Seth, please." She looked away. "Barbara loves you, while I…"

"You love me, too."

"I'm going back to Seattle. I was wrong to have ever come north."

"Don't say that, Red. Please."

She slid down into the bed and pulled the covers over her shoulders. Closing her eyes, she hoped to convince him she was going back to sleep.

Imitation became reality, and when she opened her eyes again, the room was dark and Seth was gone. A tray had been placed on the table, and she saw that it held a light meal he had apparently fixed for her.

Although she tried to eat, she couldn't force anything down. The world outside her door was dark. There was very little sunlight during the days now, making it almost impossible to predict time accurately. The sun did rise, but only for a few short hours, and it was never any brighter than the light of dusk or dawn.

She was still awake when Seth returned. His limp was less pronounced as he let himself into her apartment.

"What are you doing here?" She was shocked at how weak her voice sounded.

"Barbara's got the flu," he murmured defeatedly. "I only got to see her for a couple of minutes." He sighed heavily as he lowered himself into the chair.

Instantly Claudia was angry. "You beast! You

don't have any business being here! You should be with her, not me. She's the one who needs you, not me."

"Barbara's got her father. You've only got me," he countered gently.

"Don't you have any concern for her at all? What if she found out you were here taking care of me? How do you think she'd feel? You can't do this to her." A tight cough convulsed her lungs, and she shook violently with the spasm. The exertion drained her of what little strength she possessed. Wearily she slumped back and closed her eyes, trying to ignore the throbbing pain in her chest.

Cool fingers rested on her forehead. "Would you like something to drink?"

She looked up and nodded, though the effort was almost more than she could manage. The feeble attempt brought a light of concern to Seth's eyes.

The tea he offered hurt to swallow, and she shook her head after the first few sips.

"I'm phoning Jim. You've got something more than the flu." A scowl darkened his face.

"Don't," she whispered. "I'm all right, and Jim's so busy. He said he'd stop by later. Don't bother him. He's overworked enough as it is." Her heavy eyelids drooped, and she fell into a fitful slumber.

Again the rays of the sun appeared in her dream, but this time with an uncomfortably fiery intensity. She thrashed, kicking away the blankets, fighting off imaginary foes who wanted to take her captive.

Faintly she could hear Jim's voice, as if he were speaking from a great distance.

"I'm glad you phoned." His tone was anxious.

Gently she was rolled to her side and an icy-cold stethoscope was placed against her bare back. "Do you hear me, Claudia?" Jim asked.

"Of course I hear you." Her voice was shockingly weak and strained.

"I want you to take deep breaths."

Every inhalation burned like fire, searing a path through her lungs. Moaning, she tried to speak again and found the effort too much.

"What is it, man?" She opened her eyes to see that Seth was standing above her, his face twisted in grim concern.

Jim was standing at his side, and now he sighed heavily. "Pneumonia."

# Chapter 10

"Am I dying?" Claudia whispered weakly. Cooper and Ashley stood looking down at her the side of her hospital bed.

Cooper's mouth tightened into a hard line as his gaze traveled over her, and the oxygen tubes and intravenous drip that were attached to her.

"You'll live," Ashley said, and responded to Claudia's weak smile with one of her own.

"You fool. Why didn't you let me know things hadn't worked out here?" Cooper demanded. "Are you so full of pride that you couldn't come to me and admit I was right?"

Sparks of irritation flashed from Claudia's blue eyes. "Don't you ever give up? I'm practically on my deathbed and you're preaching at me!"

"I am not preaching," he denied quickly. "I'm only stating the facts."

Jim Coleman chuckled, and for the first time Claudia noticed that he had entered the room. "It's beginning to sound like you're back among the living, and sooner than we expected." Standing at the foot of her bed, he read her chart and smiled wryly. "You're looking better all the time. But save your strength to talk some sense into these folks. They seem to think they're going to take you back to Seattle."

Claudia rolled her head away so that she faced the wall and wouldn't need to look at Jim. "I *am* going back," she mumbled in a low voice, though she felt guilty, knowing how desperately Jim wanted her to stay.

A short silence followed. Claudia could feel Cooper's eyes boring holes into her back, but to his credit he didn't say anything.

"You've got to do what you think is right," Jim said at last.

"All I want is to go home. And the sooner the better." She would return to Seattle and rebuild her life.

"I don't think it's such a good idea to rush out of here," Jim said, and she could tell by the tone of his voice that he'd accepted her decision. "I want you to gain back some of your strength before you go."

"Pastor Reeder introduced himself to us when we arrived. He's offered to have you stay and recuperate at his home until you feel up to traveling," Ashley added.

"No." Claudia's response was adamant. "I want to go back to Seattle as soon as possible. Cooper was right, I don't belong in Nome. I shouldn't have come in the first place." The words produced a strained silence around the small room. "How soon can I be discharged, Jim?" Her questioning eyes sought his troubled ones.

"Tomorrow, if you like," he said solemnly.

"I would."

"Thanksgiving Day," Ashley announced.

Claudia's eyes met her friend's. Ashley knew the special significance the holiday held for her. The day she'd left Seattle, Claudia had told Ashley to expect the wedding around Thanksgiving. And Ashley had teased her, saying Claudia was making sure no one would ever forget their anniversary. Recalling the conversation brought a physical ache to her heart. No, she'd said, she wanted to be married around Thanksgiving because she wanted to praise God for giving her such a wonderful man as Seth. Now there would be no wedding. She would never have Seth.

"If you feel she needs more time, Doctor," Cooper began, "Ashley and I could stay a few days."

"No," Claudia interrupted abruptly. "I don't want to stay any longer than necessary." Remaining even one extra day was intolerable.

She closed her eyes, blotting out the world. Maybe she could fool the others, but not Ashley, who gently squeezed her hand. Shortly afterward Claudia heard the sound of hushed voices and retreating footsteps.

The stay in the hospital had been a nightmare from the beginning. Seth had insisted on flying in another doctor from Anchorage. As weak as she'd been, she had refused to have anyone but Jim Coleman treat her. Jim and Seth had faced each other, their eyes filled with bitter anger. Claudia was sure they'd argued later when she wasn't there to watch.

She had seen Seth only once since that scene, and only to say goodbye. The relationship was over, she'd said, finished, and he had finally accepted the futility of trying to change her mind.

Pastor Reeder had been a regular visitor. He tried to talk to her about the situation between Seth, Barbara and herself, but she had made it clear that she didn't want to talk about it. He hadn't brought up the subject again.

Barbara had come once, but Claudia had pretended she was asleep, unable to imagine facing the woman who would share Seth's life, or making explanations that would only embarrass both of them.

Now she relaxed against the pillows, weak after the short visit. Without meaning to, she slipped into a restful slumber.

When she awoke an hour later, Seth was sitting at her bedside. She had hoped not to see him again, but she felt no surprise as she lifted her lashes and their eyes met.

"Hello, Seth," she whispered. She longed to reach

out and touch his haggard face. He looked as if he hadn't slept in days.

"Hello, Red." He paused and looked away. "Claudia," he corrected. "Cooper and Ashley arrived okay?"

She nodded. "They were here this morning."

"I thought you might want someone with you." She could tell from his tone that he knew he would never be the one she relied on.

"Thank you. They said you were the one who phoned." She didn't know how she could be so calm. She felt the way she had in the dream, lost and wandering aimlessly on the frozen tundra.

He shrugged, dismissing her gratitude.

"You'll marry Barbara, won't you?"

His hesitation was only slight. "If she'll have me."

She put on a brave smile. "I'm sure she will. She loves you. You'll have a good life together."

He neither agreed with nor denied the statement. "And you?"

"I'm going back to school." The smile on her face died, and she took a quivering breath.

He stood and walked across the room to stare out the window, his back to her. He seemed to be gathering his resolve. "I couldn't let you go without telling you how desperately sorry I am," he began before returning to the chair at her side. "It was never my intention to hurt you. I can only beg your forgiveness."

"Don't, please." Her voice wobbled with the effort of suppressing tears. Seeing Seth humble himself this way was her undoing. "It's not your fault. Really, there's no one to blame. We've both learned a valuable lesson from this. We never should have sought a supernatural confirmation from God. Faith comes from walking daily with our Lord until we're so close to Him that we don't need anything more to know His will."

Until then Seth had avoided touching her, but now he took her hand and gently held it between his large ones. "When do you leave?"

Even that slight touch caused shivers to shoot up her arm. She struggled not to withdraw her hand. "Tomorrow."

He nodded, accepting her decision. "I won't see you again," he said. Then he took a deep breath and, very gently, lifted her fingers to his lips and kissed the back of her hand. "God go with you, Red, and may your life be full and rewarding." His eyes were haunted as he stood, looked down on her one last time, turned around and walked from the room.

"Goodbye, Seth." Her voice was wavering, and she closed her eyes unable to watch him leave.

"Honestly, Cooper, I don't need that." She was dressed and ready to leave the hospital when Cooper came into her room pushing a wheelchair. "I'm not an invalid."

Jim Coleman rounded the corner into her room. "No backtalk, Claudia. You have to let us wheel you out for insurance purposes."

"That's a likely story," she returned irritably. Cooper gave her a hand and helped her off the bed. "Oh, all right, I don't care what you use, just get me to the plane on time." It should have been the church, she reminded herself bitterly.

Jim drove the three of them to the airport. Ashley sat in the back seat with Claudia.

"This place is something." Cooper looked around curiously as they drove.

"It really is," Jim answered as he drove. Although it was almost noon, he used the car headlights.

"I wish I'd seen the tundra in springtime. From what everyone says, it's magnificent," Claudia murmured to no one in particular. "The northern lights are fantastic. I was up half one night watching them. Some people claim they can hear the northern lights. The stars here are breathtaking. Millions and millions, like I've never seen before. I...I guess I'd never noticed them in Seattle."

"The city obliterates their light," Jim explained.

Cooper turned around to look at Claudia. She met his worried look and gave a poor replica of a smile.

"Is the government ever planning to build a road into Nome?" Ashley asked. "I was surprised to learn we could only come by plane."

"Rumors float around all the time. The last thing I heard was the possibility of a highway system that would eventually reach us here."

No one spoke again until the airport was in sight.

"You love it here, don't you?" Ashley asked Claudia, looking at her with renewed concern.

Claudia glanced out the side window, afraid of what her eyes would reveal if she met her friend's eyes. "It's okay," she said, doubting that she'd fooled anyone.

As soon as they parked, Cooper got out of the car and removed the suitcases from the trunk. Ashley helped him carry the luggage inside.

Jim opened the back door and gave Claudia a hand, quickly ushering her inside the warm terminal. His fingers held hers longer than necessary. "I've got to get back to the office."

"I know. Thank you, Jim. I'll always remember you," she said in a shaky voice. "You're the kind of doctor I hope to be: dedicated, gentle, compassionate. I deeply regret letting you down."

He hugged her fiercely. "No, don't say that. You're doing what you have to do. Goodbye. I'm sorry things didn't work out for you here. Maybe we'll meet again someday." He returned to the car, pausing to wave before he climbed inside and started the engine.

"Goodbye, Jim." The ache in her throat was almost unbearable.

Ashley was at her side immediately. "You made some good friends in the short time you were here, didn't you?"

Claudia nodded rather than attempt an explanation that would destroy her fragile control over her composure.

A few minutes later, she watched as the incoming aircraft circled the airstrip. She was so intent that she didn't notice Barbara open the terminal door and walk inside.

"Claudia," she called softly, and hurried forward to meet her.

Claudia turned around, shock draining the color from her face.

"I know about you and Seth, and...don't leave," Barbara said breathlessly, her hands clenched at her sides.

"Please don't say that," Claudia pleaded. "Seth's yours. This whole thing is a terrible misunderstanding that everyone regrets."

"Seth will never be mine," Barbara countered swiftly. "It's you he loves. It will always be you."

"I didn't mean for you ever to know."

"If I hadn't been so blind, so stupid, I would have guessed right away. I thank God I found out."

"Did...Seth tell you?" Claudia asked.

Barbara shook her head. "He didn't need to. From the moment Jim brought you into the hospital, Seth was like a madman. He wouldn't leave, and when Jim literally escorted him out of your room, Seth stood in the hallway grilling anyone who went in or out."

For a moment Claudia couldn't speak. Then she put on a false smile and gently shook her head. "Good heavens, you're more upset about my leaving than I am. Things will work out between you and Seth once I'm gone."

"Are you crazy? Do you think I could marry him now? He loves you so much it's almost killing him. How can you be so calm? Don't you care?" Barbara argued desperately. "I can't understand either one of you. Seth is tearing himself apart, but he wouldn't ask you to stay if his life depended on it." She stalked a few feet away, then spun sharply. "This is Thanksgiving!" she cried. "You should be thanking God that someone like Seth loves you."

Claudia closed her eyes to the shooting pain that pierced her heart.

"I once said, without knowing it was you, that the girl in Seattle was a fool. If you fly out of here, you're an even bigger fool than I thought."

Paralyzed by indecision, Claudia turned and realized that Cooper and Ashley had walked over and had clearly heard the conversation. Her eyes filled with doubt, she turned to her uncle.

"Don't look at me," he told her. "This has to be your own choice."

"Do you love him, honestly love him?" Ashley asked her gently.

"Yes, oh yes."

Ashley smiled and inclined her head toward the door. "Then what are you doing standing around here?"

Claudia turned to face Barbara again. "What about you?" she asked softly.

"I'll be all right. Seth was never mine, I'm only returning what is rightfully yours. Hurry, Claudia, go to him. He's at the office—on Thanksgiving! He needs you." She handed Claudia her car keys and smiled broadly through her tears. "Take my car. I'll catch a cab."

Claudia took a step backward. "Ashley...Cooper, thank you. I love you both."

"I'd better be godmother to your first child," Ashley called after her as Claudia rushed out the door.

Seth's building looked deserted when Claudia entered. The door leading to his office was tightly shut. She tapped lightly, then turned the handle and stepped inside.

He was standing with his back to her, his attention centered on an airplane making its way into the darkening sky.

"If you don't mind, Barbara, I'd rather be alone right now." His voice was filled with stark pain.

"It isn't Barbara," she whispered softly.

He spun around, his eyes wide with disbelief. "What are you doing here?"

Instead of answering him with words, she moved slowly across the room until she was standing directly in front of him. Gently she glided her fingers over the stiff muscles of his chest. He continued to hold himself rigid with pride. "I love you, Seth Lessinger. I'm yours now and for all our lives."

Groaning, he hauled her fiercely into his arms.

"You'd better not change your mind, Red. I don't have the strength to let you go a second time." His mouth burned a trail of kisses down her neck and throat. Claudia surrendered willingly to each caress, savoring each kiss, reveling in the protective warmth of his embrace.

# *Epilogue*

"Honey, what are you doing up?" Seth asked as he wandered sleepily from the master bedroom. Claudia watched her husband with a translucent happiness, her heart swelling with pride and love. They'd been married almost a year now: the happiest twelve months of her life.

He stepped up beside her, his hand sliding around the full swell of her stomach. "Is the baby keeping you awake?"

She relaxed against him, savoring the gentle feel of his touch. "No, I was just thinking how good God has been to us. A verse I read in the Psalms the other day kept running through my mind." She reached for her Bible. "It's Psalm 16:11.

"Thou wilt make known to me the path of life; in

Thy presence is fullness of joy; in Thy right hand there are pleasures forever."

Seth tenderly kissed the side of her creamy, smooth neck. "God has done that for us, hasn't He? He made known to us that our paths in life were linked, and together we've known His joy."

She nodded happily, rested the back of her head against his shoulder and sighed softly. "You know what tomorrow is, don't you?"

He gave an exaggerated sigh. "It couldn't be our anniversary. That isn't until the end of the month."

"No, silly, it's Thanksgiving."

"Barbara and Jim are coming, aren't they?"

"Yes, but she insisted on bringing the turkey. You'd think just because I was going to have a baby I was helpless."

"Those two are getting pretty serious, aren't they?"

"I think it's more than serious. It wouldn't surprise me if they got married before Christmas."

"It may be sooner than that. Jim's already asked me to be his best man," Seth murmured, and he nibbled at her earlobe, dropping little kisses along the way.

The two men had long ago settled their differences and had become good friends, which pleased her no end. Claudia had worked for Jim until two additional doctors had set up practice in Nome. The timing had been perfect. She had just learned she was pregnant, and she was ready to settle into the role of homemaker and mother.

"I don't know how you can love me in this condition." She turned and slipped her arms around his waist.

"You're not so bad-looking from the neck up," he teased affectionately, and kissed the tip of her nose. "Has it really been a year, Red?" His gaze grew serious.

She nodded happily, and her eyes were bright with love. "There's no better time to thank God for each other, and for His love."

"No better time," he agreed, cradling her close to his side. "When I thought I had lost you forever, God gave you back to me."

"It was fitting that it was on Thanksgiving Day, wasn't it?"

"Very fitting," he murmured huskily in her ear, leading her back into their room.

* * * * *

Dear Friends,

I am thrilled that *A Handful of Heaven* is available for readers again. For those of you who have read my books before, you know I love second chances—a second chance at love, a second chance at a new life and, most important, a second chance to find happily-ever-after. I strongly believe that every heroine deserves all three and Paige McKaslin, my heroine in *A Handful of Heaven,* is no exception.

Paige raised her siblings after their parents' death. She is raising her teenage son alone after her husband's abandonment. Her life is one of duty, responsibility and caring for others. Now that her son is almost grown, she believes there are few surprises left in her life. And love? She's been too hurt to ever go down that path again. Until handsome Evan Thornton turns her world upside down and just might be the man who can restore her faith in love.

As you read the pages of this story, I hope you are reminded that it is never too late for wonderful blessings to come into your life. True love and second chances can be waiting just around the corner. Never give up hope.

Wishing you peace and love,

Jillian Hart

# A HANDFUL OF HEAVEN

*USA TODAY* Bestselling Author

## Jillian Hart

# Chapter 1

"Hey, Mom!" The diner's back door slammed shut with an icy gust of wind. Heavy boots tromped across the clean kitchen floor. "I took the garbage out. The bathrooms are spotless. I even cleaned the milkshake machine."

Paige McKaslin turned from the prep table to take one look at her seventeen-year-old son who was giving her "The Eye," as she called it, the one meant to charm her. He'd been using it effectively since he was fifteen months old. Alex was tall, blond and athletic and rangy. One day he would fill out those wide shoulders of his, but in the meantime he was eating as though he had two hollow legs. "You just had supper. Do you need two chocolate doughnuts?"

"You don't wanna stunt my growth, Ma!" He pretended to be shocked but those baby blues of his were twinkling. "Can I go? The movie starts at eight and Beth doesn't like to miss the previews."

One thing a mother didn't want her teenage boy to have—aside from the keys to her car—was a girlfriend. Especially a girl who did not belong to their church or any church in the county. "You behave, and remember what I told you."

"Yeah, I know, I'll be a gentleman. As if!" He rolled his eyes, his grin widening because he'd achieved victory. "I'm outta here."

"Drive safely. It's icy out there."

"Yeah, yeah. I know. I passed my driver's test, remember?"

As if she could forget. Letting go was hard but necessary. She bit her lip. Alex was a good driver even if he was young and inexperienced. "Don't forget to call me at the diner the second you get home—before your curfew."

"Mom, I know the drill. See ya!" He pounded out of sight, whistling. The back door slammed shut and he was gone.

Off to any kind of danger.

Paige bussed the eight plates from the Corey family's party.

She'd thought nothing could be more worrying than having a toddler. Alex had been such an active little tyke, and fast. She'd been a wreck trying to stay one step ahead of him, worrying what he would try to choke on next. Or electrocute himself with next.

Or fall off of and break open his skull next. How she'd worried!

Little had she imagined all those years ago that her sweet little boy was going to turn into a teenager and do something even more dangerous than try to stick pennies in electrical sockets. He would drive. She dealt with that the way she always dealt with anxiety—she just tried hard not to think about it.

"I had that same look of sheer panic," Evan Thornton commented as she shot down the aisle. "It was right after each of my boys got their licenses. I don't think I've calmed down yet, and they're both in college now."

"No, of course you're not calm because they are probably out there driving around somewhere."

Evan chuckled, and the fine laugh lines at the corners of his eyes crinkled handsomely. "Exactly. It's hard not to be overprotective. You get sort of fond of 'em."

She heard what he didn't say. There was no stronger love than a parent's love. "Lord knows why." She balanced the plate-filled dishpan on her hip. "Would you like a refill on your fries?"

"If it's not too much trouble."

"Are you kidding? I'll be right back. Looks like you need more cola, too." She flashed him a smile on her way by.

Evan had been frequenting the diner most evenings. Bless her regular customers who gave this tough job its saving grace. She did like making a difference, even if it was only cooking or serving a meal that they weren't in the mood to fix for themselves.

On the way down the aisle, she stopped to leave the bill with a couple who looked as if they had wandered in off the interstate. They still had that road-weary look to them. "Is there anything else I can get you?"

"Oh, no thanks." The woman, who was about Paige's age, tried to manage a weak smile, but failed. Sadness lingered in her dark eyes. "I suppose we ought to be heading on."

"Will you be traveling far? I have a friend who owns a nice little bed and breakfast in Bozeman. It's the most restful place and reasonably priced. If you're staying in the area, I could give her a call for you. No pressure, I just thought I'd try to help." Paige slipped their bill on the edge of the table.

"Sounds like just what I need, but we have a funeral we're expected at in Fargo in the morning. The airlines were full, and so we're driving straight through." Tears rushed to the surface.

Paige whipped a pack of tissues from her apron pocket and slipped it onto the table. "I'm so sorry."

"Th-thank you." The woman covered her face, her grief overtaking her.

Her husband shrugged his shoulders. "We're going through a tough time."

"I know how that is. Let me know if you need anything."

Not wanting to intrude, Paige backed away, the

memory of her own losses made fresh by the woman's grief. The day her parents had died had been the day after her sixteenth birthday, and it was as if the sun had gone out.

Time had healed the wound, but nothing had ever been the same again. She was thirty-eight, on the edge of turning thirty-nine—eek! But time had a strange elasticity to it, snapping her back over two decades to that pivotal loss.

*Maybe there's something I can do to make the woman's journey easier.* In the relative calm of the late evening diner, Paige bustled into the back, where the evening shift cook was sitting at the prep table bent over the day's newspaper.

Dave looked up, his expression guilty. "I thought I got everything done I needed to. But here you come looking like I'm in trouble. What'd I forget to do?"

"Nothing that I've found. I can come up with something if you'd like."

"Are you kidding? I just got set down. It was a heavy Friday rush. I'm about done. I've been standing in front of that grill for twenty years and every night just seems longer."

Sometimes Paige forgot how much time had passed, not only for Dave but for her, as well. She'd been in this place for so long that the decades had begun to blur. She still saw Dave as the restless wanderer just back from Vietnam. He'd come in for an early-Saturday lunch and stayed on as one of the best short-order cooks they'd ever had.

In a blink, she saw not the past but the present, and the man with liberal shocks of gray tinting his long ponytail, looking the worse for wear. "Go on, get home. And don't forget to take some of the left-over cinnamon rolls with you. They'll be a nice treat for breakfast tomorrow."

"I wasn't complainin', you know. I don't mind stayin' in case you get a late rush."

"I'll handle it. Now go, before I take hold of the back of your chair and drag you out of here." Paige turned to snag one of the cardboard to-go boxes. A few quick folds and she had two of them assembled and ready.

"Well, if you insist." Dave's chair grated against the tile floor as he stood.

"I do." She split apart a half dozen of the last rack of cinnamon rolls—why they hadn't moved this morning was beyond her. Yesterday the whole six dozen she'd been regularly buying had disappeared before the breakfast rush was over. She popped the sticky iced treats into the waiting boxes and added a few of the frosted cookies, too—those hadn't moved, either—then snapped the lids shut.

"Here. Go. Hurry, before a bunch of teenagers break down the door and take over the back booth." She slid one box on the table in his direction.

"Only if you promise to call me if you get slammed."

"Deal. Now beat it." She pounded through the doorway and into the dining room where the grieving woman and her husband were just gathering up their things to leave.

It took only a few moments to fill two extra large take-out cups with steaming coffee, stick them in a cardboard cup holder, and fill a small paper bag with sweetener, creamer and napkins.

"That sure hit the spot." The husband slid the meal ticket and a twenty on the counter by the till. "That was the best beef stew I've had in some time."

"My Irish grandmother's family recipe. I'm glad you liked it." She rang in the sale with one hand while she pushed the baker's box and cup holders in their direction. "Here's a little something to keep you alert while you're on the road. It's a long stretch between rest stops once you're past Bozeman. I'll be praying for a safe journey."

She counted back change, but the husband held up his hand, shaking his head. "Keep the change. That's mighty kind of you."

"Bless you." The woman teared up again and headed for the door, wrapping her overcoat more tightly around her.

After taking the box and cup holder, the husband joined his wife in the entryway and held the door for her. They stepped outside, the door swished closed, and they were gone.

"That was awful nice of you."

Paige startled, spinning around to see Evan Thornton watching her along the length of the serving counter. "I don't know about nice. I had extra cinnamon rolls that I didn't want to go to waste."

"Still. Not everyone would go to the trouble."

"Lord knows times like that are tough enough. We've all been there, battling heartbreak."

"Yes, we have." Evan's face hardened, and he turned away, staring at his plate.

He's known heartache, too, she remembered. She didn't know the details, but he'd been divorced long ago. She knew just how much pain that could give a person.

Maybe it was just her mood today, but the shadows seemed to darken quickly. Maybe a storm was on the way.

Night fell like a curtain until she could see the lighted reflection of the diner in the long row of front windows and her own tall, lanky form standing there, nearly as dark as the world outside.

She saw something else in that reflection. Evan Thornton turned on the bar chair in her direction. Her stomach gave a funny tingle. Was he watching her? And why on earth would he do that? When she looked his way, he wasn't studying her at all but recapping the ketchup bottle, his attention squarely focused on the task.

Funny. Maybe it was her imagination. Or maybe he'd been drifting off in his own thoughts, the way she'd been.

The back door clicked shut and the screen door banged, telling her that Dave had fled while the getting was good. It might be Friday night, but she expected it to be a quiet one from here on out. There were no games or matches at the high school. The middle school's spring musical pageant had been last week, and weekend nights were typically quiet in the lull after Easter. It didn't help that winter had decided to sneak in for a final showdown and the hailstorm earlier would keep most folks at home and off the slick streets.

Except for her son, wherever he was. She checked the wall clock above the register. Enough time had passed that he should be off the roads and safely inside the movie theater. She wouldn't have to worry about him again for two more hours when the movie was over and he'd be out on the roads again.

That left her to worry instead about the growing list of things needing to be done. Like the extra cleaning she'd been trying to fit into the quieter times, and the general ledger, which was still a mess on the desk, and the paperwork for the ad she needed to place in the paper—

She was back in the kitchen before she realized she'd made a conscious decision to go there, apparently lured by the exciting thought of cleaning behind the refrigerator, which was the first thing on her list that needed doing.

Now, if she could only find the energy, she'd be in seventh heaven. What she wanted was chocolate. Lots of cool, soothing, rich chocolate.

"Hey, Paige?" It was Evan Thornton calling from the front.

Trouble. She knew the sound of it well enough. There was no disguising the low note of concern in his rumbling baritone. Now what?

Four steps took her into the narrow hallway between the kitchen and the front. The thought of taking a chocolate break and then cleaning behind the refrigerator vanished at the sight of water creeping from the men's bathroom. Not just a trickle, but a shining sheet of water silently rushing from wall to wall and nosing like a giant amoeba toward the front counter.

There Evan was, a formidable shape of a man on the other side of the creeping waterway. "I could engineer a bridge for you."

She blinked. Was it her imagination or was he practically smiling? She'd never known Evan Thornton, an engineer, to have a sense of humor. Then again, she really didn't know him, which was the way she liked it and wanted to keep it. Getting too close to men, especially single, handsome, and apparently nice men, always led to trouble. At least, in her experience. "Uh, no, I'll risk the current without a bridge, thank you."

Why was it that some men looked better with a little distinguished gray in their hair? He shrugged those gorgeous shoulders of his, strong and straight. "Just thought I'd help. Let me know if you need me to toss you a lifejacket. Or a buoy. Or a marine? No?"

She blinked again. There he went again, and this time he was definitely almost smiling. The gentle upward curve of his hard mouth cut the hint of dimples into his lean sun-browned cheeks. She felt a flutter of interest down deep in her heart, and dismissed it. She was a woman after all, sworn to a single celibate life, but that didn't mean she was dead. "Call for help if I don't return."

"You can't deal with that yourself."

"Watch me." She swept past him, wading through the torrent streaming down the hallway. What would it be like to be free of this place? She'd been here so long, she couldn't even imagine it. But she would sure like to.

She was planning to put the diner up for sale this summer. She'd been accepted at the nearby university to begin classes in the fall.

"Do you want me to call a plumber?" He spoke with that polished baritone that could make a girl take a second look.

She absolutely refused to turn around. She didn't need a second look. She wasn't interested in Evan or in any man. "Not yet, it might be something I know how to fix."

"Are you telling me you're a good cook and a handyman, too?"

"Just because I'm a woman doesn't mean I can't use tools."

*Right.* Evan watched Paige McKaslin march away from him, all business. She was a study in contradiction. On the surface, she was brusque, crisp and coolly efficient. A man might draw the conclusion that she was made of ice.

But if he watched close enough, he'd see a different woman. A woman who was vulnerable and overworked and tender. He'd seen the look on her lovely face when the crying customer had said they were on their way to a funeral. She cared. And she hadn't charged the couple for the hot coffee and snacks to help them along on their all-night drive.

She wasn't as coolly tough as she let on, either. Not judging by the way her straight shoulders had slumped when she'd first eyed the leak cascading down the hallway. She was handling the flood now, marching up the water-filled hallway braced like a warrior facing battle. She was a small woman, and that came as a surprise. She was always moving, a busy, no-nonsense, get-things-done woman. Now, as he watched her, he realized just how lovely she was.

Why he was noticing, he couldn't rightly say. He'd given up on women and the notion of trusting them ever since he'd come home to find a quick note from his wife taped to the refrigerator door explaining why she was leaving him. That wasn't all. She'd drained their bank accounts, maxed out the credit cards with cash advances. She'd even liquidated their nest egg of stocks and bonds.

All very good reasons never to notice another woman again.

So, why was he standing here watching as Paige

disappeared into the men's restroom? Water lapped around the toes of his shoes. A smart man would go back to his seat and finish off the rest of his meal and contemplate the dessert menu. He would not be staring down the hallway, feeling as if he ought to lend a hand.

Why? That made no sense. He wasn't much of a handyman, so there was very little he could do to help, unless it was to turn off a valve. Paige had been clear she could handle the leak and any required tools. She was a competent woman; he'd have to believe her. Maybe the reason had more to do with her beauty than her competence.

No, that didn't make any sense. After Liz had broken his heart, wrecked their family, and destroyed his financial security, no woman's beauty could affect him. No, the reason he was standing here as the flood rushed past him into the dining room had nothing to do with Paige McKaslin. Not one thing. His chest constricted with a pain worse than a root canal.

He thought of his absolutely quiet, very empty house and took a step upstream. Water sloshed over the top of his shoes and wet his socks. Helping her was the only decent thing to do. It wasn't likely that she could find a plumber this time of night. And certainly not fast enough to save her entire diner from water damage. At the very least, Paige would have a serious repair bill on her hands.

He'd see if he couldn't help keep that to a minimum, he thought, as he knocked on the closed men's bathroom door and shouldered it open. Water resisted, and when he shoved harder, he saw why. What might have started as a small leak had resulted in complete erosion of the major water pipe to the sinks. Water gushed out of the floor full-force now, and Paige sat beside it, her face in her hands, her shoulders slumped.

In utter defeat.

Evan's heart twisted. He stepped forward, blown away by an overwhelming need to help her. To make this right.

# Chapter 2

This is going to wipe out the diner's monthly profit. And a lot more as well.

Paige scrubbed at her face. Tired, she was just so tired. She had to call a plumber. She couldn't do this herself—this was no minor repair. Already the water level had risen a few inches. And since the break in the pipe was below the shut-off for the sinks, the main line would have to be shut off.

Not only that, but the clean-up was going to take time—*hours* of hard work. Don't think about that, she commanded herself as she climbed to her feet. One step at a time. First she had to get this water turned off.

"Where's the main shut-off valve?" A man's voice came out of nowhere, bouncing off the bare walls.

She jumped, splashing the water around her. "Evan. I didn't know that you were there. What are you doing? You're going to ruin your shoes."

"I've had worse problems. This is an older building. Don't tell me the shut-off is underneath."

"There's a crawl space, but you can't go down there." She waded across the room, splashing and slipping, as fast as she could go.

Evan had already turned and was wading down the hall. "Evan!"

He was gone with a splash, but like the ripples ringing outward from his movements in the water, the effect of his kind presence remained.

You're only imagining that the kindness in his voice is personal, she told herself as she slogged after him. Waves washed against the tile protection along the walls and threatened to start wetting the wallboard at any time.

Evan had gone back to his seat, right? As she scurried down the hall she caught a glimpse of the nearly empty dining room. Evan wasn't in it.

Men. This was why she didn't have one. You couldn't trust them to do what you said—you couldn't trust them at all, not as far as you could throw them. She grabbed her coat from the kitchen closet and the flashlight from the top shelf.

The chill in the wind cut through her, tearing at the edges of her coat, and she zipped it up tightly as she ran. The light from the windows gave just enough light to thin the shadows as she tripped along the icy flagstone path around the far edge of the building.

The trap door was flung wide open and the scant light down below gave her no hint of what was happening. Had Evan already found the valve and turned it off?

He peered up at her from the shadows below. Dust streaked the top of his head. "You wouldn't happen to have any tools on you, would you?"

Those dimples had dug into his cheeks again and caught her off guard.

"I—" Her brain shut down. Tools. He was talking about tools. "You don't need one for the shut-off. Just let me—"

"I found the valve, but it's stuck open."

"It's stuck? No, it can't be. The handle has to be jiggled just right. It's temperamental." She barreled down the wooden steps, swiping cobwebs out of her hair. "Let me try it."

"Do you have a toolbox upstairs?"

"There's a kit in the kitchen closet by the door but—" She stumbled along the uneven ground and went down on her knees by the valve. He was already gone. It didn't matter. She wrapped both hands around the small metal handle and pulled. Nothing.

She strained harder. Nothing.

Okay, what she needed was a little more muscle. She braced her feet, used her weight as leverage and heaved with all her strength. The pipe groaned. The valve screeched a millimeter and then stuck as if it had been cemented into place.

No, this can't be happening. She took a step back and her heel splashed in something wet. Water. It was coming through the floorboards at the end near the bathrooms. What was it doing upstairs?

Before panic could set in, Evan was back, thundering down the steps and into the narrow space, stooping as he went, the toolbox clinking with his movements. He dropped the box at her feet and snapped it open. Her hand shot out for the wrench but he'd already stolen it.

"Hey, this is my job," she decided loudly.

He didn't seem to care, as he was already shouldering next to her and fitting the wrench into place. "It's just rusted some. Let's hope this doesn't break the pipe."

"And if it does?"

"There's always the shut-off at the meter in the street, but let's—" he paused as he put some muscle into his effort "—hope that it doesn't—come—to that."

Metal screeched in protest.

"Is it working?"

"Not yet. Could you aim the flashlight right here? It'd help if I could see what I'm doing."

"Sure." She moved close to point the beam at the stubborn valve in the narrow corner. "I keep imagining that I'm going to need an ark to rescue the last of the customers I left in the dining room."

He gave the wrench a little more muscle and the screech of old copper pipes told him he was making some difference. "If it comes to that, I'll engineer you one."

"Then I'll be even more in your debt." The gentle curve of her mouth eased into a ghost of a smile as she leaned closer to give the flashlight she held a better angle.

She smelled of cinnamon and roses. Cinnamon from the kitchen, he guessed. And roses from her lotion. The subtle aroma made him take notice. His chest throbbed. Heartburn, he thought, dismissing it as he felt the valve give a tiny bit. At his age, chest pain wasn't a good sign. Being forty-two was a thrill a minute.

He was no longer young, but he wasn't anywhere close to being old. Just in between. Which is pretty much where he'd been all his life anyway. Wasn't that what Liz had always mourned? He wasn't a stand-out kind of guy. Just average. Average looking, average earning...just average *everything*.

And that hadn't bothered him much over the years until this moment.

The wrench froze in place, and as he moved into a better position, he bonked the top of his head hard on a thick wooden beam. Stars lit the dimness before his eyes a split second before pain reverberated through his skull.

Great going, Thornton.

"Are you all right?" Genuine emotion softened her

lean face, and in the spare glow of the flashlight's dim bulb, he saw concern fill her eyes.

"I'm fine. I've got a hard head."

He couldn't help noticing how lovely she was. Her heart-shaped face was classically cut with a delicate chin, a straight nose and wide, startlingly blue eyes. Dark feathery bangs spilled over her forehead, making him want to smooth those silky wisps away from her eyes. A band tightened around his chest like a vise.

*That's it, I'm cutting down on French fries.*

He gave the wrench a little more torque, gritted his teeth and pushed for all he was worth. The stubborn wrench didn't move a millimeter and then slowly, with a high-pitched squeal, it began to give. The pipes groaned. Evan groaned. His arms burned as he clenched his jaw and gave it everything he had.

The valve closed.

"Oh, Evan! You did it! Oh, I never could have done that by myself. You are incredible! Thank you so much!"

"It was nothing." He removed the wrench and realized he was shivering.

"Nothing? You've only earned my eternal gratitude. It's freezing down here. Come on up and we'll get you something hot to drink." She grabbed the wrench from him, and her warm, satin fingers brushed his.

Suddenly he totally forgot about being half frozen. He noticed the faint blanket of freckles across her nose. Her skin was flawless, her cheekbones high and chiseled, her mouth full and her chin delicate.

The vise around his chest clamped so tight he felt close to suffocating. He shouldn't be noticing how beautiful Paige McKaslin was, because in the end it didn't matter. He'd sworn off women, and that especially included noticing the beautiful ones.

He cleared his throat. "No, I'm fine. And as for your eternal gratitude, why don't we call it even? You've served me plenty of good meals over the years."

"Yes, and you've paid for them."

"But I didn't have to cook 'em for myself. See?"

"That's not the same." She headed up the stairs.

He did his best to behave like a gentleman and not notice how trim she looked in her worn jeans or the delicate cut of her ankle showing above her sneakers. He hit the light switch and climbed up after her in the dark. Something cold and icy pecked against his face.

"It's snowing." She towered over him, the toolbox in one hand and the flashlight in the other, aiming the shaft of light down the ladder, growing slippery with icy snow.

"Great. That will mix nicely with the dust and cobwebs." The icy flakes slanted through the flashlight's golden beam and pelted him as he landed with his feet on solid ground. "You're going to need a plumber."

"Very observant of you." She knelt to grab the heavy trap door.

He beat her to it. "Go in where it's warm and call Phil's Plumbing. It's in the phonebook. He's my brother-in-law. You tell him I said to get over here pronto and give you a good price while he's at it."

"Thanks, Evan." She marched away, blending with the dark until she was gone.

He didn't know if it was the icy storm or the dark that made him feel keenly alone. Well, he was used to being alone these days, he thought as he hefted the heavy door into place.

There used to be a time when he'd been so busy, making a living, running after the boys, looking after laundry and meals and bills that he ran on constant exhaustion. It was painful to remember, and yet it only felt like a few days ago when he'd dropped into bed well after eleven each night and bemoaned having not a second to call his own.

Funny, how he missed that now. How he'd give just about anything to go back in time. Those days had whipped by so fast, he'd forgotten to hold onto the good in them. And now...well, his sons were grown up and both doing well. Cal was in college and Blake in law school. Grown men, or at least grown-up enough that they didn't need him like they used to.

As he made his way around the building to the back door, satisfaction settled over him like the snow. It was good to do something useful. To make a difference. There was no way Paige could have handled that valve on her own, but she certainly hadn't been squeamish about crawling into a narrow dank space.

There she was. He could see her through the window in the back door. She was talking on a cordless phone tucked between her chin and shoulder as she worked at the counter. She met his gaze through the glass. She flashed him a smile, a rare one of the sort he'd never seen from her.

His heart stopped between beats. The usually cool and collected Paige McKaslin shone like a morning star, like the gentle light that remained even when all others stars had gone out. She yanked open the door. "You're a lifesaver, Evan."

That troublesome tightness was back in his chest. He managed a shrug, but he didn't manage to breathe. "I take it you got a hold of Phil."

"He's on his way." She headed straight to the counter. He couldn't help being struck by the long pleasant line her arms made as she hung up the phone. She had beautiful hands, slender and graceful.

And exactly why was he noticing this? Dumbstruck, he padded away through the other kitchen door, the swinging one that led to the far end of the dining room, so he could avoid the pool of water.

Once he was far enough away, his ability to breathe returned, but the emotion remained jammed in his throat. At the doorway, he glanced over his shoulder at her. She was working her way around the corner and didn't seem to notice him looking.

He took one shaky step into the dining area and

along the empty aisles. Only one other couple remained in the diner, finishing up their steak dinners.
He fumbled onto the stool and leaned his elbows
heavily on the counter. The impact of her smile remained, and his heart pounded crazily in his chest
as if he needed a defibrillator.

Never had he reacted to a woman like that. Not
even to Liz when he'd first fallen in love with her.
What was happening? He didn't know. But as he
took his seat and grabbed the last of his fries, his
taste buds paled. Everything seemed suddenly dim
and distant. It was a strange reaction. Maybe he'd hit
his head harder than he'd thought.

His pastor, his friends, his sons and even his
brother-in-law, whom he'd kept in contact with after
the divorce, all told him he ought to start dating
again. That he should find some nice woman to share
his golden years with.

*I don't want to admit to being anywhere close to
having golden years.*

"Evan?

The fork clamored to the plate. His fingers had
somehow slipped. When he managed to meet Paige's
gaze, he made sure he didn't notice that she was a
beautiful, graceful woman with a tender heart. He
forced himself to see the efficient businesswoman,
who had taken his orders, served his meals and
counted back his change over the years. *That* was the
only Paige McKaslin he could allow himself to see.

"Department of Health rules. I can't be open for

business unless I have working restrooms." She set a big paper bag on the counter between them and a take-out cup, capped, next to it. "Your extra order of fries, a slice of banana cream pie, I know how you like it, and a hot cup of that gourmet decaf you sometimes order."

"Uh...thanks." What he needed was to head straight home, empty house or not, and put some distance between his stirred-up emotions and Paige McKaslin. What he needed to do was to sit in the quiet of his home, the same house where his wife had cheated on him and finally left, and then he'd remember why being alone was the right choice.

"Here." She reached beneath the counter and began dropping packets into the bag. "Let me make sure you've got napkins and a few things. Is there anything else I can do for you?"

"The pie would be fine. How much do I owe you?"

"Nothing, goodness. After your help tonight, this is on me. Please, you didn't even get to finish eating."

"No, forget it. I pay my way." He pulled out his wallet and she held up her hand.

*Men.* Paige appreciated Evan's pride and his ethics, but she had some of her own. "If you insist on paying for this meal, then I'm only going to give you the next one free. In fact, maybe I'll do that anyway." She turned toward the mature couple ambling down the aisle. "You, too, Mr. and Mrs. Redmond. I see that twenty you left on the table."

"Well, dear, we're not freeloaders, and we were

nearly done anyhow," Mr. Redmond kindly answered as he took a toothpick from the holder near the register. "You have a good night now. You still make the best steak in the state."

"My mother's secret spices." Paige made a mental note to give the Redmonds their next meal free. She had the best customers anyone could wish for—they were so understanding! She grabbed the small white sack containing the baker's box she'd filled in the kitchen and intercepted them at the front. "A little something for later."

Mr. Redmond was not opposed to the gift of dessert and held the door carefully for his beloved wife. They disappeared together into the storm.

Sweet. What must it be like to have a bond like that? Paige couldn't help the pang of regret or the pull of longing in her heart. She was thirty-eight years old, too old to believe in fairy tales, so why was she still wishing for one? The long painful years after her husband's departure and the following divorce had taken their toll, as had the years of shouldering responsibilities for her family. Working sixteen-hour days seven days a week had worn her to the bone.

What she needed was a vacation.

No, what she needed, she corrected herself, as she waded to the hall closet, was a time machine so she could go back twenty years, grab that naive eighteen-year-old she'd been by the shoulders, and make that foolish, stars-in-her-eyes girl see the truth about life. A truth that the grown woman in her had come to accept as a cold, hard fact.

There was no such thing as true love and no real knights in shining armor. Anything that looked like a fairy tale was either an illusion or simply wishful thinking.

Okay, that sounded bitter, but it really wasn't, she thought as she hauled out the mop. She sounded cold, but her heart wasn't that, either. If anything, Paige felt foolish. Think of all the time and heartache she could have saved herself had she understood that truth earlier in her life. Her road would have been so much smoother had she seen the world—and the man she'd married—for what was real instead of what she'd wished them both to be.

If she had, she could have focused on what truly mattered—and only on that. She could have avoided wasting energy on dreams that only faded, on hopes that true love would walk into her life one day.

The hope that she'd find a good man to love had faded over time, bit by bit, shade by shade until it was nothing at all.

That was how she'd been living for a long, long time. She swiped the mop through the water, thinking that she'd been happier this way. Alone was good. She was strong, capable and independent. She was also safe from all the harm a man could bring to a woman. Sad, trying not to remember the long-ago love she'd been unable to save, she wrung the mop, listening to the water tap into the plastic bucket like rain.

As she worked, she listened to the sounds of Evan gathering up the bag and ambling down the aisle. His steps were deliberate and slow, as if he were in no hurry to leave. He drew to a stop in the breezeway between the eating area and the front counter. "Do you want me to hang around until Phil gets here?"

"That's nice of you, but I'm used to being alone here after dark." She swiped the mop through the cold water and wrung the sponge head well. "I do appreciate your help tonight. Not everyone would have gotten up to help me."

"Glad I could make a difference. With my boys gone, I don't get to do that much anymore." He cleared his throat as if he had more to say, and could not.

What would it be like to come home to an empty house, she wondered? To open the door and know that her son would not be in his bedroom downstairs with his dog, listening to music or munching on potato chips or sacked-out fast asleep?

It had to be a long stretch of lonely, she thought as she went back to mopping. She didn't know what to say as Evan walked past to snag his jacket from the coat tree, she couldn't help noticing that he'd gotten pretty dirty crawling around under the diner. Dust streaked his slacks.

She bent to squeeze water from the mop head. "Uh, are those dry clean only?"

"No way. Don't even worry about it." He didn't look at her as he slid into his black jacket, pulled a baseball cap over his head and leaned against the door.

"Drive safe out there, Evan. The roads have to be a mess."

"You be safe, too." He cleared his throat, slid a ten and a five on the counter and took the sack. There was a challenging glint in his dark eyes as he ambled past, as if he were daring her to give the money back.

The bell overhead jangled as he strode into the night. "I'll see you tomorrow."

"Uh, yeah, that would be great. I'll be waitressing."

"Then I'll be ordering."

He stared at her for a beat, as the night began to engulf him. In the moment before the shadows claimed him completely, she saw the essence of him, not the physical, not the expected, but the steady strength of a good man.

The door swung shut, and she was alone. Snow pinged against the windows, driven by a cruel wind, and she swore she felt the echo of it deep in her heart, in a place that had been empty to romantic love since before her son was born.

And how foolish was that, that she was wishing for the impossible now? No, not exactly wishing, but thinking that it was possible again.

*I'm more tired than I thought,* she told herself with a chuckle as she turned the dead bolt and went back to her mopping.

# Chapter 3

The house was dark. He'd forgotten to leave a light on again. Evan fumbled along the kitchen entryway. Cal had gone off to school what? seven, eight months ago, and he still couldn't get used to him being gone. It hasn't been so bad when Blake had left, for he and Cal had made the adjustment together. But this... having them both gone, it felt like he'd walked into someone else's life.

But this was his life now. He was a free man, unencumbered and carefree. Shouldn't it feel better than this? Evan tossed the keys and his battered gym bag, and slid the sack from the diner onto the counter, pushed the door to the garage shut with his foot and listened to his footsteps thump through the lonely kitchen.

Let there be light. He hit the switch and a flood of brightness shocked his eyes. He'd been outside so long, his eyes had gotten used to the darkness. The drive home had been slow and long and pitch-black. The headlights had been nearly useless in the rapid snowfall. And now, this place seemed too bright and too glaringly empty to feel like a home.

Well, he was just feeling lonely. It was Friday night, after all. Maybe one of the boys had had time to call in. That thought put some bounce in his stride as he left his briefcase on the kitchen table and leaned to check the message light on the phone recorder. Nothing.

Okay, young men had more fun things to do on Friday nights than to give their old dad a call. He was glad for them both. He wanted them to be out there, living their lives and doing well. It's just that he hadn't figured on how his own life would stand still when they were gone.

The flyer one of his clients had sent him was sitting on the edge of the counter. He'd meant to toss it with the rest of yesterday's mail, but he hadn't gotten around to it yet. The apple-green paper seemed to glow neon in the half light and he pulled it out so he could look at it properly.

A Bible study for the rest of us. A bold carton caption stretched above a cartoon-like pen-and-ink drawing of a middle-aged man in his recliner. "The youth have their own lives, and the singles and the seniors have their activities. What about the rest of us? Come join us for Bible study, dessert and fellow-ship at Field of Beans."

That was the coffee shop in town—and Evan knew Paige's relatives owned it. That was a bonus, he suddenly realized. Plus, it was an evening meeting, something he could do after work. Something besides cleaning out the horse barn, that is.

He folded up the flyer and slid it in with the stack of bills needing to be paid. That was something he'd been meaning to do—study his Bible more. Now that he had the time. Maybe this was a solution to one of his lonely evenings. Maybe he would take everyone's advice—not to date but to get out and do the things he'd been putting off when he'd been so busy raising his sons.

The phone rang while he was on his way through the family room. One of the boys? Hope jolted through him. He snatched up the cordless receiver on the second ring. "Hello?"

"Is this Evan Thornton?"

"Uh…" In his excitement, he'd forgotten to check the caller ID screen. "Yeah. Who is this?"

"This is Michael from First National Bank, how are you this evening? I want to tell you about our new identity theft program—"

At least it wasn't bad news. "Not interested. Goodbye."

He hung up the phone, glanced around the room at the TV remote that was on the coffee table where it belonged and not flung and lost somewhere in the room, at the chairs pushed in at the table instead of all shoved around askew. There were no stacks of books or heaps of sports equipment and coats lying around, all needing to be put away.

Would he ever get used to the quiet, to the orderliness, to the emptiness? Standing alone in the family room, which had been put into tidy order by the cleaning lady, he felt at a loss. This didn't feel like home anymore.

As he headed upstairs to change out of his work clothes and into his barn clothes, he realized this was what it meant to be unencumbered and carefree, a free man again. There was no phone ringing off the hook, no kids traipsing through the house.

Just the telemarketers and him.

He'd always known his boys were a great blessing. He'd given thanks to the Lord every night as he'd lain down to sleep, but he'd never stopped to see the treasured gift that each day really was, and that, for all of those eighteen years, they were surprisingly fleeting.

"Well, that should just about do it." Phil the plumber tried to stomp the snow off his work boots. But considering the mud he'd picked up from the crawl space, it was a hopeless cause anyway. "I've double-checked the length of the pipes and couldn't find a drop anywhere. I think we've got the problem licked."

"Music to my ears. Thank you." Paige dropped

the scrub brush into the soapy bucket, where she'd been cleaning the water line against the bathroom wall. "I appreciate this so much. I know it was a long drive out here, and it's going to be worse going back."

"Before you get all misty on me..." He gave a friendly—but not too friendly—wink. "I've got bad news. You're gonna have to replace some of this pipe. It's gonna be expensive, and if you want, I can work up an estimate. I can either do it for all new water lines, or I can do it in phases and we can just do the worst stuff first. You just let me know."

Bad news? Did he say bad news? No, he had that wrong; this was *devastating* news. The small allotment she put faithfully into the savings account every month for repairs would never be enough. She didn't have to go grab the latest bank statement to know that she couldn't afford to replumb the entire diner.

She also knew how lucky she'd been tonight. The damage could have been worse, and as it was, she could open for business as usual in the morning. She'd only lost three hours of business tonight. Not bad, considering. Heaven was gracious, as always, and she was thankful. "Why don't you work up the bit-by-bit estimate?"

"Fine by me. I'll send it with my bill."

Already dreading the amount due, she handed him a sack with the last of the cinnamon rolls. "A little something for your breakfast tomorrow. You drive safely out there now."

"I've got four-wheel drive." Phil hefted his big

toolbox to the door and stopped to retrieve his parka. "I'll get the stuff in the mail on Monday. Thanks, ma'am."

When had she become a "ma'am"?

Probably about the same time her son had learned to drive. Thank God for hair color that covered the gray and intensive eye cream. Worry could do that to a girl. Stress was her middle name these days, and that combined with her age didn't help. She wasn't quite sure where all the time had gone—wait, erase that. She did. She'd spent probably seventy-five percent of the last twenty-two years right here in this diner.

After seeing Phil out and locking the door behind him, she glanced at the clock. The movie ought to be getting out about now. Great, she could get back to worrying about Alex being out there on these roads. Maybe what she needed to do was to expend some of that nervous energy and *clean*.

So she kept her eye on the clock as she scrubbed down the grill and wiped the counters, tables and chairs. Then she tackled the rest of the floor that hadn't been flooded, mopping until the tile squeaked beneath the mop head and her cell phone was ringing in her back pocket.

A quick glance at the caller ID window revealed her home number. Good. That meant Alex was home safe and sound—and even five minutes before his curfew. How great was that? "Hey there. How was the movie?"

"Good. You can stop worrying now. Notice the time? I'm calling you *before* eleven. What do you think about that?"

"It's unprecedented, and it makes me suspicious. Worry and suspicion are a mother's job."

"Yeah, yeah, I know. So, are you gonna be home soon?"

That question made her suspicious, too. "You didn't happen to notice a leak in the bathroom before you bugged out of here, did you?"

"Nope. I'd have told ya, even though Beth was waiting for me. Why? What'd I do?"

"Nothing. I had a leak in a pipe, that's all. Are you getting ready for bed, or are you going to get lost in your new video game?

"Uh, nope, I wasn't playing my X-Box, but thanks for reminding me, Ma." He sounded pleased with himself. "Just kidding. You want me to go out and feed the horse for you?"

He was volunteering to do barn work? There *had* to be something wrong. That wasn't normal teenage behavior. "Okay, what did you do?" Expecting the worst, Paige hefted the bucket toward the kitchen. "Don't tell me you dinged the truck."

"No way."

"Hit somebody on the way home?"

"Hey, I'm innocent. I'm just trying to help my poor tired mom."

Help? Now she was suspicious. She maneuvered the bucket up to the industrial sink and upended it.

"Okay. Out with it, young man. What did you do? What are you trying to soften me up for?"

"Nothing. I just thought I'd be a good son for a change." There was a grin in his voice. "Don't worry."

"Yeah, I'm still suspicious, though."

"You go right ahead, Mom. You'll see." He sounded extraordinarily happy.

Could it be her son was moving past the surly teenager stage that even the best of kids went through? No, that was too much to hope for. "I'll see you when I get home. I'll be leaving in about ten minutes. Think you can have your teeth brushed and your prayers said by the time I get there?"

"Aye, aye, captain." With a chuckle he clicked off the phone.

Yep, something was definitely up with that boy. She snapped the cell shut, slipped it back into her pocket and rinsed the bucket. Done. Well, done enough for now.

She was beat; she usually put in more hours than this staying later on weekend nights. Maybe it was the worry and upset over the water pipe. She felt as if she'd worked two twelve-hour shifts back to back.

But the moment she stepped outside and locked the back door, she saw her journey wasn't going to be an easy one. She still had to remove the snow coating her SUV and chip away at the ice frozen solid to the windows before she could even think about trying to drive. And once she was on her way, the roads would be more than a challenge.

Twenty minutes later, falling snow pelted her trusty Jeep with big wet flakes, and it was impossible to see more than a few inches in front of her. The accumulation on the road was sloppy and tricky to drive in. It caught at the wheels and tossed the vehicle every which way, so she slowed to a crawl to navigate through the town streets and along the county road where other vehicles' tires had mashed the mire down into an icy compact crust.

When she turned off onto the private road, she relaxed a bit. Almost home. The evergreens and cottonwoods lining the lane were bent low from the heavy snow and scraped at the top of her Jeep; that's when it got tough going. She fought the wheel to stay on the narrow road.

Only two other sets of tire tracks marked the way in the otherwise absolute darkness. One set, which was almost snow filled, veered off down a long, tree-lined drive. Evan Thornton's place. The remaining tracks had to be her son's and led her a few more miles into the hills, up her driveway and into the shelter of her garage.

Thank heaven. She was home and in one piece, and not that much worse for wear. Lights flicked on and there was Alex, holding open the inside door, already in a flannel T-shirt and pants she'd gotten him for Christmas. His blond hair was rumpled and in serious need of a cut. His dog panted at his side. "Hey, Mom. I was just nuking some cocoa. Want some?"

"Are you kidding? I'd love a cup."

"Cool." He flashed her a quick grin and disappeared behind the door, the dog, Max, loping along after him.

As she gave the door a shove, her back popped. Great. That was going to be the next disaster. Her back was going to go out. Every joint she owned creaked. *Wasn't life eventually supposed to be easier, Lord? Or are You trying to tell me something?*

She rescued her purse from the floor, along with the small paper sack with the last two cinnamon rolls. She had to wonder, as she elbowed through the door and into the laundry room, whether God was sending her a sign.

Every time she tried to get ready to sell the diner for good something happened to hold her firmly here. In the last six months, her sister Rachel had married and moved away, the roof had needed to be replaced and now the plumbing. Those repairs would erode a big chunk of the savings she'd been squirreling away. Not good.

Then again, it was never a true disaster, either. The Lord might be trying to tell her something, but He always made sure she had help, too. The image of Evan Thornton flashed into her mind. Tall, broad-shouldered, he had the kind of quiet strength that made a woman sigh and wish—even a woman like her who did not place any faith in the non-constant nature of men.

Sure, some men were constant, but it was a rare thing. The trouble was, it would be easy to start believing Evan was one of those kind of men. He'd helped out tonight without expecting more than a thank-you. And what was it he'd said? *Glad I could make a difference.* He had his heart in the right place. Why had it seemed that he was so sad? Not depressed-sad, just…lonely-sad. He hadn't wanted to go home to an empty house.

It hit her the moment she saw her strapping son at the microwave, punching the buttons. Hadn't Evan's youngest boy, who was a year older than Alex, gone to college this year? Maybe that's why he seemed so lonely.

Alex's crooked grin lit up his face. "Excellent, Mom. Sit down, take a load off. Want me to get that for you?"

He could have been a young, hip butler for the attention he was giving her. And while it was nice, she had to wonder what was behind his very sweet behavior. She let him take her purse, the dinner sack and her keys and then watched in amazement while he set them on the counter. He couldn't resist peeking into the sack.

"Sweet. Good call. I could use a cinnamon roll. I'm a growing boy, you know."

"I've noticed."

"Here, sit down." His hand on her elbow guided her to one of the chairs at the breakfast bar.

"Okay, what's up?" What trouble are you in now? She bit her tongue before she said it. "This is bringing to mind the time you drove into the school bus in the school parking lot and backed up traffic for thirty minutes."

"My dearest mother, now why would I be up to anything? I'm a good kid."

"*Good* is a relative term." He *was* a good boy; her heart swelled up with endless love for him, but he was a teenage boy, no matter how great a kid he was, and he needed constant vigilant guidance. Even if she was proud of the fine man he was growing up to be.

As he fetched the full steaming mug he'd obviously fixed before she'd stepped through the door, she watched him like a hawk, trying to ferret out a clue to the truth. But nothing. No hint.

She kept staring at him, but he wasn't going to crack. She took the mug he slid across the counter to her. "Okay, spill it. I want the truth."

All innocence, he opened the microwave door. "There's no truth. I just thought I'd be nice to my mom."

"I like it. I just need to know why."

"Well, let me think. I did rob a bank tonight, and I stopped by a convenience store and robbed that, too." He laughed at his own joke. "Am I funny or what?"

"Hilarious." Paige took a sip of chocolate. That hit the spot. She eyed her son over the rim of the cup.

This was a teenaged boy, home from his date with a girl she didn't approve of, and home early, despite the weather, come to think of it.

A sudden panic began to lick through her soul. He hadn't gotten into some serious trouble with his girl-friend, had he? She'd been sure to talk to him about his responsibilities toward Beth, to respect her, but— *No,* she couldn't begin to think about that!

Alex hopped onto the stool beside her. "Yo, don't have a heart attack or nothin'. You don't think I really robbed some place? I was just yanking your chain. It's my job to torment my mom." He grinned, know-ing he was perfectly adorable.

"Just like it's my job to worry and make sure you grow up right."

"I'm growing up right." He rolled his eyes. "All I did was take Beth home after the movie. That's it."

Oh, maybe they broke up. Maybe that's what this was about. He was home early, making hot chocolate and sitting next to her. Maybe he wanted to talk. Re-lief rushed through her. "How is Beth?"

"Okay. I met her mom." He shrugged, leaving her to wait while he rammed a cinnamon roll into his mouth, bit off a huge chunk and chewed.

Beth's mom? That wasn't what Paige expected him to say. Had the woman said something to upset him? She took a sip of the steaming cocoa and licked the marshmallow froth off her lip, waiting for the rest of the tale.

Finally, after a long beat of silence, Alex confessed. "I took Beth up to the door, and her mom was waiting. She was drunk, I think. And she started chewing out Beth, and I just..." He swallowed hard. "Felt so bad for her."

"Me, too." Paige knew Beth's mom worked at the local motel as a cleaning lady, and rumor had it she was a woman with a sad life.

"Beth didn't want me to see her mom like that, so she wanted me to go. But she said something to me." He hung his head. "That I was lucky. To have you for a mom. And she's right." He attacked the cinnamon roll again.

Paige let the impact of his words settle. Her heart gave another tug. "You're a pretty great kid, too, you know. I got lucky when the angels gave me you."

"I know. I am a good kid." There was that look again, The Eye, the one that made it impossible for her not to melt with adoration for him. He shoved off the counter, taking the cinnamon roll with him. "I got youth group stuff tomorrow. Did ya need help at the diner?"

"No, we'll manage without you."

"It'll be hard, I know." He was gone, bounding through the house, thumping and thudding as he went down the hall and into the basement where his bedroom was.

Leaving her alone. The warmth of the house, of her home, surrounded her as she sipped her cocoa. Alex's advanced calculus and physics textbooks were stacked on the table, ready for him to do his homework when he caught a chance over the weekend. On the counter next to the microwave was the admission booklet and information from the college he'd be attending in the fall.

High-school graduation was just around the corner, in the last week of May, and then Alex would be getting ready to leave home. She'd be putting the diner up for sale and then she'd have all the time in the world to follow her own dreams. Paige had been planning for this time of her life for a long while. She deeply wanted this new future rushing toward her.

But maybe she wasn't in so much of a hurry to get there.

She finished her hot chocolate, let the peace of the night settle around her and remembered to give thanks for all the good things in her life.

## Chapter 4

Too much time on his hands. At first Evan had filled the void of the weekends with work on Saturday and church on Sunday, but the truth was, he worked long enough hours during the week and he'd more than caught up on his workload, which was usually such that he was always struggling to keep up. Now, suddenly, he was caught-up. After six months of working most weekends, he had no reason to be at the office. And so he was wandering around the local feed store, looking at stuff he didn't need. At loose ends.

"Getting ready for summer camping?" Dalton Whitely had inherited the store from his granddad, and had been several years behind Evan in school. Even though they'd played in sports together for a year, when Evan was a senior and Dalton a freshman, Evan really only knew the man as a salesman.

Now that his life was slowing down, Evan was noticing he had a lot of acquaintances, folks he knew by name, but not nearly enough true friends. He wasn't sure what that said about him, but he knew he was guilty of keeping a healthy distance between him and most people. He'd turned into a man who didn't trust easily. Maybe, when that came to trusting a wife, that was a good thing. But he felt adrift these days. Unconnected. The flyer he'd kept, the one about the Bible study, popped into his mind again.

Maybe, he thought. Maybe it was just the thing he needed. He realized Dalton was waiting for an answer. "I'm just looking. Don't need a new tent, but those are sure nice."

"Latest models. Just put 'em out." Dalton flashed a cordial smile. "You let me know if you have any questions?"

"Yep." Looking at the camping gear reminded him of better times. Maybe he'd like camping alone. It was something he'd never done before. For more summers than he could count, he and the boys had spent most weekends up in the mountains: camping, hiking, fishing, hunting. There was nothing like riding up into the mountains on horseback. It was like stepping back a century in time. He hadn't thought about the summer to come. He was already dreading it.

As he turned his back on the brand-new pup tents

and eyed the wall of bright halters and braided bridles, he already knew how the summer was going to go. Cal would be off working to make spending money and money for books for next year; he'd probably go off with Blake and fight fires all summer. A good paying job, great for the boys, but Evan was going to be alone. He'd have to face the prospect of a long summer by himself.

His cell buzzed in his jacket pocket. He fished it out, hope springing eternal as he glanced at the screen. It was neither of his sons, but he was grinning as he answered. "Hi, Phil."

"Hey, I wanted to thank you for the business last night. Things are slow and I needed the work."

"Great. I hope you gave her a good price. Paige seems like a nice lady."

That was an understatement. Evan had thought of her on and off all morning, since she'd slipped cinnamon rolls in with his pie, and he'd had them with his coffee this morning. He couldn't get the image of her out of his mind, the softness she was so careful to hide. He'd been trying not to think of her, but things kept happening to bring his mind back to her. The cinnamon rolls, the sight of the diner as he drove past and now Phil's call. That unsettled tightness clamped back around his chest, and he didn't like it. He tried to will it away, but it remained.

"Seems. You mean you don't know?"

Okay, Phil was fishing for the truth. What truth? There was nothing between him and Paige. How crazy was that? And Phil *knew* Evan's position on women, including all the reasons behind it. Phil had been with him through the aftermath of the divorce. "I can't believe you! I don't have a personal interest in Paige. I was eating dinner in the diner when the pipe burst. That's it."

"Oh. Well, that explains it then. For a minute there, I thought you just might have found a woman who could help you get over what Liz did to you."

"You sound disappointed."

"I am, but I understand. I'm on my way into town right now."

"Here? You're coming here?" For some reason that was too much of a switch for his thoughts to take. Probably because they were still lagging, as he gazed out the store's window at the front window of Paige's diner. He realized he had a new halter and lead rope in hand, although he didn't remember picking one out, and he headed to the cash stand. "What's the deal? You're not out in this neck of the woods much, not since Cal flew the coop."

"I started work on an estimate for the diner, and realized I had to come take a second look to do it up right. I need the business, so I want to do a good job. You wouldn't want to give Paige a good word or two about me, huh? She looks savvy enough to get more than a few estimates for me to compete with. What do you say?"

"I say come meet me for lunch and I'll let you talk me into it. Or at least, you can talk to her about it."

"Done. I'm, uh, about five minutes away. I'll meet you at the diner?"

Evan pocketed his phone and set his purchases on the scarred wooden counter as Dalton slid behind to run the decades-old cash register. Funny thing how he had a better view of the diner from here. And he could see not only the diner, but also the woman who ran it, out salting down the freshly shoveled sidewalk in front of the door.

She looked as lovely as the day's sunshine. She wore a bright yellow spring coat over her standard dark sweater and jeans, and he couldn't remember ever noticing her in a bright color before. If he had, surely he would have taken a long second look. The splash of color brought out the pale rosebud pink of her cheeks, and the sheen of golden highlights in her dark brown hair. Teenagers climbed out of a minivan, calling out to her, and she greeted them with an unguarded smile.

The impact hit him like a punch to his chest.

"Should I just put that on your bill, Evan?" Dalton asked.

"Uh…yep." Rattled but not wanting to show it, Evan nodded thanks to the storeowner, grabbed his bagged purchase and walked on wooden legs to the doors. He was only distantly aware of pushing through the swinging door and into the chill of the wind. Cold penetrated his shirt, for he hadn't zipped his jacket, but it registered only vaguely. He could not seem to take his eyes off Paige.

She was talking with the kids, listening attentively, her head tipped slightly to the left, her thick fall of bangs cascading over her forehead. She was pretty. She was nice. She was a good mom. That was easy to see as her son stood at her side, tall and good-natured; Evan remembered that Alex McKaslin had played on both the football and basketball teams with Cal. He was a good kid. And Paige, as busy as she was, had made it to every game, home and away. A longing filled him as he inexplicably felt drawn to her, and suddenly the distance between them seemed intolerable.

What was happening to him? You're lonely, man, he admonished himself. And loneliness was wearing on him. Making him vulnerable. Making him wish for what he knew was impossible. For what he never wanted to try again. Marriage had been a miserable path for both him and Liz: even though he'd tried his best to make her happy, he'd failed.

It wasn't all his fault—he took what blame was his and he'd learned from it, but she'd been a hard woman to please. Selfish to the core, and in leaving she had ruined his credit and nearly bankrupted him, holding the custody of the boys over him. That's what he should be reminding himself of every time he looked at Paige McKaslin.

Except it was hard, and he didn't know why the memory of the disasters and hurts of his past weren't keeping his interest in her at bay. Paige was talking with the teenagers now, easy and open. Her son and the other kids seemed to like her so well. She ushered them inside, holding the small plastic bag of rock salt in the crook of one arm. When she stepped through the threshold and out of sight, it was as if the sun had slipped behind a cloud, and he shivered.

"Evan! Earth to Evan! Are you all right, man?"

Evan realized he'd been staring across the street as though he was mesmerized. He shook his head, clearing his thoughts, and looked around. His big burly brother-in-law was bounding down the sidewalk, his plumber's van parked six or seven car lengths up the street. He realized Phil must have called his name several times. *Do I look like a fool, or what?*

Not knowing what to do with himself, he yanked open the passenger door of his truck and tossed the bag on the floor. "Phil. You look ready to work."

"I came to get a better look in the crawl space. Didn't want to wear my Sunday best." Phil was no dim bulb. There was a knowing twinkle in his eyes as he gazed across the street. "That Paige McKaslin sure is a nice lady, don't you think?"

That sounded like a loaded question. *Just how long had he been watching Paige? And how transparent had he been?* "She seems nice enough. She runs a good business. Serves some of the best food in the county."

"All good reasons to go get something to eat at her place, right?" Phil seemed to take that in stride.

As Evan stepped off the curb, he realized that

maybe he'd been misreading Phil's statements. He was starting to scare himself. But considering the financial devastation a woman had brought to his life, he probably *should* be terrified. He was committed to being totally single. That was the way of it. Nothing was going to change his mind about that.

"I'm in the mood for some good homemade chili."

"Homemade chili?"

"It's her family's recipe. Her parents and her grandparents. It's good stuff."

"Now you've got me hungry. How are the boys?"

"Do you think I know? Good, I guess. They're busy. You just wait. Has your daughter picked a college yet?"

"She's got another year, thank the Lord, but that'll go by quick. Then Marie and I won't know what to do with ourselves." Phil hiked up onto the sidewalk, his toolbox rattling. He seemed nonchalant about the upcoming change in his life—as if it would be an easy transition.

Not so easy. Then again, Phil had a good wife. A woman who'd stood by him and worked beside him every day of their marriage. An empty nest might not be so empty in the presence of a happy marriage. But a happy marriage—those had to be rare. It certainly hadn't happened for him.

"Hi, Mr. Thornton. Welcome back." One of Paige's teenage twin cousins cracked her gum and pulled out two menus. "Wherever you wanna sit. You just go ahead and pick."

"Thanks. You might want to let Paige know that the plumber is back with some questions."

"Oh, yeah, like, I'll go get her." The teenager accompanied them down the aisle. "Paige is having a day." She rolled her eyes. "So it'll probably be a minute or two before she's free."

Evan remembered what Cal had called the McKaslin twins, who were a year behind him in school: A hundred percent clueless, but they get your order right. He'd suspected Cal had a crush on one of them—he wasn't sure if it was this one, since the girls were entirely identical right down to their hair styles and jewelry.

Evan chose a booth in the back away from the crowd of teenagers that had settled into two booths near the front. He recognized most of them from the church's youth group. Cal had been active in it up until he'd left home.

Evan opened the menu as a formality, mostly to give him a moment or two to develop a plan. Paige McKaslin had blown him away last night, and he hadn't expected that. And today when he'd seen that private side of her, it had been something he'd never seen in her before last night. What would he do if last night had changed things between them?

"I'm gonna get the chili, too. It's cold out there, and it comes with a side of cornbread. I'm a sucker for cornbread." Phil snapped the menu shut. "Oh, here she comes. Hi, Paige."

"Gentlemen." There was no falter in her step and

no flaw in her collected manner as she approached their table. "Phil, I'm told you have some questions. What can I do for you?"

"I need to take another look down below. And where's your hot-water tank?"

"Off the kitchen. Eat first, then flag me down and I'll show you what you need." She slipped two water glasses onto the table. "What can I get you two?"

Evan realized he was staring at her again. "Paige, you remember Phil?"

"Uh, of course I do. Phil, Evan braved the dark reaches of the crawl space to turn off the water for me."

"He did, huh? I wondered how a skinny thing like you could manage to turn that valve. It about gave me a hernia when I went to turn it back on."

Paige laughed; she liked the plumber. She liked that he was here to do the estimate the right way, and she liked that he was a friend of Evan's. "You two wanted to order?"

"You know where I'm going," Evan accused her. "And I'm not ordering until we come to an agreement."

"You're going to charge me for your plumbing work last night?"

"No, ma'am. I don't want you thinking you're going to give me a free meal. You charge me like any other customer, or I take my business down the street to your competitor."

"Ouch, you drive a hard bargain, but if you're

going to call me 'ma'am,' then I'm going to insist you go down the street to my competition. I just am not going to put up with anyone reminding me how old I am. I'm just not going to do it."

Evan chuckled, leaning back in the booth just enough that the sunshine streaming through the slatted blinds washed over him, haloing him in light. "I think we have ourselves a bargain. I'll have a large bowl of your famous chili, miss."

"Miss. I like that." Her face felt hot; she wanted to blame it on the sunshine, but she knew that wasn't the cause at all. She felt as if she were blushing; the good Lord knew she felt *younger.* She couldn't really explain it, but she didn't like it, and she took a step back. "How about you, Phil?"

"Make that two."

"You've got it. I'll be right back with your cornbread. Excuse me." She didn't even look at Evan as she pounded away, quick to turn her mind to the new party crowding through the doorway and the teenagers getting restless in the booths.

But as she took the kids' orders, Evan remained in the corner of her vision. She could not shake the memory of his confession last night of how he'd been in no hurry to head home to an empty house.

Her son gave her a cheeky grin as he ordered two monster burgers and extra fries, and she felt a hard pang of sympathy for the man when she realized his sons were no longer at home.

Sympathy—not interest—she told herself firmly.

She felt sympathy for the man. Maybe because she was going to be in his shoes before long. As she clipped the order to the wheel, she caught sight of Alex sitting in the booth with his friends. Beth was with him today, crowded against his side, a quiet, blue-eyed redhead who had ordered a cheeseburger in a polite voice. Remembering Alex's confession last night about Beth's mom, she had a harder time not approving of the girl.

"Paige?" Her younger sister, Amy, caught her attention through the pass-through window. "Uh… could you come back here for a minute?"

Paige's heart caught. "Are you all right? You're as pale as a sheet."

"I, uh, you're gonna have to take over the grill. I'm feeling sick." With a clatter, Amy suddenly dropped the spatula she held and dashed off at a run.

Okay, that's not good. Wanting to run after her sister, and knowing the food sizzling on the grill needed to be tended to, she hurried around into the back. She snatched up the spatula and flipped burgers and rescued a batch of chicken tenders from the deep fryer. Wasn't it just her luck that she could see Evan Thornton through the window? She had a perfect view of him, and with the way the sunshine poured through window highlighting him, it was like a sign from heaven.

*I know what you're trying to tell me, Lord.* The realization hit her like a sunbeam. Evan had become a more frequent customer over the winter. He was like so many of her other regulars, the ones who came alone, as often as not because they needed more than a meal. Friendship. Connection. Fellowship.

All her life, she'd been the one looking after others. First as the big sister taking care of her brother and younger sisters. Then as the adult in the family, after their parents' deaths. Finally she became a mom, and the role of caretaking just became hers through the years.

Heaven knew she was more parent than cousin to the twins, who were so lost, what with the way their parents lived. Somehow, her diner had become a big family kitchen in a way. And while her thoughts drifted down the hall as she wondered if Amy was okay, she quickly built the bacon, cheese and chili burgers for table eight, and held off on the incoming orders so she could run down to check on her sister.

"Order up," she called to Brianna who was just back from seating the last of the incoming customers.

"Is Amy, like, okay?" Concern wreathed the girl's face.

"I'm just going to go check on her. You'll watch the front for me?"

"Yeah, totally!"

"Thanks, sweetie." Paige started down the hall and found Amy washing her face at the sink in the women's bathroom. The way she clung to the edge of the basin told Paige everything. She caught Amy's reflection in the mirror, grabbed a length of paper towel from the dispenser and held it out to her. "I would say you've got a stomach bug, but something tells me that's not your problem."

Amy let out a watery sigh as she grabbed the paper and swiped it over her face. "I'm almost afraid to let myself think it, in case this is just an upset stomach."

"Does your new husband know about this?"

Amy's eyes filled. "This is only the second morning I've felt like this, and well, I think it's too early to take a pregnancy test."

"I'll run across the street to the drug store and get one, and we can read the instructions to see. Or, wait, no, you want to share this with your husband."

"I do."

"Whatever you need, sweetie."

The diamond wedding set on Amy's left hand caught the light, sparkling like a brand-new shiny promise. Life had been hard for Amy for a long time. She'd been a rebellious teenager, and unhappy trapped in this small town. She'd run away her senior year in high school for a bigger and more exciting life in a big city, but she'd returned unhappy and disillusioned with her baby son in her arms.

She'd worked so hard all the years since to raise her son and provide for him, and now Paige prayed for her nightly—that this new marriage and the man in her life were everything she deserved, that her road ahead would be easier and filled with love—the kind of love that could last.

"Thank you, Paige. You are the best big sister."

"No, I'm just marginal and very lucky to have you. Why don't you sit down for a bit? I'll get some ginger ale and crackers to calm your stomach. Sound like a good idea?"

"No, because the lunch rush is about to hit."

"Not your problem. It's mine."

Amy wadded up the towel and gave it a toss. It landed neat as a pin in the wastebasket. Her heart-shaped face was ashen, but her jeweled eyes were big and bright and full of hope. "I'm not sick, I don't think, and I want to finish my shift."

"Not on your life. You're going home. First you're going to sit until you're looking better and when you are, we'll discuss you staying at the diner. C'mon, baby sister." Paige put her arm around Amy's slender shoulders. "You come let me take care of you."

"I'm not sick."

"Then you're something better, and you need to take care. C'mon." She navigated them through the door and down the hall. "Go sit and I'll be right out."

"But the lunch rush—"

"Go!" Paige softened her stern tone with a smile. "Brandilyn," she called to the teen, who was standing at the till, her forehead wrinkled in concentration as she stared at the ticket and then the cash register keys. "Brandilyn, honey, go fetch two orders of cornbread for Mr. Thornton's table. I'll grab Alex to man the till."

"Like, I totally need help!"

Paige rang up the ticket, handed the change back

to Mrs. Brisbane, and thanked her for coming. It took a second to haul Alex from his friends, he came with only a half-hearted complaint, and took over front-desk duties so she could go catch up in the kitchen. She ladled out two huge bowls of chili for Evan and the plumber, and started a row of burgers on the grill. After swiping off her hands, she brought Amy a bowl of crackers and a big cup of soda. Amy looked too miserable to tackle the crackers but sipped at the pop with a look of deep gratitude.

Since Alex was answering the diner's phone, probably for a take-out order, she grabbed her cell from her pocket and dialed Amy's home number. It took only a moment to let Heath know what was going on, and before she knew it, the meat patties were done. She dressed the buns, plated the meals, added a heaping round of golden fries and rang the bell.

Out of the corner of her eye, she caught sight of Evan, digging into his chili and talking animatedly with Phil. There was something about him, something nice.

What was she thinking? She filled a basket with raw cut potatoes and lowered it into the fryer. She was *so* not interested in Evan Thornton. In any man. She didn't have time for one. Room for one. Heart for one. Her life was far too full taking care of everyone else. And that was besides the fact that she'd had enough of men. One husband was more than enough for any woman. What would she want with another?

More customers were piling in, Alex was seating them, and she turned to dress two lunch salads at the counter to go with the club sandwich for table twelve. Heath came in through the back, Brandilyn rushed in to grab the green salads and rushed right back out again, and more orders filled the wheel.

She had enough to do to fill two lifetimes. She didn't have time to waste on romance. She was just too busy for impossible dreams.

## Chapter 5

Evan scraped the last bite of chili from the bottom of the oversized bowl and licked it off the spoon. He was near to bursting, but Paige's chili had really hit the spot today. The sun had vanished and ice pellets were pounding the window next to him, dampening the lunch rush. The traffic along the main street was thinning.

It was easier to look out the window than to look around. He knew he'd catch sight of Paige hurrying between the kitchen and the front, checking on the waitresses and running the till, for she'd let her son rejoin his friends in the booth.

When she was around, his gaze kept finding her. And that was the kind of thing Phil had noticed.

Phil gave his plate a shove and leaned against the

padded back of the booth. "You're right. That was the best bowl of chili I've had since I was stationed in Texas. Say, did you know we heard from Liz the other day?"

"I thought you vowed to never talk to her again." Just like me, he thought.

"She called right in the middle of supper. Marie thought it was a telemarketer and almost unplugged the phone. Should have done it, and we would have, too, if we'd known it was her. She's in Tucson."

*I don't want to hear this.* Evan's guts tightened. The only thing Liz ever brought him was bad memories and deep emotional pain. "I know she's your sister, but I don't want to talk about her. She took what she wanted." And how. But he got what mattered, the real treasures, the real riches. Their boys. "You wanted to work on your estimate for Paige? She looks a little less busy."

"I can take a hint. I only meant to say that Liz couldn't rise to the challenge. She didn't grow up all the way. But that doesn't mean all women are like that. Look at my Marie. There isn't a better gem in all the world."

Evan's guts twisted hard with an old, bitter pain. Some losses ran too deep. Some wounds left a vicious scar. "Look, I don't need this, Phil. I've got time on my hands with both boys gone. I admit it. But I don't want to hear it one more time. A woman isn't going to be the answer. I'm better off alone."

"No one is better off alone. God didn't make us

that way. That's all I'm gonna say, and well, I've got one more thing. Marie knows this real nice lady from her Bible study. Smart, kind, has a good job. Her husband passed on a few years ago from cancer. She's a good kind of woman. We could have her over for dinner, and you, too—"

Phil meant well. There was no doubt about that. But Phil had a great wife. A woman he'd always been able to count on. A woman who did her best never to let him down.

How could he understand what it was like never to have had that? To have finally finished up the last of his scheduled payments on the nearly fifty-thousand-dollar credit-card debt his wife had left him with.

Then there had been the legal battles, the settlement he'd made in order to keep the boys…everything. If that was the way a woman who said she loved him treated her husband, then he wanted nothing to do with that again.

The trouble was, and he'd known for a long time, that not all women were made like Liz. The truth was, he just didn't think he had the heart to try again.

His gaze found Paige as she swept down the aisle with her lean, quick efficiency. She looked spare and stern and very in charge, but her manner didn't fool him; it was the same as the black sweater she wore. The color was severe, but superficial. He didn't know why last night's single glance beneath Paige's daily armor made him want to like her.

He didn't want to like any woman, right? "I'm

not interested, Phil. But I appreciate it. I know you mean well."

"Mean well? What do you mean? We're more like brothers, that's how I see you. And the boys, they're my nephews. You know how I feel about 'em. Our kids have always been close, the way cousins ought to be.

"But you know what? After a hard day's work, a good day's work, I go home to Marie. She lights up when I walk through the door. Now everything's right, she says and everything just fades into the background. I started thinkin' last night how you go home to an empty house. You've got no Marie."

Evan wanted to tell Phil that he sure wished he'd been as lucky as to have a woman like Marie in the first place, but his throat tightened with a strange aching emotion. The cynical part of him that had been hurt so hard and deep wanted to say how he was glad to be single and unencumbered by a woman who would only hurt him.

But the truth was, he was not that bitter. Not wholly. Phil was truly blessed, and that's what Evan couldn't say. What made his throat sear with emotion had nothing to do with bitterness and everything to do with a sorrow he couldn't quite explain. At least Phil knew how fortunate he was. At least he knew the value of a good woman and appreciated the difference she made in his life.

He thought of the empty house waiting for him. It wasn't the boys that had made his house a home, he knew, although they had filled it with a joy and chaos that was as equally wonderful. Finally, he found his voice, but it didn't sound at all like his, as his words came thick and gruff. "You're very lucky you have your wife. Anyone can see you got a good woman."

"Then you can see how it is. Life is about the choices we make, about doing the right thing that's asked of us or doing the easy thing. You got a bum wrap when Liz treated you the way she did, no doubt about that, but you can see that there are good women out there. Women who are alone, and who have a lot of heart to give a man. Maybe one woman who would make you happy."

"Happy. That sounds nice."

I'm not about to trust another woman just to find out. Not that he could admit that in a public place or anywhere. There was no way to really know a person, no way to peer into the future and see what choices they would make—to stay committed, to stay devoted, to stay...period.

How did he admit, even to himself, that part of the emptiness of his current life was that he had no one to share it with. No one to come home to and take care of and care for. Being a father had met those needs close enough that he didn't miss the primary relationship of marriage...not too much, anyway. Being a single father was a whole world better than how unhappy both he and Liz had made one another.

But it was hard not to notice the married couples in the diner. Men and women his age, with kids crowding into the booth with them or without, having sneaked away for a lunch alone, and it was a reminder that some marriages did last. That there were a lot of faithful, loyal, good women out there.

But knowing it and trusting it were two different things.

"Well, that's all I'm gonna say on the subject." Phil pushed his way out of the booth. "You want to wait around? I'm not gonna be long. Marie would love to have you over to supper."

"Sounds good, but I've got plans."

"Not plans with a lady?"

"As Cal would say, 'no-oo way.' I'm going to catch a movie, but I'll wait for you. Paige is a nice lady, so you're giving her a good deal, right?"

"She's a very nice lady." Phil's grin was mischievous as he backed away. "I'll do well by her, don't you worry."

Mischievous? No, Phil had jumped to the wrong conclusions, but that was okay. Evan leaned across the aisle to take the morning's paper left on an unoccupied table. He checked the baseball scores and then the local news and tried hard not to notice Paige McKaslin from the corner of his eye.

Not that he was interested, of course. She was at the front, ringing up the teenagers' orders, giving them a serious discount by the sounds of things, as the kids chorused their thanks and clamored out the door.

An icy wind skiffed down the aisle and he shivered. It felt like snow.

"Crazy weather, isn't it?" Paige had a hot cup of coffee and set it on his table. Along with his meal ticket. "As promised. Is there anything else I can get you?"

"Nope. The chili was excellent. It always is."

"Why thanks. It seemed like a good special to run what with winter thinking it can make a comeback. You just take your time here."

"I noticed your son earlier. Seems he managed last night out there driving."

She flushed. "I'm a worrier, I admit it. Lord knows I try to control it, but it gets the best of me. He's out there driving right now and it's snowing. Look at that. It's the last day of April and coming down like it's December.

"What about your boys? Do they make it home much for the weekends?"

Evan stared at the white slash of snow veiling the world that had been promising a sunny spring. Somehow, the snow keeping things frozen and isolated seemed appropriate. "You know how busy they get."

"I already do." Understanding gleamed warm and rare in her eyes as blue as a spring sky, and she set the coffee carafe on the corner of the table, a deliberate movement, as if she had something to say on the matter. "Alex isn't even gone from home yet, and he's so busy he might as well be. The youth group this morning, off with his girlfriend this afternoon.

They're going to the mall and then the Young Life night at the church. I'm catering their supper."

"If I remember right, your diner does a lot of catering for our church events."

"I do what I can." She shrugged a slender shoulder, the movement drawing his gaze to the elegant grace of her movements as she crossed her arms around her middle and gazed out the window in the direction of the main road through town, as if her thoughts were firmly with her son. "I don't think I'll know what to do with all the peace and quiet once he's on his own, and that will be too bad, because I've gotten to like the chaos."

She was gently teasing, he realized, his throat strangely aching again with emotions that he, like her, did not want to reveal. "Believe me, the quiet isn't as nice as the chaos."

"I was afraid you were going to say that. You've confirmed what I've already guessed."

It was the way she confessed that, with a genuine flash of what looked like both regret and a mother's deep love. Maybe that's what hooked him like a fish on a line and tugged him so hard through the current of his own wounds that he wasn't prepared for the speed of it. He wasn't prepared at all.

He gaped at her, as if he couldn't breathe the air, seeing the truth in Paige McKaslin in a way he'd never had the time or the reason to before. She was the woman who'd stayed when her husband left, everyone in town knew the story. She made a success of the diner with courtesy and hard work. She raised what appeared to be a great kid, and treated everyone she came across with courtesy and respect.

Why the words spilled over his tongue, he couldn't say, or where they came from, but he couldn't believe his own ears, even as he heard himself speak. "Say, you wouldn't happen to know about that Bible study over at the coffee shop on Wednesdays? I know it's hosted by a woman from our church."

"Sure. Katharine is my cousin—"

"I've been thinking about going—"

"You have?"

He paused. What was going on? Why was he trembling like a teenager asking a girl out on his first date?

He didn't want to date. He didn't want a woman, but he liked Paige. He couldn't seem to stop himself from asking the question. "Would you come with me?"

"Oh, uh, as a friendly face, you mean?" She seemed confused. Her eyebrows slanted and she took a step back. Her hands flew out and she grabbed the coffeepot as if to shield her heart with it.

*Not what I should have asked*, he realized too late. He was forty-two years old. What was he doing? He was too old to start again. Too set in his ways to think about dating. Too wounded to ever trust another woman intimately.

He *could* take the chicken's way out and agree, to say, sure, that's what he wanted, a friendly face at the meeting. He could save himself a lot of embarrassment and risk to his heart if he just corrected his impulsive question with a simple nod.

But it wasn't the truth. Not at all. "No," he said in a choked voice, while the little voice in his head kept telling him to get up and run and never come back. "I meant would you go with me. As, a, well, as a d-date."

Too late to take the words back, he watched the confusion slide from her lovely face. Horror widened her eyes. Big mistake, Thornton, he thought, surprised that the main thing he felt was remorse instead of relief. It made no sense, but it told him something. He admired Paige McKaslin. He liked a lot of things about her. It hurt to admit, but the truth was the truth.

She's going to say no. Evan saw the answer on her face. And how she bit her bottom lip as she figured out how to turn him down.

Maybe he would save her the trouble. "Hey, it's okay. I don't know why I just blurted that out. I haven't been on a date in over twenty years."

"Me, either." The tension lines around her mouth eased. "That's hysterical. Twenty years. That's a long time to be out of it. I just don't date, Evan, I'm sorry."

"I understand." He didn't meet her gaze but turned toward the window where a vigorous snowfall bordered on whiteout conditions. "We're going to need a snowplow to get home before long if this keeps up. I'd better go while the getting's good."

Somehow her feet weren't taking her up the aisle, like they were supposed to. Maybe it was shock rooting her to the same spot on the floor. Evan Thornton had asked her out? That didn't seem right. No one had asked her out in all the years since her husband had left. She always figured the reason was simple: Jimmy had always told her she was a simple small-town girl, nothing special, but a hardworking salt-of-the-earth type.

Not exactly the kind of woman men lined up to date and fall in love with, no.

As she caught her reflection in the window glass, she saw a woman whose face was too long, her nose a little too big, with a few too many character lines to be thought of as pretty.

Evan seemed embarrassed as he kept his attention riveted on the storm. The floor let go of her feet, and woodenly she stumbled down the aisle and away to the safety of the kitchen.

Brandilyn swung through the door with a full basin of dirties. She strained as if she were carrying a thousand pounds. With a groan, she unloaded the tub onto the sink counter. "So, Paige, is Mr. Thornton, like, totally cool, well, for an old guy?"

Paige leaned to the side to bring Evan in focus through the order-up window. Yeah, totally cool, to use the teenager's phrase.

But not "cool" the way Brandilyn probably meant it. Cool, in Paige's opinion, because he was the kind of man who stayed. He'd been the one to pick up the pieces when his marriage failed. He raised his boys, made them a good home. He'd provided for them and gave them a good head start in the world.

He was a nice man, handsome, strong, capable and with those wide shoulders of his, he could make a woman, even one as jaded as she, wish . . .just a little in absolutely impossible dreams.

And how foolish was that? "After you run a load of dishes, could you start prepping salads? If this weather keeps up, we're going to be dead tonight, so if you want to go early, it would be okay."

"Like, who wants to work?" The girl pitched her voice over the chink and clang of the dishes as she unloaded the bin. "But I really need the hours. Like super bad."

"Then how do you feel about managing the front tonight?"

"You mean it?" A cup crashed into the top rack as Brandilyn spun around, forgetting what she was doing, excitement lighting her up. "That'd be so sweet! Like, I can do it. I know I can. Well, except for the cash register. But I'm catching on. Really, I am."

"I know, sweetie. You're doing great. You get better every week."

"Ya think so?"

The girl brightened so much, Paige saw all of Brandilyn's potential. The teenager was so bright, when she applied herself. She only had to figure that out. "I do. Did you get your registration notice from the community college yet?"

"It came and now Bree and I have to figure out what to take. It's totally weird."

"Did you want to bring your stuff by and we can go over it?"

"That'd be so awesome." Brandilyn put all her youthful energy into stacking the dishes into the industrial washer. "So, like, are you gonna go out with him?"

The fryer-basket handle slipped from Paige's fingers and plunged back into the sizzling hot oil. She jumped back in time to avoid getting burned, but she had the distinct impression she wasn't going to avoid getting burned in a metaphorical sense. The twins had overheard Evan. How many others had?

As if thinking of him had made him materialize before her eyes, her gaze found him. A six-foot-plus flesh-and-blood man, solid and substantial and everything that could possibly be good in a male human being, and something deep within her sighed at the sight of him standing in the threshold. That sigh was absolutely something she did not want to admit she felt, especially to herself.

"You're busy." His molasses-dark gaze roamed over her like a touch. "I'll just leave this on the counter by the till, okay?"

Her gaze slid to the ticket and the twenty-dollar bill in his hand. In his big, strong-looking hands that made her wonder what it would be like to feel that hand enclosed over hers. What would it be like to feel his wide palm against hers and his thick, tapered fingers twined through hers. Would she feel safe? Sheltered? Cherished?

There I go again, wishing for fairy tales. What was it about certain men that could affect a woman so foolishly? "I'll ring that up for you right now."

It was surprisingly hard to meet his gaze, and the moment their eyes connected he jerked away as if she'd slapped him. "I'll wait out here then."

And he was gone, big athletic strides that took him from her sight. That settled it. She *had* hurt his feelings. That was so far from what she'd intended. The surprise of his proposition still rocked her. Date? Her?

It was preposterous to think of dating at her age anyway. Ridiculous. Who would be interested in a woman with too much responsibility, too much work, and too many people to take care of? And no interests, no time for hobbies, let alone letting a man woo her into believing he loved her.

Hold it, your bitterness is showing. She cast a quick prayer of forgiveness heavenward. It was not easy trying to keep a clear heart in this world where men existed.

Oops, there it was again. In truth, she was a *little* bitter toward the male gender and although it had significantly faded over the years, as she'd gotten a better handle on it, it had not vanished completely.

She vowed to work harder on it as she caught sight of Evan waiting for her at the front counter.

He looked out the window. Gazed down the aisle.

He looked at the award plaques from the local Better Business Bureau on the wall behind her. He looked everywhere but at her.

*Lord, I have hurt him.* She hadn't meant to, but what did she do now to fix this? She rang up the sale, counted back his change. But he held up his hand.

"Keep it." He looked straight ahead as he turned away. "See ya."

"Have a good day, Evan."

She watched the door swing shut, and she felt horrible. She'd been so stunned and confused she hadn't handled the situation right. She hated it when she made a mistake that hurt someone else, and she'd bungled this one but good.

This wasn't about the fact that Evan was a good customer. This was personal. She thought he was okay, for a man. Probably one of the most responsible men she knew, and responsibility was something she thought was a virtue in a man. He didn't deserve her rather cool response to him. He didn't deserve that kind of treatment at all.

And what if this stopped him from attending the Bible study? What if he'd been asking her so he wouldn't be going into a social situation alone, without a friendly face, and she'd blown that for him, too?

I have to fix this. I have to make this right. Somehow, someway, she vowed, telling herself it was her conscience that was troubling her.

And not her heart.

# Chapter 6

Evan shoveled the foot-high accumulation of wet, sloppy snow off his front walkway and grimaced as his back spasmed in protest. He'd leave the stuff to melt on its own, except that the local station had broken in to the baseball-game coverage to announce freezing temps and more snow expected overnight.

Yippee. He loved Montana weather...*not,* as Cal would say. With any luck, spring would return in full force soon and he could start planning that trip up into the foothills.

Until then, it looked as if he would spend the rest of the weekend snowed in.

Good thing I stopped by the grocery store on the way home. It looked like he might be snowed in for a day or two.

As he slipped the edge of the shovel under the block of snow and heaved, humiliation rushed over him like the bite of the north wind. He'd needed something to do after leaving the diner. He'd called Phil on his cell to say he was going without explaining why he hadn't waited. He felt bad about that, but he'd fill him in the next time they were face to face.

What he felt even worse about was how he'd come on to Paige McKaslin like a teenager asking for his first date.

It wasn't just his inexperience with these matters. No, that wasn't what was eating him up inside. It was worse than that. It was that he hadn't even given it any forethought. Any planning. The question had just rolled impulsively off his tongue—and he didn't date! He didn't want to date. He planned on never dating again.

And, of course, the worst part of all was that she'd turned him down flat.

What was it she'd said? *That's hysterical* had been her exact words, and she'd looked as if she were trying not to laugh. She didn't date; okay, he could live with that. But he knew it wasn't the truth.

Why on earth didn't Paige date? She was a gorgeous, hardworking, together woman. Come to think of it, it was strange she'd never remarried. He knew the rumor was that her husband had had enough of her and run off, but that was gossip he'd accidentally overheard around town years ago and he didn't believe it.

Not anymore, he figured, remembering the vulnerable woman he'd gotten to know last night

Unfortunately, that same Paige McKaslin didn't seem to be available when he'd asked her out. The professional, every-hair-in-place businesswoman had shown up to say no.

He didn't feel put down or even put out. But his chest was knotted up so tight and he couldn't explain it. See why he'd given up dealing with women long ago? See the kind of tangled mess they tied a reasonable man up in?

He didn't want to admit that regret was building up in him like the snow on the ground. Cold, and growing colder, he gave the contents of the shovel a good toss—and his back snapped, lightning-fast pain searing down his back and into his left leg.

That can't be good. He didn't dare move. Not at first. The pain was too searing. He took a few quick breaths and tried moving the leg that wasn't wracked with knifing pain. It made a fresh wave of agony explode in the small of his back. Great. What a treat to be forty-two.

Then, suddenly, through the veil of snow, came two golden beams of light. At first he thought it was Blake's Jeep roaring up the snow-laden driveway, but then he noticed it wasn't a black vehicle, but a dark-green new model. It wasn't Phil; he drove a van, and Cal had that undependable sports car—

The light blinded him for a split second and then the SUV turned the last curve and slid to a graceful stop in the driveway. The porch lights shone on the window so he couldn't see whom was behind the wheel until the vehicle's door swung open, turning on the dome light.

And he saw Paige McKaslin emerging into the storm, dressed in a dark-green parka and brown hat, mittens and scarf. It was all he noticed because humiliation was starting to drag him down.

What on earth is *she* doing here? He lowered the shovel with great effort. Even moving his arms made his back spasm even more. Wind battered him. Falling snow pummeled him. But neither was as hard to endure as the woman's agile progress along the freshly shoveled pathway.

"Evan! I hope you don't mind I dropped by. I tried calling. I looked your number up before I left the diner, but there was no answer."

Be strong. Stoic. Cool. Although how he was going to do that and act as if he wasn't in agony remained a mystery. "I've been out shoveling the walk. About this time, I miss the boys. They were handy for chores like this."

"And I bet it was much easier on your back when they did the shoveling."

"Now, why would you say that? There's nothing wrong with me. I'm a man in the prime of my life. A little shoveling is nothing to me."

"Is that right? Then why do you look as if you're frozen in one position?"

"I'm a little cold, is all."

"And the grimace on your face is from seeing me?"

"Uh, not so much. I think my back went out. I have a bad disk."

"I thought I recognized that particular look of torture. Can you move?" Paige shifted the heavy sack she carried to her other arm and tracked up the icy concrete walkway. "Do you need help?"

"My pride has taken a serious blow today, but I think I'll live."

Paige tried not to be affected by the sight of him. With all his wide capable strength, he didn't appear decrepit. He somehow seemed even more masculine and powerful as he lowered the shovel to the ground and leaned on it like a cane. "What brings you by?"

"I owe you an apology." She lifted the sack, concentrating on it because she didn't want to look at him in case dislike for her showed on his face. "You surprised me so much, Evan, I just didn't realize what I was saying. I'm sorry."

"Don't worry about it." He looked like a pillar of steel. Strong. Unyielding. Unfeeling.

She'd never felt so awkward in her life. Maybe she'd been wrong. Maybe he'd hardly cared that she'd said no. So how foolish was it that she was standing here, fixing something that wasn't broken and now making everything worse?

She'd never been in this situation before. Her teenage years had not been average. She'd never dated; she had the responsibilities of her younger brother and sisters. She had grownup problems and no time to date. It wasn't until Jimmy had started working at the diner that she'd had her first real taste of romance. Felt the first flutter of joy at seeing that special man's face, hearing his voice, spending time just talking and getting to know him. Experienced the first wishes for sweet kisses and holding hands and hopes for a happy marriage.

Look how that turned out. She'd been so wrong then. She was probably just as wrong now. "At least let me leave this with you."

"That looks like a meal from the diner."

"It's more than that. It's not only a peace offering, but also a chicken dinner of appreciation. You keep insisting on paying for your meals instead of letting me give you a meal in thanks, so I'm bringing supper to you. Did you think I was a pushover? That I was a woman who gave up easily?"

Evan remained motionless. "I guess I never much thought about that."

Okay, I guess that's answer enough. She was making way too much of this. No wonder he was staring at her as though he was in the greatest pain. He was put out. She'd never been to his place before, although she drove past his driveway numerous times every day.

She'd never been much more than a distant acquaintance with him, despite the fact that they'd had teenage sons in sports and school and church groups together. He'd asked her to come to a Bible study with him, not exactly the full-blown date she was making this out to be. What do you bet he's really regretting asking me to go with him now?

It was time to fix what mess she'd made and retreat. "I hope you'll accept this in good faith. Are you still thinking about coming to this week's Bible study?"

"Couldn't say."

"I don't want you to miss out because of how I've behaved."

"That's not it. Really." Okay, that wasn't exactly the truth, Evan thought as he fought the blinding pain hacking through his spine, but it was close enough. Now he wasn't sure if he would go. What if his back was still out? At least he could salvage his pride. "It was nice of you to stop by. Are you working at the diner tonight?"

She looked flustered. And if it was possible for Paige to look lovelier, then she certainly did now. A delicate pink bloomed across her cheeks and nose from the cold but also from her emotions as she glanced longingly in the direction of her vehicle. "I shouldn't have bothered you. I'll let you get back to your shoveling. Want me to put this on the step for you?"

Since he didn't want to admit he couldn't move, he nodded and made a grunt that would pass for a "yes." He gave thanks that he wasn't blocking the pathway to the porch because a herd of rampaging buffalo couldn't have forced him to move an inch out of the way.

Trying not to breathe too deeply and not to force his spine to move in the slightest, he prayed, *God, please let this pain end.* He wasn't sure if he was asking for relief from the physical or emotional agony.

He could tell Paige thought he was mad at her. That he was holding against her the fact that she'd turned him down. How did he admit that he had bigger problems, like the ability to stand tall the way a man should and not whimper? Stand tough, Thornton. It's only a little back pain.

Determined to maintain mind over matter, Evan tilted his head in her direction. The resulting strain on his lower spine wasn't too bad. Encouraging. Maybe he could fix this situation he'd found himself in with a few kind words. "That's mighty decent of you, Paige, to come all this way."

"It's all right. I owe you, too, for recommending Phil. He walked me through the first phase of repairs he wants to do, and I know he's given me an extremely low price. I suspect that might have something to do with you."

"I just told him how hard you work to keep that diner going and supporting your family is all. Phil's a family man. He knows what that takes. I'm glad you're happy with him. After all, your diner is where I eat most of my dinners these days."

"I wouldn't want that to change. Or for you to feel as if you couldn't risk coming in and seeing me behind the counter." She slipped the sack on the top step of the porch, and even in her layers of winter wear, she moved like poetry. Lithe and limber and graceful.

He felt it again, that overwhelming impulse gathering on his tongue. Just like before. He wanted to stop her from leaving. He wanted to ask her to stay, and he already knew her answer. She had a diner to run, she wasn't interested, she didn't date and she probably thought he was a dud for standing as still as a rock in his front yard. Somehow he managed to keep the words inside as she swept past, leaving a strange impression like a touch to his soul. He didn't breathe freely until she was safely buckled behind the wheel of her Jeep and backing up to turn around in the driveway.

As he watched her vehicle's taillights blink red in the gathering dusk, he felt the pain return in full force. The wintry wind sliced through him as if he were standing outside only in his drawers. He shivered, but it wasn't only the physical cold he felt. Or only physical pain.

*Why, God? Are you trying to tell me something?*

Maybe it was just loneliness, Evan reasoned, but that didn't explain that he'd never experienced this feeling around any other woman. No other had ever made him want to set aside the disaster Liz—and marriage—had brought him and try again. Because, he couldn't help thinking, loneliness was another kind of painful disaster in a man's life and maybe, with a different woman, a better woman, the outcome might be different, too.

He thought of what Phil had with his Marie. He thought of other people who seemed happy in their relationships. As Paige's Jeep pulled toward the last corner in the driveway, ready to disappear around a large stand of fir trees at the bend, he wondered if she ever wished for a different life and for someone to love, too.

Alone, in the quiet hours of the night, when no one could hear or know, and when the sting of loneliness seemed the greatest, did she, too, wish for a marriage that could work, for a happy connection to another? For that special kind of love you read about and saw in movies, a gentle, welcome place?

The shovel slipped from his fingers and thudded to the ground at his feet. Before he remembered his back, he automatically tried to bend to pick it up and then realized, as the vicious pain axed through his disk, that he couldn't move. Right. Only thinking about a woman could be powerful enough to make a man forget about a slipped disk.

Agony wrenched through his spine. He couldn't stand here forever, that was for sure, but he didn't seem able to move either. The Jeep's taillights disappeared from his peripheral vision and he was utterly alone.

The tap, tap of the falling snow, the whisper of the wind through the trees, the solemn feeling of a winter's cold settled around him.

Okay, he was tough. He could handle a little back pain. All it was going to take was a little willpower.

And, he thought, a little prayer. With Herculean effort, he shuffled his boot an inch and shifted his weight. Since it was progress, he didn't complain.

Any second now his back was going to release, his spine was going to snap painfully back into place and he'd be able to get back in the house like the man he was, the man who worked out at the gym five days a week.

That second just hadn't happened yet. But he was a patient man. He dragged his left leg, enduring the pain traveling through his hip and down his thigh, and inched closer to the walkway.

That's when he heard the roar of an engine, muffled through the heavy curtain of snow. Maybe Paige was having problems with drifted snow on the driveway. He hoped she made it back to town safely. He thought about heading in her direction just to make sure she didn't need help, but then he realized that by the time he made it all the way down the mile-long driveway, it would be midnight. She was a competent woman; she seemed as if she could handle anything.

He liked that about her. He liked the idea of being with a woman who was strong enough to face life's hardships. He liked a lot of things about Paige McKaslin, and he didn't want to. A man ought at least to have control of who he liked and why, but in this one instance, it seemed out of his hands.

Suddenly, the wind changed and brought with it the alarming sense that he wasn't alone. He knew who was standing in the driveway behind him. He knew, because apparently he wasn't in control of this either, of how his and Paige's lives were currently intersecting.

"Having problems, there, tough guy?"

"I hope you're not mocking me. My dignity's taken enough blows as it is."

"You can stop pretending. I was so busy watching you in my rearview that I didn't watch where I was going. I'm caught in a drift. You could have plowed your driveway, you know."

"If I'd gotten out the tractor, then I wouldn't have thrown out my back."

"You never know. A big, muscle-bound man like you is bound to have one weakness."

She was next to him, grabbing hold of his arm. She was a tall woman, taller than he'd first thought, but he realized, her slenderness was deceptive. She might look willowy, but there was no mistaking the strength in her grip as she helped him take another step.

Too bad his brain wasn't working right, because all he could think was, She thinks I'm big and muscle-bound. He really shouldn't be glad about that, right?

"I have no weaknesses that I'll admit to."

That made her laugh, and it was a pleasant sound. Not brassy or fake, but low and pleasant like a kitten's purr. "That's just like a man. Never show your vulnerable side. I know. It's why my son drives me nuts."

"Is that the only reason?"

"No." She laughed again. "Can you get up the stairs, or will I have to carry you?"

"I'd like to see you try." He weighed two hundred pounds. She couldn't be more than one twenty-five. "There's no sense putting your back out, too."

"My lumbar disks thank you."

"You have a bad back, too?"

"I like to blame it on carrying heavy trays of food for about two decades, but since I don't like to admit I'm over thirty-five, I can't use it as an excuse."

"You don't need the excuse, Paige. You don't look a day older than thirty."

"Careful. We'll be lucky if a bolt of lightning doesn't streak from the sky and strike us where we stand."

"No lightning, see?" He dragged his foot onto the bottom step, refusing to lean on Paige because he was no weakling, and did his best not to let on that the pain was killing him. "I wasn't lying. You're an amazing woman. You're lovely and you know how to cook some of the best—"

Lightning seared through the storm, arrowing like a bright finger from heaven to the trees behind the house. There was an explosion of thunder above and the crack of a pine tree beyond, and then there was utter silence.

Paige started to laugh. "I can't believe it. Lightning struck."

"Now don't go taking this the wrong way, Paige.

You might think I wasn't telling the truth, but I was. Why else would I have asked you out? I haven't done that since I was in college. I told you that."

What was it about this man's low rumbling voice that seemed to knock all common sense right out of her? Paige wanted to believe him, she really did, because she hated to admit it, but Evan Thornton— the *man* and not the customer—was starting to grow on her.

He could make her laugh, and she'd never appreciated the importance of a sense of humor in a man before. Tiny laugh lines crinkled around his handsome eyes, and it had a devastating effect.

Not that she could let it affect her. He was handsome, he was distinguished, and he was no thrillseeking teenager. Not this man who'd built this fine house and made it a secure home for his young boys to have grown up in.

It took a lot of character to be the parent that stayed. A lot of strength to handle the hard—although rewarding—parts of being a father. And this man looked as if he could weather anything with good humor to boot—even the back pain that he was too proud to let her see full-force.

She knelt to snatch up the diner's sack and propped open the storm door, since the handle was on her side. But Evan was taking none of that. Apparently no woman helped him. He seemed to be all male pride and ego as he grabbed the door and held it for her, even though his face went white from the strain.

"I hope you don't mind if I use your phone. My cell isn't working with this storm." She stepped into the warmth, grateful for it, but not expecting the rush of tenderness for the stubborn, strong, unyielding man who limped in after her.

Men. She'd forgotten there was a lot of good in them, too. And wasn't that the danger?

## Chapter 7

Evan craned his back the few necessary inches so he could reach the door and shut it against the shower of snow. Pain exploded once again in his lower back and, with the scrape of bone against his disk, his back was relatively back in place. Residual pain shivered through his left leg, but he gave a prayer of thanks heavenward.

"Oh, that was your back?" Paige must have heard the popping sound. Her rosebud mouth had softened into a concerned O, and sympathy shadowed her deep-blue eyes. "Evan, you need to get some ice on that. Do you have some anti-inflammatories?"

He couldn't answer. He could only stare at her as she set down her sack and her purse and untied her coat's hood. Coming closer as if naturally mean-

ing to help out. He'd been facing problems—even
something as minor as a strained back—alone for so
long, he couldn't seem to wrap his mind around it.
She was coming at him and in the half-light of the
foyer she looked mysterious, cloaked in shadow, but
also warm and vibrant with life, her heart showing
vulnerable and open.

"You've got to give that some rest. Let's get you
into the living room. Is it this way?" Again she took
his arm, but he couldn't stand to let her think he
was weak. He intended to shake his arm away from
the warm, firm grip she had, but he couldn't stand
that idea either. "I'm all right. It's been a while since
you've been around a wounded man, right?"

"Oh, you don't want my help. Fine. Limp into the
living room all on your own steam and I'll get some
ice for you. Unless you're too stubborn to let me do
that for you?"

"You think I'm amusing. I can tell. Your eyes are
sparkling."

"The male gender can be very amusing. Sometimes." She released him, trouble quirking her soft
mouth into a sweet smile. "Or maybe I just like to
see a man suffering. It's appropriate."

"Hey, I'm one of the good guys."

"I didn't say you weren't." She left him to his own
maneuvering.

Good thing. He didn't think he could keep pretending everything was all right. He limped over to
the sectional in the living room. The crackling fire

sent warm soothing radiant heat over him. He was frozen clear through, but that seemed the least of his worries.

His back was aching like a cracked tooth, and he sighed with relief as he eased onto the cushions. The fire's warmth enveloped him like an electric blanket. The tension in his back eased up a bit. Much better.

"Here's an ice pack." She bustled through the house with the same snappy efficiency that she used in the diner. "I've got two anti-inflammatories, a glass of water. If you want, I can heat up the dinner I brought over while I wait for the tow truck. Sound good?"

"Paige, you're not on duty here. This is my home. You don't need to wait on me."

"I don't mind." She handed him a sealed plastic bag of ice, wrapped in a kitchen towel, and set the glass and ibuprofen caplets on a saucer on the coffee table. "I'll be right back."

Why would any man leave her, he wondered, not because she was fetching him what he needed, but because she was so caring about it. It was easy for him to see the real Paige, the woman with a big heart she seemed to be afraid to show to the general public. She was a private person, he realized. Was she, he wondered, as lonely in her life as he was?

He popped the pills and washed them down with a swallow of water. As he positioned the lumpy ice pack against the small of his back, he could hear her in the kitchen. The whisper of cabinet doors opening. The clink of plates and the rustle of the big paper sack.

It had been a strange sensation to see a woman in his house bustling around and taking care of things. Fortunately it didn't bring back memories of Liz, because she'd never been the efficient, get-things-done type.

What it made him think of was, not the past, but the present. How good it was to hear the movements of another person in this way-too-big house. How comforting it was to hear the gentle pad of a woman's footsteps and gentle voice in the other room.

Yearning filled him. It was a sweet and rich longing, and more powerful than he'd ever known before. A longing for what he didn't really believe in. And yet it felt right there within his reach. Being with a woman—a wife—in a way that was compatible and companionable, but it was more than that. Not just love of the heart but of something deeper.

And exactly why was he thinking this way? His back must be hurting worse than he thought, to make him so sentimental.

"Bad news." She returned with a plate full of dinner salad glistening with Italian dressing. "The tow truck isn't going to be here any time soon. I'd be better off hoofing it back to town."

"I could take you."

"My rig's blocking your driveway." She slipped the plate and the paper napkin and fork onto the coffee table in front of him. "I've got a call in to Alex.

He can finish up his dinner at the church and come rescue me."

"I think I can handle freeing up your Jeep. I've got a winch on my truck. It'll be no problem."

"And what about your back?"

"It's fine. Just a little stitch, that's all."

"Sure it is, tough guy." Paige wasn't fooled one bit. "What is it with you men? You can't show an ounce of weakness?"

"Exactly. Never let your guard down. I bet you know something about that."

"Okay, now you're getting too personal." She wasn't sure what to do with Evan Thornton. He sat there with his hair tousled, looking about as rugged and welcome as a dream man, but he was real and sincere. She liked him. She didn't want to, but she did. "I don't want my reputation as an ice queen ruined. It's kept all those bothersome suitors away for years."

"Why would you want that? You like being alone?"

His question surprised her like a right hook and her knees wobbled. She sank to the couch, not at all sure what to say with her heart jack-hammering in her chest, and Evan's gaze unwavering. It felt as if he saw too much of her, and she wasn't sure how to stop him. "Now you are being way, way too personal."

"I guess you're like me. Alone is better than betrayal."

Like an ax hitting her chest, her heart cracked

wide open. Sometimes it felt as if she were the only person on earth who'd had a disappointing marriage at best, and a devastating wound she'd shown no one. Ever. "In the diner, it's like all I see are couples. Married people are everywhere. Young and old and in between. With kids, without kids and empty-nesters. It's not the happy couples I notice. It's the ones that sit in silence. They don't talk. They don't look at one another. And I think how lucky I am not to be with someone who sees past me."

"My wife saw me just fine. She just wasn't content with what she saw."

"How could that be? All anyone needs to know about you is to see what a fine job you did raising your sons."

I could kiss you, lady. Evan's chest cinched tight. Her compliment surprised him, but it did more than that. It touched him where he was vulnerable, in the deepest places of his heart. He'd tried so hard for his boys' sake. It hadn't always been easy, especially not alone, but then Paige would understand that. She would know how it felt to be alone raising kids. "That means a lot coming from someone who's raised a good kid, too."

"He is a good kid, but I keep my eye on him. I'll get your supper in the microwave and you should be set. Is there anything else you need?"

"Paige, I'm serious. Don't wait on me." He stood, refusing to acknowledge the grimace of pain in his back or the residual traveling pain making its presence known in his leg. "I think whatever popped out of place has popped back. Let me grab my keys and I'll help you out of the drift."

"You shouldn't be up moving around."

"Hey, I'm tough. That's the first lesson you've got to know about me. Not much can get me down, and if it does, it doesn't keep me there."

"Note taken. I'll never try to suggest you take it easy again."

"Excellent." Evan couldn't say why her smile lit him up inside, but the effect was like a ray of light on the dark side of the moon as he limped over to get his keys.

The storm had worsened since she'd been in Evan's house. She shivered, swiped the wind-driven snow from her eyes and tried to see him in the near whiteout conditions. The stubborn man just didn't know when to stop.

Or maybe it was just her perspective. She hadn't been around a man in a personal capacity in a long, long time, excluding her son, who was more boy than adult at this point of his life.

Evan Thornton had to be in agony, she knew because she had a slipped disk that bothered her from time to time, so she knew what it felt like. And he was acting as if he was impervious to pain, as if he hadn't just been unable to move less than twenty-five minutes ago.

He straightened from the winch on the front of

his rig, highlighted by the headlights that cast him in silhouette. Invincible, he seemed to rise up to his six-foot height and from her vantage on the down slope of the hillside, he seemed ten feet tall.

In that moment, her breath caught between her ribs and she couldn't explain what happened within her; she only knew that something in her heart felt different simply from looking at him. He cut through the beams of light and blended with the night. Although her eyes could not make him out against the dark and the storm, it was as if her heart could sense him standing there, unbowed and mighty, like some Wild-West hero brought to life.

She didn't believe in heroes. Not at all. Not in real life. Not in her experience. So why was she thinking this way? Was it simply the possibility of the fairy tale of true love worming its way into her thoughts again, after all this time and all her experience to the contrary? She'd banished the hope long ago when Jimmy had walked away from the grill and out the door with a fun, young blond thing while she'd had a crying baby with an earache, a busy diner and a call from the deputy about her younger sister in hot water again.

A woman had to stand on her own two feet in this tough world. She shouldn't be wasting her energy wishing for a white knight on a shining stallion to rescue her from her problems. The only help she needed was God's help.

The driving wind chose that moment to ram

against her so hard, she lost her balance, tumbling against the snow-driven door of her Jeep. Visibility vanished and she lost sight of the mythical man she'd woven out of old daydreams. Out of loneliness, too, she had to admit. For the business of her days and the fullness of her life, she was alone in the most fundamental way.

Maybe that's just the way life was, she'd been even lonelier when she'd been married all those years ago. She'd felt so utterly lonely, wanting the loving tenderness from her husband who would rather watch football or play his video games or go out playing pool with his buddies.

This loneliness was better, she told herself firmly, cloaked and isolated by the drifting snow and pummeled by a wildly vicious wind, she did the only thing she could. Called out a thank you to Evan, wherever he was—if he had any sense, he'd be in the warm cab of his truck right now—and she fought the gusts to open her vehicle's door, where the idling engine was blowing hot blasts from the vents—but the temperature outside was so cold, it did little to warm the interior of the Jeep.

With her teeth chattering from the frigid conditions, she hopped onto the seat and slammed the door.

And gave a jump when the passenger door opened and a dark presence slid into the other seat. The wind slammed the door shut and they sat in the glow of the dome light, the gusts shaking the vehicle and howling wildly around them.

"I can see why the drifts got so deep." Evan's low baritone rumbled as warm as firelight.

"I'm going to have a fine time getting back to town. I'd best get going. I owe you—again—for helping me."

"Then I expect you to pay up." His words were softened by a mysterious crick of his mouth in a sly—and very charming lopsided grin—as he flicked on her radio and hit the scanning button. "Thought you might want to hear this."

She already knew with a punch of certainty which channel he was scanning for—one of the local stations, which was in the middle of an emergency broadcast. All county roads were closed due to extremely dangerous weather conditions. "I left the twins in charge of the diner."

"Then call them and tell them to close up. They live right there in town, right?"

She nodded. The journey home for them would be relatively safe. "I can ask Dave to drive them on his way. He's an old hand at dealing with this weather."

"Then did you want to come back with me and use my phone?"

"No, I'd better risk getting home. Although, I'm not that sure how long that's going to take me. Could I ask you another favor?"

"Try me."

It went against her grain to ask anyone for help

like this, but she thought of the girls' safety—there wasn't anything more important than that. "Could you call the diner for me?"

"Consider it done. You'd best get going before this gets any worse, and we both know it can. Be safe." He opened the door to the fury of the blizzard conditions. "You're going to owe me big-time. How about escorting me on Wednesday night? You'd be doing me a favor. I'm shy."

"You're not shy."

"No, but help me out here. Go with the flow, like my boys say. It's a new meeting. I'm afraid to go alone."

"A big strong man like you? You don't seem afraid of anything."

"I'm big on the outside, marshmallow on the inside."

This man was *so* not fooling her. "No man is marshmallow on the inside."

"How do you know that? Are you an expert?" A quirk of humor tugged at the corner of his mouth.

Yeah, he was charming, all right. What was a girl to do? "Let's just say I have had practical experience with the species."

"Well, some men fall outside the normal bell curve of averages. That would be me."

"So, you're below average?"

That made his dark eyes twinkle. "I was thinking more of the other side of the chart. More than your average guy."

"I'm not sure that's a good thing."

"Then it's a date?"

"No. I'm not agreeing to a date. I don't date."

"Neither do I. Then how about one Bible studier helping out a wannabe Bible studier."

"Haven't we been here before? Why would my answer be different?"

"Well, you've had time to think about it. You've had time to see I'm an okay guy—I mean, above average. I at least come with morals, principles and good references."

If she wasn't careful, she was going to start liking him even more. "Okay. Agreed. I'll go to the coffee house with you, but it's not a date."

"Not a date. Two people just going to a Bible study together. Good night, Paige." He shut the door and he was gone. Not even the faintest hint of him remained as the fierce storm closed in around her, leaving her alone again. *Alone,* being the key word.

What was it about Evan Thornton that made her feel the sting of loneliness when he was gone? She hated to think about it. She didn't want to admit she had any shred of that young, foolish girl she'd once been left inside her. She was a practical, hardworking woman who knew how to get things done. What was it that she heard endlessly from people? Sensible to a fault. Yep, that was her. So why on earth was she wishing that she'd said yes to Evan as a date instead of as a friend?

*Because I'm insane.* It was the only thing that

made sense. Maybe it was some sort of mid-life crisis. Or a reaction to all the long backbreaking hours she'd been working. A woman couldn't put in horribly long work days seven days a week forever. Something was bound to give…apparently, today, it was her sanity.

I'd better schedule an afternoon off and soon.

Well…she amended. Maybe after the month's financial statements were done. As she sat forward, as if that would help her see better through the snow battering the windshield, she realized that while she was heading home, it would be no night of leisure. There was the bookwork to do. At least she had all but the day's receipts at home. She'd do a little computer work until bedtime.

Even in four-wheel drive, the tires caught and spun in the deep drifts that covered the driveway like waves in an ocean.

Driving kept her full attention, and it was a fortunate thing she had her full attention to give. Surely the youth pastor had sent the kids home before the emergency bulletin came through. She prayed that Alex was home safe.

But it wasn't worry over her son that troubled her as she battled to keep the Jeep on the road. No, for some reason she couldn't explain, the soreness of being alone remained, as if the memory of Evan's impressive presence remained like a ghost to haunt her.

*You're going to owe me big-time,* he'd said, as though it was a threat. What on earth did he mean?

She'd accompany him to Bible study, introduce him so he wasn't alone, and they'd be square, right? That's what he meant, right?

The uncertainty stayed with her on the arduous half-mile journey to the private road that took her to her own driveway. To her relief Alex's truck was parked squarely in the middle of the drive, caught in a drift, and so she parked behind him, knowing there was no way to get around.

The wind struck her like a boxer's fists, and she couldn't remember feeling a colder one, ever. The night and the darkness felt endlessly isolating as she fought her way through the drifts, and along her driveway cut between snowbound pines. The wind moaned through the snow-heavy limbs overhead, and she hurried as fast as she could manage through the blizzard conditions and to the house that emerged from the whiteout, lit windows glowing gold. There was Alex in the open doorway, calling out, glad to see her.

Not so lonesome anymore, she hurried out of the storm, hugged her son even though he protested, and gave thanks that they were safe and snug as the late-season blizzard raged on.

It was nearly an hour later by the time Evan shoveled the drifts out of the way so the garage door could close properly. He'd done as Paige had asked, returned to call the diner, given the evening cook her message and banked the fire so he could go right back out in the storm.

And why? He was frozen half to death in the sub-zero temperatures and even colder windchill, and his back hurt so bad he couldn't straighten up all the way. . .and all for a woman. A woman who made him half crazy, judging by the way he was acting.

Although the roads were beyond dangerous to drive in, what had he done? He'd followed the wheel tracks Paige's Jeep had left in the snow all the way to her driveway. Just to make sure she wasn't lost in the ditch somewhere.

When he'd come across her vehicle parked neatly in the dark behind her son's truck, unable to go any farther, he knew she must be home safe, since the walk wasn't far. Sure enough the message light blinked on the answering machine. Since he was half-stooped anyway, he didn't have much of a reach to hit Play.

"Hey Evan, I'm home safe. I hope you made it back up your driveway okay. Stay warm and take care of your back. Take another ibuprofen, okay?"

Was it his imagination, or was there more than friendly warmth in Paige's voice? The machine beeped and whirred to a stop.

Agony ripped through his spine as he marched over to the fireplace, stirred the coals and added kindling to the glowing red chunks. The cedar kindling caught instantly and flame licked through the thin slivers of wood.

He crumpled paper, trying to drown out the sound and the memory of Paige's voice and of her presence here in his house, in his home, making the loneliness so strident, it was a physical pain he could not deny.

*What are you trying to tell me, Lord?* he asked as he tossed split wood into the fire. There came no answer, although the howling winds and scouring snow against the siding and along the eaves echoed in the stillness surrounding him.

He stretched for the remote and turned on the TV just for the noise. Just to make the emptiness less dark and less shadowed.

# Chapter 8

*Tonight's the night.* It was all Paige had thought about for the last hour of her shift, and it was all she could think about now as she capped the tall chocolate-banana milkshake. The diner was quieting down, and she was keeping one eye on the door waiting for Evan Thornton to walk through it.

"Ain't it about time for you to leave?" Dave commented through the order-up window as he finished up a burger on the grill. "I've got things covered."

"Thanks. If things get busy, and you need backup, I've got my cell. You call, I'll come."

"You seem awful eager. Thought you liked that Bible study you go to."

Was that a smirk she saw beneath his mustache? Just how much did he know? She hadn't told a soul about her arrangement with Evan. After all, they were acquaintances. That was it. She was doing him a favor, because he'd done her a favor. Right?

And if thinking of Evan made her feel a little lighter, then she didn't have to have a reason for it, did she? It wasn't as if anything serious was going to come of this. She'd meet him. Take him to Bible study. Introduce him. End of story. It was no big deal.

"I'm always eager to go, you know that." She kept going on her way through the dining room. Brianna looked as though she had everything under control. She gave the teenager a smile as they passed in the aisle.

"I didn't get even one overring all shift!" The teenager beamed. "Can you believe it?"

"Absolutely. You're good, girl."

"Yeah!" She practically skipped to the front.

Well, that's progress. Paige could only hope Brandilyn's mastery of the cash register wasn't far behind. She slid the milkshake cup onto Alex's table, careful of the papers scattered over the surface.

His physics book was open, and his blond head was bent over his current problem. Lost in concentration, he scribbled madly with his mechanical pencil.

She pulled a wrapped straw from her apron pocket and slipped it next to the large cup.

"Thanks, Mom." Alex scribbled down a final number before he looked up. A deep frown of concentration dug into his forehead. "Whew. I think I nailed that. I've got one more."

"Then are you heading home?"

"You know it. Want me to check on Annie?"

The mare had figured out the latest latch on her stall door. "I'd appreciate it. Call if you need me."

"I know, Mom." He flashed her a charming grin. "You have a good time with Mr. Thornton."

"How did you know about that?"

"Little potatoes have big ears," he replied, something she always used to say when he was little. Proud of himself, he grabbed the straw and tore off the wrapper. "You left it written down in your engagement diary. The one you leave open every day on the kitchen counter. It was hard to miss."

She'd never had anything really private to write in it before. "I'm gonna ground you for that."

"Empty threat." He grinned even more widely, sure of himself. If nothing, her son was confident and steady. He was going to make a fine man one day, and that made her proud.

And sad. She had so little time left with her son. She wanted to hold so tightly to him and never let go. But that wasn't good for him.

So, instead of grabbing him close, she settled for ruffling her fingertips through his hair, the way she'd done since he was a little guy. "I don't want you to get all worried. Mr. Thornton is coming to our Bible study for the first time and I told him I'd introduce him around."

"It's not a date?" He looked crestfallen.

"No. You know me. I'm too busy keeping up with

you and this place to find time to date. Do you need anything else before I go?"

"Mom, dating might be good for you. You know, to round out your life."

"I wasn't aware my life needed rounding out."

"Sure. I saw it on TV. You don't have enough balance." He flashed her "The Eye," as if he had the power to charm her into seeing things his way. "And Pastor John said that you're going to have a hard time when I go, with the empty-nest thing, so I have to be understanding. So I'm being understanding. Go. Date. I want to support you in your life choices."

Yeah, he thought he was so funny with that glint in his eye, so confident and young. "Those are my lines, and I—"

The bell over the door chimed, announcing a new customer. Why did she automatically spin to see if it was Evan walking through her door?

"He's here." Alex waggled his brows. "And he brought flowers. Yeah, this is *so* not a date."

"He just has good manners."

"Sure, Mom, whatever you say." Alex gave her a knowing look as he took a long pull on his milkshake. Like any teenager, he thought he knew everything.

And he would be wrong. Evan wasn't interested in her. How could he be? Like her, he was probably work-weary and, since he'd never remarried, he probably liked it that way. She understood about wounds that no one could see, and they had a profound influence on the way someone lived their life.

"Paige." Evan held out the wrapped bouquet of yellow tulips and daisies, small and modest and friendly. "I noticed you always keep fresh flowers by the cash register, so when I saw these I thought you could use them."

See? Good manners, just as she'd thought. "They're lovely, and that's thoughtful of you, considering I'm the one who owes you a favor."

"After tonight, we're even." He handed her the flowers with a good-humored grin.

"Unless something else comes up and you help me out again." She brushed the edge of a daisy's silken petals with her fingertips. "Brianna, could you put these in water? And you can handle things until I get back?"

"Yeah, and Dave's, like, in charge. So chill and have a good time with Mr. Thornton." Brianna cracked her gum and waggled her brows.

It was probably hard for a teenage girl to understand. Paige knew, because she'd once been like that, too, filled with ideas of romance. But no more. She fetched her book bag from beneath the front counter and grabbed her jacket from the rack by the door. It surprised her when Evan caught hold of the sleeve and helped her into her coat.

He was only being a gentleman, which he proved again as he held the door for her. She listened to the delighted goodbyes from Alex and Brianna and rolled her eyes.

"At least it's a nice enough evening that we can walk."

"It is." Was that his attempt at starting a conversation? Paige listened to the echo of their shoes on the concrete. "It looks as if your back is doing better."

"I'm happy to say I made a full recovery."

"Now that there's no snow to shovel?"

"Yep. I want you to know I'm fit and hearty, and that was only a momentary weakness."

"I never doubted your vitality. You're just past forty."

He laughed. "Thanks. I feel so much better now."

"Glad I could help." She liked the way small, hardly noticeable character lines cut into the corners of his eyes. He really was a handsome man, she thought, in a *friendly* way. "I want to thank you again for recommending Phil. I've hired him to start renovations."

"Sounds like that leak was just the start of your problems."

"It's sad but true. Phil's promised that he can keep me open for business through just about everything. The customers won't even know he's there."

"Good. A lot of folks depend on your diner."

"I know. Some days it's just nice not to have to cook. I'm thankful that so many people come to my place when they're feeling like that."

"Are you kidding? You've got some of the best

food in the county. Why do you think I drive all the way from work, and past I don't know how many restaurants on the way, for your roasted chicken and dumplings? So, what do you do when you're too tired to cook?"

"That's not a luxury I have, but I don't mind."

They waited for a lone minivan to amble along the street. Paige recognized her cousin Karen behind the wheel, as she slowed to wave and smile. It didn't take a psychic to figure out what her cousin was thinking. Evan was standing at her side, with less than a few inches between them.

Anyone watching would leap to the wrong conclusion. It was strange, because the male at her side was usually her son. Now, she was walking through town with a handsome, eligible bachelor.

Paige waved as Karen drove by. As she and Evan stepped off the curb in sync, she gathered her courage. It might be her only time to ask such a personal question. "How did you manage after your youngest son went off to college?"

He missed a step but recovered his balance. "That's a tough question."

"Sorry. It's probably too personal. I didn't mean—"

"No, it's all right." He quickly reassured her, jamming his hands into his jacket pockets. "I could say something easy, like I finally had some peace and quiet."

"That's overrated."

"It is. I now have sole possession of the remote control. No teenager making messes in my kitchen, my bathroom or my car."

"Apparent plusses."

"On the surface, yeah. I also don't have to sit up waiting for Cal to come in at night, trying not to worry about every disaster that could happen on the road between the Youth Center in town and home. But it's not the real truth. Not at all."

Paige heard the hitch of emotion in his rumbling baritone. She wondered at the depth of feeling that lay hidden beneath the surface. "I bet your house seems empty. I know my home sure will be."

And because that hurt, she stared down at the blacktop beneath her sneakers and tried to swallow past her tight throat. It wasn't just her house that would be empty, but her life.

"The truth is, I can't get over missing them. I'm glad for my boys. They both have good starts in this world. They are smart and strong and make solid decisions. I did everything I could to raise them up to be good men. I've never been so proud."

"You did a good job."

"At the same time, I've lost my sons. They will never again be my boys running through my house, making enough noise to drive a normal person crazy."

She liked that he smiled, and dimples dug into his lean cheeks. She could just bet he was a wonderful father. She could feel all he did not say. "They're men, now."

"Yep. It's the way it's meant to be, but the void they leave behind is something that can suck you down like light in a black hole, if you let it."

"That's what I'm afraid of. I've taken care of everyone for most of my life. I raised my brother and sisters and my Alex. I used to think that I missed my chance at my own life. I went from being a child to an orphan and right into being a responsible adult. I don't regret it."

"Neither do I. Not for a second."

Paige had to like him better for his words. "I always figured when my son was raised, I would finally get my chance to do what I want. Now that that time is here, it's not exciting at all. I don't want things to change."

"It's bittersweet."

"Exactly."

Evan slowed as the sidewalk on the other side of the street neared. "Running the diner isn't what you want?"

"It was never my life's ambition, but it has kept me busy and my family provided for."

"It's a pretty integral part of this town. Folks drive for miles just for your chocolate milkshakes."

"So people tell me." She left their conversation at that, stepping up her pace until she was on the sidewalk, getting a little ahead of him.

Some things hurt too much. Her future should be

an exciting one; it was a new phase of life for her, too. It was scary to think about, but she wanted to go to college. Maybe travel a bit. But the fun things she'd always planned on doing one day did not look as exciting now as they'd been before.

The night felt colder and the dark oppressive, and she could not escape into the light and warmth fast enough, away from the hurt she knew was to come. Alex wasn't just her son. He was her whole life. And now that her sisters had married and their lives were so busy, Alex was all she had left.

After he moved away, she would be alone. Truly alone. For the first time in her life.

Evan sat at one of the small wooden tables in the town's coffee shop, unable to purge Paige's words from his mind. *Now that that time is here, it's not exciting at all. I don't want things to change.*

Change was inevitable. That was simply life. He knew that from first-hand experience. The major turning points in his life had never been of his choosing. When he looked back, it wasn't his logical thoughts that had chosen Liz for a wife. His heart had. A pure leap of faith and heart. They had been happy for a little while.

But her betrayal had been out of his control. Time passed and as the boys grew up and left home. The decades of his life seemed to be adding up. And, he feared, he was all out of turning points. All out of new directions. He wanted his life to change. He wasn't happy.

After hearing Paige's words tonight, he knew he wasn't alone. *So, Lord, what does that mean?*

He didn't expect the good Father to answer. As Karen Drake, part owner of the shop and cousin to Paige, spoke about the changes in her life, he stared at his own Bible. The black type blurred against the crisp white page.

*Lord, what do You have in store for me, which will bring me hope and a good future?*

He wanted his life to change. He'd lived for his sons. For many, many years that had been more than enough. But the endless months of solitude had become a sadness that he feared would go on forever.

He feared that the long loneliness of his future would be broken up by the occasional phone call from the boys, and, as time passed, they would come with their wives and children to visit. But when they left, the loneliness would be sharper. The sadness deeper.

The stages of life were inevitable. He could see that. The women who were wives and mothers, like Karen, managed to squeeze this Bible study into their busy schedules. One day those mothers would be where he was and Paige would soon be. Time was a relentless wheel always turning and leaving only memories behind.

He did not want to look back in one year or five or ten and see no real memories.

He didn't want to find that his heart had atrophied from having no one to love.

He did not know what the answer was. He didn't know if he could trust another woman enough to date again. He'd have to open his heart, open his life and hope that he wasn't on a path as destructive as his marriage had been.

As he looked around the room, he saw several settled couples. Husbands and wives who were raising their kids and had it together. They sat side by side, leaning slightly toward one another as if they were always just a little connected, even in public. Those secret looks, knowing smiles and silent communication spoke of the kind of bond Evan had never been privileged to know.

The hard punch of emotion in his chest, feelings he couldn't begin to sort out, left him distracted. He should be paying attention. But the lines before him seemed to brighten. Was it time to make a change?

The truth was, he'd learned the hard way that a marriage depended on both husband and wife working together. Making good choices. Renewing their love and commitment and belief in one another every day. Day by day. That was putting a whole lot of faith in another person.

What no one told you about marriage was that a man wasn't only putting his faith in the hope that love would last, but also in the woman he married. He had to have faith that every decision she would make in the years to come would be for the good.

When a man trusted a woman enough to marry her, he was trusting her with his heart, his soul, his children, his home, his finances, his everything. He'd been burned—and burned hard—by Liz.

But that didn't mean there weren't women who would never harm their husbands. Who would never hurt them. Never lie or cheat or betray the man they loved.

Why was he so aware of Paige at his side? Her presence shone through him like the warm rays of a summer sun and he felt illuminated.

Time flew. Before he knew it, he was muttering "Amen" following the final prayer. The small group was breaking up, talking and starting on their goodbyes.

It surprised him how fast Paige had popped out of her chair and was busily stuffing her book and Bible into her big floral bag. She'd purposefully turned her back to him and was chatting with one of her cousins. Evan recognized the young lady. She was one of the younger girls in the family, and she'd worked at the diner during her teenage years. Kelly, he thought the girl's name was, gazed up at Paige with unmistakable admiration.

That's when it hit him once again the kind of lady Paige McKaslin really was. She gave away cinnamon rolls and connection. She worked endlessly to cook and serve other people. Her diner supported her family and many of her cousins through their school and college years. Her business was a place in the community where friends joined, and lonely souls could find a hot cup of good coffee and kindness.

No man is an island, he knew, and he didn't want to be alone anymore.

He hadn't believed he could find a woman he could trust. A woman who stayed, who faced her responsibilities, and who did so without bitterness and resentment.

How long had he prayed for such a woman to love, to be a helpmate, just to have and to hold, after Liz had left and before the hurt she'd caused settled deep into his heart?

Forever. He'd given up. He'd let bitterness in. He'd closed off his heart to the possibility of ever being hurt like that again. And God's answer might have been in front of him all along.

## Chapter 9

Sunday morning's torrential rain chased her through the diner's back door. What had happened to May's gentle weather? Where was spring?

The last few days had felt like total chaos, and with the morning sermon still fresh in her mind, Paige slipped her Bible on the end of the counter, shrugged out of her drenched raincoat, and vowed to put order back into her life.

No more stray thoughts about Evan Thornton. No more faint wishes for fairy tales. God had given her a perfectly good life; it was enough. In fact, it was more than enough. It took all her energy to keep it in order.

Look at the kitchen. She had slipped out to the early morning service, and see what happened in her absence. Prep work was scattered everywhere. "Alex!"

Where was that boy? And, with a sting of excitement, she wondered, where was Amy? Hadn't she turned up for work this morning? Had she been able to take a pregnancy test? Was she pregnant?

Joy at that happy thought chased away her annoyance at her wayward son. He was only a teenager, and therefore innately distractible, and so she'd simply hunt him down and get him back on task.

The bulk of their Sunday-morning business wouldn't hit until after the main morning service at the town churches, and so there was plenty of time to right this sinking ship.

"Alex?" She ignored the rainwater sluicing off the jacket as she hung it up. And, speaking of teenagers, where were the twins?

She wove through the abandoned kitchen and peeked out into the dining room—there were only the old-timers finishing up a quiet breakfast before heading over to services. Their cups looked freshly refilled and their plates had been bussed, so the twins couldn't have gone too far.

"Have you seen the kids?" she asked Ed Brisbane when she caught his eye.

"Don't know what they were up to. They were in the office arguing in whispers, but we could hear 'em."

"The office?" That didn't make any sense. She was the only one who handled the paperwork.

"Then I heard the back door slam shut. Haven't seen 'em since."

That can't be good. "Okay. Thanks. How about Amy?"

"Caught sight of her running down the hall looking like a woman with morning sickness." Ed's merry eyes twinkled. "At least, that's the way it looked to me."

"Me, too." Since the restrooms were closer, Paige hurried down the short hallway and burst through the door to find the twins hovering over the sinks.

"Paige! Amy's really, really sick!" They both flew at her, talking in unison.

It was a relief to see them; at least they weren't outside in this rain, for whatever reason. "Amy, are you all right?"

"Yes," came a weak reply from inside one of the stalls.

Definitely morning sickness, Paige thought as she rounded on the twins. "Where's Alex?"

"Uh…" Brianna traded worried glances with her twin.

Both girls said nothing more for a moment, as if stumped as to what to say. "He's, uh…"

*"Where is he?"* Alarm pounded through her. His truck had been parked in the back lot. He wouldn't have gone out on foot in this weather, right? "He's supposed to be helping with the brunch prep."

"I don't wanna tell ya." Brandilyn gave a longing look toward the door. "'Cuz it'll really upset ya and stuff."

Alarm transformed into panic. A thousand possible disasters zoomed into her mind. *"What is going on?* Just tell me."

"He's. . .he's on the r-roof," Brianna stammered. "It's, like, leaking."

"What?" All she could see was disaster. It was raining so hard. "You mean he's up on the roof? *Right now?"*

"Don't worry—"

"—but we've got a bucket under the leak—" the twins said in unison.

Amy's voice sounded, thin but steadfast, on the other side of the stall. "Paige, go after him. I didn't know—" And that's as far as she got.

"What do we do?" the twins asked breathlessly.

"Brandilyn, go hold her hair if you don't mind. Brianna, call Heath, ok? Amy, I'll be right back, sweetie."

There was only a moan of misery. Sympathy for her sister's condition fueled Paige's trek through the kitchen and out the back door. She, too, had been enormously sick the entire time she was carrying Alex. Making a mental note to take Amy off the schedule in no uncertain terms—allowing her light duty only when she was feeling well enough—she slipped back into her dripping raincoat and hurried out into what felt like a hurricane.

"Alex?" The deafening hammer of the rain

drowned out the sound of her voice, even when she cupped her hands like a megaphone and tried again. Since there was no sign of him from where she stood, she circled around the side of the building. There wasn't a ladder on the premises, so that meant he'd had to climb onto the roof from the vacant upstairs apartment.

Sure enough, as she climbed the outside stairs to the apartment door, she caught sight of a flash of navy blue against the peak of the front side of the roof—she couldn't have spotted him when she pulled in. If she had, he'd be safe in the diner by now.

"Alex!" Rainwater cascaded down the asphalt shingles like a river at flood stage, and it had to make the roof impossibly slick. How exactly had he gotten up on that roof? "Alex!"

The storm was too loud for him to hear her. She could just make out the curve of his back, so she waved her arms, hoping to catch his attention. Nothing. She wasn't about to let him stay out here. The rain was bitter cold. He'd catch pneumonia if he wasn't careful, that is, if he didn't fall off the roof first.

Regretting that she hadn't had time for her usual morning yoga in the last six months, she felt her back groan as she climbed over the handrail and wedged the toes of her walking boots onto the lowest corner of the eave. Water raced in a torrent around her feet as she lunged forward and wrapped her arm around the rain gutter downspout, while icy water pounded down on her head and back.

Trying not to imagine the hard blacktopped ground two stories below, she clung to the downspout, which she seriously prayed was securely attached, and fell forward onto the roof. Her hands hit the slick surface and she began to slide, but she didn't fall.

*Alex is in so much trouble.* It was that single crisp thought that gave her enough fuel to grab hold of the gable window's eaves and inch forward. The shingles felt as though they'd been coated in vegetable oil, and she slipped her way to the top of the first peak of the gable, where Alex had apparently already spotted her.

She sank to the small crest, sitting on the frigid wetness, and tried to forget she was terrified of heights. "Get over here, young man."

He might not be able to hear her, but he knew good and well what she was saying. He gaped at her from beneath the hood of his coat; he looked wet to the skin. He held up the hammer as if explaining what he was doing on the roof.

The boy meant well. He had a good heart. But this was dangerous! She crooked her finger, giving him her best imperial look. "Now."

"I'm almost done." She couldn't hear his words, but she could read his lips.

"Move." She gave him her most severe look, the one that meant business.

He tried to charm her with "The Eye," thinking himself so grown up and manly, she reasoned, for being the one to fix the leaking roof. But that was what roofers were for. They were paid to fix roofs. She didn't relent, and finally he gave in and crawled nimbly along the dangerous roof, seemingly without a care in the world. That boy! She grabbed him the second he was in range. "Down. Now."

"Yeah, Mom, that's what I'm doing." He looked amused more than anything as he swung down, using the supports of the covered staircase roof, and landed on the top step.

If only she were that agile! Paige went to follow suit, but she couldn't get any traction as she eased down the protection of the gable window. Just at the time her boots threatened to follow the water and slide right over the full gutters to the ground below, a big male hand shot out from the gray curtain of wind-driven rain.

But it wasn't Alex's hand. It was Evan Thornton in his Sunday best, soaked and looking more handsome than any man had the right to look. Instead of appearing as a drowned rat, the way she feared *she* did, the rain slicked his dark hair to his scalp, making him look virile and capable, and when he took her hand, his touch felt as invincible as steel.

I don't want to like this man, she reminded herself firmly, surprised that she was so glad to see him. Not that she needed help, no, but his just being near seemed to take the sting out of the icy rain and the damp out of the air. She didn't like that, either! She did not want Evan to affect her in the slightest. But he did. She could no longer deny it as his hands gripped hers and held her steady as she crossed from the roof to the rail and down.

"You didn't need to come rescue me." She didn't mean to sound harsh.

"I didn't come to rescue you. I saw Alex up there, as I drove by on my way to church, and I thought he didn't belong up there. At least, not without someone who knows what they're doing on a roof."

"And that would be you?"

"Sure. I put myself through college working carpentry in the summers. Want me to take a look?"

"I want you safe on the ground. That roof is slick."

"It's a piece of cake." Only then did she realize he'd grabbed Alex's hammer, which he must have taken from him on the stairs. "Go inside before you freeze. Have a hot cup of coffee waiting for me, would you?"

And as if he had the perfect right, he climbed onto the roof and disappeared, as agile as a gorilla. A great big, pushy *male* gorilla. Why she was furious, she couldn't explain it to herself, but she wasn't about to let some man, some arrogant, know-it-all man, think he could rescue her. She didn't need help. She might have appreciated the referral to a good plumber, and though she likely could have gotten herself out of the snowdrift, she appreciated the use of his truck's winch, but *this was way too far.*

This was her roof! She didn't seem to have any trouble, other than a single slip as she cleared the gable, angrily climbing low along the slope of the roof. Rain lashed her. A cruel wind battered her as she knelt beside Evan.

He didn't seem surprised to see her. "I thought you were headed inside."

"You thought wrong. This is my roof. My problem."

"Fine. You want to hold this flush so I can hammer this flashing back down?"

There was a flicker of amusement in his dark eyes, eyes that had flecks of gold and bronze in those brown irises. Expressive eyes that seemed so…caring. Caring. She had to be wrong. Evan Thornton didn't really care about her. She didn't know why he was on her roof, but there was no way he was doing this out of some sense of fairness. Or, maybe he was just after a few free meals. That was easier to believe than the fact that a man could care about her.

She knew for a fact that a man couldn't. Men were undependable. Unreliable. And when Jimmy had left her, the pain had brought her to her knees. She'd loved him. She'd truly loved him. No, she'd been foolish ever to care, even a little, for a man.

That's when a familiar minivan caught her attention as it pulled in at an angle, taking two spots, in front of the diner. Heath emerged from the driver's door, leaving the vehicle running, and bolted onto the sidewalk. With another slam, her eight-year-old nephew followed his new dad into the diner and out of her sight. Heath had come to fetch Amy. The realization was like a terrible twisting sensation in her chest, a twisting that tightened until it felt as if her lungs were being ripped into shreds. *Some* men, she amended, were constant and committed.

"Like this?" She held the edge of the tin flashing firmly, the way he'd been doing it.

He nodded, not even bothering to look at what she was doing. His gaze latched on hers and like a brush to her heart, she felt touched in places she'd never even known were inside her. As if there was an undiscovered room in her heart— There she went, believing in things that weren't real. Things that had no substance or merit. Wishful thinking was a flaw she couldn't afford.

If it was possible, the rain came down in an even fiercer wave, the crashing downpour turning to pebble-sized hail.

"This just isn't getting any easier," Evan chuckled, as if he didn't mind at all. He slid a nail near to her fingertips and gave a competent tap.

Most men grumbled when they were uncomfortable, and squatting on top of a diner's roof in the middle of a hailstorm wasn't anything close to being comfortable. And many men thought they were pretty handy, but they weren't. Evan, true to his word, tacked down the flashing and tugged the shingles back into place competently.

"That ought to hold until the storm's over. Well,

unless it gets any worse." He grinned at her through the downpour, and the cold seemed almost bearable.

The thundering storm, the skin-chilling winds, even the cramp developing in her left calf faded until there was only Evan's steady gaze and his sincere grin and his presence brimming through her like the richest honey. It was a sweetness she'd never known and could not explain.

And certainly had the good sense not to believe in.

She felt her chin rise up, and something that felt like an impenetrable titanium shield close around her heart. "I could have hammered that down myself, you know."

"I know. I have complete confidence in you. But seeing as you're going to have dinner with me tonight—"

*"What?"* She couldn't have heard him right. The hail pounded around them, crescendoing, until the only thing louder was the wild jackhammering of her heartbeat. "We're not having dinner tonight."

"You owe me for this, right?"

"Y-yes." She stopped.

Evan watched her pretty rosebud pink lips shaped with whatever she was about to say next, and realized he was right.

Did she also figure out that he intended to make her keep her word? Evan sure hoped so. "I want dinner with you."

She looked shocked. "You do?"

Why on earth would she look so surprised? Even

with the residual rainwater streaking down her face and her hair plastered down, she looked amazing. Her features were delicate, and for all the strength she exuded, there wasn't much to her, but she was no frail beauty. She was feminine and soft and caring and it was not diminished by her capable get-things-done approach to life.

Didn't she know how attractive that was to a man like him? Didn't she know that she fascinated him? He resisted the urge to smooth a stray lock of chestnut hair that had tumbled across her cheek, and he realized with a breath-stealing punch to his chest that he wanted to get to know her better.

So he risked his pride and asked her. "Why not? You're single. I'm single. You practically have dinner with me anyway as it is. You're in the general proximity, right?"

"Well, yeah, I guess, but—" No longer so in charge and self-assured, she bit her bottom lip, as if unsure, showing her rare, vulnerable side. "With Amy ill, I can't—"

"Amy doesn't work Sunday evenings." He hoped that was true; he thought it might be. "And you take one night off a week, don't you?"

"Uh, I always take Sunday evenings off, but I work at home. It's when I do the week's books."

As if an excuse was going to work with him. He'd climbed up on this roof in the middle of a Montana spring storm, and it wasn't out of the kindness of his heart or because he had nothing better to do. "You stop to eat supper, right?"

"Well, usually I bring the plate into my office—"

He laid his hand on hers to stop her, and the instant his fingers met hers, a spark snapped like static electricity. Maybe it was something in the air from the storm, or maybe it was something more, like a sign from above. But either way he could not deny the shock of tenderness that rushed into the empty places of his heart. "You can stop for an hour or two and have dinner with me. Or I'm going to tell your sister and your son and everyone you work with that you promised to go out to dinner with me and then broke your promise."

"You wouldn't!"

He wouldn't, but he liked the way she didn't quite believe him. Good, because he would never do anything to hurt her. But when a man was standing on the peak of a roof with hail getting bigger by the minute and what looked like a thunderstorm on the way, he used what leverage he could. "So, how about I pick you up at your place around six?"

"I—" She intended to argue, to turn him down flat, he could see it. But then something on the sidewalk below stopped her.

He saw her sister Amy walking arm in arm with her new husband, her head leaning on his shoulder. Her little boy hurried ahead to open the passenger door, and there was no mistaking the protective concern on Heath Murdock's granite face as he settled his wife onto the front seat.

Paige shook her head, as if changing her mind on what she'd been about to say, and a lovely brightness swept across her face, turning her cheeks pink and her eyes full of what looked like hope. "If you're so determined to come by and take me to dinner, is there any way I can stop you?"

"Absolutely not." He saw clearly what she couldn't say. Well, there was a lot he couldn't say to her right now either.

He cared about her, and he leaned in close to gather her free hand with his. "Let's get off this roof before lightning decides to barbecue us."

"You know what they say about lightning striking twice?"

He remembered that night's storm. The sparkle of humor in her beautiful blue eyes made him grin, and he felt happy inside, not superficially, but really happy in a way he hadn't felt in so long…he couldn't remember when.

While he'd promised himself he'd never do this again, never open his heart up to the kind of devastation Liz had brought him, he *had* to know if Paige was true all the way down deep.

He led the way down the roof and onto the outside stairwell, never once letting go of her.

## Chapter 10

"Mom, where's Mr. Thornton?" Alex popped his head out of the diner's back door, ignoring the golf-ball-sized hail that was driving into them both.

"He went back to his car, I imagine, on his way to church." Bruised and battered and wet clear through from the weather, she tried to ignore the fact that her son might have very easily spotted Evan Thornton helping her off the roof. And holding her hand longer than necessary. Like all the way down the stairs.

She told herself Evan had been worried about her safety, after all, the steps were slick and coated with hail. But secretly it had been *nice*, something unexpected.

"What about you? You've got—" she glanced at

the wall clock, "five minutes to make it to the ten o'clock service."

"But the roof—"

"Is no place for you to be in a storm, young man, but church is. So go, but you drive carefully."

"I know." He rolled his eyes, giving her a grin and "The Eye," thinking himself so charming.

Okay, he was. She was biased and, as she'd been since she'd first feasted her eyes on him, totally in love with him. She couldn't help smoothing his wet bangs out of his eyes. "Think you can come back and bus tables for me?"

"Sure. But you know what?" He grabbed his sodden jacket from the hook. Uncaring of the dampness, he thrust his arms into the garment. "You could hire someone else. You know, 'cause you're short-staffed."

"When I find someone reliable, I will." Reliable was a problem when the wage for starting help was the state's minimum, and mostly kids wanted the job. "You're reliable and even cheaper."

His charming grin widened. "You know who's even more reliable than me?"

"I hate to ask."

"Beth. She works over at the drive-in, but she doesn't get enough hours there. And plus, she'd make more here because of tips, right?"

Boy, he sure could pick a sensitive subject, couldn't he? "I don't think it's a good idea to have your girlfriend work here. What if you two break up?

You'd still have to bus when we're shorthanded, and you'd have to see her—"

"It's not like that, Mom." He shocked her by smacking a kiss on her cheek. "Beth has to take care of her mom and sister. Her mom's drinking is bad again."

Paige felt a punch of sympathy hit her hard in the chest. She, too, knew what it was like for a teenager to have to carry adult responsibilities. "I don't know. Let me think about it."

"Think all you want. Then hire her." Alex jingled his keys as he grabbed the doorknob. "Hire her, and I won't say one word about you and Mr. Thornton."

With a suggestive waggle of his eyebrows, he was gone, racing into the storm before she could haul him back and set him straight.

You and Mr. Thornton. Alex had said it as if she and Evan were a pair, a couple, who were *dating*. Oh, that boy so had it wrong.

Isn't that what dinner with a man was, a date? a little voice inside her head asked. And didn't that mean she was technically dating Evan Thornton?

It was one date. Just one.

She grabbed the cordless phone and dialed Amy's number. While she waited for the call to connect, she grabbed a dishtowel and dried the rain from her face.

"Hello, Paige." Amy sounded weak and shaky. "I suppose you know what I'm about to say."

"You took a pregnancy test and it's positive?"

"Yep. Since Heath is a doctor, I suppose the result

is about as accurate as we're going to get today." She gave a watery sigh. "I've wanted this so badly, but I wasn't like this with Weston."

"Remember how sick I was with Alex?" Paige understood morning sickness all too well. But she'd always wanted another little baby. Even now, the pangs of it tugged at her, but that time in her life had gone the moment her husband had called it quits. "I know Heath is already taking excellent care of you. Congratulations, sweetie."

"Th-thank you." Amy sobbed, a result of happy tears.

It was a happiness Amy deserved. Paige had done her best to make sure her brother and younger sisters had a good life. It hadn't been easy for a teenager to raise kids only slightly younger than she was, but everything she'd done, how hard she'd worked, how hard she'd championed them, was for this, a good and happy life for them.

"I'm taking you off the schedule," Paige decided. "You stay home this week and take good care of yourself and my little niece or nephew."

"Paige, that's great of you, but we can't afford it. Heath is still working that intern position and—"

"I wasn't planning on taking you off the payroll. I just want you to take it easy. We'll square up later, okay? First things first."

"Oh." More tears had her sniffing. "You are a great big sister. I don't think there's a better one on this planet."

"Yeah, yeah. I'm sure you could find about a billion. I'll send one of the twins over with meals for the rest of the day. That way no one needs to worry about cooking, okay? Take it easy. Oh, that's call-waiting. I have to go."

After Amy's grateful goodbye, Paige answered the other call. Probably a business call. It was. A reservation coming in for the brunch. She scribbled the Corey family's name into the book, giving them the last available table.

At least business was picking up, she thought, as she went to look in on the twins. Brandilyn looked busy refilling coffee and passing out copies of the Sunday paper.

See? At least something was normal. It was going to be like any other Sunday. She'd concentrate on the cooking, hand over the dining room to Jodi when she arrived, and refuse to give a single thought to Evan Thornton…and their impending date.

Because it wasn't a real date. Not really.


The congregation was standing for the last chorus of the opening hymn as Evan slipped into the back row. He looked like he'd been drowned and beaten, and he was thankful for an inconspicuous spot. The weather must have discouraged a lot of people from coming, so that meant he had plenty of room and he didn't have to worry about dripping all over perfectly dry worshipers.

Just as the pastor was warming up to his sermon,

the back door whispered open and Paige's son sauntered down the aisle, dripping wet, and slipped into
a pew next to several kids from the youth group.

That made him think of Cal. While the emptiness
from missing his boys was still as sharp as ever, he
didn't feel quite so alone. And, remembering the way
Paige's hand had felt so right in his, he felt…hope-
ful for the future.

Someone slunk behind the last row and stopped
behind him. "Dad, what happened to you?" whispered a familiar voice.

Cal! There the boy was, looking mighty proud
of himself, and taller, wider through the shoulder.
He'd grown over the last few months, a man and no
longer the little boy Evan was so used to protecting.
"Just a little rain," he whispered back. "You didn't
tell me you were coming home."

"I thought I'd surprise you, and then I couldn't
find you here. I was just about to come looking for
you."

"Sit and listen to the minister." He was still the
dad; he couldn't help himself.

Cal gave him a sheepish grin, as if he were in-
dulging his old man, slid over the arm of the pew
and dropped onto the seat.

It wasn't until the closing hymn that they could
manage to talk again.

"Are you staying for brunch?" Evan whispered as
the first verse rang around them.

"I'm starvin'. Thought I'd come home with you,

well, after we eat, and use the washer and dryer. It's a bummer to use the dorm machines. I never have enough quarters."

"Sure you can use my machines, but it'll cost you two bucks a load. That's a bargain."

"Ha ha. You're hysterical, Dad. You know I came home to bum more money, right?"

"Right. I was a college kid once too, long ago." He resisted the urge to grab his boy in a wrestling hold, mainly because they were in church and because Cal was no longer his boy.

No, he was nineteen years old. He was a man. But, Evan thought as he followed his son down the aisle and out of the church, he will always be my son. He was glad of that fact. Like his older brother, Cal was getting top grades, he made good decisions, was active in church and in sports and behaved well. Evan was proud of his sons, and glad he was in a position to help them get a better start in life than he'd had.

"I'll meet you at the diner." He left Cal next to his bright red Mustang, a present for graduating with a perfect G.P.A. The vehicle was polished and spotless beneath the layer of sloppy ice that had been obviously falling for a while.

Evan scraped his truck windshield and huddled shivering in the cab while the traffic jammed as it always did on the trek from the church parking lot to the main street. Through the dissipating fog on his windows as his defroster blew hot air, he could see across the town park to Paige's diner.

How was he going to tell Cal about Paige? It was a date, just a date, but there was no way to minimize the significance of it. Evan had never dated while he'd been responsible for the boys; even if he'd had the inclination, he never would have had the time. More than that, though, the boys were not only hurt by the divorce, but they saw up close what their mother had done. The financial disaster was only part of it. Evan knew it was years before he managed to smile again. Longer still until he could laugh, but never had he been the same man.

How was he going to explain he wanted to take a chance again? He couldn't even rationalize it to himself. Then again, it was only a first date. The first step toward a relationship, and it was too soon to tell how things would work out.

Maybe he would wait to tell his boys; after all, he thought as he found a parking spot along the curb, he didn't expect them to tell him every time they went on a date.

The second he pushed through the diner's front door and spotted Cal talking with Paige's son, he knew the decision was out of his hands. The boys had known each other through sports, church and school, of course, and Evan tried to hold hope that the kids were talking about one of those subjects.

But as he approached, he noticed Alex's gaze widen with an uh-oh! expression and water sloshed out of the pitcher he was carrying around.

"Hi there, Mr. Thornton," Alex cleared his throat. "You, uh, want some coffee?"

"I do." And those two words sent the boy hurrying off as if Evan had barked an order. He tried to ignore his son's smirk. "After you surrender possession of my washer and dryer, are you gonna hang around for a while? Or are you heading back to the dorm?"

"I was gonna head straight back. I've got this killer chem test tomorrow, but—" That smirk turned troublesome. "I've decided to stay and help my dad get ready for his date."

I should have known this would happen.

Evan was desperately grateful that Alex showed up with a pot of coffee. He was in such a hurry to figure out what to say to his son—and now to Paige's—that he pushed the cup and saucer closer to Alex with a little too much power and the cup rocked toward the edge of the table.

Alex caught it. "Whoa, there. Don't go breaking the dishes, Mr. Thornton, or my mom'll call off the date."

The boys thought that was hilarious by the looks they were exchanging.

"Just pour the coffee." He tried to sound unaffected. They were teenaged boys. They could laugh. What did they know? He was a man; he could sit here and pretend nothing bothered him. At least Cal was taking the news well.

"Your mom won't call off the date. I caught her looking at my dad through the window. She was smiling. Dad is a good catch. I've been worrying about him now that I'm out of the house. He needs someone to keep an eye on him."

"Funny." Evan was glad that Alex had the manners to stay quiet as he filled Cal's cup and then backed away. "A chem test, you said?"

"That's old news. This thing with Paige. How long have you been dating her? She's old, but she's pretty. Hey, she's, like, as old as you!" As if proud of his brilliant deduction, Cal upended the sugar canister over his steaming cup of coffee and stirred.

"I feel so much better now." Evan stood, taking his plate with him. "I'm not that old."

"Of course not," Cal concurred diplomatically. "But you're, like, forty, Dad. Just roll with it. You don't look all that bad."

"I'm relieved to know that." That was perspective, he thought remembering that when he'd been Cal's age, how anyone older than thirty had seemed ancient. "I figure I'll try to enjoy what life is left me before the rest of my looks go."

"Ha ha, Dad." Cal stepped into the buffet line behind him. "I'm just sayin' you don't need to feel like Mrs. McKaslin won't think you're, you know—"

"Old?" Evan asked wryly as he grabbed a pair of tongs and loaded up on link sausages. "That's the last time I want to hear that word, boy."

"Okay, I wasn't gonna say it, though. I was gonna say ugly."

"Thanks for the words of encouragement. I'm glad I can count on my son at a time like this."

"You can count on me, Dad," Cal shoved his plate at him. "And can I have lots of sausages?" He was already using his free hand to pilfer the piles of crispy bacon. "So, you got reservations for tonight?"

"I don't need my son to help me plan my date." Evan finished doling out sausages and moved onto the choices of hashed or butter-fried potatoes. He took some of both. "I know how to take a woman to dinner."

"Dad, the last lady you dated was Mom. You're out of practice. Times have changed."

"What's changed? You go to dinner, be polite, have conversation and take her home."

"Not so much, Dad." Apparently a dating expert, Cal took over the spoon and loaded diced potatoes next to his mountain of breakfast meat. "You've got to have this all figured out. You don't want her to think this is no big deal."

"Well, it's a first date." And a really big deal, Evan was beginning to realize and didn't want to admit, even to himself. So he chose eggs Benedict over the Belgian waffles and tried not to think about it.

He waited while Cal took both choices, his plate nearly ready to collapse under the weight of all that food, and they headed back to their table together. "I was going to take her to that steak place in Bozeman that we like."

"That's a good place." Cal dropped onto his chair

and bowed his head for a quick prayer. As soon as "Amen" was muttered, he grabbed his fork and dug in. "If I were you, I'd pick an even better place. Classier. Mrs. McKaslin's pretty swift. She'll like something real nice."

"That place is nice."

"Yeah, but you're serious, so you have to let her know right up front."

"I never said I was serious."

"Dad, look at her." Cal gestured to the cash register where Paige greeted the newly arrived Corey family. Three generations of them crowded around the counter, as Paige chatted amicably with Mrs. Corey.

Paige. Her loveliness stunned him. Evan couldn't explain what happened in his heart as he looked at her. Yes, she was sure something. It had taken him a decade to notice, but he was finally ready, and he *was* noticing.

She'd changed into dry clothes, something she might have had on hand, he suspected, for the jeans peering out from beneath her crisp ruffled green apron were wash-worn, and it was a high-school sweatshirt she wore. Her hair was curlier than usual, probably from the rain and wind, and every time he looked at her she became more beautiful. Not in a cool, distant kind of way, but he noticed warmth and heart in her that he'd never taken the time to notice before.

His son's words haunted him. Serious. Am I serious about her?

How could he not be?

"Look, Dad, a friend of mine works at this great restaurant in Bozeman. I'll give her a call, get you a cool table, and on the way home we'll stop by and get some flowers."

"Flowers?" He had a hard time focusing on anything because Paige was coming his way, leading the Corey family down the aisle, chatting with Mrs. Corey over her shoulder as she went. Paige was elegance and she fascinated him.

On the way past his table, she surprised him by flashing him a warm knowing smile. One that made his soul lurch. One that made him feel alive all over again.

"Dad? You are one sorry dude. But it's gonna be okay. I'm gonna take care of you. Help you out with this."

Evan tried to focus on his son and had a hard time doing it. "Help? Nah, I got this all wrapped up. You need to study for your chem test."

"Dad." Cal shook his head like a parent who knows best when confronting a clueless teenager. "You have *so* much to learn. It's a good thing you have me. Who knew all my dating expertise was going to pay off? Now, what is it you're always telling me? Respect the girl. Mind your manners. Be a gentleman. I don't have to tell you what that means, do I?"

Evan felt his face burn. "No, I think we can safely say that I'll be a perfect gentleman. Let me think.

I'm trying to remember why I was glad you came home? All that quiet I've been enjoying sounds good about now."

"Yeah, yeah. Face it, Dad. You need me." Cal stuffed a forkful of waffle into his mouth, enjoying this way too much.

Evan's gaze roamed across the dining room to where Paige was helping elderly Mrs. Corey into a chair and when Mr. Corey insisted that was his job, Paige simply melted.

In that brief moment he saw something new about her. Paige McKaslin was an old-fashioned girl.

Well, she was in luck, because he was a hold-the-door, treat-a-woman-right, old-fashioned kind of guy.

## Chapter 11

"Mom, you're gonna be late for your date!" Alex's voice echoed down the long hallway. "Mom!"

"I'm in here." She checked her reflection in the big beveled mirror over her dresser.

The woman who gazed back at her looked ready for a meal at a fine restaurant. Her hair was tidy, her jewelry sedate—except for her earrings, maybe those were too much. And maybe the black rayon jacket and pants set made her look too severe. She had time. She should pick something else. There was that pretty pink dress she'd worn at Easter, and it had been a flattering color on her.

No, I'm not going to be one of those women who dress to suit some man, she told herself firmly. This is just dinner. Just a thank-you for all he's done. He's a customer. He's a man. He's not really interested in me.

But am I interested in him? She couldn't quite answer that question truthfully, and she was glad for the interruption of her son bounding through her open bedroom door, looking windswept and bright-eyed. "What have you been up to?"

"No good." With a wide grin, he dropped into the overstuffed chair by the picture window. "You know me. Robbing banks. Holding up old ladies."

"Sure. Did you play basketball at the church?"

"When it finally stopped raining. I told Beth to stop by the diner tomorrow on her way to school. She has work release so she doesn't have to be there until noon."

"I never said I'd hire her." Paige decided black was the perfect color for a woman with a teenage son who had a girlfriend. The perfect color for a woman who was not going to believe in love again. The perfect color to remind her that this dinner wasn't a genuine date. "And before you say anything, I am short-handed, but I can't hire her just because you like her."

"There's a reason I like her, Mom. She's a good person." Her teenaged boy flashed her a telling look. "Isn't that what you always say is important?"

Paige rolled her eyes. "Aren't you supposed to be doing something? Your homework, maybe?"

"Yeah, yeah, I'll get to it. What I need to do—" he rose up to his full six-foot height, "is help my mommy get ready to go out with her new boyfriend."

That he seemed pleased with the idea only made her laugh. Laughing covered up her embarrassment. She snapped the back off her left earring. "If I ever hear you say *boyfriend* again, you'll be grounded so fast, it'll make your head spin."

"Ooh, I'm afraid." With a wink he caught her hand. "Leave the earrings. They're pretty. Just like you."

Her heart melted. "You stop trying to charm me."

"It's just the truth, Mom." Sincerity shone in his eyes, as blue as hers, when their gazes met in the mirror. "Cal told me his dad's like *waaay* serious about you. And I figure, this'll be good for ya. Get out. Be with a nice guy your own age. I raised ya right. I trust ya."

Before she could begin to figure out what on earth she should say to that, the doorbell chimed. Nerves skidded through her like cold ice. Her fingertips felt frozen as if she'd been hours out in the cold and she had a tough time getting the earring back on.

"That'll be him." With a delighted grin, Alex dashed from the room.

Paige gripped the edge of the dresser, holding on for dear life as her son's words replayed in her head. *Cal told me his dad's like* waaay *serious about you.*

That can't be right, can it? Paige clicked on the earring back. *And if it is, oh, Lord, what am I going to do?* Because she had mentally prepared herself to have a friendly conversation over a meal with Evan. To keep her shields up and her hopes, as tiny as they were, securely in place. What she wasn't ready for was a big first step on a path that was uncertain and risky.

No, she told herself firmly, Alex's words were nothing more than the result of two boys speculating on their parents' relationship. It was nothing to worry about. She took a steadying breath, heard the front door close and the rumble of male voices in conversation. It looked like Evan was waiting for her, so she grabbed her evening bag and headed down the hall. She was ready for a casual, friendly dinner. She wouldn't think about the rest.

"Evan." His name spilled from her lips at the sight of the fit and handsome man standing in her foyer, wearing a striking black suit and coordinating black tie, and holding a vase of long-stemmed red roses. There were so many perfect buds, she could smell the beautiful old-fashioned aroma as she stumbled the last few yards down the hallway. "Oh, you brought flowers."

"You like 'em?"

"Y-yes. Thank you." The flowers were exquisite, but it was the man who captivated her. The man whose dark eyes widened with visible appreciation as she stepped into the fall of the overhead light. His was no casual look, but one that frightened her for all its sincerity and warmth. She saw the man's steady heart and kind nature in the slow sweep of his smile.

"Paige. You look beautiful."

The way he said it, made her think that he believed it. She couldn't remember any man who'd ever said that to her. It wasn't true, and she couldn't let herself read anything into his misguided belief, but deep down, it mattered. She knew she was beaming as she smiled at him. "You brought me flowers?"

"I was told by my son it is important to make the right impression. How am I doing?"

Wonderful. "Passable."

Alex stepped in to take the flowers. "That means she's pleased. You two have a nice time. Drive safe. Oh, and Mom, don't forget you have a curfew."

"You are enjoying this way too much, young man." Her hand shook as she reached into the hall closet for her Sunday-best coat. "I want all your homework done before you turn on the TV."

"Roger, captain." He disappeared into the kitchen. "Call if you're gonna be late. You know the rules."

Thank heavens for her son. She was chuckling instead of trembling as she slipped her arm into her coat sleeve and missed. She was rattled, that was all. More nervous than she expected to be. The evening had turned more serious than she had imagined.

"Let me." Evan was there, a big powerful presence behind her, holding her coat so she could try again. He was so close she could smell the pleasant spice of his aftershave. She felt small next to him, feminine and womanly, something she hadn't felt in so long. It was as if a part of her was awakening, and there was more light for her eyes to see by and more heart for her to feel alive.

Evan settled the coat around her shoulders with care. "Since you have a curfew, we'd best get going."

The low rumble of humor in his voice seemed to draw her closer. "I noticed Cal was with you at the diner. What does he think of this?"

Evan held the door for her. "I didn't get a curfew, but I have to call him with a report as soon as I get home. He tried to give me advice. He thought I needed it."

"Do you?"

"Considering I haven't dated for two whole decades, I think that's a yes." Evan shut the door and followed her down the steps. "Cal gave me advice all day long. When he stopped, Phil called in with even more advice."

"So, how does everyone know about this?"

Evan opened the passenger door for her. "I'm sure my son is to blame. I'll beat him thoroughly the next time I see him."

"Yeah, I'm sure you will." Paige didn't look as if she believed it for a second.

And she would be right. He took her elbow as she climbed up into the cab, and he could feel her muscles tense beneath the layers of clothes. She was small-boned, hardly anything at all to her, he realized, and a hard surge swelled through him, bringing with it the need to protect her. To take care of her.

Strong needs for so early in the game. He didn't trust feelings, and so he did his best to hold them back as he closed her door and circled around to the driver's side.

He had to be careful. This was how it had all gone wrong with Liz, or at least that was his theory. He'd been overwhelmed with those strong male traits to love and protect. Liz wanted to be taken care of and he wanted to love and protect her.

He'd fallen too hard too fast, and he hadn't noticed the small signs and clues along the way until she had his ring on her finger and it was way too late to step back.

He had to tread carefully. He would not make that mistake again.

Had she ever been so nervous in her entire life? If she had, Paige couldn't remember when. It wasn't like her at all. She was never rattled. She was a single parent, a business owner and responsible for her employee's salaries every month. She couldn't afford to be anything but rock-solid.

It was Evan. He was putting her right out of her comfort zone.

And to make matters worse, he kept getting the doors for her. Didn't he know she was perfectly capable of getting them for herself?

She walked through the heavy wood-and-glass doors to one of the nicest restaurants in the area. Evan's hand settled on her shoulder as he followed her into the lobby. The lights were low, and restful piano music added a tasteful background. The décor was Western and expensive.

Nice place. A fire crackled in the central stone fireplace in the dining area of high-backed booths and the firelight reflected in the long row of windows that overlooked the spectacular mountains.

A hostess tended to them immediately and Paige managed what she hoped was a composed appearance as she followed the college-age girl past the fireplace to a window table. Tucked in the corner, it was cozy and private and offered a stunning view of the up close Bridger Peaks and the rugged Rocky Mountains. The pewter sky was swept with broad strokes of magenta and gold from the setting sun.

Evan had pulled out all the stops. There was no possible way she could call this a casual friendly meal, not considering this elegant restaurant. He held out a chair for her, indicating she should take the better view. Wordless, she slipped into the chair and the solid warmth of his presence so undeniably close had her trembling all over again.

She wasn't prepared for this. Not at all. But she didn't want to stop it from happening, either.

Evan seated himself across the table, and while she accepted the menu from the hostess and tried to concentrate on the specials, she felt as if the room were spinning. Alex's words kept replaying in her head. *Cal told me his dad's like* waaay *serious about you.* Why had the boy told her that? She didn't want to hear things like that! She felt as if she were standing on the edge of a tall cliff with the earth crumbling away around her feet.

As soon as the hostess stepped away from their table, Evan leaned closer. "Did you happen to catch what she was saying?"

"No," she confessed. "I was too blown away by the view to listen very well."

Not exactly the truth, but she didn't feel comfortable confessing just how anxious she was. Would he understand? He looked sure and confident, as always. The menu he held open in his wide, capable hands was steady, unlike hers. This dating thing is for the birds, she decided. Why on earth would anybody do this to themselves?

Evan studied her with a small smile, as if he had a secret. "The view? I didn't notice. All I can see is you."

The air evaporated from her lungs. Her heart forgot to beat. Thought fled from her poor befuddled brain. This was not friendship; this was not safe ground. The earth was crumbling faster around her metaphorical feet, and she didn't like knowing she was about to fall.

"Cal said the steaks here are great." Evan kept talking, his tone calm and steady and everything a dream man should be. "That's not the exact words. I think he said they were awesome."

Their boys. This was safe ground; safe conversation. She groped for what normalcy she could. "How is your son liking MSU?"

"Cal's thriving. Busy. Wasn't homesick for a minute. He got a good roommate in the dorms, and he's made friends. I think he manages to study in there some time. Actually, he's doing well. Growing up and away."

"Kids tend to do that. Alex is going to be spending the summer working as a camp counselor up near Glacier National Park. And so after this graduation, I'll be sending him off into the world. Now that it's getting closer, I don't think I'm going to like that as much as I always thought."

"I know what you mean. I raised my boys to be good men. They are. I'm proud of them. But they were my life."

"As they should be." They had this in common. Not only were they the ones in their marriages who had stayed the course, they were also the ones who had had the reward of spending their lives day by day with their children.

That's what real love was, the holding on when it was hard to do so. Evan had a steadfast heart. And, after feeling the sting of a husband who'd bailed, there was nothing more important to her in a man.

A perky waitress arrived, obviously a college girl from the nearby campus, who introduced herself as Caitlin. Fortunately, she repeated the specials for Evan, who considered the choices and indicated that Paige should order first.

She chose the smallest steak, thinking the less food, the quicker the meal would be finished and the sooner she could get this over with. A suffocating ache had dug in deep in the center of her chest. An ache that was pure emotion, a little of the past hurting, and mostly fears she could not put into words. They were fears she didn't want to acknowledge.

While Evan ordered one of the evening's special Angus steaks, Paige watched the sunset. The pewter clouds turned nearly purple as the last of the light burned into the glacial peaks of the Rockies. It was stunningly beautiful, but she felt a little like that sun slipping into the unseen beyond and treading in unfamiliar country.

Relationships—even a first date—required vulnerability. Exposing an honest piece of who you really are to another person. She'd done that once, and gotten burned where she was most fragile. She'd decided long ago that nothing—*nothing*—could ever be worth the risk of hurting like that.

Except one thing.

As Paige reached for her water, her attention caught and held on the couple one table over, just visible some distance behind Evan. They were in their retirement years, seated together on the same side of the table, leaning toward one another instead of away.

How sweet. The wife gazed up at her husband with honest adoration, and her husband took her delicate hand and kissed her knuckles tenderly, the sconce light reflecting on the slim gold wedding ring she wore.

A great love. Wasn't that what every girl dreamed of finding one day? It hadn't happened to her; she believed that it could not. But she'd seen plenty of people who seemed to have marriages that worked. And some couples had something more, something special. That true love was so special and rare, it had to be like holding on to a little piece of heaven.

"That's really something, isn't it?" She hadn't realized Evan had finished speaking with the waitress, who had turned out, apparently, to be a friend of his son's. Embarrassed to be caught watching something that was so private, she reached for her water goblet. "It's heartening to see that some marriages really last," he continued.

She nodded, for that was just what she had meant to say. "It's so easy to see the bad divorces and the painful marriages and love that has broken apart."

"Especially when that's what happened to you." Evan's deep baritone resonated with understanding. "What happened to Alex's father?"

"He decided he'd had enough of responsibility and left in the middle of the breakfast rush." Her hand was trembling again and she tried to still it as she lifted the water glass. Somehow she managed to get a sip of water down without choking.

"No," Evan said gently. "What really happened?"

*I don't want to tell you what really happened.* Her hand wobbled. She set down the goblet before she dropped it. "No one knows that story. It's not very interesting."

"I'm interested."

Her heart gave a lurch. She'd never been so glad to see a waitress. Caitlin arrived with their house salads, with ranch dressing for her and Italian for Evan and fresh ground pepper, giving Paige enough time to prepare herself. While time had dulled the pain, the scars had gone deep. All the way down to her soul.

She'd never told anyone the truth. She didn't know if she could open up so much now.

Instead of taking up his salad fork, Evan laid his big, warm hand over hers.

His touch was as unsettling as it was comforting, because she was used to neither. She'd been alone in the most essential way for so long, the connection of his hand on hers felt like everything she could ever want and at the same moment everything she was afraid of. "There's not much to tell. I married Jimmy when I was nineteen and he was twenty. We thought we were in love.

"But in a ycar's time, I was pregnant, there had been a kitchen fire in the diner and we were in debt up to our ears from the repairs. I was raising Amy and Rachel; Ben was in and out of trouble and acting out. I had more responsibility than I could handle, and Jimmy just had enough one day. He walked out with half our morning regulars listening to us argue. That's it."

Technically, her story was correct. But it left out the real things, the painful arguments and disappointments that she did not want to remember. Because if she did remember what love had brought her, then she would also remember how she'd vowed never to go through that devastation again.

"That's not it. You loved him."

She knew that surprise showed on her face. "I was too young to know what love is. I thought he was something he wasn't. It was my mistake."

"You thought he was the kind of man who stayed, even when the better turned to worse?"

She swallowed hard. *The truth, Paige.* Evan had asked for the truth, and he was waiting patiently, the silent demand of his touch seeped into her like the heat from his skin on hers. She studied his hand, his knuckles were thick but not beefy, his fingers well-proportioned and so capable looking. He knew the unspeakable sadness of a failed marriage. Of a broken love.

She was going to trust that he would understand. "I thought he loved me enough to stay. Until I found out he didn't love me at all. Not really. He just wanted someone to take care of him. You know, do his laundry, put a roof over his head and food on the table. He said that I was good at taking care of other people. It's what I do. And he was right. I think that's what hurt the most."

She tried to tug her hand free.

He held on tight. "I've been there, too. Liz went from her parents' house to her college dorm at her school to marrying me. She'd had a sheltered childhood, and she was looking to be taken care of. It was my mistake, because I was looking for a real helpmate in a wife, in a best friend."

"I thought that's what marriage was."

"Me, too." Evan couldn't explain why, but he could feel her truth like the bright cast of light from the setting sun on his face. In a blinding moment, he understood. She'd been raising her younger brother and sisters, running a business on her own, responsibilities he'd never had at that age, and she'd been looking for a man. Had hoped that's what her husband would be. The same as he'd done with his wife. "Being let down like that, why, it does something to a person."

"Yes." She shook out her napkin, hand trembling, and turned to stare longingly out the window.

Was she dreaming of escaping him, he wondered, or was it escape from remembering the past? She'd said yes to the date; she must want to be here. But that didn't make it any easier to risk trusting him. He knew that. "I want you to know up front, that I've never intentionally let someone down in my life. Just so you know."

He released her hand then. "Do you want to say grace? Or do you want me to do the honor?"

"Y-you." Paige cleared her throat, thankful she was able to get that one word out. Her throat felt as if it had closed shut and she knew she'd never be able to say a blessing. He'd gone and said the one thing that mattered the most. "N-neither have I. Let anyone d-down."

As the last ray of sun slid behind the Rockies, the twilight and shadows lengthened everywhere but in her heart.

## Chapter 12

Paige felt a mix of relief and regret when Evan turned his truck into her driveway. Clouds blotted out any starlight, and the night stretched black and ominous as the headlights slashed twin paths through the dark woods. A movement blurred just beyond the reach of the light.

"My horse is out."

Evan saw it, too, and braked to a sudden stop just in time. The shadowed movement became an Arabian that bolted across the road, turning golden in the beam of the headlights.

"That mare." Paige rolled her eyes and popped open the door. "You can just leave me here. I've got to get her."

"You've got to be kidding." Evan shifted into Park

and set the parking brake. "Didn't I tell you at dinner? I'm not the kind of man who bails."

I've noticed. Paige didn't want to feel the tug of appreciation that made her throat ache and burn. It was easier just to hop out into the gusting wind and night and feel her good shoes squish in the mud on the shoulder of the graveled driveway.

She heard Evan's door close as she wrapped her coat around her and called out to the mare poised in the middle of the road like a deer caught in the headlights. "Annie, baby. Did you get your stall door open again?"

The mare's nostrils flared as she scented Evan.

"Do you want me to herd her toward you?" he called from the other side of the truck.

"No, she's just having some fun. Baby, come with me." Mud sucked at her shoes as she approached, hands out, palms up.

The mare pressed her nose into those hands and her head against Paige's stomach. Spotlighted by the headlights in shades of gold and platinum, woman and horse came together, a revealing moment as she rubbed her mare's long nose. The animal's trust and affection for her mistress was unmistakable. As was the realization that hit him. He was short a horse-riding partner.

Paige rode horses.

"Hey, girl." Her voice was tender and her slender hands gentle as she grasped the nylon halter the mare wore. "Evan, I'm just going to walk her up to the stable. Thank you for an unexpected evening."

"Unexpected, what does that mean?"

"I mean that I'm glad you asked me."

As if shy that she'd said too much, Paige dipped her head, turned her back and hurried down the driveway. The big mare at her side ambled with her, her hooves crunching in the gravel.

*She's glad she went out with me.* Slow joy spread through Evan as he hopped back inside the cab and put the truck in first gear. There was a lot to like about Paige, the private woman who kept her real self well hidden, but he'd seen the part of her she protected so well.

Her confession came back to him, what she'd said when she'd spoken of her husband's betrayal. *He said that I was good at taking care of other people. It's what I do. And he was right. I think that's what hurt the most.* But who had taken care of her through the years? Had anyone?

It was amazing, too, that she was the one woman he just might be able to trust. A woman who'd been through something similar. Who'd been hurt in the same way. A woman with a gentle heart and a kind spirit who made him want to hold her...just to hold her.

The road curved, and Paige and her horse veered off through a path in the trees. He put the truck into Park and hopped out to help with the gate that gleamed just within the faint reaches of the head-lights, but it was already open.

"Did you get that untied all on your own?" Paige didn't even seem annoyed as the mare disappeared into the paddock.

He waited while the first drops of cold rain pelted him on the head. He waited while the drops became steadier and by the time Paige had emerged from the dark shadows, he was wet clean through. But he didn't mind. He opened her door, so she could hop inside.

"Evan, I'm muddy. I don't want to get your interior dirty."

"It's happened before. And this date isn't over until I see you to your door."

"Isn't that an old-fashioned rule?"

"Sometimes old-fashioned is the best." He tucked her hand in his, and the connection that zinged through him hit him right in the soul.

*Please let her be all that I think she is, Lord.*

It had been a long time since he'd wanted anything so much. His spirit ached with the power of it. They'd had a solid conversation over dinner about their kids, their jobs and their church. They'd lived in the same town all their lives; there were plenty of things to discuss, from the yearly Founder's Day celebration to the fundraiser for the county library Paige was catering.

And as Evan cupped her elbow to help her into the truck, he felt something greater than he'd ever felt before: a tender desire to take care of this woman who worked so hard. His feelings were moving way too fast for his brain. He needed to take his time. Neither of them was in a hurry. Love was best, he'd learned, when it was meant to be instead of when it was rushed into being.

He made sure she was in and gave her seatbelt a tug so she wouldn't have to search for it, before shutting the door. He'd never expected the evening to turn out so well. He'd never expected to feel an emotional connection so strong. He didn't know why it was there, but he figured it made sense in a way.

He'd always known Paige, from a distance to be sure, but she was everything he admired in a woman.

Tonight had only shown him she was even more amazing on a deeper level.

They drove the rest of the way in silence. The hum of the heater and the rhythm of the wiper blades were deafening. Evan knew he wanted to ask Paige for another date. The question was, would she say yes? It was tough, but he only had a few more moments with her, so he had to gather up his courage now or it would be too late.

He steeled himself, preparing for her rejection. "I hope I wasn't too boring tonight."

He put the truth of what he was thinking right out there for her to comment on. What would her reaction be? He waited the infinitesimal beats between one second and the next.

"Boring?" She turned to him, highlighted by

the dash lights enough that he could see the surprise clearly on her lovely face. "I was worrying
you thought the same thing about me. I work, I take
care of my family, I work some more. That's hardly
exciting."

"It is to me." He pulled into the graveled spot
next to the house and shifted into Park. "That's just
about all I do."

"Don't men at your age have a mid-life crisis?
You know, sports cars, excitement, twenty-year-old
wives?"

There was a gentle lilt to her words, as if she
were kidding him, but he could feel the dead seriousness beneath. "I'm happy with my life. A sports
car wouldn't haul my horse trailer. I think a quiet
evening reading at home is exciting. And I would
only bore a twenty-year-old, aside from the fact that
my youngest son is nineteen. That would be beyond
wrong."

Okay, that was a good answer, Paige thought
while Evan hopped out and circled around the vehicle. Although Jimmy hadn't left her for a mid-life
crisis, he'd been having another sort of crisis, and it
had left it hard for her to trust any man.

Evan opened her door. "Do you think I got you
home before your curfew?"

"It's only nine o'clock. I think I'm safe from my
son's wrath." She liked the way he chuckled easily
and the sure way he took her hand. She felt as light
as air as he accompanied her up the walkway.

Those pesky nerves returned. Did she invite him in? Did she let him kiss her good night?

"About Wednesday evening." Evan stopped on the top step, clearly meaning to leave her by the door. "I'll pick you up at the diner around seven?"

He wanted to see her again. Why did that make her feel like she'd filled up with helium and was about to float away? She was way too practical for romantic foolishness. "I don't remember saying that I would go with you. But then again, I'd hate to be the reason you decided not to go to Bible study."

"Then it's a date." The way he said it, wasn't a question but a confirmation. As was the deliberate step he took in her direction.

Was he going to kiss her? Something between panic and wonder held her locked in place as his mouth slanted over hers. The first brush of his warm lips to hers was the sweetest she'd ever known.

Tenderness filled her like a slow, sweet waltz, and when he moved away into the shadows off the porch, she swore she could hear music.

"Good night, Paige. I'll see you soon." He left her standing in the glow of the porch light, bathed in raindrops and alight with hope.

Max was breathing on the other side of the door, a happy welcome-home pant that, since he was such a big dog, was louder than the rain tapping all around her. She felt wrapped in a warm pure glow, staring into the direction of the idling truck.

A dark figure cut through the headlights, the

dome light appeared and disappeared. She spun and bolted through the door. Max was bounding up and down on all fours, his doggy mouth stretched in a happy grin.

She stroked the top of his wide head with her hand. The puppy Alex had begged her for had grown into a one-hundred-and-twenty-three-pound giant, and he was still growing. The sleek, powerful dog took up most of the available space in the foyer, and she had to reach around him to hang her jacket up on the set of hooks by the door.

Only when she saw the streak of mud across the side of the garment did she remember she'd been out in the muddy field. And her shoes were caked with it. She'd completely lost her mind, apparently, and tracked mud into the house.

Great going, Paige. A single kiss was all it took for her to lose control of her good sense.

Oh, well, it had been a lovely evening. And Evan—why, she really liked him. Too much for her own good. Too much for the safety of her heart. He was a good man, she knew that. But it was a long rocky road to trusting a man enough for...well, whatever lay ahead. If they made it that far. Her future and what direction it was going to take was a big question mark.

As she kicked off her shoes and set them to dry by the heater vent, she saw Alex's light on downstairs. If he was studying, she didn't want to interrupt him. That was her excuse. She really didn't want to interrupt him, because she didn't want to answer any questions about her date.

Not that she could avoid questions forever, but she needed time to make sense of things. Nothing had been what she'd expected tonight. She couldn't remember a time in her adult life when a man had more than exceeded her expectations in every way.

The phone rang. When Alex didn't pick up, she gave away her presence in the house by snatching up the kitchen extension. "Hello?"

"Paige?" Someone was crying—one of the twins. "Paige? Are you, like, really busy right now?"

"Of course not. Where are you? I'll come over."

"N-no." Brianna sobbed, stuttering. "We're almost to y-your house. Mom and Keith got into this b-bad fight—"

Paige ached for the girls. Their mother had married a man who was better at drinking and gambling than at holding down a job, and Paige constantly worried about the girls' welfare. There was only so much she could do, but she did what she could. "Of course, you come right on over. The porch light is on, and I'll whip up some hot chocolate."

"With sp-sprinkles?" she asked through a sob.

"Absolutely. You girls drive safely. Promise?"

"O-okay. Brandilyn's dr-driving. She's, like, way b-better at it than me."

After saying goodbye, Paige left the cordless receiver on the counter and went in search of the special secret recipe cocoa mix she'd brought home from the diner. There was a jar of it somewhere.

"Hey, Mom." Alex startled her. He was in the entryway next to his dog. "Who's coming over?"

"The twins. How's the homework going?"

"It's going. Why are you all muddy?"

"Annie got out again. She figured out how to open the gates. Could you go figure something out to hold her in until the morning?"

"Sure. Oh, I forgot. I need this form thing signed for school tomorrow." He shoved a piece of paper toward her before he dropped into one of the bar chairs on the other side of the counter. "It's for our field trip to the Museum of the Rockies. So, how went the big date?"

"Fine. We had dinner. We talked. We came home." Paige opened the drawer next to her, pulled a pen out of the organizer, and signed the form. "Is that field trip this week?"

"Friday. You changed the subject."

"No, I was finished telling you about my date." She pulled a saucepan out of the lower cabinet and plunked it on the stove. "Wait, I can see those wheels turning in your brain, so listen up. No, I'm not in love with him. No, I'm not planning on marrying him—"

"He'd be like my stepdad. Never thought I'd get one at my advanced age."

"You can't look into the future. I can't look into the future, so drop it. Are you worried about that, about me marrying one day?"

"Worried? Nah, I'm not worried. I just don't want to go off to college and leave you alone."

"It's your job to grow up and move away. It's mine to make sure that you do—" She took the milk from the fridge and set it on the counter as the doorbell rang. Max barked joyously. "Could you get that dog?"

"He's so well-trained." Alex rolled his eyes, grinned, and jogged to hold the black-masked rottweiler back so Paige could muscle open the door.

The girls were rain-soaked and tearstained and in emotional tatters. Setting her thoughts of Evan aside, she helped them carry their overnight bags down the hall to the guest bedroom next to hers, drew each girl a bath in separate bathrooms and got them to soaking.

Such was her life. She took care of others first and didn't get a moment to herself until it was after midnight.

Evan. Just thinking his name lessened the shadows in her soul.

Paige. Evan had thought of little else in the last twenty-two hours.

It had been a typical Monday with disasters by the truckload, but he'd tackled meeting after meeting and one conference phone call after another with unusual efficiency. Nothing had dimmed his happiness. He was in a good mood because he couldn't get Paige out of his mind. Or their kiss.

Tenderness filled him. He pulled his truck to a

parking spot in front of the diner and checked his reflection in the visor mirror. His hair was still a little damp from his shower at the gym, but he'd had a good day, a good workout and he was looking forward to a good evening—because he'd be seeing Paige in about two minutes.

The evening was cool and bright as he stepped onto the curb and spotted her through the rose-hued window. Sunset blazed overhead, painting the street with a soft glow, and the light seemed to find Paige in the dining room, falling across her lovely face like a touch from heaven.

*I'm not ready to care so much so soon.*

This was not the take-it-slow, one-step-at-a-time pace that he'd planned. As he pushed through the door and she turned as if she sensed his presence, he felt a click in his heart, like a key turning in a long-unused lock, like a door opening and sunlight flooding inside for the first time. He felt renewed as their gazes locked.

There was no hiding the gleam of warmth that lit her sapphire eyes or the secret quirk of a smile in the corners of her soft mouth. Remembering their kiss, remembering the connection they'd shared last night, he took one step forward and another to his usual seat at the counter.

"I see you found your way here tonight." Paige brought her smile and a menu. "You know the usual Monday specials, and we also have a grilled salmon special."

"So, that's how you're going to greet me, huh?"

She blushed. "Now you want preferential customer treatment? How about a complimentary soda?"

When she looked down at the counter, as if it held some great interest, he could feel as plainly as if the emotions were his own, her shyness. This was new to them both. "I seem to remember how we said goodbye last night."

Her cheeks blushed harder, but there was a twinkle in her eye as she reached for the soda cups. "Oh, and you thought you might get something similar with a hello?"

"A guy can hope."

"This is a place of business, I'll have you know." She filled the cup with ice and then cola. "If it's not on the menu, then it's not served."

Okay, he had a sense of humor, too. "So, what do I have to do? Ask for a rain check?"

"Maybe." She slipped the beverage on the counter in front of him. "I'll be back. The twins are not having a good day."

"Is there anything I can do to help you?"

His question took Paige by surprise. He wanted to help her? *Evan, I'm going to fall so hard in love with you if you keep saying things like that to me.*

The pathway was so familiar, she could probably do an entire shift with her eyes closed tight, but suddenly moving forward seemed to take tremendous effort. It was as if the air had suddenly become heavy and she had to wade instead of walk.

Why did her entire being want to keep her from moving away from this man?

Because something in him drew her and the hold was stronger every time she was around him. She was a practical woman; she always prided herself on her good sense. Those traits seemed to have abandoned her now. One date and she was smitten. One kiss, and she'd hardly been able to focus on her day's work.

Brandilyn was in deep conversation with the Whitley family at table sixteen. She'd gotten their orders wrong. While the customers had been polite, Brandilyn burst into tears.

Paige laid her hand on the girl's shoulder, gave her a quick hug, and told her to take a much-needed break. By the time she'd sorted out what had gone wrong and how to fix it, and apologized profusely, several tables had finished and were heading up the aisle to queue up at the front counter to pay.

Instead of her mind being focused on asking Dave through the pass-through window to get a rush on the Whitleys' changes and hurrying to the till to ring up the sales, what was she doing?

Watching Evan. Noticing the way he sat so strong and straight. How those wide shoulders of his looked solid enough to carry any burden.

What should she do? He was a dream, and she didn't have time to dream.

# Chapter 13

The next time Paige was able to catch a breath, she noticed Evan's chair was empty. Brianna was bussing his plate. The rush had hit, she'd been caught in the back, and now, an hour later as the dinner crowd was thinning, he was gone. And she hadn't gotten the chance to say goodbye.

"He left about five minutes ago." Dave gave a New York strip a flip on the grill and sprinkled seasoning across it. "Seemed to be looking around, like he was trying to find you to say goodbye. But that's when the twins' stepdad came to the back door and you went outside with him. Don't worry, Evan'll be back tomorrow."

"He'll be back as a customer."

"As a customer only? Nah, no customer looks at you the way he does."

"And what way would that be? As someone too busy to talk to him?"

"Nope." Dave grabbed a baked potato from the warmer. "As a man who's serious."

*Serious.* There was that word again. She'd never felt she had much in common with Cinderella before, but that's what this reminded her of. Last night's outing had been wonderful but it was way out of the ordinary. She was no beauty to make a man fall in love with her. She was no princess. Paige McKaslin had lines on her face, and gray hair she had her hairdresser color, and more responsibility than she would ever have free time.

Last night she'd put her bookkeeping aside to go out with him, thinking she could do it when she came home, and then the twins had landed on her doorstep. The girls had been in tears most of the night, distraught over their stepfather's drunken behavior and his terrible fight with their mother.

Tonight looked to be filled with even more drama and upset for the girls. And now the bookwork needed urgent attention.

Everything needed urgent attention.

The door swung open, jingling the welcome bell overhead. Paige automatically put a smile on her face, ready to greet whoever had stepped into her family's diner, and saw with relief that it was Alex and his girlfriend. She'd had a good talk with Beth before the lunch rush and had seen some real character in her. She was willing to work hard, and her reference from Misty at the drive-in was stellar.

"Thank you for hiring me, Mrs. McKaslin." Beth's thick hair was tied back at her nape and she'd come in comfortable shoes. "Here's the paperwork that you wanted, all filled out."

"You'll have to call me Paige, since you're working for me. Go ahead and put your things in back. Alex will show you where. Grab a bin and we'll start with bussing."

The teenagers headed off into the back, and Dave had an order up. Paige served the Monday meatloaf special and a cheeseburger to the young married couple she recognized as being new to the area, and hurried to tell the twins they should head on home—to her house. They were emotionally distraught, they'd gotten enough hours in to meet their income needs, and, as she reminded them, they'd had little sleep last night. A little relaxation was in order.

The twins seemed grateful about that, and Paige hugged each girl between ringing up the Redmonds' dinner, and sent them on their way. She kept an eye on Beth, who looked well practiced at bussing, while she whipped up a milkshake for Alex to nourish him while he studied at a table in back.

Already exhausted, she kept going, relieving Dave at the end of his shift. Taking calls for to-go orders, a follow-up call from Phil, who had put the estimate for the plumbing repairs in the day's mail for delivery tomorrow, and a frantic call to her CPA at his home, explaining the taxes were going to be, again, a last-minute thing. Good thing he was an understanding sort.

Then there were the bills to gather up to take home, orders to serve, customers to look after, especially old Mr. Corey who'd come in, alone and confused, to meet his wife for sundaes.

Paige sat him down to wait for his Rosie, who'd been buried eight years before, asked Beth not to let him out of her sight, and called his daughter. Shirley was frantic; her dad had wandered out of the house again. Dementia was a cruel enemy, and Paige sat with Mr. Corey trying to comfort him as he became more upset and saddened worrying over why his wife was late, until Shirley and her husband arrived to gently guide him home.

"That's so sad," Beth commented as the door swished shut behind the family.

"It is. There's a list of phone numbers tacked to the wall next to the register. Shirley's number is on it. Just so you know what to do."

Paige then seated the Everlys, who were out with their new baby girl. Family, she thought, was not only everything, it was the only thing. She'd taken care of her family for so long, and what would she do when they no longer needed her? She was losing them.

Her son was growing up. Her sister Rachel was now married and living in Florida, with a Special

Forces husband and a stepdaughter she was close to. Amy was married and happy, and it was Heath's job to take care of her now. And her brother? Soldier Ben had finally married his high-school sweetheart and was currently serving in the Middle East.

One day Alex would be like this couple, she thought, as she took their beverage orders and took time to admire their newborn wistfully. Alex would be a strong, good man with a wife and family of his own.

All things change, but somehow the passing of time came bitterly. Maybe it was the punch of sadness over seeing poor Mr. Corey, who could not find his dear wife, and who had spent the last three years, as his mind deteriorated, looking for her always.

While she was sorry for Mr. Corey's condition, she couldn't help thinking what a great love he must have known. Real love. She believed in it.

She wasn't so sure if she believed it was possible for her. Or was it?

It was such a risk. Relationships failed all the time. Her gaze strayed to the chair where Evan usually sat in the evenings, occupied now by a couple of junior-high girls downing milkshakes and giggling.

When she was near to him, it seemed easier somehow to believe—just a little. The day was brighter, the shadows gentler with him nearby.

But now, as the night deepened and the demands of life remained, she didn't know how if she could possibly find the heart—or the faith—to really believe.

\* \* \*

Evan pulled his truck to a stop in front of Paige's ranch house and killed the headlights. The night shadows were so thick, he could see nothing except for the thin line of lamplight between the seams of one of the large picture windows.

He imagined her sitting behind those curtains with her hair falling loose around her face as she bent over her bookkeeping.

His chest cinched up tight. Yep, he definitely had it bad. Whether he wanted to or not. Whether he was ready or not. He cared for the woman. So much for going slow and careful.

He opened the door, and his movements echoed in the stillness around him. He shut the truck door, careful not to spill the contents of the large grocery sack he carried. The night air was chilly, but the pungent aromas of greening grass and rising sap scented the darkness. The change of seasons rustled in the limbs overhead like a promise.

Paige. He could see her through the crack in the curtains. She sat at the kitchen table with paperwork spread out all around her feeding numbers into an adding machine. Her head was bent to her task with her dark hair spilling over her shoulders and hiding most of her face. Those dark rich strands shone like burnished silk in the lamplight, and he'd never seen anything more beautiful than this woman. His spirit stilled.

*She's the one.* He felt the truth deep in his soul. She'd brought him back to life.

He rapped lightly on the door. He could see her look up from her work and squint in his direction. Their gazes met. He felt her intake of breath and watched her eyes widen in surprise and then pleasure. Her smile was enough to jump-start his heart. She pushed away from the table, rising in her graceful, confident way and disappeared from his sight.

When the door opened, it was all he could do not to draw her into his arms and never let go. "Surprise. Someone has had a long work day."

"Longer than most, not that I'm complaining." She swept a shock of lustrous hair out of her eyes and stepped back, as if to welcome him in.

He stepped into the warmth and the light. "I've come to interrupt you."

"Good. I'm trying to come down with a headache."

"Accounting will do that. There is a remedy."

"I'm afraid to ask."

"Lead me to your kitchen and I'll show you."

"I'm not sure I should let you into my house. Maybe you should turn around and go back where you came from."

His eyes laughed at her as he closed the door. "Smart woman. But if you don't let me in, you'll never know what you missed."

"Oh, I'm not falling for that. I'm perfectly aware of what you want."

"I came to collect on my rain check. Remember?"

Oh, she remembered, all right. He'd wanted a hello kiss at the diner right in the middle of the dinner rush. "I don't seem to recall that kisses were offered on the menu."

"Something so rare and fine wouldn't be."

It was a sweet thing, how he came to her. Her heart fluttered with longing. It seemed unbelievable that he was here, that his warm hand was twining with hers, but this moment was real in a day that hadn't been the best.

Every heartache, every trouble, every worry eased as he brushed his lips across hers. And then there was only the silence of her soul, and a single moment of perfection.

When he moved away, it was as if he took a piece of her heart with him.

She was falling for him, and if she wasn't careful, she was going to fall so hard, she would never be able to get up again. What if this didn't work out? True love took time. Strong relationships took work. She couldn't go rushing into something she couldn't trust.

It was smarter to take a step back. "Now that you're here, can I get you something? I have hot tea."

He set the bag on the entryway table and stepped behind her. "Tea is fine, but let's get something straight. You will not wait on me."

"I won't?"

His hands settled onto her tense shoulders and

began to knead at the knots there. "Did you stop long enough to eat supper?"

"I've been busy. I'm shorthanded down at the diner—"

"I bet you're always shorthanded at the diner. That's no excuse not to take care of yourself." His fingers dug into the sore flesh around her vertebrae.

*I could stand here forever.* She let her eyes drift shut. She hadn't realized her neck muscles were so tight. Stress, that's what it was. She knew she needed to slow down, but there would be time for that later. She had to get the diner in good enough shape to sell it. And once the business was off her shoulders, then she could take time.

But until then, all she could see was full steam ahead. It was as simple as that. As wonderful as Evan's neck massage was, she told herself that she didn't have time for closeness.

Or maybe, a small truthful voice said inside her, it was safer to step away.

"Did you want to come into the kitchen?" She took a step, twisting to break his hold, but his grip was like iron.

"I want you to take five minutes off." His words tingled against her ear. "I'll stay and help you for five minutes to make up for time lost."

"What do you know about bookeeping, exactly?"

"Uh, nothing. But what I lack in knowledge, I make up for in the willingness to work." His fingers stilled, and his hand settled against the curve of her neck, a heavy, possessive touch.

It was nice. It took every ounce of willpower she owned not to lean into him. Not to move closer. It was what she wanted so much. "Tea. I'll pour some tea. What's in the sack?"

He grabbed it with his free hand as he steered her toward the kitchen archway. "I noticed when I was at the diner that you were pretty busy. It's my guess that you work all evening serving other people their meals and never take the time to get dinner for yourself."

Good guess. But was she going to admit that? No! "I've been taking care of myself for a long time. I eat when I'm hungry. And when I can fit it in."

"Not good enough." Evan set his grocery bag on the counter and released his hold on her.

She stepped away with an odd sense of disconnection. Distance was what she wanted, but as she handed down two cups from the overhead cabinet, her heart wasn't so sure. She had to take down the tall walls she'd built so thick and sturdy that she would be safe from every harm.

Well, not *every* one. Evan. There he was in the edge of her peripheral vision, pulling covered plates from inside the paper sack. His powerful masculinity shrinking the large kitchen until he was all she could see. Every breath felt squeezed into her too-tight chest. She didn't want to feel this way. She couldn't help feeling this way.

He moved behind her and took the cups from her, his touch like warm steel against her. His voice was an intimate hush against her ear. "Take five minutes off. I meant it. Now go sit."

"I *am* taking five minutes off. You don't see me working do you?"

"This is what you do all day. Go to the table and let me do this for you. Please."

She twisted around to get a better look at him, and the affection she saw on his handsome face made something melt inside her. She was afraid it was a section of her defensive walls, and that just couldn't be good. "This is my kitchen. I don't take orders from men here."

"There's a first for everything." Humor tugged at his mouth as he leaned to brush a kiss to her forehead.

Sheer tenderness. It flowed from him and into her heart like the rising of a tide.

"You like honey and cream, right?"

She blinked up at him, her mind strangely blank. Oh, in her tea. "Uh, yes."

Call her stunned, but he was actually working around her. He poured the tea and then opened the fridge for the small container of half-and-half. Her taxes were calling her, but for some reason she didn't care so much about the work needing to be done as about the man moving around her kitchen. See why it was a bad idea to let a man into her life?

Her senses honed to his every movement in her

kitchen. She heard the rasp of the utensil drawer being opened. She couldn't remember the last time someone had served her something to eat.

He removed foil from the plates he'd brought. "Is Alex ready for graduation?"

Somehow she found her voice. "He's ready. I'm not. It's a good thing I'm so busy. That way I can't think too much about what it's going to be like when he's gone."

"Believe me, you'll have plenty of time once he is."

"That's what I'm afraid of." Her confession felt as dark as the night shadows, and she wished she could take back the words.

Evan turned, as if to come to her in comfort. Too overwhelmed, she slipped into the shadows on the other side of the counter. He studied her for a minute before going back to his work. "That's why I care about you so much, Paige. You deeply love your family and the people in your life."

She recognized the shadowed pain in his eyes, because it was so much like her own. "I guess we both know how important that is."

"It's everything." He slid two cups of tea across the counter. He said nothing more as he turned to fetch the plates he'd brought.

Paige took one look at the roast beef sandwiches on thick wheat bread and her jaw dropped. He was busy at the microwave and when she leaned across the bar chairs to hit the switch for the overhead track lighting, she caught the aroma of split pea soup. Sure enough, when the machine dinged, he withdrew a bowl of the thick, fragrant soup and fished through the drawers for a spoon.

When he returned, he swung into the bar chair across from her. "Is there anything else I can get you?"

"You could get me a time machine so I could propel myself into the future." She reached for the nearby paper-towel roll and ripped off two sheets.

He took the paper towel she offered. "Sorry, I left my time machine at home."

She folded her paper towel and laid it in her lap. "Maybe after the meal we could go over to your place so I could borrow it?"

"Why do you want to go back in time?"

"If I could, then I'd have my books done and I could put my feet up and not move for the rest of the evening." She bowed her head and said grace before she dipped her spoon into the hearty soup. "This is really good, Evan. Did you make it?"

"My grandmother's recipe. I have a few secret recipes in my family, too." He'd only made a half sandwich for himself, and he bit into a corner of it.

"This hits the spot. I hadn't realized how hungry I was. Thank you for being so thoughtful."

"I aim to please. It's the least I could do for all the times you've brought me a meal."

"That was at my restaurant and you were a paying customer."

"Well, I appreciate it." He grinned, emphasizing the dimples that dug into his lean cheeks.

His jaw had darkened with a five o'clock shadow, and Paige fought the urge to lay her fingertips there and feel that wonderful, manly texture. There were so many things she wanted to know about him. He obviously cooked. Did he like cooking? What did he do with his evenings? She wanted to know everything about him.

"If I really did have a time machine, I don't think I would use it." Thoughtful, Evan stirred more sugar into his cup of tea.

"There's nothing you wouldn't change in your life?"

"No. I *should* want to go back to college and instead of proposing to Liz, I would break up with her. That would have saved me major heartache. But if I hadn't made the choice to marry her, then I never would have had my boys. Having them to raise was worth anything."

There was no mistaking Evan's love, and Paige understood what he meant. Romantic love had brought her nothing but pain in the end, but it had also given her Alex. "My son is my world. Even when he moves away, I'll have had eighteen years with him. The best years I have ever known."

"The years ahead will be as good. Different, but good, too."

Emotions clawed to life in her chest, and she grabbed her tea, hoping the soothing hot liquid would calm them. But no such luck. She drained the cup, fighting down something she couldn't name that felt surprisingly like panic. She needed the seventeen-year-old pain that still darkened her heart to have never existed. And how was that possible? She wouldn't have the best blessing in her life without her greatest heartbreak.

"Let me refill that for you." Evan was up and taking off with her cup before she could think to stop him.

Now there's a change. She remembered Jimmy and how he'd never thought a man's place was in the kitchen. Oddly enough, he was the day-shift cook at the diner but when he came home, he expected to be the king of his castle. And that meant she was the maid, the cook and everything else. It was strange to see a man looking at home in her kitchen, as if pouring tea and stirring sugar and cream into the cup was no big deal.

He set the cup into its saucer with an easy smile. "Why do you look so sad?"

"Oh, it's because I don't like bookkeeping. It bums me out and that makes me remember things best left forgotten."

"I had a lot of those things, too. Things that are better off buried from the light of day." He returned to the bar chair beside her, moving slowly, as if he felt her sadness. "I would never have come here and brought you a meal if I knew it reminded you of your ex."

She closed her eyes against the past and the pain. It was over and done with; she'd let the wounds heal and went on with the demands of her life. "You don't remind me of Jimmy at all. He never would have brought me a cup of tea, let alone made sure I had supper after a long day on my feet."

"What on earth could be more important to a man than his wife?"

How could he be real? He had to be a figment of her imagination. A piece of fiction projected like a movie in front of her. He said the right things. He did the right things. He was everything he was supposed to be, but she'd believed in a man once who had seemed so strong. Who had seemed like everything she'd ever prayed for in a man.

And now she had no excuses. No man had ever measured up to her ideal, and she believed that no man ever would. So that made it easy. She didn't have to risk. She didn't have to trust. She didn't have to put the most vulnerable parts of herself on the line.

She didn't know if she ever could.

"It was nice that you came over. And this meal. This is the nicest thing a man's done for me. Really. Evan, I truly like you, but I don't have time for this. For dating and as much as I want—" Oh, she couldn't finish that one. Time to think before you speak, Paige, or you'll be spilling your heart to this man. Evan was a good man, but he was still a man. She couldn't allow herself to look at him and see eternity. She leaped to her feet in panic. "I've got to get back to work. Let me rinse off your plates."

"Leave it." He sounded harsh. He stared up at her as if thunderstruck.

She'd hurt him. She didn't want to hurt him. "It's not you, Evan. I just—" She couldn't finish the sentence or the thought. What she wanted rang in her heart. *I want you.* But what she wanted was a good, decent, unfailing man. And few men were like that.

In a flash, her mind leaped back in time. She shook as images of late-night fights flashed through her mind. Wee hours of the night when she'd been too exhausted and stressed and miserable. When she'd managed to get the baby back to sleep—*again*—and Jimmy still wasn't home.

Worse images of what had happened when he did come home, drunk and in a mood. He would start in on her, yelling and criticizing, angry that everyone and everything else was more important to her than he was.

"I'm just trying to pay the bills, Jimmy," she'd tell him. "We need to pull together, not apart." But there was always something that kept their world off kilter: Ben being dragged in by the local sheriff, Amy suspended from school, the baby was colicky again and the endless demands of the diner. It *was* all work and no play. But that was life, right?

It was not the life Jimmy wanted. Paige knew she was a decent and hardworking woman, but she wasn't enough. She wasn't prettier, more interesting, and, as time proved, she wasn't enough to love. He'd gone outside their marriage, he'd cheated, and he'd had fun, as he told her on their last day as man and wife. His parting words replayed in her mind as they had a thousand times since that heartbreaking night. "The only special thing about you is that you can work. You're useful, but what man would really love you?"

She was terrified that if she risked so much of her heart on Evan, one day he would finally get to know the real her.

And think the same thing.

So, what did she say to Evan? He'd come here with his caring and his heart and his thoughtful meal. She wanted…it didn't matter what she wanted. She swiped the bowl beneath warm water and scrubbed it with the pre-soaped scrubber she kept on the back of the sink. The running water drowned out the sound of him moving toward her. The wild thumping of her heart drowned out the sound of him moving away from her.

When she shut off the water, he wasn't at the door. He was putting her untouched sandwich on a plate he'd found in the cupboard and wrapping it in cellophane. His movements were deliberate and confident. "I'll leave this for later. You may get hungry after you're done figuring out your books."

"Or need consolation only good food can provide."

With a nod, he placed the wrapped plate into her

refrigerator. The dependable line of his shoulders and the straight plane of his back blurred as she dried his bowl and handed it to him.

"Th-thanks." The words came out stilted and resonating pain. She winced. She didn't want him to know that his kindness was hurting her. Because he was the wished-for dream she'd stopped believing in long ago.

He placed the bowl with his plates into the grocery sack and rolled down the top. "When I give my word, I mean it. When I give my heart, I give it completely. And just so you know, I don't scare off easily. Good night, pretty lady."

With a lopsided grin that was at once both serious and charming, he walked out of her house and into the night.

# Chapter 14

The shrill ring of her bedside phone woke Paige out of a dreamless sleep. Confused, she groped in the dark for the phone. Her hand hit something hard—not the phone, she realized too late as it hit the floor. Probably her devotional.

The receiver rang again and she snatched it up, her thoughts coming at the speed of light. Alex was downstairs asleep in his room. Amy and Heath had stayed home tonight. That meant something was wrong with Ben. He'd been shot in combat again? Her pulse fluttered with fear.

Or what if something had happened to Rachel's husband, who was also on active duty? "Hello?"

"Paige?" It was a man's voice she recognized, but

she couldn't place it. She sat up in bed as he continued. "This is Cam Durango."

*The sheriff.* "What's wrong? What happened?" Her mind groped at the possibilities. Amy was pregnant. Had she been rushed to the hospital?

"It's the diner. I'm sorry to have to tell you this, but it's on fire. My deputy was driving by on patrol through town and saw the flames. He called the fire department and started in on fighting it—"

"I'll be right there." She slammed down the phone before she realized she hadn't let the sheriff finish. A thousand unasked questions zoomed through her mind. She was suddenly awake and moving too slowly. She couldn't seem to move fast enough. She pulled on last night's jeans and sweater.

"Mom?" Alex was bounding down the hall when she stumbled through her bedroom door. His hair stood up on end and his dog ran along at his side. "What's wrong? What can I do to help?"

"I need you to stay here. It's the diner. It's on fire. The sheriff said—" *It can't be on fire.* It seemed unreal to be shrugging into her jacket so she could drive to town and watch her diner burn. She wanted to offer up a prayer, but she didn't even know what to pray for.

"Mom? I'm driving you." Alex took her keys from the hook above the entry table. He'd already jabbed his bare feet into a pair of boots by the door. He grabbed the door and his coat at the same time.

His hand at her elbow felt steady and strong. Her

boy was turning into a fine young man. She let him lead her outside, leaving the dog behind to whine. It seemed just like a nightmare as she settled into the passenger seat of her SUV and waited to see smoke and flames.

She wasn't disappointed. As they rolled down the deserted street into town, she saw the smoke cloud blotting out the constellations. The acrid scent filtered into the vehicle as the black ribbon of the street led them to the strobe of sirens. A fire tanker from Bozeman was pulling in beside the city and county vehicles. Flames writhed like orange monsters, giving eerie flashes of illumination into the burning building.

This was no dream. She gripped the seat belt like an anchor. There was a horrible thundering sound and men's voices rose in alarm. A split second later, the roof crumbled into the ruins of the diner, and fire surged up into the night sky like rockets.

Tears blurred her vision as she watched the building that had been both burden and blessing burn into ember and ash.

Although her back was to him, Evan recognized Paige in an instant. Even with his eyes closed, he felt her nearness in the deepest places of his heart, as if she were the reason it beat. He pocketed his truck keys and hurried down the sidewalk, past the grocery and across the street to where she stood at the barrier a few yards from the fire trucks.

She looked defeated, Evan thought as he hopped out of the truck and onto the blacktopped street. She looked beaten, and he hurt for her. With her. He hated how her head bowed forward and her shoulders drooped as if she'd lost her best friend. He knew what that diner meant to her, her great responsibility to her family, and as the building rubble burned, he knew she felt as if she'd failed them. He knew because he could feel the heaviness of her emotions in his chest. He felt the black void inside her as if it were inside himself.

*I love her.* The simple fact didn't amaze him. He knew the fall had been inevitable. It had only been a question of when. As he crossed the last yard of distance that separated him from her, he had to hold back the fierce need to make her world right. It was all he wanted to do for the rest of his life.

The last steps he took toward her were certain. Unwavering. He laid his hand on her nape. "How can I help you?"

The muscles beneath his touch tensed even more, but she didn't jump. As he thought, she'd sensed his approach. "What about that time machine? I could really use that right now—"

There was no mistaking the anguish reflecting darkly in her eyes. Before he could answer, her sister did. Amy stood huddled against her husband's side, her face streaked with tears. "This isn't your fault, Paige. Stop second-guessing yourself."

"I don't remember if I double-checked my night

list. I had a lot on my mind. I could have left the fry-
ers on. I could have—"

"You never forget anything. Stop torturing yourself. Please."

Paige's tension surged through Evan as she turned
to face him. Soot streaked her beautiful face. "Evan,
it's two-thirty in the morning. You should be home
in bed. Why? Why are you here?"

"I got a call from your son."

"Alex? What was he doing calling you? I sent him
home. It's too bad he's not still here, or I'd make him
apologize for disturbing you—"

"Disturbing me? No! I'm here because I care
about you." *Because I love you,* he wanted to say
but he wasn't ready. But he already knew he *was*
ready to be the man who stood beside her through
this. The man who was never going to let her down.
"I've told you before. I'm not the kind of man who
bails. So what if it is two-thirty in the morning? I'm
tough. I can handle it."

Evan's hand settled against the small of her back,
a steely comfort so wonderful, she was afraid to accept it for fear that comfort would vanish. She didn't
want to feel that harsh sting of disappointment when
she found out Evan was just a man, after all, used to
taking and not giving.

*Not every man is like that, Paige, you know that.*

She did; but the heart had no logic and fear had a
life of its own. She stepped up to the barrier, trying to

trust the steady pressure of Evan's hand on her spine and his iron presence at her side as he followed her.

Some of the firemen were leaving. The Bozeman department began to roll up their hoses. The flames were gone, and only the glowing embers within the black rubble seemed to be left to deal with. The local department appeared very busy. The wind changed direction, and the acrid-scented air thickened.

"I'm glad you're here, Thornton." Heath, Amy's husband, met his gaze over his wife's head. "I want to get Amy home, but Paige—"

Evan nodded, and a moment of understanding passed between them. Paige was a strong woman, but she was also vulnerable. She needed care. And he was the man to do it.

After the sisters said goodbye and embraced, he watched in silence as Paige turned away from him. She wrapped her arms around her waist, as if she had no one else to hold on to. "You should go home, Evan. It was good of you to come, but there's nothing you can do. There's nothing anyone can do at this point."

"No, the fire can't be undone."

"Some things are so devastating, the damage can never be undone." She sounded hollow.

He knew she had to be in shock. To her, the diner wasn't only a building made of wood and drywall, he knew, it meant so much more. It represented an important part of her past. Her parents had run the place. It was also her future. She had to have been counting on it as her livelihood for the years to come.

He could feel the pain rolling through him as if their hearts were connected. This was something he'd never felt before. Something he'd heard about from Phil and Marie and some of his friends at the office, a special God-given connection that was rare and wondrous.

Love in all its forms was a blessing, but this, he realized, was extra special. Like a piece of heaven brought to earth just for the two of them.

Her hands were ice when he cupped them. "You're not alone, Paige. Remember that."

"I can't even think about what this means. The twins. They need the job to stay in school. And Jodi, my morning waitress? She's been with me since we both were in high school. What's she going to do?" She wrenched her hands from his and covered her eyes. She wasn't crying, but the agony reflected in the tight line of her jaw said everything.

He tried to imagine the woman he'd been married to caring so much about other people, but it was difficult, for she'd been so concerned in looking out for her own interests that she'd even neglected their sons. But Paige was the exact opposite. She was giving and loyal and strong. She was everything he admired and respected in a woman.

If he made a list and wrote down on a sheet of paper every trait he'd hoped for in a wife, the kind he could trust with his life and his heart, she would meet every criterion. But being with a woman in a long-term relationship was about more than admiring her good traits. Much, much more.

And that emotion sang through him, like a hymn coming to life in a quiet sanctuary. Love. The real kind that filled a man up and wasn't whole until it was given away. Rare, pure tenderness swelled in his soul until he couldn't breathe, until he couldn't think, until all he could see was Paige. Paige, who was hurting. He wanted to ease her pain. He wasn't going to let her stand alone. Not tonight. Not for the rest of her life.

"Evan. Paige." It was Cameron Durango, the town sheriff and captain of the volunteer fire crew. He swiped the soot from his face as he approached the temporary barrier. "We've got the fire out. It's a total loss, as you can see. I am sorry."

"Do you know what started it?" Her voice trembled as if she were afraid of the answer.

Evan curled his fingers around hers. She needed him, and he would be here for her, now and always.

Cameron shook his head. "Not until the county fire marshal comes to take a look at it. I'll tell you this, though, it didn't start in the kitchen. The worst damage is in the wall by the electrical panel. My best guess is that a short in a wire started this. I'll be in touch tomorrow. You might as well take her home, Evan."

"No, I want to stay—" Paige began.

Evan tightened his hold on her. "Cameron's right.

There's nothing you can do, baby. Not until the ruins cool down."

"The ruins. My diner is in ruins."

He wanted to protect her; he wanted to take care of her. He wanted her in the most fundamental ways and the most emotional. "Thanks, Cam. I'll take her home."

As the fireman moved away, Evan pulled his beloved to his chest and held her. She was trembling, as if from more than the chill night. As if from more than fear at the uncertain turn her life had taken. When the right time came, he would reassure her. He wasn't going anywhere; he'd stand by her. He would move heaven and earth if he had to, if only to make sure she was well and secure.

As he led her to his truck, his grip was constant devotion that kept her from stumbling when she tripped. He opened the passenger door, and the dome light spilled over her like a blessing. She was a light that hurt his eyes to see, and yet he could not look away. He took a ragged breath, finally squeezing air into his lungs. What did a man do when he was struck so hard? When love rendered him powerless?

When heaven was within his reach right here on earth?

A man stood tall, that's what he did, to protect and preserve this rare gift. Tenderly, he helped Paige into the truck and pulled the seat belt for her. She looked too dazed and exhausted to do more than offer a quiet thanks.

"Any time, gorgeous." That made her smile, if only a watery weak one, but it was enough.

He could feel the change in his spirit like calmness coming to this turbulent night. Committed love filled him, slow and steady, and he knew, from this moment on, his life would be devoted to her, come what may.

Paige covered her face with her hands and closed her gritty, burning eyes. The truck bounced along the ruts at the end of her driveway and eased to a stop in front of her house. Alex had left the porch light on, which broke the endless blackness of the night, and she gave thanks for her fine son, who was already such a reliable young man. He'd been wonderful tonight, taking charge and taking care. He'd called the rest of the family. His only mistake was in calling Evan Thornton.

What was she going to do about Evan? She glanced at him out of the corner of her eyes as he killed the engine and switched off the headlights. He sat straight and tall behind the wheel, moving with a masculine confidence as he unbuckled his seat belt and reached for her hand. His touch was as warm as comfort, and there was something awesome about him, and it broke her heart.

She wished she *could* rely on a man, one who would never let her down again. Evan was a steadfast man. She admired him. She respected the man she'd come to know, but the future was an uncertain place.

And trusting a man enough to really love him, trusting him enough to let real, true love happen, was a complete risk.

*Don't do it!* every instinct within her warned as she opened the door and climbed out into the cool night. She shivered, but not from the wind. She felt broken, as if something within her had crumbled to ashes right along with the diner.

It took her a moment to register that Evan's steps sounded behind hers on the concrete walkway. "Go home. It's late. You have work tomorrow."

"No way. I'm not going anywhere until I know you're all right."

Please, don't be wonderful to me. It would make it too hard to resist placing her trust in him completely, and she couldn't do that. She felt battered and lost and vulnerable enough that she would reach right out to him and let him into her heart. And she couldn't do that. She couldn't risk that.

As she opened the door, she blinked against the blinding light and wondered where her defenses had gone. The iron willpower she'd used to stand on her own two feet for seventeen long years seemed to have crumbled.

For the first time since Jimmy had walked out on her, she felt as if she were falling through thin air, sure of certain impact. If she reached out to stop her fall, it would be Evan she grabbed. Evan, so good and dependable, and she didn't want to need him.

She couldn't let herself really need him. Why did she think she ever could?

"Here. Let me take your coat." He was calm and in control, and it felt just right to be so close to him that she could rest her cheek against his chest if she wanted to. His fingertips scraped the nape of her neck as he helped her out of her sooty jacket and hung it over the closet doorknob.

She was too dazed to do more than turn toward the kitchen. She didn't know what to do. How was it that everything around her was exactly as it always was, when something so catastrophic had happened? It didn't make any sense.

Evan's hand gripped the curve of her shoulder. "Come sit down. Let me make you some tea."

She moved woodenly, hardly aware of making her way to the small round table in the shadowed nook. The table where her taxes sat in a pile. Was it just a few hours ago she'd been here with Evan? How could everything seem so normal, when so much had changed?

"All settled?" Evan towered above her, haloed by the glare of the light slanting in from the entry and, cast in silhouette, he seemed to radiate more might, if that were possible.

This man had come to her in the middle of the night. He'd stood at her side and never wavered. He'd comforted her, helped her at every chance, and was, at 4:10 in the morning in the process of nuking her a cup of water.

Don't get too used to it, a small voice inside her whispered. It was neither a wise voice nor a kind one, but, she feared, it was a sensible one.

She'd learned before that men could be one way and then, over time, or when their reasons were different, they could let you fall to the ground faster than you could see coming.

Evan's not like that, she argued, managing what she hoped passed for a smile as he slid a steaming mug with a floating tea bag onto the table in front of her.

"Thanks. You've been pretty wonderful tonight."

"Yeah? I'm glad you think so. This is only the start, Paige. Just the beginning."

Oh, how she wanted to believe him completely. To grab tight to his words, and to him, as if she could keep this moment, when he stood over her so tall and invincible and committed, and make it last forever.

The deepest places in her *wanted* to believe.

"Want honey and cream?" His rough, intimate baritone made her soul shiver.

"Uh, n-no." She hardly tasted the sweet soothing warmth of the chamomile. Her senses seemed to freeze. And then empty.

And fill with him. Evan's voice. Evan's deep bronze-flecked eyes. Evan's warm, male-textured hand covering hers as he knelt at her side. He overwhelmed her. He filled her. He made it impossible to push him away, impossible to pretend she didn't need anyone, especially him.

Her throat ached with the knot of emotions, wanting to need him and being afraid to, so that she couldn't speak, only nod, in answer. The tea was fine. The tea wasn't the problem.

The problem was the man who was as true as could be. She'd never had a man stay beside her as if a tornado couldn't unseat him.

Or a man with such a heart. A man she could love with every bit of her soul.

"I'm sorry about your diner. It's a terrible loss. I know it's how you make your living. Whatever you need, I'm right here for you. Money. Moral support. Prayer. More tea."

Oh, I could so love this man. The enormity of it terrified her. "I have to deal with the insurance people. I have to—"

"Don't worry about that now. You're not alone with this, baby. You're not alone any more."

She felt as if she were plunging through thin air, falling fast and hard toward the canyon floor below. She feared that when she hit, the impact would blow her apart. It felt as if her life was already in pieces. She didn't feel as if she could take another heartbreak.

She'd thought she could try to find love with this wonderful man. But she'd only been kidding herself with falsehoods.

The truth was that men left, and she wanted to push him away and take out on him the pain she knew he would bring her one day. The same pain

Jimmy had given her when he'd told her she wasn't enough for him, or for any man.

But that wasn't the truth at all. She scrubbed at her eyes, burning and gritty from the smoke. Be honest, Paige, she ordered herself. Not all men left women. There were plenty of good decent men who stayed with their wives, who stuck with their families through thick and thin.

The truth was, men left *her*. She felt the night's shadows creep into the empty places in her soul. In places that had been hurting for too long. What if she *wasn't* enough? She wasn't worldly or gorgeous or exciting and never would be. Doubts were like a small crack in a bone that grew and grew until the sting of it had her eyes watering. She loved him completely, this man who had stolen every last piece of her heart. What was she going to do when he turned away from her? When he said to her that she wasn't fun enough or exciting enough to love?

She'd lost a major part of her heart when Jimmy headed for the door. If Evan left her, what would he take with him? A part of her very soul? That's how much she loved him now. What about in time, as she came to love him more? What would she do if he left her to fall? What would she do on the day to come when he no longer cared if he hurt her or not?

*I can't go through that again, Lord.* She swiped at her tears, but they came too fast and too hot and she couldn't see as she put down the cup with a clink to the tabletop.

"Hey, it's going to be okay. I promise." He said those words with the greatest of convictions, as if he would move mountains stone by stone just for her. "Here, lean on me."

She wanted to. She ached to be weak, just for a moment, and sink against his strength. To let him hold her up just for a bit. She wished she could rest her cheek against the invincible plane of his chest and feel his arms around her and simply hold on. Maybe then she wouldn't fall.

Who was she kidding? Leaning on a man was the greatest danger of all.

Terror filled her. If she could just give in. Just trust. Believe that he would hold on to her forever, come what may.

Surrender, Paige. She willed herself to lean toward him. His chest felt strong. His arms would hold her tight. He wouldn't fail her. He wouldn't move away. He wouldn't buckle and let her fall.

*I can't do it, Lord.* Terror clawed through her like a hunted animal trying to escape, and she turned away. "I need you to go. I just need—" She squeezed her eyes shut. She couldn't take seeing his strong arms or his iron-hard chest or the rejection in his eyes when she pushed him away.

Since it was inevitable, she covered her face with her hands. "Go home. Evan. Please."

"But you're not okay."

"S-sure I am." She bit her bottom lip to keep in the sob. "I'm free. That diner has been a weight around my neck for too long. Alex graduates in two weeks, and he'll be gone. I can finally do whatever I want. I'm free. That's my d-dream, you know."

Liar, she called herself. Evan was her real dream. And a dream was all it could ever be. Ever.

She couldn't trick herself into wishing for impossible dreams. Fairy tales were fiction, and so were the heroic men in them. This was real life. Evan, as good as he was, was an everyday, ordinary man. And she was too broken and scarred.

She'd lost her heart long ago and there wasn't enough left of her to try marriage again. "I'm sorry. I really am, t-to have d-dated you. And let you think—"

She couldn't go on. His jacket sleeve rustled when he lifted his arm. He was reaching out to pull her close. Panic blinded her. She bolted out of the chair. He gaped up at her with hurt blazing in his eyes, still kneeling, his arm frozen in midair.

I've hurt him. The impact rocked through her. She'd been afraid of being devastated and look at what she'd done. She'd drawn first blood.

I want to love him more than anything. She scrubbed the tears out of her eyes so she could see enough to walk away from him.

# Chapter 15

For a moment, his faith in her wavered. She was finally free? She wanted freedom? This was news to him. Yet she'd talked about her son leaving. She'd talked about needing to fill the emptiness left behind by her son.

Maybe she's telling the truth, he thought, as pain crushed his heart. Maybe he was only someone to pass the time with until she was free of her responsibilities?

And then the shock of her words wore off. What she was saying didn't make sense. Paige hadn't dated once in the seventeen years since her husband ran out on her. She was nothing like Liz. He knew. Paige didn't use people, she didn't give excuses; she was his dream come true.

A dream he still believed in.

She held up her hands helplessly, tears streaming down her face. "I was wrong to let you think this c-could work between us. I didn't mean to h-hurt you. I really thought—"

"Why can't it work between us?" He was already on his feet and crossing the room. "Everything was all right until tonight. Until I was trying to hold you and I felt you tense up. I felt it, Paige, and I'll be—" He bit his bottom lip, determined not to curse. Frustration burned like an ulcer in his guts. His heart still felt as if it was being axed apart. He had to take a deep breath and try again. "I won't let this go. Do you understand? I love you."

"No, you don't love me."

"Don't tell me what I feel." He knew she'd had a terrible blow tonight, but didn't she know she was throwing away something that was real? When he opened his heart, she was there. Where she would be forever.

"Maybe it's my fault for not telling you sooner. But it isn't easy for a man like me. I've been alone for a long time, and I've gotten used to keeping my feelings below the surface. And you—" How did he tell her all that was in his heart? "You are the sweetest thing I've known. You make my day brighter. My life better. And me, you make me happy. I love you so much."

"You love me?"

"Why do you think I came to you tonight?"

"I don't know." If her brain would start working right again, then she might be able to tell him. She fought to take a normal breath and to dig beneath the panic threatening to swallow her in one great bite. "Alex called you. He told you about the fire."

"But I came because I wanted to be with you. To stand beside you. Because that's what a man does when he loves a woman more than his own life. He sticks by her. He's her rock when she needs strength. He's her soft place when she needs comfort—"

"No." His words hurt as if they were a thousand tiny arrows piercing her skin, drawing blood and digging deep. "Those are only words. Love isn't like that."

"Yes. Real love is."

"You can't make me believe—"

"That's going to be my job for the rest of my life." Incredibly, he cupped his warm palm against the curve of her face, breaching the distance between them. "To make you believe."

"I c-can't believe you." He was stealing every last bit of her heart and she couldn't stop him. Her feelings were out of her control; she couldn't stop the love bursting up through the shroud of doubt and fear, shining brighter than any light and more certain than any dawn. But she could not let go of her fears. "I can't go through that again. I just can't."

"It's an unconscionable thing, what people do to one another. He hurt you deeply. I know, because I've been hurt like that, too. *Hurt* is too small a word when the one person you love and trust beyond all else on this earth betrays you, and it cuts you down to the soul." Instead of moving away, instead of buckling like water beneath sand, he moved closer, a towering strength that did not yield.

"You're never the same when someone does that to you," she confessed.

"No. I'll never understand how some people can have everything that matters and not be happy with it. I'm not like that. I know how valuable you are. I see you, Paige, clear down to your soul, and loving and honoring you is a commitment I will make to you every single day to come. Because you are worth it."

No, a voice deep inside her cried, because it could not be true. *He* could not be true. She could not believe in dreams and flattery.

But this was Evan, stalwart, steadfast Evan, and his goodness was breaking her will. His love was breaking her heart.

The voice of her past, the one she'd internalized for so long, was Jimmy's voice. How did she silence it? How did she erase his damaging words from the broken places in her soul? *No one can love you,* he'd told her and she'd let those words in, and she'd believed them.

She didn't want to believe them anymore.

"I love you so very much, Paige McKaslin." He was honesty and faith and commitment, a dream that she could not believe in.

A dream that seemed too rare to be true. Too

amazing to happen to her after being alone, and without romance, for so long. Love was a dangerous risk. There were no guarantees, and love demanded a person's everything—her vulnerability and her openness. Romance needed belief to have a chance. And she so wanted this to have a chance.

Terror filled her. But the power of it was nothing compared to the warmth that seemed to surround her like a glowing, iridescent cloud. A shimmering brightness of love that she could not deny, although it was felt and not seen, emotional and not tangible, but it was there all the same. Love, true and pure, in Evan's gaze, in Evan's words, and, once again, in his touch resolute against her cheek.

And then she knew. If she did not risk, she would hurt him. If she did not trust, she would break his heart. If she did not love him truly, then she would be turning her back on the precious, committed love he offered her. And she would rather die before she caused Evan the tiniest pain.

In the end, wasn't love like faith? They were both unseen, but felt. And both were more powerful than any force in the universe. And that force rose up from her soul.

As if Evan could feel the change within her, he leaned closer. Her pulse fluttered in anticipation. There was a man strong enough to stand beside her in this life, and that man was Evan.

His kiss was a warm certain brush against her lips. His tenderness unmistakable.

Yes, her heart knew for sure. *He is the one.*

Dazed, she opened her eyes and met his gaze full-force. Flat-out, nothing held back, all defenses down, she could not stop the sting of emotion rising up within her.

True unshakable love shone through her, chasing away every shadow in her soul.

This was her chance. God was giving her this man and his love and it was up to her. All she had to do was trust and take the biggest risk of her life.

"I love you, Evan Thornton. With all of my soul."

*Thank you, Lord, for this woman.*

Evan gently tucked his beloved against his chest. Peace filled him. Holding her was like finding the missing part of himself. Like filling a place that had always been empty within him. Pressing a kiss to the crown of her head was tenderness and commitment and a dream all wrapped up in one unbelievable blessing. Tears wet his shirt as she pressed against him, leaning into him, holding on.

He ached with a love so pure, he could not begin to describe it to her. So he simply held his dear Paige, feeling their breathing slow and fall into rhythm together.

He couldn't stop the images that poured up from his soul. Images of marrying her in the old-fashioned church in town. Of making a home together. Of coming home to her every evening.

Their sons would be stepbrothers. There would be marriages one day, grandchildren…family.

And he would be happy, he knew, because he would spend each day to come with this woman, with his incredible Paige. Love burned like a super-nova within him.

"This is forever," he vowed and kissed her sweet lips.

# Epilogue

*The Sunshine Café's Reopening Day, Late August.*

Paige pushed through the swinging doors into the brand-new kitchen. The sight of her sister Amy and her husband side by side at the grill brought a smile to her face and happiness to her whole heart. "Are you ready to take a break yet, Amy?"

"Are you kidding? I'm just getting started." She glowed in her fourth month of pregnancy, now that the tough stretch of morning sickness was past. "It looks like a full house from here."

"I'm going to open up the patio. Customers are still arriving." As she spoke, the bell on the front door jangled, announcing new arrivals. She swept

four house salads onto her tray. Her two-carat emer-
ald-cut diamond sparkled cheerfully in the generous
sunlight from the windows, a constant reminder of
Evan's love and faith.

Life is good, she thought as she drizzled dressing on the fresh greens. She would always be grateful for the blessing of Evan's love. She'd never been
happier. She hefted the tray. "In ten more minutes,
you take a break, sister dear. Or I'll come hunt you
down and make you take one."

"Promises, promises."

The dining room was cheerful and full of light.
Families gathered together, talking and laughing
and enjoying their meals. The long row of garden
windows on two sides of the building gave the din-
ers lovely views of the park across the street and of
the small woods at the side of the property. It had
been the right decision to rebuild, she thought as
she hustled down the wide aisle. Jodi, who'd been
the morning waitress for nearly twenty years and
was practically family, was now set to buy the place.

"Hey, Mom. Are you sure you don't want me to
get up and help?" Alex, back from his summer as a
camp counselor, looked so grown-up and suntanned,
even she hardly recognized him.

He grinned at her from the sunny booth where
he sat with Westin, Amy's son. They were playing
a game of Battleship while devouring a platter of
French fries.

Oh, it was good to have her boy back home again,

even if it was for only a few days before she and Evan would be taking him to college. "Are you kidding? You just got home. Relax for a change."

Over the din of cheerful conversations, Paige hustled down the wide aisle. Brianna was seating the Brisbane family while her twin sister rang up the Whitley family's ticket at the front counter.

God is gracious, she thought as she served the Corey family their salads. The diner was beautiful, a new start for the building and the business, and although her life was going to take her in new directions, this place would always remind her of sweet memories. She'd grown up here, underfoot as her parents worked. Alex had grown up here, playing his electronic games in the corner or lost in a book while she ran the business.

Everything changed. That was life. And changing brought the sting of loss and the joy of new beginnings.

She promised the Corey family that their New York steaks would be coming soon. The front bell had her looking toward the door. A petite woman, slim and fashionable, stood in the light of the windows, looking too mature and confident to be her other little sister. A little girl with bountiful curls clutched her hand and gazed around wide-eyed.

Rachel! Paige was running, her heart wide open, her vision blurring. She had her sister in her arms and gave her a tight squeeze. "Oh, you're here. What are you doing here? I can't believe it! You look gorgeous!"

"I wanted to surprise you. Did I?" She stepped back, sun-browned and trim and happy.

Happy. Paige was so grateful for that. She'd worried so at first, when Rachel had met Jake, that he had ulterior motives for proposing marriage. But there was no mistaking Rachel's deep contentment. She'd known Rachel was happy and that her marriage was working well, because they talked on the phone every chance they got. But there was nothing like seeing in person that it was true. Rachel had found her happily ever after.

"Jake's on temporary duty in Afghanistan, but Sally and I decided to fly up and see the new place. Didn't we, baby?"

"Yep." Sally nodded, a little shy, and leaned against Rachel's hip, a clear sign the girl had finally come to trust and love her new stepmother. "I'm real hungry. For a chocolate milkshake?"

Ah, a little niece to spoil, Paige thought. What fun. "With lots of whipped cream on top and chocolate sprinkles? Did you want to go sit with Westin, sweetie?"

"Okay."

A squeal rang through the restaurant behind them. It was Amy, flying down the aisle to wrap Rachel into a sisterly hug. While they cried and chatted excitedly together, Paige took Sally to Alex's table with promises to return soon. "With Tater Tots?" the little girl asked, with the cutest grin.

"Hey, beautiful," a man's voice murmured against her ear as she slipped Sally's order to the wheel. "Whatcha doin' later?"

"I'm having dinner with my handsome fiancé."

"He's one lucky guy. Handsome huh?"

"Very." She turned in his arms, feeling the quiet rush of joy brimming her soul. Her dear Evan. He was her forever love. Her hero of a man. She ran her fingertips against the roughness of his jaw. Because of this good man, she knew what love really was. It was like the mountains she could see from the window, majestic and unfailing. Her life was better because of him. She was better because of him.

He took her left hand and dropped a tender kiss to her engagement ring. "How's the new engagement ring feel?"

"Like a dream come true. I can't believe I get to be your wife."

"Are you kidding? I get to be your husband. December can't come fast enough." Evan wanted to be married to her now, but they were going to wait until all the family could be together. The boys would be home from school. Her brother would be back from active duty in the Middle East. His parents were planning to drive up from their retirement home in Scottsdale.

It was right that they say their vows before the witnesses who mattered the most, because this was it. It was forever. A once-in-a-lifetime love that he wanted to celebrate not just on their wedding day, but for every day to come. She wasn't just the kind of woman he'd never thought he would find, but she was more wonderful than he ever could have imagined. Where once his life had been steady and predictable and his future a long vast stretch of emptiness, now there was her. And she was everything.

He brushed the hair from her eyes, so he could better look into their dazzling depths. Forever with her would not be long enough. "I know you're busy, but we have reservations for six o'clock."

"Jodi promised she'd take over at six."

"That's in five minutes from now."

"I know. Don't worry. I wouldn't miss time with you for anything." She brushed a kiss to his lips. "There's Cal now. I see him driving up. You two go get settled, and I'll be right out. The Coreys' steaks are up."

Evan. He was her life now. Paige finished her shift by serving the Coreys and made sure they had everything they needed, steak sauce and extra sour cream and refills on their drinks. Then she untied her apron, hung it in the office, and left the responsibility of the dinner rush in Jodi's capable hands.

Her family was waiting for her. Beth, who was off tonight, had wedged into the booth at Alex's side. They were busy talking across the table to Cal, who sat next to his father. A table had been pulled up to the corner booth, to make enough room for Rachel, who was still talking with Amy. Westin and Sally were beginning a game of Battleship.

"Right here, baby." Evan had kept a spot for her at his side and he held out his hand, tender as he'd always been and would always be.

She settled at his side, where she would be for the rest of her life. The front bell chimed again, and it was Blake, Evan's first son, sauntering through the doorway. He waved when he spotted them.

So much in her life was changing. Her son was a man now. The diner would be Jodi's to run. Her sisters were married and happy. Next month she would start her first two classes at MSU in Bozeman, a thirty-nine-year-old freshman who was planning a Christmas wedding. Finally, she had her fairy-tale ending. Her happily ever after.

And all because of the man who leaned close to kiss her cheek. She shivered down to the bottom of her soul. This was simply another beginning.

The best one of all.

\* \* \* \* \*

*A fractured family comes together during Christmas in an uplifting new Love Inspired® story from* USA TODAY *bestselling author Jillian Hart.*

*Read on for a sneak preview of* REUNITED FOR THE HOLIDAYS.

* * *

It was good to be home, Dr. Brian Wallace thought. The long trip from rural Texas had tired him. He missed his kids—although they were grown, they were all he had left of his heart.

He dialed his daughter's number first. A muffled ringing came from what sounded like his front porch. The bell pealed, boots thumped on the front step and joy launched him from the couch. His kids were here? He tugged the doorknob, and there were his three children.

Maddie tumbled into his arms. "Dad, you have no idea how good it is to see you."

"Right back at you, sweetheart. I was gone a little longer than I'd planned this time."

"A little? Dad, you have no idea what we've been through over you."

"Where have you been?" Grayson, his oldest child, stepped in.

"We've been looking for you." Grayson's hug was brief, his face fighting emotion, too. "We found your wallet in a ditch and we feared you were missing. The police—"

"I was in rural Texas, you know that. I would have gotten a message to you kids, but I lost my cell."

"I know. We found your phone, too." Carter, his youngest from his second marriage, stepped in.

"We feared the worst, Dad," Maddie said.

"I never meant to worry you." He shut the door, swallowing hard. His illness had been severe and there'd been days, even weeks, where it hadn't been certain he would live. "I survived, so it wasn't so bad."

"This is just like you. Always keeping us out instead of letting us in." Maddie sounded upset.

He hated upsetting her. "I'm on the mend. That you're here means everything."

"Oh, Daddy." Maddie swiped her eyes. "Don't you dare make me cry. I'm choked up enough already."

"What do you mean?"

"Dad, you'd better sit down for this."

He studied Carter's serious face and the troubled crinkles around Grayson's eyes. "Something happened while I was gone. That's why you were trying to reach me?"

"It's not bad news, but it could give you a real shock. There's no easy way to say this, so I'm just going to do it. We found Mom."

*Separated for more than twenty years,
can Brian and Belle find the love they lost?*

*Pick up REUNITED FOR THE HOLIDAYS
by Jillian Hart, available November 13, 2012.*

## celebrating 15 YEARS

# *Love Inspired®*

## INSPIRATIONAL ROMANCE
### TO WARM YOUR HEART & SOUL

# Save $1.00

on the purchase of

**REUNITED FOR THE HOLIDAYS** by Jillian Hart,
available November 13, 2012,
or on any other Love Inspired® book.
Available wherever books are sold, including most
bookstores, supermarkets, drugstores and discount stores.

---

# SAVE $1.00

on the purchase of
**REUNITED FOR THE HOLIDAYS**
by Jillian Hart, available November 13, 2012,
or on any other *Love Inspired®* book.

Coupon valid until February 28, 2013. Redeemable at participating retail outlets
in the U.S. and Canada only. Limit one coupon per customer.

**52610569**

**Canadian Retailers:** Harlequin Enterprises Limited will pay the face value of this coupon plus 10.25¢ if submitted by customer for this product only. Any other use constitutes fraud. Coupon is nonassignable. Void if taxed, prohibited or restricted by law. Consumer must pay any government taxes. Void if copied. Nielsen Clearing House ("NCH") customers submit coupons and proof of sales to Harlequin Enterprises Limited, P.O. Box 3000, Saint John, NB E2L 4L3, Canada. Non-NCH retailer—for reimbursement submit coupons and proof of sales directly to Harlequin Enterprises Limited, Retail Marketing Department, 225 Duncan Mill Rd., Don Mills, ON M3B 3K9, Canada.

**5 65373 00076 2** **(8100)0 11815**

**U.S. Retailers:** Harlequin Enterprises Limited will pay the face value of this coupon plus 8¢ if submitted by customer for this product only. Any other use constitutes fraud. Coupon is nonassignable. Void if taxed, prohibited or restricted by law. Consumer must pay any government taxes. Void if copied. For reimbursement submit coupons and proof of sales directly to Harlequin Enterprises Limited, P.O. Box 880478, El Paso, TX 88588-0478, U.S.A. Cash value 1/100 cents.

# REQUEST YOUR FREE BOOKS!

## 2 FREE NOVELS
## FROM THE ROMANCE COLLECTION
## PLUS 2 FREE GIFTS!

**YES!** Please send me 2 FREE novels from the Romance Collection and my 2 FREE gifts (gifts are worth about $10). After receiving them, if I don't wish to receive any more books, I can return the shipping statement marked "cancel." If I don't cancel, I will receive 4 brand-new novels every month and be billed just $5.99 per book in the U.S. or $6.49 per book in Canada. That's a saving of at least 25% off the cover price. It's quite a bargain! Shipping and handling is just 50¢ per book in the U.S. and 75¢ per book in Canada.* I understand that accepting the 2 free books and gifts places me under no obligation to buy anything. I can always return a shipment and cancel at any time. Even if I never buy another book, the two free books and gifts are mine to keep forever.

194/394 MDN-FELQ

| | | |
|---|---|---|
| Name | (PLEASE PRINT) | |
| Address | | Apt. # |
| City | State/Prov. | Zip/Postal Code |

Signature (if under 18, a parent or guardian must sign)

### Mail to the **Reader Service:**
**IN U.S.A.:** P.O. Box 1867, Buffalo, NY 14240-1867
**IN CANADA:** P.O. Box 609, Fort Erie, Ontario L2A 5X3

Not valid for current subscribers to the Romance Collection
or the Romance/Suspense Collection.

**Want to try two free books from another line?**
**Call 1-800-873-8635 or visit www.ReaderService.com.**

\* Terms and prices subject to change without notice. Prices do not include applicable taxes. Sales tax applicable in N.Y. Canadian residents will be charged applicable taxes. Offer not valid in Quebec. This offer is limited to one order per household. All orders subject to credit approval. Credit or debit balances in a customer's account(s) may be offset by any other outstanding balance owed by or to the customer. Please allow 4 to 6 weeks for delivery. Offer available while quantities last.

**Your Privacy**—The Reader Service is committed to protecting your privacy. Our Privacy Policy is available online at www.ReaderService.com or upon request from the Reader Service.

We make a portion of our mailing list available to reputable third parties that offer products we believe may interest you. If you prefer that we not exchange your name with third parties, or if you wish to clarify or modify your communication preferences, please visit us at www.ReaderService.com/consumerschoice or write to us at Reader Service Preference Service, P.O. Box 9062, Buffalo, NY 14269. Include your complete name and address.

**HARLEQUIN**® A *Romance* FOR EVERY MOOD™

## We hope you enjoy this great story!

From passion, paranormal, suspense and
adventure, to home and family,
Harlequin has a romance for everyone!

Look for all the variety
Harlequin has to offer
wherever books are sold,
including most bookstores,
supermarkets, discount stores
and drugstores.

*Enjoy!*

THNYTIBC12

ISBN-13:978-0-373-18060-8

*P.H.*

## BESTSELLING AUTHOR COLLECTION

*Classic romances in collectible volumes from our bestselling authors.*

## SOMETIMES LOVE WORKS IN MYSTERIOUS WAYS...

Before Claudia Masters even meets Seth Lessinger, she leaves him a message from the Psalms: "May the Lord give you the desire of your heart." She knows there's something different about this man. Something special. And meeting him only confirms it.

For his part, Seth, who is a new Christian, immediately recognizes that Claudia is the woman for him—the woman he wants to marry and take back to Alaska. But Claudia is torn between Seth and her life in Seattle. How can she give up everything familiar, everything she's always worked for? And yet, she can't bear the thought of losing this man she's come to love…. Only when she acts with faith and hope does she find her true destiny.

> **"Macomber has a gift for evoking the emotions at the heart of the genre's popularity."**
> —*Publishers Weekly*

## BONUS BOOK INCLUDED IN THIS VOLUME!

*A Handful of Heaven* by *USA TODAY* Bestselling Author Jillian Ha

Responsibility was Paige McKaslin's middle name—until her diner burns to th ground, leaving Paige free to discover herself…and a relationship with ranche Evan Thornton. Could life still hold some surprises for her?

**HARLEQUIN**
BESTSELLING
AUTHOR
COLLECTION
www.Harlequin.com